THE WATERGUARD

Richard Hernaman Allen was born in Loughborough in 1949. He attended Merton College Oxford and subsequently worked in the Civil Service, where he was a Commissioner and member of the Board of HM Customs & Excise. He also worked in the Treasury, Cabinet Office, and the Departments of Social Security and Environment, Food and Rural Affairs. He retired early in 2005 to work as a consultant and fulfil ambitions to write books and music.

He is married to Vanessa (a former special needs teacher) with two daughters, a professional violinist and an English teacher in Rome. When not writing or playing music (violin, guitar, mandola), he is a long-distance runner. *The Waterguard* is the first in a series of eight books about Nick Storey's exploits in HM Customs & Excise.

THE WATERGUARD

Richard Hernaman Allen

THE WATERGUARD

Olympia Publishers
London

www.olympiapublishers.com
OLYMPIA PAPERBACK EDITION

A CIP catalogue record for this title is
available from the British Library.

ISBN: 978-1-84897-234-6

First Published in 2012

Olympia Publishers
60 Cannon Street
London
EC4N 6NP

Printed in Great Britain

*To Vanessa, for her love, support
and encouragement*

INTRODUCTION

I spent twenty-five years or so of my career working for HM Customs and Excise. I began my career in Headquarters (the Secretaries' Office as it was still called then) in 1970, a few years after the time when I have set this story. I never worked in the 'Outfield', so experienced Customs Officers will undoubtedly notice errors and solecisms, for which I apologize. My purpose was to provide a setting and an atmosphere rather than strive for complete accuracy. Similarly, I have simplified and altered the geography of Harwich port and Customs buildings and facilities and pressed HMRC 'Vigilant' and 'Valiant' into service a year or two early. Various other addresses have been culled from a map and I have no reason to expect that the buildings that exist there resemble those that are mentioned here in any way. All names are fictitious and not intended to refer to anyone living or dead.

Like many organisations, customs and Excise had peculiar jobs titles and jargon – often using acronyms. I feel it would be inauthentic and stilted to spell these out constantly or try to draft round them. The first time an acronym appears, I have explained it. There is also a glossary at the end for reference purposes.

Certain characters are deliberately intended to reflect former colleagues, most of whom are now dead and I have aimed to draw them in a way as to pay tribute to them. I have tried to reflect the hierarchical nature of the Department as it was then. What I couldn't portray in a book of this sort was its ability to change and respond to a changing environment effectively, meeting massive challenges with speed and a willingness to get stuck in, while invariably treating whatever happened with immense humour. Whether the dismemberment of the Department in recent years will have enabled a more effective and efficient performance of the tasks HM Customs and Excise performed will and can never be known. But as an organisation, it was unique, with its own failings and strengths.

Though through this book I want to pay tribute to all those who worked in the Department, I would particularly like to raise a glass or two to:

Ken Ball, Chris Mann, Tony French, Sidney Silverstone, John Robinson, David Howard, Don Bryars, Lewis Hawken, Bill Coghill, Jim Galloway, Mike Newsome, John Parkin, Diana Barrett, Martin Brown, Lance Railton, Judith Cook, Ian Strachan, Denis Battle, William Parker, Graham Hooker, Jim Williamson and Jen Brailey.

I also dedicate the book to Vanessa (my "Rosemary"), for her constant encouragement and love, and to Jo for her editorial help and both Jo and Kat for their encouragement.

Richard Hernaman Allen
February 2010

ONE – HARWICH CUSTOMS

Two of the uniformed officers – both APOs (Assistant Preventive Officers) – were squaring up to each other. One was tall, a rugby player of some renown, I later learnt. The other was six inches shorter, but broader and more muscular. Suddenly the latter grabbed the other at chest height and squeezed. Even from where I was standing I could hear his ribs crack.

"Bloody hell!" exclaimed one of the POs (Preventive Officers). "Let him go, Morry or you'll crack him in half!

Morry relaxed his grip and his opponent almost fell backwards.

"You little runt, Gold! I never knew you had it in you!" he growled and tried to step forward. But the pain in his ribs was too much and he grimaced and let out several oaths.

"Don't ever call me a yid again, Wilson! Or anyone else!" retorted Morry Gold, his head moving quickly round to survey all of us.
"Not that we would," replied the PO evenly, "but I reckon this morning's little display would've stopped us, even if we'd thought about it."

Then he looked round and saw me.

"And who the hell are you, matey?"
"I'm Nick Storey," I replied. "I've just come from Holyhead. I'm fixed here as an OCX (Officer of Customs and Excise) on freight."
"An OCX, eh? A grammar school boy! You don't want hairy-arsed preventers like us, you want to see Jim Round, the Freight Surveyor in the Custom House."

I looked blankly. I had absolutely no idea where the Custom House was in Harwich.

"Over there. The other side of the dock."
"Ta."

13

I made my way past the APOs and POs, now heading for a shack near an empty ship's berth where presumably they brewed tea and sheltered from the elements when neither freight nor passengers were coming through the port. The Custom House was not one of the more historic custom houses, but a large, two-storey brick construction that at some stage had been painted white, but now had received the full force of the North Sea weather and the attentions of the local graffiti artists as well. The only words I could read were "love me don't" by the corner of the building. Whether it was aimed at HM Customs and Excise or at some lost love was impossible to tell. But unconsciously it made *Love Me Do* rattle through my brain as I entered Portcullis House, as it was called.

"And who might you be?" demanded a wizened, uniformed Revenue Constable, seated in a small cubicle immediately inside the door.

"Nick Storey. I've been fixed here as an OCX. I was told to report here at 9 a.m., to the Surveyor – Bill Garlick – but the PO outside mentioned a Jim Round?"

"Don't expect the Chief Inspector's Office to know owt! Bill's on the late shift. Jim's on early. It's him you'll need to see. But they're just finishing clearing the last of the entries, so you'll have to wait a bit. They should've said ten – or six. In between it's complete mayhem."

So I sat where he indicated – on a metal-framed chair with a canvas seat that had evidently seen better days. I suspected it made its way outside in summer and only returned indoors when someone realised that the storms of autumn had well arrived.

"So you're Storey?" demanded a deep voice with a strong Yorkshire accent. It was about a quarter to ten and a thickset man stood over me. Actually, as he was virtually as tall as he was broad, he wasn't far short of looking me in the eye. But he had the look of a rugby front row forward, not a man to be trifled with.

"Yes," I replied standing up. "I've been fixed here…"

"Ah lad, I know. I got the form last week. How are you fixed up for accommodation?"

"A B&B not far from the station."

"Calls itself 'Beaumanoir'? You'll find it a bit pricey! Now you're fixed, you'll get nothing like the same subbies you got as a UO (Unattached Officer). There's a couple of boarding houses many of the lads use at less than half the price – but you've got to get your own breakfast!"

"Sounds good to me. Are there any vacancies?"

"Always vacancies for the Cuzzies. The owner used to be one of my Purchase Tax traders when I was an OCX, so he knows the score."

"Do you know what my job will be here?"

"What've you done as a UO?"

"Landing Officer and worked indoors on freight clearance. I also helped out on some of the passenger movements in Holyhead and Stansted."

"We don't have much to do with the Waterguard here. You only have to mix and match in piddling little stations like those… and as you'll be on freight clearance indoors, you'll hardly see them at all."

"Not even in the pub? They seem quite a lively lot. A couple of APOs were wrestling as I came past and one broke the other's ribs."

"We usually drink in different pubs. Did you get the name of the chap who got his ribs cracked?"

"Wilson. I think it was Wilson."

"Not bloody Geoff Wilson! Our best bloody wing forward! We're playing Hull in the Carruthers Cup next Saturday! Why can't the arsehole ever keep out of trouble! You don't play rugby do you?"

"Centre or wing three-quarter."

"Wing forward's not that different. Can you play on Saturday? No fiancées or girlfriends to be placated?"

"If I've got my kit…"

"That's splendid. Now I'd better show you your desk and the other chaps in the office."

He led me along a corridor, past a small room with a large boiler and a small sink, a room that was evidently some sort of rest room, judging by the glimpse of dartboard I saw as we passed, the gents and then into a large room full of tables, desks and mountains of files and papers.

"Welcome to the Harwich Long Room!" declared Jim Round. "Nick Storey our latest OCX, everyone!" he announced. "Bill Strevens and Ted Robins – the other OCXs, Derek Chalmers, Ken Byrne, Alf Veale – DCOs (Departmental Clerical Officers), Bert Gill, Vernon Turnell, Terry Taylor and Len Mair – DCAs (Departmental Clerical Assistants). That's the team on earlies today. You'll meet the late shift after lunch. Here's your desk – next to the *Venturous*."

It was perhaps the only decoration the room boasted – apart from a portrait of HM the Queen. A watercolour, faithfully copied from a photograph of HMRC *Venturous*.

My desk had a small clearing in the middle, where a tea-stained mug, that might or might not have originally been white, stood. The rest of the desk was occupied by various metal racks containing either files in buff or pallid green covers or bundles of paper. It only took one glance to confirm what I knew already, the papers were import entries, with a few export documents, and masses of supporting documentation.

"You've inherited import entries P to Z," explained Bill Strevens, a rangy middle-aged man, with grizzled hair and a wolfish grin. "And export entries F to Q, and MIB (merchandise in baggage). You handle the lot – apart from the actual exams, of course – penalties, compounding, even prosecutions…"

"Not that we've had any of those," added Ted Robins, a bespectacled middle-aged man of middling height and curly, light brown fly-away hair. "Never found an agent yet who doesn't take compounding and a restoration penalty."

"You've done this stuff before as a UO?" asked Bill.

"Yes – at Holyhead and Tilbury."

"I did a stint as a UO in Tilbury. They were all a pain in the arse there – dockers, agents – and the bloody surveyors most of all. Was Jack Reeve there when you were there?"

"No. I heard about him though. He's in the CI's Office at present."

"Oh hell! Let's just pray he doesn't come out here to inspect us!"

"We'd better introduce you to the agents in the next day or so," added Ted. "They're mostly well trained here. Just a couple of fly boys."

"You'll find your instructions and OWOs (Omnibus Weekly Orders) in the cupboard by the window under Neville Davenport. Your predecessor. Gone to do PT (Purchase Tax) back home in Walsall."

They went back to their desks. I picked out an entry from the nearest rack – marked 'In' in red ink. It was an import entry for eight boxes each containing forty-eight magazines.

"Who pulled this one?" I asked the DCOs at the desks next to me.

"I did," replied Alf Veale. He was a tall, scrawny young man, about the same age as me, with an inappropriate Beatles haircut and a brown knitted tie.

"Why?"

"It's for Wrynesses in Cambridge. They tried to import dirty books last year, so I thought they might be at it again."

"How did it come in?"

"Part-load on a lorry off the last Hook ferry. It's waiting examination, if you agree."

"You know the patch better than I do. Let's have a look at it!"

I opened the desk drawers and, among the paper clips, treasury tags, stamp pads and stamps, pencils and pens that I expected to find, discovered a filthy and disgusting ancient pipe – presumably the property of my predecessor – and what I was looking for, the appropriate form to authorise examination. My experience as a UO was sufficient for me to fill it in and it didn't take too much searching to find the appropriate date stamp. The form initialled and duly stamped, it went into my "Out" tray, where, five minutes later, it was collected by an ancient messenger and continued its way to the examination shed, where a couple of POs would take great delight in opening up the boxes, in keen anticipation of what they might find.

The interest element in my paperwork declined thereafter. Most of the entries pulled out were for cut flowers or root vegetables from Holland, subject to Min of Ag (Ministry of Agriculture) checks pretty well on a 100% basis. As I knew from my brief stint in Tilbury, the Dutch were a thorough lot who didn't want to damage their reputation by sending diseased plants or using dodgy certification. So, every consignment not only had the correct health certificates, but was also invariably declared free from disease by the Min of Ag boffins. Memos had reportedly been sent to the CI's Office and even the Secretaries' Office recommending less than 100% checks, but whoever took the decisions in the Min of Ag was immutable.

By lunchtime I had worked my way through all the entries for goods still awaiting examination. My colleagues headed off for a café that was used by dockers, drivers, ships' crew, agents and port authority workers alike. Known as Canute's, it was located just outside the dock area in Coller Road. Denigrated by the more refined as running a "greasy spoon" operation, Les, the owner, provided generous helpings of sausages, bacon, liver, black puddings, fried bread, baked beans, fried sausages and eggs, fried, scrambled or poached. I told them I would join them but I thought I'd just spend ten minutes going to the examination bays to see whether anything had emerged from the Waterguard inspection of my entries.

As I arrived at the examination bays, a burly CPO (Chief Preventive Officer) approached me.

"And who might you be?"

"Nick Storey. I'm a new OCX in the Long Room. I wanted to find out the results of the exams of the entries I sent you earlier."

"Your Commission, please."

I pulled my Commission from my jacket pocket.

"Ok. You can come in. But don't get in the way... I'm Wally French, by the way. Was it you that sent us the suspected dirty mags?"

"Yes. Were they?"

"Depends what your tastes are. They were all legal, if that's what you mean. All the naughty bits air-brushed out, so all these naturists *in Sun and Beauty* are playing tennis with lots of little low level-clouds floating around in front of them."

"Do you get much of it?"

"A fair amount. Things like that liven the monotony of constantly checking cut flowers and plants for the Min of Ag, which is just a complete waste of time."

"I'm sorry I sent you a fair few of them too."

"Well, as the Super isn't here I can tell you we only cast an eye over them when there isn't someone from the Min of Ag – or from the IGW's (Inspector General of the Waterguard) office – here. Doing a full inspection wastes so much time – and you can damage lots of the cut flowers in the process. Are you on your way to lunch? We'll all be knocking off in about ten minutes and going to the Jolly Jack Tar in Station Road. You'd be welcome, if you can stand a bit of ribbing about grammar schools."

"Thanks – but as it's my first day, I'd better have lunch with my colleagues. Another day, perhaps."

"Fine. Expect to buy the first round!"

I rejoined my colleagues. The main topic of conversation appeared to be football – notably a lively discussion about the respective merits of Norwich City and Ipswich Town. The only neutrals were Jim Round, who professed a total ignorance of a sport played with a round ball, and Ted Robins, a Fulham supporter who maintained that Johnny Haynes was worth more than both East Anglian sides put together. As a Charlton Athletic supporter, I felt I was safer keeping my head below the parapet.

"Was my predecessor really keen on PT work?" I asked Jim. "Or was it just he wanted to go back home? As far as I'm concerned, working in a port is much more interesting."

"He hadn't been very well. Don't know what it was. He said it was his nerves. I think Walsall was a bit of an excuse. I think he'd've taken pretty well anywhere to get out of here. Don't know why though. He always seemed to get on with everyone OK. A bit of a loner was our Neville, but if he wanted out, I don't think it was to escape from us lot... Are you a Londoner?"

"Woolwich. Probably why I like port work. I was born within sound of the River."

"Well, my advice to you would be to get to know people here and get them used to you before you ask too many questions – unless it's about the work, of course."

I realised he wasn't annoyed by my question, but was just advising me as a senior officer to his junior.

"I assume our Estabs Section will get your file eventually. You seem a bit long in the tooth for getting your first fixed post? National Service?"

"Yes. Stupidly, I did it straight after school. Then I went to college. If I'd done it the other way round, I'd've avoided it... Not that I mind."

"Where did you serve?"

"Germany, including West Berlin. I'd done German for A level, so the Army messed up and actually sent me somewhere where I'd be useful. When I was in Berlin, they taught me Russian too. But then they came to their senses and sent me to Kenya, where I hated the heat and didn't much like what we'd been doing there either."

"You must've been there just after the Mau Mau stuff?"

"Just a bit of 'tidying up', as they put it. I fired a few shots in anger, but I don't think I actually killed anyone. They gave the sergeants pistols, so the enemy would have to get pretty well within spitting distance for you to finish him off. By the time I was there, the Kikuyu were trying to avoid fighting rather than spitting at us."

"So you're a college graduate! We don't get many of them coming as OCXs."

"I'm not the academic type. I did languages because I like using languages. I tried for the Foreign Office and the Administrative Class of the Civil Service, but I didn't get in. No good on the theoretical stuff and a bit too much 'saarf lun'un' for them! Customs seemed like a good place to use my languages and not spend all my time in an office."

"Which is how you ended up here in Harwich, working all day in an office!"

19

"Well, it's not for life – and I can get out from time to time and keep an eye on the physical exams. I like to visualise what's written down on paper. I feel it helps me get better at spotting wrong 'uns."

"Just try and avoid being seen hanging around the exam shed when Eric Shepherd's there. He's the Waterguard Superintendant. He doesn't think much of us – and the feeling's mutual."

There were just a couple of passenger ships in the afternoon. All that brought was a couple of MIB entries. One was technical drawings claiming TI (Temporary Importation) status and the other was a small package of high quality diamonds coming from Amsterdam and on to London. It struck me as a curiously cumbersome route to move such expensive goods, rather than flying directly to Heathrow. But, according to Alf Veale, it was fairly regular and always for Silberstein in Hatton Garden.

"We reckon they vary their route so the diamonds don't get stolen en route. None of the packages have been worth less than fifty thousand quid. Pity we can't get any duty on them, as they're under TPR (Temporary Processing Relief)."

"Does the same chap always bring them through?"

"A nondescript little man called Sydney Small. But we suspect he has a couple of travelling companions to keep an eye on him. No idea who they are though."

And that was it for the day, a day which ended rather more quietly than it had begun. As I walked back to the B&B, I reflected that the interest in this station was likely to be the people rather than the traffic. It all seemed fairly predictable – from the routine nature of the freight passing through to the continuing rivalry between the Waterguard and the 'Excise', as they tended to call us: at least, when they were being polite. If the merger of the former Customs and Excise in 1909 had been intended to create a single, new, unified Department, it was still a long way to go after more than fifty years. However, since I wished to make use of my languages, a career in the Waterguard would make more sense than in the 'Excise', so I needed to think out ways I could transfer before someone started to encourage me to go and do Purchase Tax in London or Birmingham.

What was needed was some problems with German or preferably Russian speakers. I suspected that the Harwich station contained at least one German speaker, as a significant proportion of trade was with West Germany. But I doubted whether anyone knew any Russian. Unfortunately, no Russian ships called in at Harwich, so encountering a Russian-speaker with a Customs problem was likely to be infrequent, to say the least.

But what did I know?

TWO – LEICESTER: AN EXTRAORDINARY DISCOVERY

By the end of my second week at Harwich, I was already settling into a routine. I had moved to a boarding house in Orwell Road, run by a Mrs Donaldson, with a complement of lodgers all employed by HM Customs and Excise. Apart from Mike Downing another OCX on freight, all the others were from the Waterguard – Phil 'Taffy' Lewis a CPO, Jerry Wilshire and Hywel Jenkins, the PO who I'd met on my first day. Not to my great surprise, Taffy and Hywel were stalwarts of the Harwich Customs rugby team , for whom I played on my first Saturday in the place, enjoying the relative freedom from fear that goes with the position of wing forward compared with that mixture of fear and anticipation you get playing in the backs. I could look forward to several weeks playing in that position until Geoff Wilson's ribs healed. Whether I would get a game after that would probably depend on whether other team members got injured. But rugby wasn't a passion, so whether I played or not was of no great importance.

In theory I should have been returning to south-east London when I had the chance, as I had a sort of fiancée, Barbara Colley, who lived in Maze Hill, and with whom I had been 'going out' in a somewhat desultory way ever since I met her in my second year at London University. But my peripatetic existence as an Unattached Officer moving all round the country to gain experience had put something of a strain on what was, in truth, a somewhat tepid relationship. She was too like me – even-tempered, rather cold-blooded – when what I needed was the opposite, a headstrong, passionate woman. Being who we were, we had yet to summon the energy to pronounce the relationship ended, but were letting it pursue a lengthy, silent course to its grave.

My father was a Communist former docker, now unemployed/retired, who regarded my position working for the repressive bourgeois state as rank treachery to my class. Rather than expect my mother to put up with his constant sniping at me and me studiously ignoring it, I preferred to put the Thames and the best part of a county between them and me. It also avoided the sniping, of course – though, by and large, it was water off a duck's back.

I'd seen enough of a worker's paradise when I was stationed in West Berlin to realise that my dad's view of Communism as practised in the Soviet Bloc and the reality was as alike as Elvis Presley and Marlene Dietrich. Unfortunately my peripatetic existence meant that I wasn't registered to vote anywhere, so I missed the opportunity to vote for Harold Wilson and Labour, who would at last pull Britain out of its complacency. My father, of course, would have voted along with a hundred others for a Communist candidate whose lost deposit didn't matter, as the whole party existed almost entirely on funding from the Comintern.

I didn't have enough money to afford a car – even an old banger. And even if I had, I lacked the mechanical skills or interest to do up an old banger and keep it going. While I saved for something that would give me trouble-free transport, I bought a cheap racing bike from the local police and spent my spare time at weekends exploring the locality. Going south, I had quickly put the delights of Frinton and Clacton behind me and found a more gemütlich place at Tollesbury, with a friendly pub selling local beer. The following Sunday I explored inland and discovered countryside so rural that it was too much for a "townie" like me, so I headed back early to Harwich.

On the Monday I received mail from HQ. A Mr D K Mummery, Executive Officer in Section 3B of the Valuation Branch (VB), had been 'directed by the Commissioners of HM Customs and Excise' to inform Mr N. F. J. Davenport that there were inconsistencies in the description and valuation of two import entries which he had cleared on 21 June and 3 July 1964. The items – four cases of scrap jewellery – had been valued at a total of £44 12s 6d on each occasion. But, as declared under the relevant tariff heading and in the quantity stated, the value should have been at least twice as much. Mr Davenport was requested to re-examine the relevant papers and furnish the Commissioners, in the person of Mr D. K. Mummery, with an explanation.

"Do you know anything about this?" I asked Alf Veale and Bert Gill, who generally worked to me.

"I recall one of the entries," replied Alf. "But Neville dealt with it himself. I don't know about the other one. He could've picked it out himself. I had a week's leave in July."

"Never seen either of them," added Bert, a mournful, taciturn soul at the best of times.

"Oh well, I suppose they must be filed away. Can you see if you can dig them out, please, Bert?"

But after half an hour's diligent searching through various metal filing cupboards, Bert returned to say that the relevant papers were nowhere to be seen. So I spent the next twenty minutes searching through my desk and the cupboard I had inherited from Davenport, but with no greater success.

"I suppose I'd better phone him at the Walsall PT office," I suggested.

No-one disagreed. So, having found the relevant telephone number, I rang. A woman's voice, with a thick Black Country accent answered.

"My name's Nick Storey. I'm ringing from Harwich Customs. I need to have a word with my predecessor, Neville Davenport, who joined you recently."
"Neville who? I don't know any Nevilles working here."
"Could I possibly speak to the Surveyor or one of the OCXs please?"
"OK. I'll put you on to Brian Traynor, the Surveyor."

There followed several minutes of alternating silence, buzzing and clicking.

"You're from Harwich Customs, ye say? I'm Traynor. Perhaps ye can tell me what's happened to Davenport. I know he had a week's leave due between postings, but he was supposed tae show up here last Monday and we've not seen hide nae hair of him." Traynor was a Glaswegian and, I reckoned, of the Presbyterian rather than the "I belong tae Glasgie" sort.
"I was going to ask you the same thing," I replied. "I took over here after he left and I've got a difficult letter from the VB about some entries he seems to have mislaid."
"Well, he's nae here. I'll try tae see what's happened at this end. Perhaps ye'll do the same at your end. Good day to ye."

I went in search of Jim Round.

"I've had a memo from the VB about some entries Neville Davenport dealt with. We've searched everywhere we can think of, but can't find any trace of them. So I thought I'd have a word with him over the phone, but the Surveyor there says he hasn't turned up yet. He said Davenport was going to take a few day's leave. Did he say where he was going?"

"I thought he was going to do some house-hunting in the Walsall area... It sounds a bit fishy to me. Neville wasn't the sort not to turn up when he was supposed to. He and his wife had a bungalow in Manningtree. I wonder if his file has a phone number. Let me see if I can find out anything."

I went back to my work, intrigued. About twenty minutes later, Jim summoned me to his office and told me that, as the phone line in Manningtree had evidently been disconnected, he had rung round the local estate agents to see if they knew anything about Davenport's current whereabouts. He had been told that the Davenports had been renting the house in Manningtree and, from what the agents understood, had been proposing to return to a house he owned in Shire Oak, on the more rural borders of Walsall.

"So I went back to his file and realised that he'd been claiming rent allowance and only some minor costs rather than a full Crown Transfer... And before you ask, his file doesn't have a phone number for the Shire Oak address. Besides, that's Temperance Traynor's patch. Let him do the phoning around and any leg work!"

"You know him?"

"We were UOs together in Glasgow Excise. We used to control the distillery at Port Dundas – a vast place, a huge temple to the production of grain whisky! I assume you've never been there? He used to treat the place and everyone in it as though it was one of the outer reaches of hell full of minions of the Devil. Every time we'd try to slope off to the pub, he'd give us a lecture on the sins of alcohol and pamphlets – the same pamphlet actually – on the virtues of temperance. Not an easy man to get on with."

"So we just wait for his phone call?"

"Yep. He'll probably ring me and complain I allowed an OCX of mine to phone a Surveyor... Yep, he's rank-conscious as well."

Not long before we were due to hand over to the late shift, Jim summoned me again.

"I've just had Brian Traynor on the phone. They managed to get a number for the Shire Hill address, but got no answer. As it's on his way home, he says he'll call in and see if he can find anything out... I must say it's all rather fishy."

The next morning Jim was attending a meeting called by his AC (Assistant Collector), so I had the dubious pleasure of answering Brian Traynor's phone call.

"I'll ask ye to pass this message on tae James Roond. I went tae Davenport's hoose in Shire Hill yesterday evening. There was naebody there. However, there was an elderly man working his garden next door, sae I had a few words with him. He told me that since the people renting had moved oot three weeks ago, naebody had been tae the place. He thocht Mrs Davenport had kin in Leicester, sae perhaps they had gone there. This morning I've spoken tae my AC and we've agreed tae seek the advice of the polis. Will ye please tell James Roond that I'll let him know what transpires. Then perhaps ye'll find oot aboot your lost entries. Good day to ye."

I passed the message on to Jim and also discussed whether to inform Mr Mummery. Jim told me to hold fire at this stage. The VB wouldn't start to concern themselves about our reply for a couple more weeks at least. If they contacted me by phone, I could truthfully say that I was new and still finding my way round Davenport's papers and filing system.

Two days later, Jim summoned me into his office again.

"I've just heard from Brian Traynor. Neville Davenport is dead. Apparently he was the victim of a hit and run motorist in the Aylestone district of Leicester, where he and his wife owned a house, I gather her parent's house bequeathed to her. His wife was also hurt, but apparently left hospital about a week ago. I suppose it's not surprising she wasn't in a state to tell anyone at Walsall about what'd happened. She's staying at the house in Leicester where she's got old friends who can look after her, apparently. Traynor spoke to her on the phone and she told him Davenport had a suitcase full of various office papers and if someone wanted to examine them, they could collect them from the house in Aylestone. Traynor said there couldn't be anything there of any interest to him, so if we wanted to see whether this suitcase contained your missing entries, that was a matter for us."

"I suppose we could ask Leicester Excise…"

"Not on your nelly! I don't want it all round the Department that Harwich Customs can't keep hold of our papers. No. I'm sending you to get hold of whatever poor Neville had stashed away in his suitcase. There may be a lot more than just your entries."

"Tomorrow?"

"Yep. I'll give you a chitty for the accounts people so you can get your T&S (Travel and Subsistence) refunded."

"Then I'd better start looking at train timetables."

"And I suppose I'd better break the bad news. Neville wasn't exactly popular – but it's still pretty awful when something like that happens to one of your colleagues."

My route to Leicester was tortuous. If I hadn't been so keen to avoid going to London, it would almost certainly have been quicker – even given the tube journey from Liverpool Street to St Pancras. As it was, I had to change at Manningtree, Ipswich, Norwich and Peterborough, travelling by a series of noisy, uncomfortable stopping trains, except for the brief interlude of the London express which took me from Ipswich to Norwich. I had a distinct feeling that if Dr Beeching had his way, this journey might well not be possible for much longer. On the other hand, if some of these stations in one-horse towns and oversized villages were closed down, at least the journey might have been considerably faster.

Though I was aware that Marsden Lane, Aylestone was several miles from Leicester railway station and that the quickest way to get there would be by taxi, I was under no illusion that a claim for a taxi fare would be allowed, so after two bus journeys and a short walk, I finally reached number 23, a 1930s bow-fronted semi-detached which looked very much as I imagine it had then.

I went up to a door painted in mid-green gloss and knocked on the brass knocker. After a couple of minutes, the door opened and a tall, scrawny woman in her forties peered out at me.

"Who are you?" she demanded.

"I'm Nicholas Storey from HM Customs and Excise," I began. "I believe you've spoken to one of my colleagues on the phone. I've come to look at your late husband's papers and take them back to the office if necessary. I'm afraid I never met your husband, but I'm very..."

"Sorry, I know. But as you never met him, you can't be that sorry, can you? But come in anyway. I'd prefer Nev's papers were looked at by someone who didn't know him... Would you like a cup of tea, Mr Storey?"

"Yes, please."

"Where have you come from?" Her accent told me that she was local to these parts.

"I've come from Harwich today. I followed your husband as the OCX on freight there."

"I assumed you would have come from the Leicester office. Why did you need to come all this way?"

"I was contacted by the VB – Valuation Branch – about some entries, but I couldn't find them. That was why I tried to contact your husband last week."

"Well, if they're anywhere, they'd be in the suitcase we brought with us here."

"Do you mind if I have a look?"

"No. I'll go and get it from the glory hole."

She reappeared a couple of minutes later with a medium-sized brown leather suitcase that had evidently seen better days.

"This was my dad's," she explained. "Nev began to use it after he died. It's not locked. We never could find the key after my dad died."

I pushed the locks holding the metal holders apart and the suitcase opened. At the top were several buff files stuffed with papers. There were various items of office equipment, including an ancient steel hole punch, a stapler and one of those long cylindrical ebony rulers that always resembled a Government-issue cosh rather than an instrument of measurement. There were a couple of framed photographs – a ten-year-old one of his wife, the other – fairly recent, I'd reckoned – of both of them together in a back garden somewhere. Then there were several A4 size brown envelopes, a couple of Agatha Christie crime novels and a Bible. Lastly there was a package which looked like an envelope folded over several times with a piece of string coming away from it, as though it hadn't been very well tied.

I picked up the files. Putting them on my knee, I gave them a cursory 'face' inspection. They were all Departmental papers, many of them entries or supporting documents. I couldn't immediately see my missing entries, but it seemed a reasonable proposition that they were there somewhere.

"I think all these properly belong to the Department," I said. "Do you know why he had taken them away with him, Mrs Davenport?"

"I've no idea. We never talked much about his work. Knowing him, I'd expect it was work he'd been unable to complete before he left Harwich and was going to finish off and send back to you."

I decided not to mention that the first few papers were several months old and, judging by the stamps and signatures, looked as though all the necessary work had been completed.

"Do you mind if I open the other envelopes, just in case there's anything else belonging to the Department in them?"

"No."

The envelopes all contained entries, curiously all relating to imports of diamonds by Silberstein of Hatton Garden. All the entries had been passed and formalities completed. So why had Davenport felt the need to take them away with him?

The small package was, however, a total surprise. As I began to open it, I realised that there were several small objects inside rolling around. So I tore a small hole in the corner and poured the contents out on to the tray where Mrs Davenport had put the teapot, milk jug, sugar bowl, and two cups and saucers. These were now joined by several dozen sizeable uncut diamonds, worth, I would imagine, many thousands of pounds.

"What the…!" I began and managed to refrain from blasphemy in front of the recent widow. "Did you know anything about this, Mrs Davenport?"

She was breathing heavily, at a loss for words. Her face certainly suggested that this was as much a shock to her as it was to me.

"No. Where in heavens did those come from? They are diamonds, aren't they?"

"Yes. Uncut – and these entries suggest they were intended for a Hatton Garden jewellers."

"What was Nev doing with them…? He isn't a thief, you know, Mr Storey! I'm sure there's an explanation."

"Unfortunately the person best able to give it can't. Can you tell me why you came here, rather than going to your house in Walsall? After all, that's where your husband was going to start in his new post."

"He had a week's leave and he suggested coming here to check up on the house. The last people who rented it moved out about six weeks ago and he wanted to look the place over before we let it out again… Or at least, that's what he said. It seemed a perfectly reasonable thing to do at the time."

"Did he seem all right in the last few weeks?"

"He was a bit tense... But he was often affected by his nerves... He didn't really like working on the Customs side... he'd always done Purchase Tax or Excise since the early days..."

"But nothing out of the ordinary?"

"Not that I'd noticed. But when you're moving home from one part of England to another, you tend to be thinking more about the day to day things..."

"I suppose so..."

"You're not married?"

"No. Harwich is my first fixed station."

"Oh well. I suppose you'll find out... What are you going to do about all these?" She waved her outstretched hands towards the diamonds, glittering among the floral tea service.

"Hmm... I don't know whether to hand them over to the police or to the Department? Do you have a phone here for me to ring my Surveyor?"

"Yes. It's in the hall."

I rang Jim Round and explained what I had discovered. There was a long whistle and an obscene exclamation at the other end.

"Give her a full, detailed receipt and bring it all back here, lad," he concluded.

I explained what he had proposed.

"Is that OK with you, Mrs Davenport?" I saw her grimace slightly at the Americanism.

"I'll write two receipts and we'll both sign them. Then you've got a copy and so have I."

Within a quarter of an hour the receipts were written and duly signed, diamonds were recaptured and sealed in an envelope and cups of tea duly drunk.

"I'd better be on my way, Mrs Davenport. I've got a complicated journey back to Harwich."

"Of course. I hope you won't mind if I ring your Surveyor tomorrow to check that everything has arrived safely."

"Certainly. I'm not planning to flee the country..." I shut up, realising that it was a joke in somewhat poor taste.

30

We went into the hall and I opened the front door. Just as I was about to go through it she said,

"Thinking about it, I'm now quite convinced my husband was deliberately run over. As you try and work out what all this means, take that into account, please."

She then turned away, evidently not prepared to vouchsafe any more. I pulled the door to and left. I wasn't the right man to eke any more information out of her.

The journey back to Harwich was even slower and, a little spooked by Mrs Davenport's parting shot, I felt weighed down by the suitcase with its astonishing contents. Were they really the cause of my predecessor's death?

THREE – HARWICH: THE INVESTIGATION BRANCH

"I hope this doesn't turn out to be a police matter," I remarked to Jim Round as I brought the suitcase into his office the following morning. "I don't think they'd be very keen about me carting evidence halfway round the country." Though neither of us was rostered to work on a Saturday, our presence was barely noticed.

"Let's worry about that if and when, lad," he replied. "Now have you had a look at the papers?"

"Yes. I did it in my room last night. Two files are either MIB entries or supporting documents, all relating to imports for Silberstein of Hatton Garden. One contains entries for nursery plants from Holland. The other one is much thinner and more varied, but it does include the two lost entries relating to scrap jewellery. There are three or four other entries also for the same stuff, all intended for David Weissman of Hatton Garden. There were several envelopes, all containing entries of diamonds for Silberstein – though they were ordinary entries, not MIB ones. And last, but not least, there was thousands of quids worth of uncut diamonds."

"The first thing we'll need to do is to check all the entries. We'll need to know whether the goods were received and whether the importer is what it says on the entries… and I don't think I can afford to use anyone here, other than you."

"Uh?"

"Well, though I didn't know Davenport well, he didn't strike me as the sort of chap who'd get involved in cheating or stealing, either from importers or the Revenue. Any explanation may be…"

"I think I should tell you that his wife told me she believes he was deliberately run over and killed."

"Whether or not that's true, that settles it. There are others here I'd be less certain about, naming no names. But you're new and clearly can't have been involved… Hmmm, I think I need to call upon the services of an old friend in the IB (Investigation Branch)."

"And the diamonds? And the police?"

"No-one has been belly-aching to us about any lost diamonds, so there's no evidence Davenport stole them. For all we know, they may have been his... his way of saving for a rainy day..."

"Those stones must be worth thousands, as much as fifty thousand, I'd say. I'd like to think you could afford that much on OCX money."

"Well, perhaps he inherited it... All right, it's a bit thin. But I don't want to bring the police in unless I'm sure. After all, they didn't think Davenport's death was suspicious, did they? They could've interviewed Mrs Davenport and got hold of the suitcase themselves. It's not as though they haven't had the opportunity. But if we can keep the police from rooting around in the Department's affairs, so much the better... Anyway, leave the suitcase with me and when I've spoken to Iain Coggy, we'll start trying to see what it all means. I think it'll fit in my combination."

The 'combination' was a six by four metal cupboard with a combination lock, the setting and re-setting of which required an operation of fiendish complexity and a special key. Twice as a UO I had managed to foul up this delicate manoeuvre and had to send for a supercilious Revenue Constable to undo my incompetent handiwork and do it for me. However before Jim had shut the briefcase away, I got him to let me keep at the ebony ruler, of which I thought might come in handy for defensive purposes in future.

The following Monday morning, I was summoned yet again to see Jim. Standing in the corner of the office was a short, spare man in his late thirties, with sandy hair, bright, intelligent eyes and an unassuming, but alert manner.

"Morning lad. This is Iain Cogbill, Senior Investigator. Iain – this is Nick Storey."

"Pleased to meet you," said Cogbill, with a Scottish accent which I associated with Edinburgh.

"You'll be pleased to know that from my conversation on the phone with Mrs Davenport, you're not going to be charged with walking away with any unowned diamonds," added Jim. "But, down to business. First, we need to check the various entries in the suitcase against the records. Second, we need to discover what we can about these diamonds. And third, second and first, we need to be bloody discreet."

"The IB is not formally taking over this matter – at least, not for now," said Iain. "Until we know what we're dealing with, the Chief is happy for it to be left with you."

Iain Cogbill and I were given a separate office at the rear of the Custom House. The story apparently was that one of my former cases had been turned over to the IB and I was helping them out. Deliberately vague, but with a ring of plausibility. It would, of course, have taken the locals about half an hour to find out who Iain was, even if no-one had met him before. And if we said nothing, a few phone calls and the putting of two and two together would certainly lead to a plethora of rumours, which might even have included the truth.

"I've been on excise and PT so long, I've forgotten what happens to entries. Perhaps you can enlighten me," Iain began.

"There's supposed to be an audit trail. The agent gets a copy, we keep the top copy and file it here; a copy goes to the A&CG (Accountant and Computer General), to the Statistical Office and, if necessary, to the VB."

"Well, if we're going to check all of these, we'd better have some sort of story. All we need to do is to find out whether these entries have reached their destination and there are no discrepancies – unlike your two VB ones. You say there haven't been any previous enquiries by the VB of a similar nature?"

"No, Jim checked. Either Davenport made a mistake or…"

"Let's see what the evidence shows up. I'm not one for theorising in the absence of facts."

"Do you reckon we need to check each entry with every possible destination?"

"Hmmm… No. I think we could ignore the Stat (Statistical Office). From what I hear, the trade stats are invented anyway. I think the most useful area would be the A&CG and the agents. But we're going to need a plausible cover story for the agents – and possibly the importers."

"And the A&CG's?"

"I've got a former colleague working there. There's a fair prospect he can do our digging there for us. Let me give him a bell and you start to draw up a chart of goods, agents and importers – with dates as well… Is MIB treated in the same way?"

"Essentially yes."

From what I overheard of his next phone call, his former colleague was another Scot. It had been said to me that compared to the stranglehold the brotherhood of Scots had on the Department, Masonic influence in the police was but a daisy-chain.

By lunchtime, I had drawn up the requested chart. It made an illuminating picture.

Entry method	Agent, etc	Goods	Importer	Country of origin
MIB	Courier – Sydney Small	Uncut diamonds	Silberstein & co	Netherlands (Amsterdam)
Import entry	Blatherwick (Harwich)	Nursery plants	White House Nurseries, Belsize Park	Netherlands (Haarlem)
Import entry	Kersey (Harwich)	Scrap jewellery	Weissman	Netherlands (Amsterdam)
Import entry	Kersey (Harwich)	Uncut diamonds	Silberstein & co	Netherlands (Amsterdam)

None of the entries in Davenport's suitcase failed to fall into one or other of these categories.

Jim Round joined us, bringing a couple of plates of sandwiches and large mugs of strong tea.

"I thought you might need these. How are you getting on?"

"Storey's chart covers all the entries found in Davenport's suitcase. Mean anything to you?"

"We've always thought that MIB traffic was a bit fishy – but without any evidence. Blatherwicks are one of the two agents here who cover the Dutch flower trade. They keep their noses pretty keen. I don't think we've caught 'em at anything…"

"…yet!" added Iain Cogbill, demonstrating a traditional Departmental opinion that all agents, importers and PT traders either had, were currently or would in future attempt to cheat the Revenue.

"Kerseys have been here about three years," said Jim. "Not liked by the older agents for trying to pinch their traffic. We've never got them for anything, but something there doesn't smell quite right. We don't really know anything about the importers – though why would you import plants through Harwich to go to Belsize Park? Wouldn't it be easier to go from Rotterdam to London Port or Tilbury?"

"Perhaps they get a better deal going to the Hook and driving at this end?" I suggested.

"What's also interesting," observed Iain, "is why there are entries relating to nursery plants. The rest is high value/low volume stuff. But there can't be much money in plants… unless they're being used as a concealment… Well, it's an idea to bear in mind."

During the afternoon, I checked through the local files to see whether these entries had been logged, and, if so, what was the information held about them and whether it tallied. Meanwhile, I imagined that Iain's contact in the A&CG's Office was doing something rather similar. Iain went off to do a bit of snooping, as he called it, round the examination sheds, the QW (Queen's Warehouse), the bonded warehouse and any other areas under Customs control. He also took a wider stroll round the harbour to get the lie of the land, as he termed it. Jim did whatever Surveyors do in places like Harwich.

As I began to realise once I started examining the records, it was quite possible to have gaps or dummy entries placed in the filing cabinets without anyone really knowing. Unless someone sought a particular entry or there was some sort of inspection or audit, no-one ever checked up what was there.

I had a total of thirty-eight import entries and ten MIB entries from Davenport's suitcase. All the MIB entries in the filing system had a copy or dummy entry, with a note written, so Jim told me, in Davenport's handwriting explaining that the original copy was held by the Officer pending conclusion of certain unspecified post-importation formalities. All the information on the copies tallied with that in the originals. All of the fourteen entries for nursery plants were completely missing, without a note or any copy. The eleven entries for scrap jewellery had been replaced by copy entries. There were no accompanying notes, but the copy entries looked as though they had been written up by Davenport. The remaining thirteen entries, for uncut diamonds, had no documentation except for a note in Davenport's hand stating'"entry number 26014664, 23601664, etc, potential evidence in IB investigation. CONFIDENTIAL. Refer AC Harwich Customs (Freight)."

"I'll check within the IB, but as far as I'm aware, we've no current investigations involving Harwich," Iain observed.

"And I'll check with Jock Imrie," added Jim. "Though I'd trust him as far as I could swing a cat, at least I reckon I can tell when he's lying and when he isn't."

"The AC?" I asked.

"Yep." Jim said. "You'd do well to steer out of his way. Jock Imrie is out for Jock Imrie and anyone who stands in his way is likely to get trampled on. If you do well, he claims the credit. If you foul up, the shit lands on you. I worked for him when he was a Surveyor in Greenock, so I know of what I speak."

"I'd keep what you tell him to a minimum," advised Iain.

"Believe you me, that was my intention. I don't want him getting his snout into this. And we'd better do a full check on the entry filing systems and get them all tidied up. If there's any more shit going to emerge, I'd like to know about it first. Ken Byrne can do it. He's methodical, slow-witted and completely without ambition – all the requisite qualities for this sort of work!"

Later that afternoon, Iain informed me that the A&CG's Office reported that their records reflected what I had found in the filing system in Harwich. The copies of the MIB entries were complete and correct, those for scrap jewellery complete but all appeared to have been completed by the same person. There were no copies relating to the imports of nursery plants and the jewellery entries just had a number and a reference to an IB operation, with a phone number which turned out to belong to Jock Imrie.

"On reflection, I believe we should all go and see Imrie," said Jim, after Iain had related his conversation with his contact in the A&CG's office. "It's not clear to me why anyone would use his phone number without good reason. So a couple of witnesses strikes me as a wise precaution."

He rang Imrie and when he mentioned Davenport's death and some missing entries, we were summoned immediately.

Imrie's office was on the top floor, a vast, corner room which looked out over the harbour and across the River Stour. It boasted an enormous double-sided mahogany desk with matching floor-to-ceiling bookcases, full of books of instructions, Acts of Parliament and subordinate legislation going back decades and a large mahogany table with eight chairs fitting round it easily. Behind the desk in a large leather chair was Jock Imrie. Though I realised I had seen him, I hadn't known who he was. He was over six feet tall, big but not fat, with dark ginger hair and 'full set' (i.e. beard and moustache). If he had been wearing naval uniform, I would have taken him for a ship's captain. His eyes were small, green and beady. They seemed to miss nothing.

"You're the new OCX, Storer, aren't you?" he demanded of me, in the gritty accents of an Aberdonian.

"Storey," I replied.

"Same difference," he barked, giving me an unpleasant look. "Weel, you're here now, Mr Round, wi' your accomplices. Better tell me what you're up to!"

"Have you met Iain Cogbill, SIO (Senior Investigation Office) from London, sir."

"He may be from London now, but I ken he hails from Leith once upon a time."

"Good day to you, Jock. It's been a few years."

"I was Iain's Surveyor when he cut his teeth on Speyside. Which distillery was it, Iain?"

"Macallans mainly, but as a UO I could be sent anywhere in the District."

"Weel, enough of times past. What are you up to, boys?"

"You know Neville Davenport was killed in a hit and run accident a couple of weeks back, sir? Well, we were trying to get in touch with him because of a couple of files which the VB had queried," Jim began.

I could tell Iain Cogbill at my side almost visibly straining to encourage him to say as little as possible. Plainly he didn't trust Imrie an inch.

"After we tracked down what happened, we discovered that Davenport had a case with some Departmental property in it, so Storey collected it from his widow. We've been checking the files – both in the registry here and, through a contact of Iain's…"

I could feel Iain's almost invisible wince.

"…in the ACG's Office. Mostly the stuff tallies. But both in the registry here and in the ACG's, there's a note been placed against certain entries that they're part of a confidential IB investigation and contact should be made through you. We were wondering what you knew about this, sir?"

"What were these entries for?"

"Uncut diamonds. Imported from Amsterdam for Silberstein of Hatton Garden, agents Kerseys."

"When?"

"First half of this year. Last one in August, I believe."

Imrie paused for thought, looking around at us with a mixture of hostility and contempt.

"I know nothing about any entries of this sort. If anyone's put my name as a contact, they've done it without my knowledge. If anyone knows whether an IB investigation is involved, it's that man yonder!" he exclaimed, pointing at Iain.

"That's indeed what I am endeavouring to do," replied Iain icily. "But as your name came up, we thought you should be apprised of it."

"Well, duly apprised am I! So what's going on? Something crooked?"

"At this stage, we've no idea, sir," said Jim, trying to interrupt the staring contest that had developed between the two Scots. "There appear to be no goods missing and the uncut diamonds seem to have been correctly entered and valued. What Davenport was up to we've no idea – and we may never know."

"Is that all?"

"Yes, sir. Thank you for your time."

"Don't mention it," said Imrie sarcastically. "If anything untoward comes up, inform me instantly. You understand?"

"Of course, sir."

We left and returned to Jim's office.

"Make sure I've got any relevant papers – including your charts and notes, Storey. I'm going to keep all of them locked in my combination safe. Come to think of it, I'll change the combination this evening... With a man like that, you really can't tell whether they're being straight or not."

"That one's never straight. But whether he was lying to us, I don't know," added Iain.

"So what do we do now?" I asked.

"Well, I'll go back to Fetter Lane and make sure there is a genuine investigation going on into these diamonds," replied Iain. "And, if you don't mind, I'll take four or five of your diamonds to see if I can ascertain their origin."

"I suggest I take you over to meet Kerseys and Blatherwicks in the morning, to introduce you to them formally as the new OCX. I'm sure we can slip in the odd pertinent question while we were with them."

The phone rang. It was Sylvia who operated the phones.

"Have you got a Mr Cogbill with you, Mr Round?"

"Yes."

"He's wanted on the phone by his DCIO (Deputy Chief Investigation Officer), name of Williamson."

Iain took the phone and, as by habit, turned away from us so we couldn't hear what was said. In any case the conversation was brief and we were apprised of its content immediately.

"My DCIO tells me that the police have just informed the Leicester office that Mrs Davenport has apparently committed suicide."

FOUR – LEICESTER: POLICE INVESTIGATIONS

"Good God!" exclaimed Jim. "When?"

"Yesterday evening, apparently."

"They're certain it's suicide?" I asked, conscious of her parting comment. I began to wonder whether the suitcase or something else Davenport had in his possession was so valuable, sensitive or important it was worth the price of murder.

"I didn't question it. Why?" demanded Iain.

"Just as I was about to leave, Mrs Davenport said she thought her husband had been run over deliberately."

"So you think she might also have been killed? Did she strike you as someone who might be going to kill herself?"

"I only saw her for an hour, so I really couldn't tell. She seemed calm and in control of herself, I thought. If you'd asked me before I'd heard this, I'd've said she didn't strike me as the sort of person to kill herself. But…"

"Well, I imagine the police will want to interview you. There can't've been all that many people who visited her before she died. I imagine you were the only one from the Department."

"Do you think I should contact them?"

"In the normal course of events, I'd advise you to wait until they contact you. But if there is any suspicion that she didn't commit suicide, it'd be worth getting a chance to look at the house. So you could get in touch, explain you took some Departmental papers which Davenport had taken with him from Harwich and say you want to check whether there are any other things belonging to the Department in the house. I'd come with you, but I did a fraud case at Players in Nottingham a year or so ago, so my face is known round those parts and questions might be asked. At this juncture we need to keep it low key until we've got a clearer idea – any idea – about what's been going on and the Departmental interest. So I'd advise you not to inform the police what Mrs Davenport said to you about her husband being murdered. After all, it's just words said by a woman who killed herself not long afterwards, isn't it!"

"Just go along with Iain's advice, lad," added Jim.

So I telephoned the Leicester police shortly afterwards and, having hung around for about half an hour, was summoned to attend the Granby Road police station the following morning.

Fortunately, the police station was close to Leicester Midland station. I was beginning to detest the cross-country journey from Harwich and vowed if I ever had to travel to Leicester again, I'd go via London.

I was kept waiting a fair time, initially on a bench opposite the counter ruled by a couple of ancient policemen who grunted in almost unintelligible East Midlands accents, who in their turn were ruled by a very fat and studiously unhelpful desk sergeant. After about twenty minutes, I was escorted to a windowless interview room and left to twiddle my thumbs for a further quarter of an hour. Then a bored-looking man in his early forties, with a moustache, thinning hair and a drunkard's nose entered the room.

"Afternoon. I'm Detective Constable Sedgwick. I'm looking after the Davenport cases. You are… Storey from Customs? Is that right?"

"Yes. Nicholas Storey. I'm a Customs Officer in Harwich. As I told your colleague on the phone, I saw Mrs Davenport last Friday…"

"All in good time. Let's have your full name and address."

"Nicholas Vladimir Storey…"

"Vladimir? Are you some sort of foreigner?"

"No. I was born in Woolwich. My father was a great admirer of Lenin – you know 'Vladimir Ilyich Ulyanov', known as Lenin."

"So you're some sort of Commie?"

"He is. At least both my father and Lenin were Communists. I'm not. He thinks I'm betraying my class by working for Customs and Excise."

"Well, if you're like anyone else in the Customs, you're probably betraying someone! Just my little joke. We don't get on all that well with your lot, as you probably know."

"My address is 14 Orwell Road, Harwich. It's a boarding house. I've only been in Harwich about a month. Before that I worked all over the place."

"Eh?"

"I was what we call an Unattached Officer. Generally I worked where I was sent, partly to get training, partly to fill in where there were vacancies. But recently I got a fixed appointment to Harwich Customs. Before that I spent four months in Holyhead."

"I see. So why did you come all the way from Harwich to see Mrs Davenport?"

"I took over from her husband. I discovered that some papers seemed to be missing and I wanted to check whether he knew where they were. It was then I discovered that he'd been run over and killed. The Leicester office contacted Mrs Davenport and she said her husband had some papers that might belong to the Department in a suitcase. As he had nothing to do with the Leicester office, they suggested that I went to see her to find out whether these were my missing papers."

"And were they?"

"Yes."

"So why do you think he had them?"

"I can't really say. I never met him. We've been checking to see if there was anything untoward, but we haven't uncovered anything as yet. It seems possible he may just have got them caught up with his personal possessions and was planning to send them back to us when he started in his new post in Walsall."

"If he was going to work in Walsall, what the hell was he doing in Leicester?"

"I understand he owned a house in Walsall and also the one in Aylestone. Mrs Davenport told me he had some leave due. The house in Aylestone had been let and the lodger had moved out about six weeks ago, so they were checking it was OK."

"I see. Did that seem plausible to you?"

"I'd no reason to doubt it. Mrs Davenport seemed open enough to me. And her accent sounded like yours, so I guess she was from these parts. It was her parents' house I believe."

"Did she seem like someone who was likely to kill herself?"

"Well, I was only with her for about an hour. She seemed quite calm and in control. She made me a cup of tea. When we talked about her husband, she wasn't tearful. But she could've been putting on a front. I'm told that when Mr Davenport worked in Harwich, they lived in Manningtree, which is about ten miles away and didn't mix much with their colleagues, so she was barely known."

"How long had they been there? Do you know?"

"I checked in case you might ask. Nearly five years. I gather basically he was waiting to get a posting back to Walsall, where he came from."

"Anything else you can tell me relevant to her death?"

"Not that I can think of… But, as I said to your colleague I spoke to on the phone last night, I wonder whether it'd be possible for me to go to the house in Aylestone just to check there aren't any Departmental papers there that should be accounted for?"

"The sarge agreed that was all right. WPC Johnson will take you there. She's the only woman driver we've got on the force, so don't do anything that'd distract her."

"Do I need to make a statement?"

"I'll get my notes typed up and you can sign it when you get back from Aylestone. If you think of anything else when you're at the scene of the crime, so to speak, you can always write it in then."

I returned to the front desk, where a young WPC was waiting. She was the first member of the police force who I would willingly have allowed to arrest me. Even with the unflattering policewoman's hat, I could make out her jet-black hair, cut short in the way of sportswomen. She had brown, amused eyes and an ironic smile.

"You are Mr Storey from Customs, I take it?"

"That's so. You are WPC Johnson?"

"All day. Would you come with me, please. My car is round the back."

She wasn't more than five feet five inches tall and had a slightly 'jolly hockey sticks' manner, but I reckoned if I had the chance, I could put up with that.

"I understand you're the only WPC driver in the Leicestershire Constabulary," I began, making idle conversation.

"Yes. I beat all the men in my police drivers' class, so while they get given Rovers and Zephyrs, I get this tyre-burning Mini!"

"Well I suppose it allows you to go where bigger cars can't."

Ignoring that observation, she led me along a couple of dingy corridors and out through a locked rear exit. In a small compound at the back were three cars – two large Rovers and a Mini.

"I suppose it could've been a Morris Minor," she remarked. "But it still looks rather pathetic, don't you think?"

"I dunno. The Rovers look a bit middle-aged and ponderous. The Mini is more a young person's car."

"Do Customs run some sort of charm school?"

"Not that anyone's ever mentioned. Generally the opposite, in fact."

"Well, get in – and try to avoid banging your head on the roof."

I got in, without failing to notice a pair of slim legs in regulation dark WPC stockings. "If she looks this good in that unflattering uniform, she must look sensational in ordinary clothes," I thought to myself. "Those legs were made for miniskirts."

"I must say I'm grateful for the lift. When I went to see Mrs Davenport last week, it was two bus rides and a fair walk."

"Not a taxi? I thought all the Customs people only used taxis."

"Only the higher ranks – and I suppose the IB – Investigation Branch – might. Not humble Customs Officers like me."

"Are you humble, Mr Storey?"

"Not exceptionally. And please call me Nick."

"I think we'll stick to Mr Storey."

"Oh well," I thought to myself as she drove efficiently out of the city centre and into the suburbs, "it was worth a try. Better to fall at the first hurdle than be left two from home, never knowing whether you might have got there or not."

Naturally we reached the house in Aylestone considerably faster than on the previous occasion I had been there. WPC Johnson had a key and let us in.

"Have your lot finished with the place?" I asked.

"As far as I'm aware. The detectives and experts were all here yesterday, but they said they'd found all they needed."

"Do you know where she was found and how she died?"

"She was lying in bed, apparently she'd taken the contents of a bottle of sleeping pills and several glasses of brandy."

"And was there a note of any kind?"

"No. I don't think so... Why are you so interested?"

"It's only a few days since I met the poor woman for the first time. She might have said something about the Department in a note. I felt I needed to know, just in case."

"Well, at least there was nothing to blame Customs and Excise for her death."

I took it she was being ironic.

"Do you mind if I have a look around and see if there are any papers or other things that might belong to the Department?"

"That's why we're here. Of course, anything you take away will need to be receipted."

"Of course."

It was only at that moment that the thought struck me that somewhere in the house, or already in police possession, was the receipt which I had given Mrs Davenport for the contents of the suitcase. If nothing else, if the police had read it, they would know that I had certainly not told them 'the whole truth' in my interview. On the other hand, if they did have it, why hadn't they just produced it and asked me about the most interesting item – the envelope containing many thousand pounds' worth of uncut diamonds?

We were in the sitting room where Mrs Davenport had given me tea. It was still extremely neat and tidy. I noticed that a painting, a copy of a van Gogh landscape, was slightly askew – something I hadn't noticed when I was there before.

But the bureau made me more suspicious. Davenport was meticulous in the way he filed his papers, both in the files in the suitcase and at work. Yet the papers in his bureau – almost all concerning the renting of the house – were not in date order. They were tidied away neatly, as though someone had made an effort for them to appear untouched, but four items were out of place. From what I had seen of Mrs Davenport, I did not believe she would have been any less meticulous than her husband.

I searched through the rest of the bureau, which mainly contained stationery and several ancient photograph albums dating mainly form the 1920s and 30s, to judge by the clothes. I guessed that I would find pictures of the late Mrs Davenport in her childhood and youth here. But I had neither time nor inclination. One compartment contained a few household bills – again, not wholly in date order.

But my receipt was nowhere to be seen.

"Anything there?" asked WPC Johnson.
"No, nothing. I'll have a quick look at the bookcase."

The bookcase, an ugly Victorian mahogany monstrosity contained almost entirely paperback thrillers published by Penguin. Inevitably, the books were organised alphabetically by name of author and then title. Of course, I hadn't taken the two books I'd found in Davenport's suitcase and I assumed that Mrs Davenport would have replaced them in their correct places. *A Murder is Announced* and *Cat Among the Pigeons* had, indeed, been replaced in their correct locations. But, as my suspicions had already been aroused, I worked my way along each row and found *The Mysterious Affair at Styles, The Body in the Library"* and Dorothy L Sayers' *The Nine Tailors* were all misplaced. As casually as I could, I opened each one to see whether anything might have been concealed in them. But nothing was.

Unfortunately, I had lingered too long in front of the apparently innocuous bookcase.

"Mr Storey, what are you up to? Why are you looking at those books? And don't tell me just casual interest, or I'll have to report it back to my sergeant."
"OK. Have you noticed something odd about the books in this bookcase?"
"What apart from the fact that the Davenports seem to have been obsessed with reading crime novels?"
"Yes. All the books are located as though it was a library. They're all in order – except for the three I was looking at. I was wondering why they were out of place. Perhaps there was a note in one of them – a clue to Mrs Davenport's death…"
"And was there?"
"No."
"Did you think she might have put a suicide note in a misplaced book? Seems rather far-fetched, if not bizarre!"

"I was thinking more about someone else searching for something. Mr and Mrs Davenport seemed inordinately organised to me. I find it hard to believe that she would put books away out of place. Whereas someone searching for something, however meticulously they went about it, might just make the occasional error, especially if they had limited time."

"Perhaps Mrs Davenport made a mistake while she was upset."

"Well, the two books that were in Mr Davenport's suitcase, along with the Customs stuff I took away, have been replaced in exactly the right places."

I pulled both of them out. It was a convenient excuse to see whether anything had been concealed in them. I prayed that my receipt wouldn't fall out of one of them. But, as before, they contained no surprises.

"That's rather a leap to suggest that someone has searched the bookcase. Why? What are you suggesting?"

"Well, it may have been your detectives. But I doubt whether they would've been so careful about putting virtually every book back in its right place. Besides, as they believed her death was suicide, I doubt whether they would've had any reason to search the bookcase… The papers in the bureau are similar. Very carefully put away and almost entirely kept in the right order, with just a couple of papers out of place."

"You weren't going to tell me about that were you?"

"No. I'm here to find any papers that belong to the Department, not do the police's job for them."

"So you think she didn't commit suicide? She was murdered?"

"I don't know. I'm not a detective. I'm just telling you what I've seen. Shall we have a peep in the other rooms?"

The kitchen, which looked barely changed since the 1930s and the dining room, which appeared to be barely ever used, contained nothing out of the ordinary. The cupboard beneath the stairs – the 'glory hole' referred to by Mrs Davenport – revealed brushes, mops, cleaning cloths, dusters and various cleaning fluids and powders, but nothing untoward.

The first two bedrooms were evidently guest rooms and appeared not to have been used for several years. The main bedroom, where Mrs Davenport had been found, looked out over the back garden. The bed was a bare mattress. Presumably all the bedclothes had been taken away for expert analysis. In the drawer of the dressing table were the usual lady's knick-knacks. The two wardrobes were only partly filled with the Davenports' clothing. Unsurprising, as they were paying a visit, not planning to reside here permanently.

"I reckon these have been examined by someone," I remarked. "There's a suit out of place in his wardrobe and a coat in hers. As you can see, they have a pattern of hanging garments, with shirts or blouses on the left, with trousers or skirts, suits or dresses, then coats on the right. In both cases, one has been put back out of order."

"That could easily have been detectives having a quick look round."

"More than likely."

The bathroom like the kitchen appeared to have resisted any temptation to modernisation, apart from a wooden-framed medicine cupboard with a mirrored front, which had been placed directly over the washbasin. In it were largely what you'd expect, an unwrapped cake of soap, toothpaste tubes, shaving requisites including an astringent aftershave. There was also a small packet of aspirin, a tin of Andrews Liver Salts, a tin of Bisodol, a half-empty bottle of Friar's Balsam and a virtually empty bottle of Metatone tonic – and an almost full bottle of prescription sleeping tablets.

"Now, you're the policewoman – what does that tell you?"

"Who do you think you are, Sherlock Holmes? And you think I'm Dr Watson! Think again! I've been doing this job about eighteen months and I've had no chance to do any detective work in that time. If you can see something clever, out with it!"

"Very well. Assuming that these things belonged to the Davenports, I'd say both suffered from indigestion. You wouldn't use both Bisodol and Andrews Liver Salts at the same time, surely? One or both also suffered from anaemia, judging from the Metatone – I'd guess Mrs Davenport. But the oddest thing is the bottle of sleeping pills. They're on prescription from a chemist in Manningtree, so presumably the Davenports brought them with them."

"So what?"

"If they were supposedly only staying here for a week or so and, from all we've seen, only brought with them enough stuff for a short period, why did Mrs Davenport have another bottle largely full of sleeping pills which she used to kill herself? Why didn't she use these? Do you know where the bottle of sleeping pills she used to kill herself came from?"

"Of course I don't!" But I could tell from the tone of her voice, she was beginning to have the same doubts I had.

"Wait a moment!" I cried, running downstairs. "There's something else."

"Wait for me… What now?"

I had gone into the dining room and looked again in the massive mahogany sideboard.

"Look. There's a tea service, a dinner service, various serving plates and bowls and just a set of cut-glass wine glasses and a similar set of sherry glasses. There's nothing to drink brandy out of… and in the kitchen, there's a bottle of Emva cream and that's all… I suppose you don't know what size the bottle of brandy was that Mrs Davenport poured her last drink of brandy from?"

"No. The detectives must've taken it away as evidence. Along with the brandy glass she drank it from."

"It wasn't a brandy glass. It was the little tumbler she used to put her toothbrush in. There was one missing from the bathroom. You can see the holder where it normally sat. Someone had tidily put both toothbrushes in the same tumbler, but the other one was clearly missing."

"So you're saying, if there weren't any brandy glasses, why was there a bottle of brandy in the house…? It could've been medicinal brandy. A lot of people keep a quarter bottle in their medicine cabinets."

"That's why I asked about the size of the bottle recovered after Mrs Davenport's death."

"You've got me going now… So you think… what? Someone forced Mrs Davenport to drink the brandy and swallow the sleeping pills? Why?"

"I don't think I'm suggesting that. All I'm saying is that there are inconsistencies here that seem to me to need fuller investigation before someone concludes it was suicide. But if it was murder, it seems to me it was done by someone who was very experienced and professional at doing such things."

"That still doesn't explain why."

"As to why, I haven't the foggiest idea. But it seems to me that if that is what happened, someone was looking for something – and who knows whether they found it or not."

At that instant, the icy thought darted into my brain that perhaps what was being sought was among the contents of the suitcase I had taken back to Harwich. Moreover, as I hadn't turned up my receipt and the police probably hadn't either, if there was a highly skilled and professional murderer seeking the suitcase and its contents, I was likely to be the next person on his list.

"You are wondering whether someone is searching for something among the papers you took back to Customs?" said WPC Johnson, regarding me intently.

"How did you work that out?"

"You suddenly went as white as a sheet. Besides, I'm perhaps not as dim as you think I am."

"I'm sorry if I've given that impression. I didn't mean... But all the papers were Customs entries and we have other copies. We've checked... so I don't think it's likely..."

"Anyway, is there any reason why anyone would know you'd taken any papers away?"

"I left a receipt with Mrs Davenport. It's not here. It identifies me by name and where I work."

"But if it shows you only took papers relating to Customs, I assume Mrs Davenport can't've been killed for something in them, surely?"

"I can't see so."

"Well. Are we finished here? I should get you back. You probably don't want to be travelling in the dark this evening." She smiled gently. I was very tempted to kiss her.

We got back in the car and headed back along Marsden Lane. We'd gone no more than twenty yards when she suddenly braked hard.

"If Mrs Davenport was murdered, do you think Mr Davenport's accident was actually on purpose?

I would love to have told her what Mrs Davenport had said to me, but caution, the advice of my senior colleagues and the fact that I should have told Detective Constable Sedgwick earlier made me dissemble.

"If you're going to mention what we've talked about to your colleagues, it'd be a thought worth mentioning, I'd think."

"Well, I'll talk it through with my sarge. No detective is going to give me the time of day."

We were back to the Granby Road police station too quickly and she handed me back to the desk sergeant with another of those smiles that gave me goosebumps.

"That was certainly an interesting afternoon, Mr Storey. Perhaps we might do it again sometime."

I couldn't imagine when. But was it some sort of private invitation? I would have to reflect when I was back on more familiar territory.

Within ten minutes I had signed my statement and headed on my way. I decided not to travel back the way I had come, because I felt that if I was being followed, returning the way I had come would make it too easy for whoever it was – and there were too many stations where I had to wait for a connection. So I exchanged my tickets for a route via London and hopped on the next express to St Pancras.

I took a seat in the most crowded compartment, but when a tall, lean man in a trenchcoat got in immediately after me, I convinced myself that he was following me and moved to another with only a middle-aged couple in it. As the train rumbled towards London, my thoughts whirled around in my head – a mixture of fear of an unknown, but deadly, menace and a strong desire to take WPC Johnson in my arms and give her the first kiss of many. I was already trying to work out ways I might be able to get in touch with her again, most of them fanciful.

At St Pancras I rushed along the long underground corridors before reaching the Tube station, reckoning that if I was being followed, speed was a better ally than cautiously trying to identify who was following me. At Liverpool Street I used the same tactic, with the variation that I waited until the departure whistle was being blown for the Norwich express before dashing on to the train. However, as I sat congratulating myself, I realised that if any pursuer had the receipt I had given to Mrs Davenport, he would know where I was heading and could easily have placed himself on the train already. I spent the next hour and a half, as we headed through the gathering gloom of the monotonous suburbs of East London and the equally undistinguished Essex countryside, surreptitiously eyeing my fellow-passengers, especially when people came and went, to see whether I might be able to identify my potential assailant.

Needless to say, I was particularly concerned about having to change trains at Manningtree and wait on that rather isolated station in the dark for the connecting train to Harwich. I would liked to have taken a taxi, but I knew our accounting office wouldn't accept the expense. Curiously, when faced with a choice between unidentifiable peril and certain additional expense, I chose to remain on the station.

By the time I reached Harwich, I knew Jim would have finished for the day, so I headed for my lodgings and was relieved to find several colleagues already there. After a good meal and a couple of pints in a nearby pub, I almost began to believe that my fears were groundless – almost.

FIVE – HARWICH – THE SHIPPING AND FORWARDING AGENTS

The following morning I reported back to Jim Round what had happened in Leicester. Iain Cogbill was still at the IB HQ in London.

"I don't think we need trouble Imrie with any of that," stated Jim. "After all, it's a matter for the police, isn't it lad?"

After we had completed the morning's freight movements, Jim took me to meet a couple of the local forwarding agents who arranged the passage of freight through Harwich. First we went to Blatherwicks, based in a converted and extended house in Foster Road, within sight – and more important – sound of the new refinery that was just completing construction. Jim had rung in advance and we were met at the front door by Alf Blatherwick, middle-aged son of the ancient but reputedly still very active Bert Blatherwick, founder of the firm, and Pieter Rust, Alf's son-in-law.

"I thought I'd introduce Mr Nicholas Storey to the agents here, as he'll be dealing with a fair number of your entries over the next few years. He's the Customs Officer who's replaced Mr Davenport," Jim began.

"I heard that Mr Davenport had sadly been killed," said Blatherwick, a stocky, balding man with the red-faced, weatherbeaten look of a typical East Anglian peasant farmer.

"Yes. Killed in a car crash in the Midlands."

The formalities concluded – during which time I realised from his accent that Pieter Rust was either Dutch or just possibly Afrikaans – we entered the Blatherwick offices, where we were immediately offered tea or coffee. It came dark and strong in large blue enamel mugs.

"Have you worked on freight clearance before, Mr Storey?" asked Blatherwick. "It sometimes seems odd to us that some of the Customs Officers have almost no knowledge of freight clearance before they come here."

"I've worked at Holyhead, Stansted Airport and Tilbury, so I know a fair amount. But there's still lots to learn. Every port is different, so they say."

"That's true enough. After Tilbury, you'll find our traffic rather limited. We really only get stuff from Holland, West Germany and Denmark."

"Don't you get anything transhipped in Rotterdam?"

"A bit – but most of that stuff goes to places like Tilbury and they're starting to ship by the lorry load through Dover."

"You must get a lot of the Dutch cut flowers and nursery plants. I've seen lots of entries of yours for those."

"It's the bulk of our work. Thank heavens for the Ministry, I say. If they didn't insist on so much paperwork and all those physical checks, that's the sort of stuff that'd sail through barely touching the sides. But as it is, it puts the meat on our table – and the veggies and the gravy."

"It's always nice to find someone who likes 'em," remarked Jim. "If you talk to any of the farmers round here, they'd happily throw the whole lot of 'em into the Stour."

"Do you deal with the same shippers in Holland?" I asked.

"Mostly. Piet used to work for Schouwers in Rotterdam, so we've got good contacts over there."

"I noticed quite a bit of your stuff goes to London. Wouldn't it be quicker for them to send it via Dover or London?"

"Some do it that way," replied Piet Rust in a thick Dutch accent. "But many send them through shippers they know and trust. Schouwers and Blatherwicks have been around a long time. So they know what to expect."

"Is it the same for flowers and for nursery plants?"

"Mostly. Most comes through Schouwers or van Keert."

"Do you take single or occasional shipments from smaller shippers or exporters?"

"We'll take anyone who provides the proper paperwork and pays up on time."

"You don't check up whether they're bona fide at all?"

"If the paperwork is satisfactory, the goods match the paperwork and the money comes in on time, that's enough for us. If we ever felt someone was using shipments we were entering to smuggle contraband, we'd either tell you or the Dutch authorities. But because someone only ships occasionally does not automatically mean they are smuggling, you know."

"I suppose it's the same for the importers?"

"Ja. Mostly they are regulars, but we get some that import only occasionally. For example, if a nursery here loses stock for some reason and cannot replace it from English suppliers, they may have to get stock from Holland."

"I suppose an entry that I was checking the other day – for plants for a White House Nursery in London – might be one of those? Or are they regulars?"

"Occasional, I should think. Most of our flowers and plants go to Vandenburg or Hatch in Covent Garden… and there's a large nursery just outside Ipswich… Nutbush at Martlesham… They get a lot of plants too."

"That's very helpful. I think I understand your traffic a lot better now."

We moved on to Kersey's. They occupied the first floor of a small new office block in Station Road. There was a small entrance lobby inside the front door, with a bored young woman who evidently modelled herself on Diana Dors sitting at the receptionist's desk. As we entered she put on a pair of trendy black and white rimmed spectacles.

"Who are you for?" she demanded.

"We've an appointment with Mr Kersey," explained Jim. "He should be expecting us."

"Oh well, I'll ring up and let him know. Go through the lobby. The stairs are on the left."

When we reached the lobby at the top of the stairs, a youngish man was waiting to greet us. He was slightly shorter than me, but tanned and stocky, with the air of a middleweight boxer. He led us into a bright office filled with modern, Scandinavian-style furniture and a stainless steel coffee percolator. He offered us a cup each. It was strong enough to blow the top of your head off.

"Mornin' Mr Round… and this must be Mr Storey. What d'ya think of 'Arwich then, Mr Storey?"

"It's OK. I like working in a port."

"Well, I'm a Londoner and I think it's a dump. But you go where the money is, don't ya! I've bin 'ere three years and when I've made enough, I'm goin' back to the smoke."

"London? The port of London is dying."

"Nah. Tilbury. I come from Grays and I learnt the business off my uncle at Tilbury."

"What sort of stuff do you deal with? Do you take anything? Or do you specialise? I've just met people at Blatherwicks and they seem to do almost entirely flowers or plants from Holland."

"Old man Blatherwick's pretty well sewn up that market. I'll take anything I can get if I can make a few bob on it. I suppose because of people I know in London, I reckon I do all the diamonds and jewellery from Amsterdam. Blatherwick's got 'is daughter married off to a Dutchman from Schouwers. My brother-in-law does the transport for Silbersteins, Gutmans and Weissmans of 'Atton Garden. So I've got a foot in the door. When I got that business, Blatherwicks weren't too 'appy. Thought they'd got it sewn up between them and Eastons. Don't invite me to their little sherry parties, they don't. I'm the only shipping and forwarding agent not a member of the local FFA (Freight Forwarders' Association) branch, even though I reckon the value of my businesses is bigger than any of them, except perhaps for Blatherwick. Still, they can't stop me workin' 'ere and as I'm not a member of their club, I don't 'ave to abide by their rules, do I?"

"One of the things that I'm responsible for is MIB. I've seen a few shipments of uncut diamonds for Silbersteins going that way. I didn't think you did any of the formalities."

"Silbersteins are an odd lot. Very cautious and safety-minded. They 'ad a big consignment stolen about ten years back, so I was told. Since then, they use lots of different routes to transport their stuff. Some of it goes by air. Some by road through Dover. Some goes in freight. Some as MIB."

"Lots of different suppliers too, I suppose?"

"I suppose so. I just deal with a Lev Goldman from Amstelveen near Schiphol. I only know 'oo supplies the actual stuff when I see it in the documents. Frankly, I don't care 'oo they are as long as I get my dosh on time."

"All the MIB stuff seems to be brought in by a Sidney Small. Is he from Silberstein or does Goldman employ him?"

"I dunno. I don't ask too much around any of the Silberstein business. I reckon if they thought I was gettin' nosey, they'd take their business elsewhere before you could say Bobby Moore!"

"But they haven't lost any consignments lately have they?"

"Not so I'd 'eard. Once in ten years – twenty years – is more than enough for them!"

"And Weissmans – are they the same?"

"Weissman's is lower value stuff – scrap jewellery mainly."

"And is the way things are done different?"

"Yeh. Goldman put a firm called de Wet on to me. They're quite big in the scrap jewellery business in Amsterdam and their partners in 'Atton Garden are Weissmans. I was able to offer more competitive rates and a better service than what they was gettin', so I got the work. Bin doin' it about eighteen months, I suppose."

"Do you ever go over to Amsterdam? I did some of my National Service in Germany and always meant to go there, but I never got the chance."

"You can get a dirt cheap crossing from 'ere to the 'Ook, if you know the right people. Never bin there myself. I did all my National Service in Germany – the most boring and depressin' time of my life. I couldn't wait to get 'ome and I 'aven't bin abroad since."

"Well, if you peace-time soldiers have finished reminiscing," interrupted Jim. "It's time we got back to work."

"Thank you for your time, Mr Kersey. That was very helpful in understanding what the paperwork I see actually means."

"Any time."

"Well, what do you make of them, lad?" asked Jim as we made our way back to the Custom House.

"Blatherwicks have got a nice bit of business going, but they're complacent. I couldn't see them spotting anything out of the ordinary. If a dodgy importer sent nursery plants through them, they'd look for all the right documents, but not whether the import might be a front for concealing something else."

"And Terry Kersey?"

"A chancer. Though he's not a crook himself, he'd look the other way if he suspected something was fishy if there was enough money in it… or at any rate, that's my opinion."

"It's mine too."

When we got back, there were two messages from people who had telephoned me. The first was from Iain Cogbill who asked me to phone back.

"I thought as I was in London, I should pay a visit to Silberstein and Weissman – and this White House Nursery. But it'll raise fewer suspicions if you come too. You can always be doing some sort of post-importation check. Can you make it tomorrow?"

"If Jim okays it."

"Assume he does. Meet me at Fetter Lane. It's handy for Hatton Garden."

The second call was from Rosemary Johnson, asking me to call back. This name meant nothing to me. As far as I was aware, I knew no-one called Rosemary Johnson. It was only as the switchboard dialled it for me that I realised that it was a Leicester number and the caller had been WPC Johnson. The moment the call was answered, my mouth began to go dry.

"Leicester police station here," said a woman's voice in a heavy East Midlands accent. "What do you want?"

"I'd like to speak to WPC Johnson. I'm returning her call. My name is Storey."

Even with my thumping heart, I retained sufficient nous not to advertise my connection with HM Customs and Excise.

"WPC Johnson here. Who is it?"

"Nick Storey. You rang me."

"Oh yes." She sounded formal. I could hear conversation in the background. "Would it be possible to meet? I could come to London on Saturday. I'd rather go there than anywhere that requires complicated travel."

"That presents no problem," I replied, realising that when it came to a choice of playing rugby or meeting WPC Rosemary Johnson, the latter won hands down any day of the week. "If you could let me know what train you're catching, I could meet you at St Pancras."

"That would be kind of you. I don't know London very much. I expect to be on a train that arrives close to eleven o'clock. Will that give you enough time to get there?"

"Yes."

"See you then."

"Yes."

Unconvinced of my animal magnetism, I suspected that WPC Johnson wished to tell me about Mrs Davenport's suicide. But at least it was an opportunity to get to know her better – and off duty, out of uniform. Even if she was intending to hurry back to Leicester, I should surely be able to persuade her to join me for lunch – and somewhere nicer than the dingy so-called restaurant on St Pancras station.

SIX – LONDON – THE DIAMOND IMPORTERS

I made an early start the following day, as Iain Cogbill wanted me to be at the Investigation Branch HQ in Fetter Lane by 10 o'clock. As I got on the train, I idly reflected that when one's fears failed to materialise, how rapidly they drifted into one's unconsciousness. The fact that over the last couple of days no assassin had attempted to kill me or recover Davenport's suitcase was already making me believe that my fears had been unfounded.

I was not allowed to enter the IB HQ. Iain was waiting for me in the entrance lobby and hurried me off to Hatton Garden. There was barely enough time to tell him about my suspicions about the death of Mrs Davenport when we were in Hatton Garden and standing outside Silberstein & Co, on the corner of Greville Street.

"I've told them we're going to visit them this morning," Iain explained, "not least because I want this to appear completely routine. I've told them it's a routine post-importation check and that you'll be undertaking it. I said that you're quite new at this and I'm your senior, observing you and helping out as necessary. So you should do most of the talking. I take it you know what to ask?"

"I believe so."

We went in. A slim, blond young man was behind the counter. I was slightly surprised, as in my mind, I'd expected all the employees of the firm to be Jewish.

"Yes. And how can we help you?" asked the young man, with a Central European accent and a rather high voice.

"Cogbill and Storey from HM Customs and Excise. I spoke to Mr Klugman on the telephone yesterday."

"Certainly. If you'll just wait there a moment, I'll let Mr Klugman know you've arrived."

Within half a minute a small, grey-haired man with a long grey beard arrived. He was exactly my idea of a rabbi. He was wearing a suit of black cloth, so dense and dark that it looked impenetrable. We went into a small office at the back. There was a table with four chairs. Three walls of the room were cupboards with many small compartments, presumably where diamonds were kept. The room had no window and smelled of a mixture of furniture polish and hair oil. On the table had been placed two large leather-bound books, which I guessed were ledgers of some sort.

"I'm grateful to you for sparing the time for us to carry out this work," began Iain. "I'm Mr Cogbill. We spoke yesterday. This is my colleague, Mr Storey, of whom I spoke."

"It is no problem for us," replied Mr Klugman. "Martin Klugman is my name. I'm happy to answer what questions I can. But I will need to finish by eleven."

"I hope that will be sufficient. Mr Storey, do you wish to commence?"

"OK. Mr Klugman, this is what we call a post-importation control check. What it involves is that we extract a number of files, pretty well at random, from our records and check up whether the paperwork held by the shipping and forwarding agent and the importer are consistent and show that the importation has taken place and the goods reached their destination. As you may know, we don't physically examine every importation, so we like to assure ourselves that the reality tallies with the documents which we've seen. So what I'll be doing is asking you some questions about a few importations which you have undertaken earlier this year, if that's all right?"

"Certainly. Please go ahead, young man."

"OK. First, there's an importation of uncut diamonds from Edelmann in Amsterdam, declared value of £48,211 17s 6d on 18 May of this year."

"Yes. You can see it here. Imported through Harwich, shipping agent Kersey in Harwich, Goldman in Amsterdam."

"Importation also of uncut diamonds from van Heller of Amsterdam, declared value £47,447 9s 3d on 8 June."

"Yes. Here it is. Same agents as the previous one."

"These values seem very precise for such high value items?"

"Purely based on weight. There is a current price for uncut diamonds of a particular quality – in pounds and guilders. The scales for weighing diamonds are extremely precise, because of the high value, as you say. So the figures for value are necessarily very precise. It is on such things that profit and loss may depend, young man."

"I see. How can you tell what the appropriate quality is? And therefore the price?"

"I can see you've never had anything to do with diamonds, young man. An expert can tell the difference, an ignoramus not. Look – here are two uncut stones. Can you tell which is worth more than the other?"

"No. Not at all."

"Then you could lose yourself over a thousand pounds in this business. This one is worth five hundred pounds, but this one is worth three times as much. If you haven't been taught, if you haven't got the nose for it, you'd do well to steer clear of buying diamonds – unless you get yourself an expert."

"But I'd still have to trust my expert. When things are so expensive and vary so much in value, it wouldn't be that hard to fool a dupe out of a lot of money."

"Such happens, of course. But you have to trust somebody sometime, young man. After all, if you don't take a risk, you don't make a gain."

"I've got a different entry next. One that you sent with a courier, Mr Sidney Small, on 14 June."

"From Edelmann, valued at £38,818 4s 8d."

"That appears to tally… Might I ask why you use a courier and import through freight?"

"Security. Eleven years ago a consignment got stolen. Now we use several different routes, by air and sea and by courier. God be thanked, we've not suffered a loss since."

"Are there many lost consignments?"

"Very few. After our misfortune, the other importers all tightened up their procedures as we did. I haven't heard of any going missing for two or three years – though there was a rumour going round that something had happened a couple of months back, in the middle of the Election campaign. But it wasn't anyone I know and it all seemed to die away quickly."

"Can you tell where diamonds come from? Originally, I mean?"

"Of course, young man. In the same way you might tell a claret from a burgundy, I can tell a South African from a Russian diamond from a Brazilian diamond."

"Where do yours come from?"

"That's a commercial secret that I doubt HM Customs and Excise needs to know."

"You're quite right, Mr Klugman. I'm sorry for my colleague's inexperience."

"I guess you're thinking I trade in Russian diamonds. Well, I don't. I do a lot of business with Abramovitch and with Feldmann in New York and I wouldn't possibly do anything to put that business at risk, even if I was not concerned about breaking this country's laws. England has been good to me and my family and we willingly abide by its rules and regulations."

"I'm sure that's the case. Let's go on with the checking," replied Iain.

I ran through another four of Davenport's entries. But all were matched in Klugman's ledger. I was about to draw a halt, but Iain nudged me to run through all of them – with the same result. Just before eleven o'clock we finished. Mr Klugman hurried us out – not, I felt, because he had anything to hide, but because he needed to get on with his next piece of business. No doubt it would be a lot more profitable than the hour he had spent with us.

"Well, what did you make of that?" asked Iain. Evidently he wasn't going to mention the error of my ways.

"I couldn't really tell whether he was lying or not. What seems odd is that all those entries that Davenport had appear to have gone through as normal. I can't see why Silberstein's ledgers would tally so exactly with our paperwork... unless..."

"Unless?"

"Well, if someone was committing fraud, the obvious place to do it would be the valuation of the diamonds. Then everything would have to tally on paper – even though the diamonds were twice as valuable."

"Or those weren't Silberstein's real ledgers. It's an old trick – two or even three sets of books. I was trying to gauge whether it was a dummy set, but if it was, it had been well done. The entries looked as though they had been written in at different times. That's partly why I wanted you to ask about every entry, because he had to turn over a page. I'd really like to have seen some of the earlier pages – just in case they were blank."

"Partly?"

"It already seems to me possible that we're just dealing with a single or couple of entries that are the key to Davenport's death and the envelope of diamonds he had in that suitcase. Either he didn't know which they were or he took a load of similar ones to create a smokescreen. If we take a short cut and just ask about a few, we might miss the right ones."

"I see. And what did you make of his response about Russian diamonds?"

"Methinks he doth protest too much. It's well known that the Russians launder their diamonds through Zurich and Amsterdam, usually by way of Stockholm or West Berlin. There must be a bigger margin on such stones, so I don't believe any business as canny as Silbersteins washes their hands of it. And who's to tell? As he said, you need an expert to tell. And where

63

are the experts? In Hatton Garden and its equivalents in Amsterdam, New York and so on. And most of the traders are related one way or another."

"I wonder whether that rumour about some diamonds being lost had anything to do with Davenport's? There were also those notes in the files about a confidential IB investigation into several of the entries which appeared clearly in Klugman's ledger and were no different from others where Davenport hadn't left a note like that."

"Hmm... I think Klugman could've provided some refreshment. We're due to see David Weissman at 11.30, so let's grab a coffee. There's a newish Italian place round here somewhere."

At 11.30 we duly presented ourselves at David Weissman and Co. On the corner of Cross Street and the narrow dingy alleyway known as Saffron Lane, it looked several leagues below Silberstein. In the window were second-hand watches, rings and other jewellery, along with a notice that proclaimed that Weissman would give good prices for second-hand gold, silver or jewellery.

"I suspect they also act as undeclared pawnbrokers," muttered Iain.

Inside there was a large counter, with more wares displayed under glass. A thin-faced woman in her mid-thirties, with peroxide-blonde hair stood behind it.

"Mornin' gents. Sellin' or buyin'?"

"Neither," replied Iain. "I spoke to Mr Weissman on the phone yesterday. We're from HM Customs & Excise to carry out some routine checks."

"Okey dokey. I'll get 'im."

Mr Weissman could have been a second-row forward. Six foot two and big with it, he was in his late thirties, with curly, black, brylcreemed hair and the beard of an orthodox Jew.

"Mr Cogbill? Do come through with your colleague. I've got an office out the back."

We followed him past a couple of heavily padlocked doors to a room with a small desk and chair, with three comfortable, if elderly brown leather chairs in front of it. Behind the desk were a couple of ancient wooden cupboards and on what looked like a pedestal for a plant pot perched a small Russian-made TV.

"Do sit down," he said, switching the TV off. "I follow the gee-gees."

"You remember why we're here, Mr Weissman?"

"Yes. Some sort of check on some of the stuff I've been importing. I'll just get my ledgers."

He went over to the desk and pulled out a ledger that looked remarkably similar to the one used by Silbersteins.

"Mr Storey here will ask the questions, if you don't mind. He's quite new to this and I'm supervising him while he picks it up. Is that satisfactory?"

"Yes."

"Because we don't physically examine every consignment that goes through the port, we carry out occasional post-importation checks to satisfy ourselves that the documentation which we have matches yours – and the goods arrived as declared. That sort of thing."

"OK. Fire away."

"The first one I've got is an import entry for 19 April of this year for scrap jewellery from de Wet in Amsterdam valued at £17, 315 11s 6d. Is that in your ledger?"

"Yes. You can see it here. Shipping agent Verhaeren in Rotterdam and Kersey in Harwich."

"Yes. That tallies. What about 23 May, also scrap jewellery from de Wet worth £23,222 14s exactly."

"Yes. Same as before."

"And 18 June?"

"Same as the others. Worth £14,877 4s 6d. Is that the value you've got, Mr Storey?"

"Yes. They match. Do you do all your imports of this stuff through Harwich?"

"Yes."

"Do you mind if I ask why?"

"Not at all. It's cheaper. Terry Kersey's cheaper than anyone at Tilbury. Air freight is much too expensive for my sort of stuff. I get all my stuff from Jan de Wet. He's handy for the Hook."

"But you use Verhaeren in Rotterdam?"

65

"My Dutch Terry Kersey, that's Frans Verhaeren – though actually he's Flemish not Dutch. He's cheap and reliable. The agents at the Hook are too bloody greedy!"

"Do you ever get any stuff from anyone other than de Wet?"

"No. He and I have what you might call an exclusive deal. I was stationed at Osnabruck during National Service and I met Jan while I was there. He and I helped each other out, you might say. Jan de Wet and I go a long way back. We trust each other – and that's important in this business. Scrap jewellery can be anything from nickel silver to a ruby worth a hundred grand, so dealing with stuff you haven't seen requires trust. Of course, my stuff is in the middle – no trash, no stars."

"I've got a couple of rather odd entries – 21 June and 3 July, four cases of scrap jewellery valued at a total of £44 12s 6d on each occasion. The entries suggest they were imported by you."

"Hmmm… Let's see. I vaguely recall something… As you can see, we're importing quite a lot. I also get stuff from my cousin in Dublin and a second cousin in Marseilles… Ah, here we are…! Yes, I remember it now. It wasn't really a commercial importation. A friend of Jan de Wet's has a daughter who was marrying an English bloke and wanted to send her some family jewellery. Four cases sounds a lot, doesn't it? But it was just a necklace in an old presentation box, a silver bracelet watch in a similar box and so on… But I've only got that once – an import arrived 23 June. I've no record of the later one. Are you sure your records are correct?"

"It could be a mistake. Sometimes agents forget and misplace an entry or it slips in with another one," said Iain hastily. "We'll check with Kersey."

"It seems rather a low valuation for four cases," I suggested.

"Oh well… suppose they may have pushed the value down as it was for family. I imagine they were just trying to keep the customs duty down. I never actually opened the stuff. Just sent it on to Genevieve van Hoogstraaten, Jan's god-daughter. If there's any duty to pay, let me know and I'll pay it."

"There will be – and a penalty for misdeclaration," said Iain coldly. "I'm content for you to pay as the importer, but I'll need Miss van Hoogstraaten's address. We shall need to see the jewellery to get it valued correctly."

"Well, she's Mrs Denton now. Mrs Philip Denton… of Flat 2 24 Markham Street, SW3. I'm afraid I don't have a phone number."

The atmosphere had become decidedly chilly. I went through the remaining entries, all of which were reflected exactly in Weissman's ledger.

A sudden thought came into my mind and I decided to pursue it a little.

"Do you only import second-hand and scrap jewellery, Mr Weissman? Or do you bring in other things, like diamonds for example?"

"If only! I may be on the edge of Hatton Garden, but I'm not really part of it. The diamond trade is sewn up between half a dozen families who wouldn't welcome interlopers."

"But I imagine you must know what goes on."

"I keep my ear to the ground, as they say."

"Well, you may know that one of the jobs of Customs and Excise is to keep an eye out for smuggled Russian diamonds. Do you reckon there are any here in London?"

"I'd be surprised if there weren't. The Russkies have to sell them cheap to get the hard currency, so there's a bigger margin, since the eventual punter can barely tell the difference between a diamond and a piece of cheap crystal... Not that I know anything specific. But if you got an expert to examine in the uncut diamonds within three streets of here, I'd bet you at least one in ten were from Russia."

"And if any consignments of Russian diamonds got nicked, presumably no-one would really be able to go to the police or to Customs and Excise?"

"If anyone was stupid enough to nick Russian diamonds, I expect they'd have more to worry about from the KGB."

"The last place we went to said there'd been a rumour of a consignment of uncut diamonds going missing a few months back. Did you hear anything about it?"

"I make it a rule not to believe idle gossip. If there was a rumour, it was very quickly squashed. You may make of that what you will."

We parted in a slightly more cordial atmosphere than had seemed likely at one stage.

"I believe we could do with a spot of lunch," remarked Iain. "And if that was the real set of books, I'm a Dutchman too!"

"But if they were a dummy set, why would he leave the van Hoogstraaten stuff in there to be found? Or not got it right?"

"The trick of a good set of dummy books is to be as accurate as possible in most things, so that the incurious examiner fails to spot the small number of large lies because of the convenient truth that lies in front of him. The question for us is, where were the large lies?"

67

We walked back towards Fetter Lane, but headed beyond the IB HQ into Cursitor Street, to what appeared to be a Victorian pub called the Lamb and Flag. Nodding to the barman as he went in, Iain led me through a door marked 'private' down a flight of stairs into a basement room, set out with tables and benches, each one cut off from the rest by a dark wooden dividing wall. There was no-one else there. At the end of the room was a blackboard with "today's menu" inscribed on it in chalk. There appeared to be no choice. It was Lancashire hotpot, apple crumble and custard and tea or coffee – or not.

"I was going to say 'do you come here often'," I began, "but evidently you do."

"This room is almost exclusively for the use of the IB. The landlord gets a good trade from us and Richard Sawyer, one of our Deputy Chiefs, encouraged him to convert a former storeroom into somewhere we could have private conversations outside the office."

A middle-aged woman in a white apron appeared.

"Good afternoon, Maisie," said Iain. "Lunch for two please."

"If you want drinks, you'll have to go upstairs today, Mr Cogbill. Ivy's sick, so we're short-handed today."

"Thank you. That's fine. I take it you don't want a beer or a glass of wine?"

"No thanks. At the moment I feel particularly in need of keeping a clear head."

"What did you make of David Weissman?"

"I doubt he's much scruples about making money where he can. But if he's in the big league, like Silbersteins, he's disguising it well. I imagine he knew more than he was telling us. But apart from that odd shipment which the VB picked up, I don't see him being seriously involved in whatever Davenport was mixed up in."

"I think we might chase up that little story this afternoon – though I expect it's probably right. I would like to know whether it was two entries or one, though. It's just possible that it's meant to look like that – and the under-declaration was made – all to provide a smokescreen for a small consignment that was of very high value. When you get back to Harwich, put Kersey on the spot about it. Although I fear Weissman will have tipped him off. I might just pop into the office after this and ring Jim Round and see if he could get over to Kerseys this afternoon... but even then, it'll probably be too late."

"So you think that Weissman might've been the one who brought in the uncut diamonds in Davenport's suitcase?"

"If I was trying to bring hot Russian diamonds into the UK, I think I'd use a number of routes – both apparently straightforward and more devious... You know, putting the same value for both those sham consignments the VB picked up was either very sloppy or quite brilliant."

"I suppose we ought to try and find out whether Davenport's diamonds actually are from Russia."

"Easier said than done. We have no experts ourselves and it's a tight community. If we get someone in to examine them – even one of them – two and two will be put together, especially if people know that a consignment went missing. I think we may have to be a bit devious ourselves about that... .But I'll need to think a bit more..."

"I meant to ask you – is there any IB investigation going on relating to any of the files Davenport took with him? You remember, the note in our registry and the A&CG's files?"

"So far I've found nothing. I suspect it was just a convenient smokescreen put up by Davenport. There will be one soon, though."

The food was excellent, as I'd expected. It struck me that the IB did themselves pretty well. I was beginning to wonder whether my career should not move in that direction.

Afterwards we took a taxi to Markham Street, just off the trendy King's Road in fashionable Chelsea. No 24 was in a large, elegant Victorian terrace, presumably originally built for large families with servants, but now divided up into flats for wealthy couples.

Iain rang the bell for Flat 2 and within a minute, a young woman opened the window upstairs and asked who we were and what we wanted. We explained, so she came down and let us in. She was short, blonde-haired, quite pretty and very Dutch.

"Do you mind if I see some identification, please?" she asked in a husky Dutch accent.

We showed her our commissions and Iain introduced us.

"We've been to see David Weissman earlier today about some family jewellery which we understand he imported for you from the Netherlands," he began. "Our Valuation Branch has queried the value of these items and

Mr Weissman said that he had imported them for you and that the value may have been under-declared because they were a family gift."

"That's right. They were my grandmother's things. My father said it would be safer if my Uncle Jan shipped them, rather than sending them by post or courier. I know nothing of the value that was put on them."

"We would like to see the items, if you please."

"Certainly."

She took them out of a cupboard. To my mind, they were so easily accessible, because she had already been warned of an impending visit from us by David Weissman.

"Here they are: four boxes – a necklace, a bracelet-watch, a bracelet, another necklace and matching earrings. As you can see, they're rather old and not very valuable. I believe my grandmother hid them in a hole in the ground in our garden under the German occupation."

"Were they a wedding gift?"

"Yes and no. My Grandmother left them to me in her will, so I should have had them five years ago. But as I had no interest in them, because they're so old-fashioned, my mother held on to them. It was only when I agreed to marry Phil and remain here in London that she said that she wasn't going to store them anymore and I should have them and decide what to do with them."

"I don't think we could regard such a transaction as a wedding gift."

"Very well."

"We will have to take them away with us, to get them properly valued. We'll then contact Mr Weissman if there's any extra Customs duty to pay. Once that's paid, we can arrange for you to get them back."

"Keep them as long as you like. I wasn't planning to wear them. If I didn't think my parents would check, I'd sell them tomorrow."

"That was all? There wasn't another lot of boxes?"

"No. that was all. It was enough, believe me!"

Did I believe her? Probably. Either she was a very good actress or she was far too talkative to risk involving in something secretive, especially if it was important and valuable.

"This is a very nice flat," I remarked. "And in such a fashionable area."

"Phil is part-owner of a boutique in Carnaby Street. I work part-time at the London School of Slavonic and East European Studies, as a secretary."

And that was that. I made out a receipt for the four boxes of jewellery and she kindly provided a paper shopping bag in which I could carry them away.

"I think I'll talk to some colleagues at Box 500 about this matter," said Iain. "Much as it might be worth you coming along, Storey, you haven't the necessary clearance, so I suggest you make your way back to Harwich. I'll try and make it up there tomorrow. But if not, see what you can do to chase up this second entry. If you go by way of the river, you could drop these boxes off at Vintry House and get the VB to do the valuation for you. After all, they started the whole thing off."

So I took the Tube from Sloane Square to Mansion House and walked to the south side of Southwark Bridge. At the entrance to the Customs and Excise premises in Vintry House, I presented myself to the Revenue Constable, who looked to me more like what my mother would've called a "spiv", and asked for Mr Mummery.

After about ten minutes this gentleman, a thin, pallid man with mousey hair and a pair of thick round NHS spectacles appeared.

"I'm Mummery. You're Storey?"
"That's right. You wrote to Davenport, my predecessor, about a couple of entries of scrap jewellery. Sorry it's been a while, but we've had to follow quite a long trail. At the moment, it seems possible there was only one entry and the agent submitted it twice by mistake. Also, it was misdescribed as scrap jewellery. It was actually second-hand jewellery. I've got it here. I suggest it might be simplest if you value it for us. Then we can get any Customs duty that might be required off the importer. I'm going to chase up exactly what happened with the other entry tomorrow. Is that OK?"

"It's all a bit irregular. There are forms and procedures, you know."
"But doesn't it seem a bit complicated and time-consuming if I take this stuff back to Harwich and then send it to you along with the various forms? If you give me a receipt for the stuff, I can send you the appropriate forms tomorrow."
"Well... really, you are supposed to get the stuff valued and we –"
"But if I get it valued and you don't agree or aren't sure I've got it right, you'll want to see the stuff and get it valued yourselves anyway, won't you? Won't this just get it done a bit quicker?"

"I suppose so. But you must send form V205 first thing tomorrow, along with a formal receipt AG32 which I'll sign and stamp and regularise the position. It's a pity you Outfield chaps don't value the importance of proper procedures more. We'd get a lot less work that way."

He sighed and took the four small boxes back to his office. I made my way back to Liverpool Street and was fortunate in catching a boat train direct to Harwich. By the time I got there it was getting dark and I was knackered. A hard day's bloody night indeed!

SEVEN – HARWICH: – KERSEY CONFESSES

Of course I had the Beatles LP! Practically everybody aged under thirty did. Though my teenage years had been formed by *Rock Around the Clock* and skiffle, I was as enthusiastic about the new type of music epitomised by the Beatles and the Mersey sound. Indeed, observing today's teenagers, quite a lot of me felt I wished I'd been born ten years later.

That morning *Things We Said Today* kept buzzing round my brain, as I wondered whether I should perhaps have waited for a fixed appointment in Liverpool Customs where I could have got into the Mersey scene at weekends. If I could play slap bass, as I had in my later teenage days, surely I could master the bass electric guitar. If I'd had the money, I might've invested in a Rickenbacker like George Harrison's, but the cold-hearted realist in me knew that when I got enough cash together, I'd buy something like a three-year-old Ford Anglia in decent running order.

As I arrived in the Custom House, I wondered whether Jim had been to see Terry Kersey the previous afternoon.

"Couldn't get away," explained Jim. "Bloody Imrie had us all at a meeting with the refinery people to try and work out how we could best manage our controls. Bit bloody silly when a Hydrocarbon Oils expert hasn't even been posted here yet. I don't suppose you ever did refinery work as a UO?"
"No. I did the Courage brewery in Reading, Players in Nottingham and Gordon's gin distillery in Wandsworth as my Excise training, but no HC oils I'm afraid."
"Given the choice of booze and fags, who would want to be a control officer on oils…! Anyway, you'd better get round to Kerseys after we've completed the morning's clearances. You've got the background after all."
"You want to come?"
"No. I'd better catch up on what didn't get done during a wasted afternoon."

I had been wondering whether Davenport's death and the inevitable police enquiries, not to say our recovery of possibly incriminating documents, might have caused the traffic in uncut diamonds and scrap jewellery to have changed its route. But that morning we got entries for both and I insisted on a full physical examination. I went over to the examination shed to observe. I wasn't unduly surprised to find that the goods appeared to tally with the entries. Of course, as far as the diamonds were concerned, it wasn't possible to tell from the sort of inspection the Waterguard could give what quality they were or whether they were Russian. Talk about looking for a needle in a haystack with a blindfold on!

On the other hand, I did have the minor satisfaction of pulling an entry which might cover the import of pornographic magazines and watching my hunch being confirmed and the goods formally seized.

"You seem to be developing a revenue nose," observed Wally French. "I should let Morry Gold deal with the importers. He'll scare the shit out of them. The only other person in this place who can do that is your boss. When Jim gets his teeth into some hapless importer who's erred, I've seen them shaking like jellies and weeping like little girls!"

Just before lunch I made my way to Kerseys. I decided to go unannounced, even though I suspected Terry Kersey would already be expecting a visit. Just as he had when I visited with Jim Round, he met me at the top of the stairs and took me into his office, offering me a cup of extraordinarily powerful coffee.

"What can I do you for?" he asked with a cheery grin.
"I had a recent enquiry from our Valuation Branch about the valuation of some scrap jewellery that you handled the entries for, imported by Weissman of Saffron Row, London. They were two quite small consignments, four boxes, imported on 21 June and 3 July valued at a total of £44 12s 6d each time. A colleague and I went to Weissmans yesterday to find out more about it, but he claimed that it was only a single entry and that you must have mistakenly put the entry in twice. Perhaps it got caught up with another, later entry."
"I can certainly check. Which was the one that 'e said 'ad definitely been imported?"
"The 21 June one."
"Okey dokey. We'd better go round to where I keep my records. I'm not bang up to date at the moment. My secretary's off havin' a baby and as

74

she's family, I can't really replace 'er. I got rid of 'er brother, 'oo was my filing clerk, 'cos 'e was completely useless. That's another reason why I can't bring someone in instead of 'er. So I've been doin' most of the work 'ere for the last couple of months."

It certainly looked like it. The room where the files were kept had eight filing cabinets in it, with files supposedly stored in date order. But there were piles of entries and other documents on the floor and on the small table and chair in the middle of the room.

"I suppose you don't want to come back when I've 'ad a chance to sort myself out…? No, I didn't think so somehow."

While he tried to work out where the files might be, I wondered why he was renting the whole floor, when more than half was left empty. I suspected that some of his clients might have been rather less enthusiastic to use his services if they knew the extent to which his business seemed to run on a wing and a prayer. It also struck me that the secretary I'd seen but a few days previously had suddenly become so very pregnant.

After about ten minutes, he came up with the entry for 21 June. This didn't surprise me. If there was something fishy going on, it would be imperative to find the entry that tallied with Weissman's story.

After another twenty minutes or so, Kersey said, "I've looked in all the likely places, Mr Storey. I can't find anything. I think Mr Weissman must've been right. I must've got the earlier entry caught up with another entry. So I don't think there's any point in me looking any further, is there?"

"I think there's every point. I checked earlier, you didn't put any other entries in on 3 July for it to have been caught up with. Also, if it was the same entry, how come we have two top copies with different dates? If it was the same entry, why was the date changed?"

"I suppose if I'd seen it and thought I 'adn't put the entry in, I might've changed the date."

"Wouldn't it've been easier just to give us a ring and find out?"

"You're not always very 'elpful. Besides, it might've been a black mark against me."

"Better than forging an entry, I'd've thought. Anyway, I'm not going to leave here until there's been a thorough check of all these entries. If I might use your phone, I'll ask two or three of my people to come over and do it, if you like."

"They won't find anything." This wasn't said in a spirit of defiance, but of sudden resignation. It was as if the middleweight had just received an unexpected blow to the solar plexus and had all the wind knocked out of him.

"Why not?"

"I destroyed it a couple of months ago, after that bloke Davenport started asking questions – the same sort of questions you've been asking today and you asked Dave Weissman yesterday."

"Did Weissman know you'd destroyed the entry and presumably any relevant documentation?"

"You bet! It was 'im 'oo told me to destroy the stuff in the first place?"

"So what was in the consignment?"

"I dunno. Jan de Wet just told me there'd be two small consignments, low value, one coming a week or so after the other. The first was genuine, the second was 'special'. If I was sensible I wouldn't ask what was in it – or look, for that matter."

"What happened to it?"

"It went through without examination and the van took it on its merry way to Saffron Lane, as far as I know."

"When did Mr Davenport start asking questions?"

"A few weeks later. I can't really remember when. 'E asked why Weissman 'ad suddenly taken to importing in such small quantities, and why two consignments of something so variable in value as scrap jewellery should have exactly the same value? I told 'im I couldn't lay my 'ands on the entries at that very moment and rang Dave Weissman. That was when 'e told me to destroy the second entry and to use the story I tried on you."

"Did Mr Davenport come back?"

"Of course. Persistent if nothin' else. I shot 'im the line and 'e looked as though 'e didn't believe a word of it. But if there's nothin' to be found, you can't find nothin'. 'E said e'd 'ave to check the shipping record. So I rang Jan de Wet. 'E said not to worry as the consignment 'adn't featured on the manifest, so even though Davenport was suspicious, 'e 'ad no evidence to prove anythin'."

"Were any other consignments sent this way?"

"You must be jokin'! After Davenport began snoopin' around, whatever was being shipped that way found another way to get in. But it may just've been a one-off, you know. I never got asked to do anythin' like it before – or since."

"What do you think it was?"

"I've got no imagination. Trying to guess things like that could be very bad for my 'ealth. I'll leave that to blokes like Davenport and you."

"And after asking these awkward questions, Davenport gets killed by a hit and run driver. Do you wonder whether that's a bit too much of a co-incidence?"

"That's precisely why I don't ask questions like that. I don't see why they should be connected. Wasn't 'e movin' on to a new job?"

"As his wife killed herself the other day in suspicious circumstances, perhaps the police might require rather more informative answers."

"There's nothin' I could say that'd 'elp 'em. What are you goin' to do, Mr Storey? I suppose you realise that I'll deny anythin' I've said to you today. And you 'aven't got any evidence."

"No – and I'm not an investigator so I don't know the rules about getting statements out of witnesses. But you mightn't find such an easy way out from our investigators, who I'll be phoning the moment I get back to the Custom House."

"I could try to stop you."

"Exactly how? And what good would it do? My boss – Jim Round – knows I was coming over here. Don't you think he might get just a little suspicious if I don't return? Besides, you would then have definitely broken the Customs & Excise Act and you could be arrested and charged. Do you really want to do that?"

I was also ten years younger, faster and fitter, and still retained some of the benefits of three months' unarmed combat training when I was doing National Service.

He said nothing. So I turned and made my way out. Would he phone David Weissman and tell him what he'd told me or would he decide it was safer to say nothing? As Weissman must be expecting us to ask Kersey some questions about the supposedly missing entry, he would be foolish not to let him know I had been. If he said that he'd used the story Weissman had suggested for him and though I wasn't satisfied, there was nothing I could do about it. In the absence of any positive evidence, he might get away with it. However, if he believed that Davenport had been murdered because of his involvement in this matter, I think I might now be gathering my most valuable belongings together, getting my savings out of the bank and setting off for somewhere I couldn't be found.

But wasn't I now in exactly the same position as Davenport?

I returned to the Custom House and, once he had returned from lunch, told Jim what I had learnt.

"An interesting tale," he observed. "But if the consignment got through to Weissman safely, how did Davenport get his hands on £50,000 worth of uncut diamonds? And if it wasn't diamonds, what was in the bogus consignment?"

I felt a little more relieved. After all, if whoever had killed the Davenports knew I'd told my colleagues, they could scarcely go bumping us all off. Besides, wasn't it more likely that it was the diamonds someone was after?

"Are you going to inform Mr Imrie?" I asked Jim. "If this blows up into something big, as it seems it might well, he's going to give us the most almighty bollocking for not keeping him properly informed."

"Not on your nelly!" he replied. "Or at least, not yet. Jock Imrie could easily mess all this up trying to get himself noticed by the CI's Office and the Board. Either that, or he'll reckon it's too hot to handle and persuade the Collector we should hand it all over to the boys in blue."

"In whom you have little faith."

"My limited experience is that when the police get involved in matters that have a significant Customs element, they don't understand what they're doing and foul up any chances we might have of getting any convictions or decent compounded penalties."

"So we keep it to ourselves."

"For now. Iain Coggy is coming up on Monday, so we'll see what he's come up with and what he proposes to do next. I'm sorry you're not able to play tomorrow…"

"I'm meeting a girl in London."

"Oh to be young again! Enjoy yourself, lad."

EIGHT – LONDON: UNOFFICIAL SLEUTHING

I certainly hoped WPC Rosemary Johnson would allow me the opportunity to enjoy myself, but I suspected that any enjoyment would be limited in how far it went. I rose early, put on my leather jacket (the first fruits of regular employment) and jeans and caught a train that would get me to Liverpool Street by around 9 o'clock. I wasn't planning to be late to meet WPC Johnson.

St Pancras was dismal. I got there just after 9.30 and spent a tedious hour and a quarter sitting in the station buffet drinking tea. Not that it was particularly good, but experience of British Rail coffee ruled that out as a possible alternative. I occasionally wondered why the makers of Camp Coffee hadn't been lynched. But evidently plenty of people were content to drink it, but after the coffee I had drunk in Germany and, especially Kenya, most English coffee tasted mediocre, at best. I sat reading the paper and idly watching people come in, get something to eat or drink, consume what they'd bought and depart for their trains. I bought a copy of *The Guardian*, staunch in its support for Harold Wilson, the new Prime Minister. I could picture my father, avid reader of, occasional letter writer to and complete believer in everything written in, the *Daily Worker* remarking that it was always pseudo-social democrats like Wilson, aided and abetted by uncritical press admirers like *The Guardian*, who persuaded the working class into believing they were working in their interests when actually they were working in the interests of business and the bourgeoisie. His view was that at least with the *Express* and the *Mail*, your enemy didn't disguise his true colours. On the other hand, I told myself, most of these people coming in and out of the station buffet had been offered the chance to vote for the party of their choice rather than for the Communist Party or a one-way ticket to the gulags as in the Soviet Union. Probably my father saw the replacement of Khrushchev the previous month by Brezhnev and Kosygin as a welcome return to the orthodox Communist ways, but I suspected it would be a turn for the worse for ordinary Russians.

I went over to the station barrier. The arrivals board told me that the next train calling at Leicester would arrive on Platform 2. It was quite a nippy November day, grey and raw, which poured in under the great canopy of glass and steel that had undoubtedly seen better – and cleaner – days. I hoped I would be able to recognise WPC Johnson. The WPC uniform and hat were unflattering – unless you like that kind of thing – and she would look very different in civvies.

But in the event, she was instantly recognisable. Short, jet-black hair, a short grey coat with a black velvet collar, a miniskirt which I could barely see beneath the coat, black stockings or tights and black leather boots, which came almost up to her knees. At least as attractive as she had appeared in my mind's eye.

"Good morning, WPC Johnson. Welcome to the smoke."

"As we're off-duty, I think we can drop the formalities. I'm Rosemary... You are called Nick, as I recall."

"Sorry, I was probably pushing it a bit."

"It was nothing. When you work in a man's world like me, you expect it and it doesn't bother you."

"There was something you wanted to tell me?"

"Yes. But not here. I could really do with a coffee. There weren't any refreshments on the train."

"OK. But not on the station. The coffee here is diabolical. The area round here is pretty grubby too. If you can hang on for twenty minutes or so, we could go somewhere in the centre of town. Is there anywhere particular you wanted to see?"

"I've seen all the obvious things, like the Tower, Buckingham Palace, Westminster Abbey and St Pauls. You're a Londoner, aren't you? You certainly sound like one. Why don't you suggest somewhere?"

"Well, we could go and see Scotland Yard and the original Scotland Yard in Whitehall?"

"I hope that was a joke! I'm off duty today."

"Well, if you want to be educational, we could go to South Kensington or Bloomsbury to one of the museums. If you want arts or shopping, the West End? We could go to Carnaby Street, if that interests you? Or Oxford Street? Or one of the big department stores, like Harrods?"

"Let's go to Carnaby Street."

"If we get the Tube to Oxford Circus, we can get a coffee in a coffee bar near there."

"Sounds OK to me."

At the Tube ticket office, she insisted on buying her own ticket.

"You didn't say whether you really are a Londoner?"

"I'm from South-East London originally. I was born and brought up in Woolwich. You sound as though you come from Leicester or near there."

"Thurmaston. It's a little village, a few miles from the city."

"You said you hadn't been in the job that long. Were you at college before that?"

"I went to a teacher training college in Loughborough. Then I taught for a couple of years in Leicester. I quickly realised I wasn't suited for it, so I decided to try the police instead. What about you? Is this your first job?"

"Yes – in a way. I've been in the Department for over two years. Before that I was at college and before that I did my two years National Service."

"But couldn't you…?"

"Couldn't I have avoided doing National Service if I'd gone to university first? Yes. I suppose I wasn't really ready for it, but I wanted to get away from home. I didn't mind being in the Army. I had an interesting time – and learnt some useful skills."

"How to kill people?"

"Of course. But also more useful ones, like how to drive, how to use a compass and map read, how to speak Russian…"

"How to be a detective? You seemed to do a better job than any of our detectives the other day."

"Thank you. I get that from being an avid reader of Sherlock Holmes when I was a boy. The Army do teach you to be observant, though. The unwary soldier tends to be the dead soldier, they used to tell us."

"What subject did you do at college?"

"German mainly, with a bit of Russian. I tried to get into the Foreign Office and the Civil Service, but I don't think I've got the sort of mind they're looking for. What subject did you teach? Or was it a junior school?"

"Music. I'm a fair piano player and a better violinist. But not good enough for the Royal Academy here in London. The trouble with teaching music in a secondary modern is that the girls treated it as a break. Instead of doing anything musical, I was spending all my time trying to keep them in order."

"You haven't taken up the electric guitar then?"

"I've got a room in a house of WPCs. They'd probably arrest me and confiscate my guitar – if I could afford to buy one. Do you play one?"

"I used to play bass in a sort of skiffle band when I was in the sixth form. Basically I was one of those children that regarded music lessons as free time."

We had arrived at a little coffee bar, one of many that had appeared in and around Oxford Circus over the last five years or so. It was half full. We took a table on its own at the back. Rosemary allowed me to buy both of us an "Americano", as recommended by the man behind the counter. It came with complimentary dry biscuits which tasted of almonds.

"Amaretti. Italian. Very tasty!" explained the waiter. Whether he was really Italian or from Stepney, no doubt Sherlock Holmes would have been able to tell. But not I.

"This is very nice. But I mustn't forget why I came," Rosemary began. "Detective Constable Sedgwick summoned me to see him after you'd gone. He asked what you'd done, so I explained you'd just searched to see if there were any Customs papers or anything else that belonged to Customs around, but you'd found nothing. Eric Sedgwick is a pig and there was no point mentioning your suspicions to him. I did ask him whether the bottle of brandy which Mrs Davenport had drunk from might have been smuggled – and he showed me a full-size bottle. 'If you can tell whether that was smuggled or not, you can send it back to the Customs,' he said. 'But they'll only drink it themselves.'"

"That was a clever idea."

"I thought so too. I did speak to my sergeant about your suspicions. He's only a year or two off retirement and he's about the only man in the whole station who hasn't tried it on with me. He also seems to be pretty straight. So I told him what you'd found. But he went all formal on me and said that it's more than likely that Mrs Davenport had done it herself while the balance of her mind was disturbed or perhaps one of our lot on the scene had done it. He laughed at the idea of the brandy bottle. He said there was no reason why she hadn't just got the bottle specially to get drunk enough to kill herself or, if it was normally kept for medicinal purposes, perhaps it was kept downstairs and the Davenports liked to economise by buying a full-size bottle. 'Everyone doesn't have to keep their medicinal brandy in a medicine chest,' he said. As for the sleeping pills, he suggested Mrs Davenport may have got hold of two bottles to make sure she killed herself. I'm afraid I didn't see the bottle they took away from her bedroom, so I don't know where it was bought or whether it was on prescription or bought from a chemist. Whether he has said anything to Sedgwick I don't know. But no-one has said anything more on the subject."

"Well, you did your best. We've subsequently found out that one of the entries Davenport had taken away with him related to a bogus import that he'd been asking questions about. But we don't know what it was yet. I guess it was valuable – as many of the entries were for imports of uncut diamonds worth thousands."

"I think Sedgwick has made up his mind it was suicide. They've all got plenty of other cases which appear to be less straightforward, so they want to draw a line under Mrs Davenport and get on with some real work, as they put it. There's an inquest sometime next week – I'm sorry, I don't know which day – and that'll be the end of it."

"What do you think?"

"You encouraged me to have doubts – and I have. I wouldn't like to say Mrs Davenport was murdered, but you found enough loose ends that if I was Sedgwick, I'd want to do a more thorough job."

"Well... I hope I can trust you," I said lowering my voice, "but the last thing Mrs Davenport said to me was that she thought her husband had been run over deliberately."

"Oh! Did you believe her?"

"I'd no reason to believe or not believe her. I'd no idea what she was like as a person except for meeting her not long after her husband had been killed."

"Did you tell Eric Sedgwick this?"

"No."

"Don't you think you should've done?"

"Yes and no... Can I trust you, Rosemary Johnson? I'm not going to mess things up just because you're so pretty am I...? Sorry... But I really need to know if I can tell you something important in confidence and you won't tell a living soul, unless I agree to it. Do you trust me enough to promise that?"

"Well, I suppose I ought to confess that I rather liked the look of you. Otherwise I'd just've rung you from outside the office. I don't think I could tell a straight lie to any of my colleagues. I hope you're not asking me to do that. But if it's more about not telling them something, I can promise. But if it's something that's at the heart of the Davenport deaths, I don't know..."

"Well, I think I'll trust your judgement. You know that Mrs Davenport had a suitcase belonging to her husband containing things that belonged to the Department? Apart from the various Customs entries and other papers was a small envelope containing thousands of pounds' worth of uncut diamonds. As several of the entries concerned uncut diamonds, my boss told me to bring the whole lot back to Harwich so we could try and find out how Davenport had got hold of them. We'd had no complaints about any diamonds going missing before, during or after their passage through Harwich, so it wasn't obvious whether any crime had been committed. It was only when Mrs Davenport said she thought her husband had been murdered that the diamonds took on a more sinister character. They are now safely under lock and key in Harwich."

"And you couldn't tell Eric Sedgwick about what Mrs Davenport said because you'd have to come clean about the diamonds, which I take it you didn't mention in your statement?"

"No."

"Well, you and your boss are undoubtedly guilty of withholding evidence. So you're going to have to come up with a pretty good result."

"We believe the diamonds were smuggled – so at least the original offence was under the Customs & Excise Act – and that Davenport seemed to be trying to find out about them. I'm beginning to believe that he'd worked out how uncut diamonds had been smuggled and intercepted a shipment. Why he might've done it on his own and what he thought he was up to I've no idea."

"Well, I suggest that as far as we're concerned, you haven't told me any of this. If anyone asks, you and I got on when we met in Leicester and agreed to have a day out together in London. That means that I don't need to drop you in it – and also I don't lose my career because I should've passed on what you've just told me."

"Fine by me. Shall we do what we're supposed to be doing? Carnaby Street is only a short walk from here."

We wandered up and down Carnaby Street and some of the neighbouring ones, full of boutiques selling trendy and sometimes rather alarming clothes at extremely high prices. Quite a few of the clothes were visibly on young people we passed. Beatlemania was being hotly pursued by worship of the Rolling Stones, so every item of clothing that could be seen when they appeared on TV or, in the case of the Beatles, in *A Hard Day's Night* was widely copied, as were the clothes seen on the girls who danced on *Ready, Steady*, Go or *Top of the Pops*.

Rosemary looked, even picked up a few things, but never tried anything on and certainly didn't buy anything.

"I like Mary Quant stuff, but most of this isn't very good quality for the prices they're charging," she remarked. "I'm not badly paid as a WPC, but I'm not going to waste my money on something as badly made as this stuff. It'll be out of fashion by this time next year anyway."

"I'm starting to feel quite old," I said. "I'm twenty-six and I look at this stuff and I think it's for kids."

"It's probably having a job. I'd probably have worn this sort of stuff when I was at college, but now I want to save to get a flat of my own."

"And there isn't some bloke to share it with you...? Sorry, that's me being too forward again. Ignore the question."

"No. It's all right. I've had a couple of serious boyfriends, at college and when I was a teacher. The teacher turned out to be rather a creep. He was one reason why I decided to give up teaching. What about you? How come you've got to the ripe old age of twenty-six and some woman hasn't got her claws into you?"

"I've had a long relationship with a girl from near home. It's been dying a lingering death for more than a year. We met at college. Since I joined Customs I've been moved all round the country every few months, so I've not had much chance to get to know anyone... I'm not generally as pushy as I've been with you..."

"I'm glad you were... I think."

Both of us, I suspect, thought about kissing, but didn't. The moment passed and we agreed to have lunch.

As we were within walking distance, I took her to Greek Street in the hope that there might be a free table in the Gay Hussar, which I had read about in *The Guardian* earlier that morning. It seemed rather trendy and I doubted whether we would get in, but there were plenty of other restaurants in the vicinity. I was fortunate – or perhaps it was just because it was Saturday, grey and cold – and a table was found for us. Weaving our way past a series of wood and metal structures that evidently were holding the place together, we found ourselves at a table for four that was better suited to two.

Knowing practically nothing of Hungarian food, we ordered goulash, because we had both heard of it, and a glass of a red wine recommended by the waiter – not Bull's Blood, fortunately. The goulash was delicious and, to my relief, not too hot. A couple of weeks before I had unwisely gone with the Harwich Customs rugby team to an Indian curry restaurant in Ipswich after a match and had regretted it for a couple of days afterwards. I could easily see why such restaurants were few and far between.

I had rather hoped we might see someone well-known eating there, but though it was pretty full, there was no-one I recognised. But then, half the new Cabinet could be lunching there and I wouldn't recognise them.

"You Londoners do choose the strangest places to eat," observed Rosemary. "I'd've been happy to eat in a Lyons Corner House, you know… though this was a lot better and a lot more interesting. Why did you choose to come here?"

"It was mentioned in the paper this morning as somewhere all the politicians and Fleet Street reporters go. I thought it'd be nice to go somewhere different. I don't really know the West End very well and I don't eat out very often."

"Maybe when you get the bill you'll realise why?"

"I don't mind spending money, at least, I don't mind spending money on you."

In that instant, our eyes met and the moment I'd been dreaming about ever since I first set eyes on her happened – we enjoyed a long kiss.

"Your bill, sir." A waiter with a central European accent, possibly bogus, interrupted us.

The bill was less than I had feared, more than I had hoped.

"What would you like to see this afternoon?" I asked as we left the restaurant.

"I was planning to get a train shortly after four and it's after half past one now. I'm not feeling very sight-seeingy or like wandering round galleries or museums. You're the Londoner, what do you suggest?"

A sudden inspiration hit me.

"I know it's our day off, but one of the importers whose entries Davenport had in his suitcase was a nursery – for plants, not babies, of course – in Belsize Park. We could always have a look at it."

"A bit of amateur sleuthing! I rather fancy that. I can be Miss Marple and you… Hercule Poirot? Hmm… perhaps not… Inspector Alleyn?"

"I'm far too common."

"You'll just have to do your Sherlock Holmes impression again."

"OK – but it'll be quicker if we travel by Tube rather than horse and carriage."

I liked the way she put her hand in mine as we walked to the Tube.

I knew I could remember the name of the nurseries, "the White House Nurseries". But I had no idea where they were in Belsize Park. I could deduce it, but it would probably be easier to ask someone. Fortunately there were a few shops close to Belsize Park Tube station and a woman in a laundrette told me it was in Lawn Road a short walk away.

It seemed a rather plush residential neighbourhood, if perhaps a little run-down. Most of the large Victorian houses had been converted into flats. I supposed it was a notch or two below Philip and Genevieve Denton's neighbourhood, but doubtless estate agents described flats here as 'Hampstead borders'. The White House Nursery was actually down a short alley between two houses, sufficiently well disguised for us to have walked past it the first time. The alleyway was wide enough for cars and even small trucks to get through. At the end was a metal gate with a notice-board advertising the nursery and its opening hours. On Saturdays between October and March, it closed at 4p.m. The only vehicles parked there that I could see were a Land Rover with 'White House Nurseries' written on the front door and a truck. We appeared to be the only customers.

As we opened the gate, it struck me that it was a very small operation. There was a large wooden hut with a greenhouse of a similar size attached to it. In one corner was a low barn with a small aluminium shed inside. Otherwise there were eight rows of plants, some growing in the ground, others in clay pots of various sizes. It being November, there was nothing in flower and most of the plants looked well advanced in a state of winter decrepitude. But for all the apparent low value of the contents, there was a high metal fence all the way round.

A burly young man came out of the wooden shed.

"We're closed," he stated in a hostile tone.
"Oh! I thought you didn't close until 4. We wanted to look at roses."
"Bad time of year to plant roses. But we're closed anyway. I'm just about to lock up."
"OK. We're on our way."
"Do you ever get perdonias?" asked Rosemary. "You know, they have wonderful little yellow and purple flowers in the summer."
"Yeah. I think so. But we don't get 'em in until the spring."
"Thank you."

We left. As we closed the gate at the front, the unfriendly young man padlocked it behind us.

"They can't do much business with someone as grumpy as that," I observed. "But it was a very strange place. Something didn't quite fit."

"He knows nothing about gardening anyhow," said Rosemary. "It'd be perfectly OK to plant roses in November and there isn't such a plant as a 'perdonia'. I just made it up. It confirmed that whatever he does there has nothing to do with plants."

"You have a nicely devious mind, Rosemary Johnson. That was very worthy of Miss Marple – though you are altogether too young and pretty for the role."

"My mother used to work in a florists in the village. For some reason it was called 'Les Fleurs'. The owner was called 'Les' for years. His real name was Trevor."

"I know it's fairly early November, but you'd expect a nursery to be getting ready for the Christmas trade. But that looked more like a plant graveyard. I can't see how it can be making any money."

"So it's either a front for something else or it's used for other purposes as well as being a nursery, so they don't need to make too much money."

"Exactly. It's also far too small, you'd think, to be going to the expense of importing plants from Holland. So what was that all about?"

"None of this seems to be getting any clearer."

"Well, there's nothing more we can do about it today. It's just after 2.20. If we keep walking up Lawn Road we'll get to Parliament Hill where I think you can get quite a good view right across London. Do you fancy a bit of a walk and a bit of a climb?"

"Sounds OK. Any girl who goes around with you had better not wear high heels, that's all I'd say."

We enjoyed a pleasant walk up Parliament Hill and then through Dartmouth Park to Tufnell Park Tube station.

"I'm sorry we didn't have time to go through Gospel Oak," said Rosemary. "It sounds so creepy and Victorian, like something out of Sherlock Holmes or Wilkie Collins."

"I fear it might disappoint – rather like Primrose Hill and Strawberry Hill. The best hill in London anyway is in Greenwich Park, from near the Royal Observatory where you can see the Thames with the Royal Naval College and Maritime Museum in front and the cranes of the dockyards behind. Of course, I may be a bit biased."

"I'd like to go there with you sometime."

Unfortunately, the Tube form Tufnell Park took us directly to King's Cross/St Pancras and Rosemary's train back to Leicester.

"We shall see each other again?" I said, fighting back tears.
"Definitely," she replied. "I'd like to see a lot more of you... But I may not be able to make London every weekend. Let's sort it out on the phone."

We embraced and kissed, tears falling down both our cheeks. She rushed on to the train, sensibly not looking back. I stumbled to the Tube and Liverpool Street for my lonely journey back to Harwich, with a mixture of intense happiness and the barely endurable pain of parting.

EIGHT – LONDON: RUSSIAN DIAMONDS

Iain Cogbill appeared in Harwich the following Monday morning. He was sitting, slightly smugly I thought, in a chair in Jim's office to which I had been summoned after we'd finished clearing the morning's entries.

"That was useful stuff you got out of Kersey, Storey. But you should remember always to take another colleague with you as witness."

"The trouble is – only Mr Round is in the know here – and I'm not sure Kersey would've said anything if he thought it could be used against him in court."

"You may be right. Anyway, I've got some hot information for you. At least some of the diamonds that Davenport had are Russian in origin. After you went off to Vintry House, I went over to see a contact in Box 500, who put me on to someone in Special Branch. He gave me the name of a jeweller they use to value and identify diamonds. Of course, he has an entirely legitimate business, so we sent one of our fellows with one of the secretaries along to pose as a couple who'd inherited four uncut diamonds from an uncle who'd lived in Brussels. Ostensibly they wanted to know what the diamonds were worth – but they also said they'd heard that importing Russian diamonds was illegal and wanted to know if they were and what they might do about it. The diamond merchant gave them a valuation, and stated his opinion that all the diamonds were of Russian origin. His advice was that he would buy them off the couple at about two thirds of his valuation. So much for his legitimate business! Anyway, the couple refused and said they'd take them back to Brussels and sell them there. The diamond merchant said, good luck and see if you can do any better if you want, but everyone will tell you the same thing. I hope we didn't raise any suspicions. At least the diamond merchant is in the West End rather than the City. Sometimes, you just have to hope."

"And this Box 500 chap?" asked Jim. "Or aren't we allowed to know?"

"Not much. The Russians do want to sell as many diamonds in the West as they can to get hard currency. They are keeping an eye on several interesting individuals and businesses. The KGB are involved in it."

"Well, thanks for that! I'd never have guessed any of that!" said Jim with an ironic chortle. "On the other hand, I can tell you something you don't know. On Sunday, someone tried to break into the Queen's Warehouse (QW). Sawed their way through some of the bolts and tried to jemmy the rest, but they must've been disturbed. A Revenue Constable said he thought he heard some noises, but he didn't see anyone – and then he saw the broken bolts and raised the alarm."

"What was in there?" asked Iain.

"Quite a lot of seized booze and fags. Some red diesel seized from a local garage. Some watches and the cannabis we pulled off that Dutch sailor a month or so back."

"So you've not put the diamonds in there?"

"No. Two reasons. One – it's the obvious place anyone who knows about Customs would think to look. Two – more forms and people who don't need to know about this having to be told."

"But you believe someone was trying to retrieve the diamonds?"

"Don't you? It's a bit too much of a coincidence, as far as I'm concerned. We've got booze and fags and watches in the QW all the time. And it wasn't enough cannabis to be worth breaking in for. So what, if not the diamonds?"

"Hmmm… I wonder whether they're safe where they are? They're likely to be vital evidence. Perhaps we should take the rest of them to the QW in Custom House. The IB can put things in there under a dummy name, so we don't have to reveal what they are."

"If you wish. In many ways, I'd prefer it if they didn't leave Harwich, but the security in the Custom House QW is a lot better, I know."

"I'll collect them next time I'm up here."

I wondered briefly why he couldn't take them now.

Then I recalled what I'd been doing on Saturday.

"Well, I have a little extra to add to the pot," I began. "I was in London on Saturday and I called in at the White House Nurseries in Belsize Park. It's small and looked as though it couldn't make ends meet as a nursery business. It seemed too well protected by a metal fence considering the state of the plants. And why they would have the need or money to import plants all the way from Holland. I'd say it was some kind of front. Oh and the unfriendly bloke there knew nothing about plants."

"Did you go around asking questions?" enquired Iain.

"No. The bloke told us the place was closed. So we left."

"Us?"

"I went with my girlfriend. The only question she asked was whether they ever got any perdonias in."

"Perdonias! What the hell are they?"

"They don't exist. That was what told us the bloke didn't know anything about plants. My girlfriend knows a bit about gardening."

"Your girlfriend comes from the East Midlands?"

"How do you know?"

"After you and she blundered into our surveillance, one of the IOs (Investigation Officers) followed you in case you had some links with the owners. You tired him out with all that traipsing around Parliament Hill, but he kept up enough to see her get a train to Derby. You never guessed you were being followed?"

"No. Not an inkling. It was my first serious date with her."

"Well, if you're planning to do any more amateur investigating, let me know first. You could've messed our surveillance up completely. At least you didn't go round snooping on your own. By the way, the IOs say to pass on their compliments on your taste in women!"

I decided that as they knew enough already, I wouldn't volunteer any information about Rosemary's job.

"Anyway," Iain added, "we've had enough of surveillance. We're going to have an unannounced look at Weissmans and follow that up with a search at the White House place. If you can spare Storey, Jim, I'd like him to come along. I need someone who knows the Customs side of this and has an idea what to look for."

"That's no problem. I can re-jig the roster. Is that all right with you, Storey?"

"Fine. What time will it all start?"

"Weissman's at 6 a.m.," replied Iain. "So you'll need to stay in London tonight. There's a couple of cheap places I can recommend that we use. Or will you go home?"

"Definitely not. I'd prefer to be somewhere near where you're meeting in the morning."

"We'll go from Fetter Lane. You'll need to be in the lobby by ten to six."

"I'll bring an alarm clock with me."

It was a strange day. I'd spent Sunday mooching around until the cheaper time for phone calls before having a conversation with Rosemary which was, inevitably, too short. Obviously, I couldn't ring her from the office, besides I was quite busy, but with routine tasks. The only thing that truly took my mind off Rosemary was the arrival of Sidney Small with an MIB entry for uncut diamonds worth more than £40,000. The entry details and the number of diamonds tallied, but whether their value was as stated or not, I now realised I had no way of knowing. As Sidney Small got back into the train, I got the distinct feeling that he was being shadowed, not just by the man we had all designated as his 'minder', but by someone else. I also thought I caught sight of Iain Cogbill's face in the window of the next compartment. Evidently the IB were putting a lot of people on this case.

I travelled down by a late afternoon train and checked into a nondescript and dingy small hotel in Clerkenwell. My room was clean and comfortable enough and the place had a payphone, so I was able to have a brief conversation with Rosemary after she finished her shift. Consistent with our decision that officially she knew nothing about what I was, or had been, up to, I didn't tell her where I was or what I was about to be involved in.

Inevitably, I left my hotel before they could lay on any breakfast. So I left shortly after five and walked a few streets to Smithfield and had a large cooked breakfast in one of the many cafes there that seem to stay open pretty well all night. All around me, market porters were accompanying their eggs, bacon, sausages, fried bread, black puddings and fried tomatoes with pints of Guinness. What with the size of my breakfast, I thought if I followed suit I would be unable to move and would probably fall asleep by 7 a.m. At any rate, fortified by nothing stronger than a mug of dark brown tea, I arrived outside the IB HQ by quarter to six.

There were already a couple of men standing around inside. Within a couple of minutes five more joined them – and finally Iain Cogbill and another slightly older man appeared.

"This is Customs Section B," said Iain. "And this is Nick Storey from Harwich Customs who's got us much of the way here. If you've any questions about what you find at Weissmans, ask him or me. Right. Let's go."

I had expected that the IB would travel in cars. But for a journey of little more than a couple of streets, we walked. Most of the IOs were between five and ten years older than me. Several struck me as having been

Armed Forces regulars. One, who I took to be Iain's HIO (Higher Investigation Office), looked just like my Sergeant-Major when I was in training camp at the start of my National Service.

We got into Cross Street and halted.

"You know what to do. Campbell, Cockburn and Mahoney round to the rear. The rest in the front with me. Remember, if anyone starts waving guns around, don't try to be heroes. Keep down low and get out sharp. All right?"
"Stay close to me," he whispered to me.

We made our way up to the front entrance of Weissman & Co. There were no lights on. One of the IOs knocked hard on the door. About twenty seconds later a light went on in an upstairs window. He knocked again. The window opened.

"Who the hell are you? What do you want? Can't you see we're closed?" demanded David Weissman, resplendent in shiny yellow pyjamas.
"My name is Lowe. HM Customs & Excise. We intend to search these premises. Come down and let us in or we'll break the door down!" called out the HIO.
"Where's your warrant? You can't come in here without a warrant!"
"I have a Writ of Assistance. Under the Customs and Excise Act 1952 that gives me powers to enter your premises and search them. Are you going to come down and let us in?"
"OK. OK. Give me a moment."
"Half a minute, Mr Weissman. Then we're coming in. We don't want you trying to dispose of anything before we get in, do we?"

Within the time allotted, Weissman opened the door.

"You're making a big mistake. I'm clean. I'll be writing to my MP."
"Feel free to do so, Mr Weissman," said Iain coolly, "but please keep out of our way while we search."
"If anything gets broken, I'll sue!"
"Unless you can prove it was wilful or negligent, you won't have a cat's chance."
The IOs were already expertly searching both the shop and the various rooms behind.

"Is there anyone else here with you, Mr Weissman?" asked Iain. "It's more than likely we may wish to search upstairs, as the documents we seek are often not retained on the business premises."

"Just my wife. She's upset."

"Well, I suggest you go upstairs and comfort her. It would be a good idea for her to get dressed and come downstairs. Shreeve, will you go with Mr Weissman, please, and keep a constant eye on him."

"I may need to go to the toilet. Will your man come with me in there?" said Weissman with a smirk, bordering on the hysterical. It struck me that he plainly had not been expecting anything like this.

"Not unless he thinks you're trying to conceal or dispose of something." Ian's sense of humour was like him: there was a proper time and place for it.

Iain wandered round through to the offices and store rooms at the back. I followed.

"Mr Cogbill, there's a tin box here with a whole load of records in it and ledgers and accounts."

"Where was it?"

"Behind these empty jewellery boxes in the cupboard in the corner there."

"Recent? 1964? All right. Bag them up and seal them. Note the seizure record and make out a receipt. Just let me have a glance first…"

"Yes," he murmured to me. "This looks like the real set of books. Now we may be getting somewhere."

I noticed that the older man who had been with Iain at the start wasn't doing any searching. I began to suspect he was from Special Branch or one of those secretive organisations. That suggested hopes of finding material linking Weissman to the Soviets.

"I wonder whether all jewellers use pouches like these?" I remarked. "These look just like the ones Sidney Small uses to carry Silberstein's diamonds from Amsterdam to London."

"I suppose we might get some fingerprints off them. Mahoney – pick them up carefully and bag them please." Iain appeared less than happy. "There's got to be more than this," he muttered.

"There's a locked cupboard out the back," said Cockburn, one of the IOs who had entered by way of the rear entrance. "Do you want us to break into it?"

Weissman was back downstairs with his wife, the blonde who had met us when we arrived on our previous visit. She had a cigarette dangling from her lips. She had put on brown slacks and wrapped a large ocelot fur coat round herself. She seemed bored, rather than upset or annoyed.

"Will you unlock it, Mr Weissman?" asked Iain. "Or shall we break into it?"

"The key is in the top drawer of my desk, in the middle. The one with the coin attached to the keyring."

Within a minute or so, the IO returned.

"There's an old safe in there. Combination variety. Can you give us the combination?" he asked Weissman.

"Sorry. Haven't used it in years. Can't remember it at all," replied Weissman, but even an observer as inexperienced as I could tell he had become very uneasy.

"Don't worry about it," said Iain evenly. "We've got people here who can overcome problems like that."

An IO approached me with a couple of rather tatty box-files containing a mass of documents.

"Can you look at these, please? They look like import entries, but I don't know whether they're relevant to this enquiry."

"I'll have a look," I said. "They go back a few years…"

"Don't bother about that now," Iain interrupted. "Campbell, bag them up and seal them. I think we've got enough for a van-load, so will you ring Francis Ames and get him to send a van round here?"

There were a few muffled noises and a couple of curses in the back room. I went to see what was going on, to be met by Lowe carrying various bundles of paper, held together by thick rubber bands. I followed him into the main room, where Mr and Mrs Weissman were sitting. He laid the bundles down on the table. Within seconds he was followed by an IO with a sizeable cash box and another with a smaller metal box, locked with an oversize padlock.

"This is dated October this year… So you somehow forgot the combination within the last month, Mr Weissman?" remarked Iain icily. "What's this? Is that German?"

"No," replied the man who I thought of as 'the Secret Agent'. "It's Dutch. But those are in German."

"And this lot are in Russian," I added. "I don't know what it means though. My Russian is mainly conversational. It looks official though."

"Right. Bag them and seal them and get them back to the office. We can find out what they mean soon enough. Will you open these other two boxes, Mr Weissman? And don't tell me you've lost the keys."

Weissman looked a defeated man.

"In the same desk drawer. Next to where the cupboard key was."

The boxes were swiftly opened. In the cash box was at least a thousand pounds, mainly in ten-pound notes. In the other box were forty or so uncut diamonds.

"And you told my colleague that you weren't involved in the diamond business!" exclaimed Iain. "I wonder how many more lies we're going to catch you out in?"

But despite a thorough search, that was all we could discover that was remotely suspicious. About twenty minutes later a van arrived at the rear and the various items of evidence were taken out to it. Mr Weissman was asked to sign the list of what had been taken and was given a receipt. Then he was taken by a couple of the IOs by car back to Fetter Lane.

"Ring Julius Keller, will you, love, and tell him what's happened," he told his wife as he was taken out.

"He's our brief!" snapped Mrs Weissman.

"No phone calls for the present," replied Iain. "We can't have anyone tipped off. I know Keller of old. I'm afraid you'll have to accompany us back to the office for a few hours, Mrs Weissman. There'll be a few questions for you, too."

"I don't know nothing about Dave's business. 'E keeps that to 'imself. You've no right to arrest me!"

"We're not arresting you, just using our legal powers to detain you, Mrs Weissman."

Her accent seemed so familiar.

"Do you know Terry Kersey?" I asked.

97

"'E's my brother. Why d'you want to know?"

"When we were talking to your husband the other day, he never mentioned the family connection. Curious, don't you think?"

"Was that guesswork or did you know?" asked Iain as we walked back to Fetter Lane.

"A hunch. Her accent sounded so much like Kersey's and it just seemed obvious to me that if you're involved in any dodgy imports, it'd be best to keep it in the family."

"Hmmm… So you think Weissman may have set Kersey up in Harwich?"

"I hadn't thought about it before, but it's possible. He's got far more office space than he needs and his whole office seems pretty chaotic. If Weissman had set him up, he could probably afford to undercut his rivals, because he didn't really need to make a profit."

"But he'd have to get other business, otherwise his dependence on Weissman would be too obvious."

"Only he does Silberstein as well…"

"And Weissman was sitting on a stash of uncut diamonds. It's beginning to look as though Silbersteins are up to their neck in this as well."

"You hadn't planned to raid them?"

"No. We didn't have much on Weissman, but enough to use the Writ. So far I haven't got sufficient evidence to go over Silbersteins. They're not the sort of trader you can raid without plausible evidence. They're far too well-connected."

When we got back to Fetter Lane I expected to be consigned to some waiting room, but Iain had arranged a pass for me and I went in the lift with him up to the fourth floor, where his sections were based. Though it was a post-War building, it already looked old-fashioned and the functional Civil Service furniture did it no favours.

"We'll let Weissman stew for a bit while we have a look at the papers we've picked up," said Iain. "Will someone get Mrs Weissman a cup of tea and get her something to eat if she wants it."

The 'Secret Agent' joined us.

"I suggest you make out what you can of the German and Russian stuff," he said to me. "I'm Jones," he added, as though that explained all I needed to know about him.

So I started to wade through a couple of bundles of papers that we dropped on a desk they gave me in one corner of the Section Room. As it was easier, I started with the German stuff. It was mainly about trade in second-hand and what in the German was described as *unerwarteter glüecksfall* or 'windfall', which I imagined was code for stolen jewellery and precious metals. There was a trader called "Loeb und Schmidt" based in Dortmund and Braunschweig, who appeared to be the funnel for all these goods, some, at least, of which were passed through Jan de Wet in Sloten, just outside Amsterdam and on to Weissman in London. The Amsterdam shipping agent, Verhaeren, wasn't mentioned, but I would have bet my bottom dollar that there was a family or perhaps wartime connection. Without a sight of the goods, it was impossible to tell from this what exactly was going on. It certainly suggested that stolen jewellery was being got rid of into London and possibly that there might be large-scale misdescription and under-declaration going on. But I'd have to see the relevant entries to know for sure. And I had yet to come to anything which related to the 'special' import on 3 July which Kersey had confessed to destroying his copies of the documents.

"Have you got anything?" asked 'Jones'.

"I've only had a chance to read the first third of the German stuff. I'd say that Wessiman is part of a route which sends stolen goods from West Germany into the UK. So far it seems to be just jewellery and precious metals, described as 'windfall' in German – as opposed to 'second-hand'. Braunschweig is, of course, the closest big city in West Germany to the Helmstedt crossing with East Germany. So, in view of the Russian documents as well, it seems more than likely that some of this stuff has come from the East. Of course, if it's just criminal, it's probably what it says it is. But if it's an unofficial way the Soviets are using to acquire hard currency, who knows what things are really being transported by these people?"

"You haven't looked at any of the Russian stuff yet?"

"Give me time."

"Time is what we haven't got. We're going to have to start interviewing Weissman soon and we need all we can to throw at him."

"Well, I'll need the best part of an hour to look at the German stuff. There's no point skimming it and missing something vital. Though the Russian stuff is much less, I don't know Russian anything like as well as German, so it'll take me some time. You should've brought along one of your Russian experts, Mr Jones."

"Well, crack on with it. What can you give us to be going on with?"

"You've already got Kersey's confession about the package on 3 July and Weissman telling him to destroy the records. You can also ask him about the top half dozen of these documents. I've been scribbling down a rough English translation as I've been going along. The main things you can ask is what does 'windfall' mean? Where does all this stuff come from? Who are Loeb and Schmidt? What sort of stuff is it? Where does it go on from him? You can also ask him about the stash of uncut diamonds, I imagine. If I get anything more I'll get a message in to you. Are you interviewing with Iain Cogbill?"

"I shall observe. Paul Lowe will assist. I suggest you examine the Russian stuff first. That's what may contain the dynamite."

So I began to struggle my way into the Russian documents. They certainly felt authentic. I recalled the unique quality of Russian paper from when I was in West Berlin. The first document appeared to be some sort of invoice from NPO Sovyakutalmaz, an organisation which meant nothing to me, from a town called Mirny, which equally was unknown to me. The goods concerned were *almazi*. What the hell were they?

"Do you have any dictionaries and atlases here?" I asked the IO at the desk nearest to me.

"There's a library on the ground floor. I don't know what's in there. What are you after?"

"A Russian dictionary. These papers are full of words I don't know."

"I'll go down and see."

Meanwhile, I returned to the German stuff. But it was just more of the same.

He returned.

"You're in luck. There's two. Russian-English and English-Russian. I brought both, just in case. And a world atlas."

"Thank you."

I turned the pages hurriedly to get to *almazi*. To my astonishment – and pleasure – it meant 'diamonds', specifically 'unpolished diamonds'. Mirny turned out to be a town in Siberia, in the Yakutsk region. Hence, presumably, the name of the organisation.

The document, as far as I could tell with the help of the dictionary, set out the transfer of a substantial quantity of diamonds from NPO

Sovyakutalmaz to a Juwelgrosshandlung Gesellschaft of Magdeburg in East Germany. I recalled that Magdeburg is the first city of any size in East Germany if you travel from Braunschweig through the crossing point at Helmstedt. The next document was from the Almazjuvelierexport Foreign Trade Association, based in Moscow concerning the granting of licences for exports of diamonds to specified COMECON members, which also referred to a directive from the State Committee of Precious Metals and Gemstones, of the Ministry of Finance of the Russian Federation without giving any details other than a reference and date. The next two documents appeared to concern arrangements for transporting diamonds from Mirny, deep in Siberia, to Magdeburg.

It already seemed to me that the only purpose for such traffic had to be to export these diamonds to the West illicitly. It scarcely seemed credible that Magdeburg should be the diamond cutting centre of the Soviet bloc. It would be useful to have known anything more about this Juwelgrosshandlung Gesellschaft there. But I doubted whether the IB library contained that sort of information, though I suspected Mr Jones's organisation probably could dig it up relatively quickly. But he was now 'observing' Iain Cogbill's interview with David Weissman.

I was about to examine the next document when a large man entered the room. He was big, burly and had a commanding, bullying manner about him and the complexion of a seasoned drinker.

"What's going on here?" he demanded. And, seeing me, "Who the hell is this?"

"We've just raided a second-hand jewellers in Hatton Garden and Mr Cogbill and Mr Lowe are interviewing the owner now. Mr Storey is from Harwich Customs. That's where the smuggling took place. He also reads German and Russian and we picked up German and Russian documents on the raid," replied one of the IOs, called Shreeve, I thought.

"Well, shove a note into Cogbill and get him out to see me. Pronto!"

"What's this all about then, eh?" he demanded of me, his face about six inches from mine, an aroma of stale alcohol on his breath.

"I'd say illicit smuggling of Russian diamonds through West Germany and the Netherlands. But there are still quite a lot of unanswered questions."

"So that's why James Bond is on the premises."

"Yes, there is a bit of *From Russia With Love* about this, isn't there."

He withdrew his face, glowering.

"I don't like civvies on my patch. Get on with what you've got to do. Where's Cogbill?"

He departed, harrumphing like a rogue rhino.

"Who on earth was that?" I asked my helpful neighbour.
"The DCIO. Barry Williamson. Iain Cogbill's boss. Not just an arsehole, but a shit too!"

I felt that Iain Cogbill's coolness and intelligence would easily cope with a braggart like Williamson. It seemed to me that I'd seen too many men at that level in the Department who appeared to substitute rank for intelligence or courtesy. The only point of pulling Iain out from an important interview was to demonstrate Williamson's superior rank, surely?

I returned to the Russian documents. There was a letter from the State Committee of Precious Metals and Gemstones, of the Ministry of Finance of the Russian Federation to a Sergei Vorokhin of the Russian Trade Section of the Embassy in London about making 'suitable arrangements' for a Mr Louis Davidson with the Moscow Narodny Bank, based near the northern end of London Bridge. There was also a letter of introduction from the Ministry of Finance of the Russian Federation for Mr Louis Davidson, address the same as Weissman's shop. Mr Davidson also had a set of bank statements from the Moscow Narodny Bank, showing more than £35 million paid in and withdrawals amounting to less than £50,000. There was a chequebook for Mr Davidson's account with several cheques used, with varying amounts written on the stubs. But who the cheques were written out to was impossible to tell. Each one went to 'X3' or 'Z7', etc.

A middle-aged woman came into the room. She was short, plump, with straggling, greasy hair and a cigarette dangling from her fingers.

"Anyone here name of Storey?"
"Yes. That's me."
"There's a Mr Round on the phone for you. You can take it outside."

I went to a small office a few yards along the corridor.

"Morning, lad. How's it going?"
"We seem to have picked up quite a lot of stuff. Mr…"

"Don't say any more over the phone. You never know who's listening in. I'm just warning you that you'll need to be back here first thing tomorrow. Some twat at AC level in the IB has phoned Imrie and complained about lack of co-operation and involvement of Harwich Customs in IB operations. It's all bollocks, of course. But it's got Imrie in a lather and he's demanded to see you and me tomorrow first thing."

"OK. I'll make sure I'm back."

"There was one other thing. A chap called Mummery from the VB rang the office and got Alf Veale. He told him to tell you that scrap jewellery was worth £18 3s 4d more than they declared it for. The forms and the jewellery are on their way to you here. You'll have to get the sum owed from the importer, or failing that, the shipping agent. Bit of a problem with the latter, I reckon. It was Kersey wasn't it? Well, he's done a bunk!"

"And the importer has more things to worry about than underpayment of £18 quid."

I nearly broke out laughing. This whole affair had been started by Mummery suspecting an under-declaration that turned out to be worth less than £20! But if he hadn't sent the original query, this whole matter might never have come to light.

I returned yet again to the remaining handful of Russian documents, conscious that I still had nearly half of the German ones to work my way through. I was just about to start when Iain Cogbill appeared.

"I'm sorry my boss has caused difficulties with your boss, Storey. But I reckon Jim Round will be able to handle it. How are you getting on?"

"I've got a sort of tenuous trail from a Soviet diamond mining company through an East German organisation that deals with jewellery. The other side of the Helmstedt checkpoint is a German firm that supplies de Wet who supplies Weissman. There are also Russian documents enabling a Mr Louis Davidson, based at Weissman's address, to run an enormous account at the Moscow Narodny Bank in the City. Davidson, whoever he is, has paid in over thirty-five million in the last year or so and taken virtually nothing out."

"Do you reckon that Weissman is this Davidson?"

"Impossible to tell. But he can hardly have this stuff in his safe without knowing something about it. Has anyone looked through the ledgers and the other documents to see whether that supposedly duplicate entry of 3 July is recorded and what it says?"

"Shreeve and Mahoney are working their way through that lot."

"They'll need to cross-reference with the Harwich entries I assume? In which case, they'll need to talk to me."

"I think I'd better tell them to ring Jim Round. I'd like you to join us and ask Mr Weissman a few questions, based on what you've discovered from these documents. We've had enough delay. I've got a raid on the White House Nurseries planned for two o'clock and I'd like to have squeezed most of the juice out of Weissman before then."

We went into the interview room. It felt uncomfortably warm and stank of sweat. Weissman was on one side of a table, looking drained and greasy with perspiration. Iain sat down opposite him in an empty chair. Next to him was seated Paul Lowe, with 'Mr Jones' at one side of the table. I sat down in an empty seat opposite him.

"Right. For the record, Iain Cogbill has re-entered the room along with Mr Storey OCX from Harwich Customs," said Lowe, scribbling in a notebook.

"Has Mr Weissman had anything to say in my absence?" asked Iain.

"No. Apart from requesting his lawyer."

"All in good time, Mr Weissman. We're entitled to ask you some preliminary questions before you contact your lawyer."

"Not for hours, you're not."

"But it's been a deal less than two hours yet. Anyway, we've been examining papers found in your establishment. Mr Storey has some questions to ask about some of them."

"Mr Weissman, I've been looking particularly at the German and Russian documents which were in the safe in your back office –" I began.

"These are the documents," interrupted Iain. "Do you recognise them?"

"Yes. But I can't read German or Russian, so I don't know what they say," replied Weissman.

"When we met last week you said you were a close friend of Jan de Wet, who you say you met in West Germany. Does that mean you speak Dutch?"

"No. Jan speaks good English."

"And you did all your National Service in Germany?"

"Yes."

"And you spoke no German all that time? Didn't learn a word of German?"

"I picked up a bit, obviously. But I've seen those documents. I couldn't understand one word in ten."

"So when you said earlier you'd forgotten the combination of the safe and hadn't seen the documents therein, you were lying."

Iain sat back.

"You told us last week that you deal exclusively with Jan de Wet. Do you know where he gets the merchandise from?" I began again.

"He has his contacts. I don't know who they are."

"You mean you expect us to believe that you don't know where valuable jewellery comes from? You must know that importing stolen goods is an offence. Surely you take some trouble to know where the stuff comes from?"

"I trust Jan."

"Do you know where it comes from?"

"Holland and Germany, I guess."

"Mr Weissman, why are these documents in a safe in your office?"

"Sorry, I don't understand?"

"Well, if as you say, you can't read German or Russian, why do you keep documents you can't read in your safe in your office? How did they get to be there?"

"They belong to one of my customers."

"Why should one of your customers leave documents like these in your safe, Mr Weissman?"

"To keep them safe."

"Why? Hasn't he got somewhere safe he could keep them himself?"

"I suppose not."

"If they need to be kept in a safe place, not on his own premises, but in yours, they must be important or very valuable. Wouldn't you agree?"

"I don't know. I don't know what's in them."

"You mean your customer asks you to put German and particularly Russian documents in your safe and you don't ask what they're about? There's a Cold War on. There are supposed to be Russian spies all over the place. Didn't you think it was rather odd? Didn't you ask what they were, just to make sure you weren't holding something that might be treasonable?"

"No. I trusted my customer."

"You're a very trusting man, Mr Weissman. You trust Mr de Wet that he's not sending you stolen goods and your customer that he's not involved in spying. What's the name of your customer?"

"I can't say."

"What do you mean? Can't say or won't say? Or perhaps he doesn't exist at all?"

"He does – but you won't get his name from me."

"Then perhaps if we bring Mr Louis Davidson in for questioning, he'll deny it's his name mentioned in the documents written in Russian?"

"Who's this Louis Davidson? Never heard of him."

"He's mentioned several times in the Russian documents. He has a large account with the Moscow Narodny Bank in the City. How come documents containing his name, and at your address too, are in your safe and yet you know nothing about him?"

"He must be someone my customer knows."

"Well, when we talk to him, he must surely know the name of this anonymous customer."

"You're already withholding evidence, Mr Weissman," added Iain. "Why don't you just save time and tell us who this customer is?"

"No. I'm no stoolie."

"I take it you've never heard of a West German company called 'Loeb und Schmidt'?" I continued.

"No."

"Or an East German company called Juwelgrosshandlung Gesellschaft, based in Magdeburg?"

"No."

"Where did the diamonds in your safe come from?"

"I imported them for a customer. I'm holding them for him until he collects them."

"Is this the same anonymous customer who's left the German and Russian documents with you?"

"It might or it might not."

"But I take it the same customer left all the documents? One customer didn't leave the German ones and another one the Russian ones?"

"It was the same customer."

"Do you charge your customers for keeping these valuable things safe for them?"

"No. I do it as a favour."

"How did the diamonds get into the country? What was their origin?"

"I've no idea where they were mined, if that's what you mean."

"We can check that. But you didn't answer the other part of my question. Who did with you deal with on the other side of the Channel about these diamonds?"

"Jan de Wet, of course."

"So how did it work? Did this anonymous customer ask you to contact Jan de Wet to arrange for some diamonds to be imported? Or did Jan de Wet contact you? Or did the customer have the contacts and you just had to use your normal contacts – de Wet and Verhaeren?"

"The customer had the contacts. I gave him Jan de Wet as my contact in Holland. His contacts abroad would get in touch with Jan."

"As you say you don't understand Russian, perhaps I should tell you that the Russian documents in your safe indicate the illicit export of Russian diamonds – in large quantities – into the UK via East and West Germany. You have these documents in your safe. You also have a considerable quantity of uncut diamonds in the same safe. If these diamonds turn out to be Russian, and I'll bet you all the money in your cash box that they are, you'll've been the principal in an illegal importation and facing a long gaol sentence."

"But you don't want to talk – and that's your right," said 'Jones'. "Of course, we can keep you here until we've located this Louis Davidson. Then we might let you go, free of all charges. Of course, your anonymous customer and his various contacts might be a little curious how Mr Davidson came to be detained while you walked scot free."

"You don't scare me, whoever you are," retorted Weissman. "If a Davidson is named in the papers you took from my safe, my customer must know that. So if you arrest the Davidson, he'll know I didn't squeal to get out from under."

"Right," said Iain. "We'll leave it here for now. These notes will be typed up in the form of a statement and you'll be asked to sign it, Mr Weissman. After that I'll consider whether to let you contact your lawyer. You should know it's likely you'll face a number of serious charges under the Customs and Excise Act 1952 which bring with them both gaol terms and heavy fines. Some are absolute offences, which means that the only discretion a court has is whether to gaol you or fine you – or both."

We left Weissman with one of the IOs keeping an eye on him. Another one was despatched to tell his wife that he would be detained for at least another hour and that no contact with his lawyer was yet permitted.

"Actually, it'll be more like three hours before I let Keller get anywhere near him. I want to see what we get out of the White House place first. The owner is supposedly a man called Smith. But who knows, he might turn out to be Davidson or even Weissman's mysterious customer," remarked Iain.

"He did pretty well confirm that the people he's involved with are extremely ruthless. He's plainly more scared of them than he is of us," I observed.

"Well, even if we can prove what we think he's been up to, he'd only get banged up for six or seven years, I reckon. Compared to being killed, that's the easy option... Now before we set off for Belsize Park, I've got to brief my DCIO, so you might as well get a bite to eat. There's actually a modestly good canteen down in the basement. I'll pick you up there."

"I think that means us," said 'Jones' to me.

While we ate a more than passable Irish stew with the added choice of pickled red cabbage and apple pie and custard, I was dying to ask Mr 'Jones' whether that was his real name and what organisation he worked for. I was also certain he knew what I was thinking. He also probably knew, therefore, that I wouldn't actually ask. So we ate in virtual silence, except for a few words about the food and the quality of the canteen which, he pointed out, probably had to provide food for investigators at all sorts of odd hours.

We had not been finished long when Iain Cogbill joined us. He grabbed a plate of chips with a rather tired-looking hamburger, splashed a large dollop of HP Sauce on it, and started to devour it.

"The Chief has got interested in this, doubtless because Williamson started moaning to him. He wants to talk to his oppo in your outfit," he said to 'Jones'.

"Do you mind if I just pop upstairs and warn my boss? I briefed him over the weekend, but he doesn't like surprise phone calls and your Chief isn't the sort of person he'd take to his club."

"I take it you can't tell me where Mr 'Jones' is from?" I asked.

"He's from Box 500, which I assume you've guessed is one of the Security Services. And, though you evidently think otherwise, his name really is Jones. I have it on good authority."

"I wondered whether he might've been Special Branch."

"The trouble with bringing the police in is that they want to take over. I know there are those dead bodies in the Midlands, but this is primarily a Customs case. Apart from the murders, the offences are all Customs and, if the killers are who we think they are, the police aren't going to be able to lay a finger on them anyway... And, come to think of it, even the murders are, in a sense, the by-product of the original Customs offences."

"Let's hope that when all this comes out in the wash that's how they see it."

Within ten minutes we were on our way by car to Belsize Park. Two Ford Zephyrs and a Ford Cortina sped up the empty alley and into the open central area of the White House Nurseries. Nine of us got out and various IOs hurried round to the back of the premises. Iain Cogbill, Paul Lowe, Mr Jones and I went up to the entrance to the main hut. The door was padlocked. There was evidently no-one there.

"Break it open!" called out Iain.

That task quickly and professionally accomplished, we went inside.

"I hope they haven't heard about this morning's events and done a bunk," said Iain.

But his fears appeared to be groundless. A little filing cabinet behind the serving counter revealed a large stack of documents and a combination safe in a store room brought out some more. These were bagged and dumped in the boot of one of the cars.

"Now let's have a root around the plants and that little metal shed over in the corner there. We're looking for any plants in containers that are being used as concealments. Roses are the most likely. I seem to recall it was mainly roses that were on Davenport's entries. But it's not inconceivable they've buried the stuff, so look at any patch of ground that looks suspicious."

The tin shack was empty, except for the sort of small metal box that the Army uses to carry ammunition around in. The oddity was that the markings were East German.

There were no plants remaining in containers and the clay plant pots, some with "van Beek" painted on them, were all neatly stacked in a corner of the barn. The IOs dug up a sample few roses, but there was no evidence of anything being concealed.

"Short of digging up the whole place, that's the best we can do," Iain concluded.

"It might not be worth doing, but sheds like these don't sit directly on the ground," I suggested. "To stop the floor rotting, there's usually something placed under the structure to keep the floor from touching the soil below. It would be possible to hide something underneath."

"It's worth a try," replied Iain. "Let's also see if we can move that little metal shed and see what's underneath it."

Despite several IOs staring underneath the shed in the light of torches and poking around, nothing was found. However, there was a neat little concealment under the metal shack – an oil drum with a tight-fitting lid. Unfortunately there was nothing in it – except the fact that it was clearly a long time since it had been used for its original purpose.

"It's a pity we couldn't lay our hands on someone to question about the papers we picked up. Still – Paul, you've got a copy of the Writ. Leave it on the counter where it's bound to be seen. Cockburn, will you stay behind with Shreeve until six-ish, keeping an eye out and detain anyone who comes in? I still don't see why the front gate was left unopened but the main shed padlocked."

It was about half-past three by the time we got back to Fetter Lane.

"Would you be able to spend an hour or so looking through those remaining documents?" asked Iain.

"OK," I replied.

I settled down to examine the remaining Russian stuff. The first document was odd. It seemed to involve the grant of permission by the State Committee of Precious Metals and Gemstones, of the Ministry of Finance of the Russian Federation, to the Almazjuvelierexport Foreign Trade Association for the export of four unspecified items of jewellery valued at the equivalent of £8 million. This was followed by a consignment note from Almazjuvelierexport Foreign Trade Association to the Juwelgrosshandlung Gesellschaft of Magdeburg for a small consignment of jewellery, of low weight and no value given. The date was May 18 1964. As these two documents were together, I wondered whether I could make the assumption that they were concerned with the same thing. I thought I would cross-check with Mr Davidson's statement from the Moscow Narodny Bank. This showed a deposit of £7,875,000 on 16 July.

Continuing to add two and two and possibly make five, I felt that there was a distinct likelihood that it was these very high value jewels that had been in the 3 July consignment, which the Valuation Branch had queried. Presumably the jewels had been concealed with the cheap stuff that had been imported ostensibly on behalf of Genevieve van Hoogstraaten. But how could they be sure that the entry wasn't pulled for physical examination – or examined anyway by an eagle-eyed APO or PO with the famous "revenue nose"? Was Davenport somehow involved in this? I had always considered him to be a victim, but perhaps he had been part of the smuggling operation and either got too greedy perhaps, or possibly just knew too much? But how would he have ensured that no Waterguard officer did a random check – unless he had an accomplice there?

The final document was from the KGB. I nearly fell off my chair when I realised what the Russian was! I had never imagined I would ever see any document emanating from such a notoriously secretive organisation. From what I could tell it was a 'laisser passer' for Louis Davidson to travel within the Soviet Union, Poland and East Germany. Unless Weissman was an actor so accomplished as to rival Laurence Olivier, he clearly wasn't a big fish like Davidson. I could also understand why someone so well-connected might appear more fearsome to Weissman than the combined might of HM Customs and Excise and the British Security Services.

I hoped that those who were examining Weissman's books would find the relevant ledger entries and accompanying documents that would confirm the importation of the consignment of jewels through his hands. I did not hold out much hope. I realised that, in our ignorance, we had chased up Kersey about this consignment, and my visit to him the previous Friday had probably ensured that any remaining evidence had been destroyed. But on the other hand, these incriminating documents had been left, as well as what Iain thought were Weissman's real ledgers. I suppose it was possible that they needed to retain full evidence for their Russian paymasters that they hadn't been up to any fiddling.

I decided I had better inform Iain about what I had found. He was in his office with Paul Lowe and Mr Jones.

"Ah, Storey. Have you found something? We were just debating whether to have another go at Weissman or whether to charge him and let Julius Keller wrap his dirty little arms round him."

"The last few Russian documents cover the export of a small consignment – four items – of jewellery worth around eight million pounds. They seem to have used the same route as the diamonds. The timing looks as though they could have been imported, concealed in the consignment of 3 July we were trying to track down. About a fortnight later, a sum of almost £8 million was paid into the Moscow Narodny Bank here. The final document was from the KGB, giving Louis Davidson freedom to travel within the Soviet Union, Poland and East Germany."

"Davidson isn't Weissman then," observed Lowe.

"No. A much bigger fish," said Jones. "He is being sought as we speak. But, of course, once all this started – even before Davenport got killed – he may have deemed it safer to be overseas."

"Do you know what he looks like?"

"No. But everyone who enters any door of the Narodny Bank is automatically photographed. So with the information we now have about the use of the bank account there, we should be able to identify him."

"How soon?" asked Iain.

"By tomorrow morning."

"But it also raises another question," I broke in.

"What, exactly?"

"If you were going to bring eight million pounds'worth of jewellery – only four items –"

"Faberge probably," remarked Jones.

"– into the UK, concealed with some third-rate stuff like that they imported a few weeks earlier, surely you'd want to be certain that it wouldn't be physically examined. The Waterguard would certainly have found anything concealed in those little boxes. So it seems to me that there must have been at least one person in Harwich Customs – possibly in the Waterguard too – who was in on it."

"Davenport?" exclaimed Lowe.

"We shouldn't jump to conclusions too rapidly," cautioned Iain. "He may look the obvious person – and you could envisage circumstances where he might be killed, because he was trying to blackmail them or just because he knew too much. But he might be a decoy."

"If the KGB are involved in this, that certainly isn't out of the question," added Jones. "Assuming they want to continue this traffic, they might well want to draw attention away from people who can assist them in future."

"You'll have to tread very carefully on this when you're back in Harwich, Storey," said Iain. "Trust no-one with this information. Not even Jim Round. I'd believe it likely that Jim was involved in this as much as I'd believe it was my own dear mother, but let's keep this Faberge stuff within a tight group. If anyone asks you, just tell them nothing had been found about it as yet. But keep a mental note about who asks about it."

"I probably should be heading back to Harwich in the next half hour or so," I reminded them.

"I'd rather you finished reading all the foreign documents first, if you don't mind.. If you're happy to dine somewhere around here, I'll get one of the drivers to drive you back to Harwich later."

"OK."

So I went back to the German documents. A couple of transport documents confirmed the East German end of the relationship between Juwelgrosshandlung Gesellschaft and NPO Sovyakutalmaz. There were several invoices from Juwelgrosshandlung Gesellschaft to Loeb und Schmidt covering the transport of 'second-hand jewellery and semi-precious stones' during the first nine months of 1964. The value was consistent with the description of the goods. There were then a series of export licences from East German Ministry of Trade and import licences from the Land Niedersachsen (the West German region of Lower Saxony) office of commerce. These tallied with the various consignments of diamonds, as far as I could recall.

I wondered why all these documents were being kept by Weissman in his safe? I could understand that he might need to retain documents covering his part in this operation, so that his hands could be seen to be clean. But why did he have all the Russian and German stuff? Not only was it unnecessary, it also placed in one place records that enabled the whole chain to be identified. While we might not have full evidence or the ability to lay our hands on many of the links in the chain, we now understood the nature of these transactions, which might enable us to catch those involved when this was attempted again. Perhaps this was an isolated series of high value transactions because the Soviet Union required a large amount of hard currency urgently? That explained the reason for the operation, but not why all the documents should be in Weissman's safe. The only explanation I could think of for that was Louis Davidson. If he was the central cog in this machine, perhaps he needed this information readily available. Perhaps Weissman was telling the truth when he told me he was holding them for one of his customers, presumably Davidson?

Finally I came across what I had been hoping for. There were a set of shipping documents linking Loeb und Schmidt with Jan de Wet. His business was called 'Juweel en Edelsteen Import/Export' and that might have disguised his identity for a while, but several of the documents were addressed to 'Jan de Wet, Directeur'. That completed the chain and conveniently reached the end of the bundle.

For an operation apparently run under the auspices of the KGB, it seemed rather sloppy to give so much away. But then, I suppose the British authorities weren't expected to find these documents. Perhaps Davenport had forced their hand in some way? Perhaps whatever he was up to had made them finish up what they were doing and tidy up those loose ends which they could before escaping out of harm's way. The Davenports were no doubt two of the loose ends, killed because they knew too much, or were suspected of knowing too much.

I thought I had better inform Iain Cogbill and his colleagues of what the German documents revealed. Iain and Mr Jones remained in his office, along with one of the IOs. They were all peering over Weissman's ledger.

"You've finished?" enquired Iain. "Do the documents tell us any more?"

"They provide confirmation of the links between the East German business, the West German business and Weissman's Dutch contact, Jan de Wet. Once we get into East Germany, using German rather than Russian, the goods concerned stop being diamonds and revert to second-hand jewellery and semi-precious metals. So the whole of the chain is documented, though I doubt you could prove that the diamonds that left Siberia necessarily travelled along this chain all the way to Weissman, with Davidson selling them here and the Moscow Narodny Bank getting the proceeds... I've been scribbling notes as I went along, so if I leave them here, you can see roughly what each document means."

"Well done. That'll be very useful. I fear that the ledger just confirms what we already know. The real one does confirm that there was a second consignment on 3 July and that it was 'special', as Weissman records it. But he was quite cagey even about what he put in his real ledgers. If he had any copies of entries or other import documents, they're either well hidden or he's destroyed them."

"Which leads to the question why all these incriminating documents were left in Weissman's safe." I said. "I don't understand why someone didn't destroy them once it became possible that this was starting to unravel?"

"Overconfidence, maybe," replied Jones. "Or perhaps in some way Davenport forced them to finish off the operation a lot faster than they intended and Davidson had to get out before he had time to get rid of those documents."

"So you think he's fled the country?" asked Iain.

"I would in his shoes."

"Shit!"

"Well, we can always hope that he's complacent or can't leave."

"If it was just a single urgent operation, presumably he'd be free to go back to wherever he came from anyway," I commented.

"A single urgent operation?" said Jones. "Have you got that from the papers you've been going through?"

"Partly. The documents show a series of transfers of a very large quantity of diamonds along with the consignment we've called 'Faberge'. But it was over quite a short period. We've seen no documents earlier than March or April this year. I just wondered whether the Soviets had needed a lot of hard currency urgently and this operation was set up to provide it."

"The earlier documents might just have been destroyed," suggested Iain.

"Or perhaps it was needed to persuade the right people within the Party and the Army to get rid of Khrushchev and put Brezhnev and Kosygin in power. I should think the KGB would be much happier with them ruling the roost," said Jones. "As a theory, it certainly makes sense… and I think I'd better get back to the ranch to see how we're getting on and spread the good news among my colleagues… a pretty good day's work, I believe. Good evening, gentlemen."

With that he departed. I realised it was nearly six o'clock. I suddenly felt both ravenous and tired.

"I suggest we have a pie and a pint downstairs," said Iain. "Then you can get your drive back to Harwich."

We were joined by Paul Lowe in the canteen in the basement. I had a decent steak and kidney pie and mash, washed down by a pint of Ind Coope bitter. To be honest, I would have eaten and drunk virtually anything at that point. I was also too tired to say much. Iain and Paul said little about the case – more about a whole series of unknown people within the IB, which seemed to be a hotbed of intrigue and cliques.

"Where is Weissman now?" I asked, as I finished off my pint.

"In custody. We got him charged at Bow Street and he's safely under lock and key. No doubt Keller has been to see him and they're busy cooking up a story. But we've got enough on him to get him sent away for a good many years," replied Lowe.

"Besides, he's only a small fish. I'd still like to hope we could net the big 'un," added Iain.

"What about the White House Nurseries? Was there anything useful in the papers we seized?" I asked.

"We've only just starting to look at them. Everyone's been on the stuff we got at Weissman's – and I had to send two of them to replace Cockburn and Shreeve. I meant to ask you – why didn't you ask Weissman whether he knew about any of the Russian organisations involved in this?"

"As he was denying all knowledge of the documents, I didn't see any point getting another series of denials on record. Besides, I'm sure he's sharp enough to work out from our questions what we know and what we don't, so why give him unnecessary information he could pass on through his lawyer?

"Hmmm. Though your interrogation technique could be sharpened up, you'd make a good investigator I think. Do you fancy a wee dram before you go?"

"Thanks, but it's been a long day and I've got a difficult meeting with Mr Imrie first thing tomorrow."

I remember little about the journey back to Harwich except the driver, Eric, drove extremely fast, racing through the rain-soaked evening streets of the London suburbs as if he was at Brands Hatch – and once we got out on to the A12, it was like the Monte Carlo Rally, only twice as fast. I was relieved to get to my lodgings in one piece – and then devastated because I'd been unable to ring Rosemary and it was now too late to do so.

NINE – HARWICH – THE INCONVENIENCE OF UNTIMELY DEATHS

I arrived in the Customs House just before 6 a.m. in a bad mood. This resulted entirely from the fact that Jerry Wilshire, one of my fellow lodgers, had told me that a young woman had phoned me at about eight o'clock and, informed that I had been in London all day and wasn't back yet, had left no message other than to remind me not to ring after 9 p.m. I was also still tired, having found sleep hard to come by, what with my annoyance at having been unable to speak to Rosemary and all that had happened during the day whirling around in my brain.

"We're summoned to see Imrie at 6.30 sharp," explained Jim Round cheerily. I suspected it took a lot to dampen Jim's natural good humour and appetite for life. "You'd better get me up to speed about what went on yesterday. Imrie is bound to ask, not least because some DCIO (Deputy Chief Investigation Officer) appears to have phoned him to complain that you were on his premises without proper notice and authorisation from him. It's pure bollocks, of course, but it'll mean Imrie will want to know what you were up to."

"I joined the IB in a raid on Weissman's place. We found a lot of documents, including his real records, and some documents in German and Russian in a safe. We also found a load of diamonds and a thousand quid or more in cash. Because I appeared to be the only one there who could read German and Russian, I spent most of the day translating the foreign documents. I also joined in the interview with Weissman and asked him some questions, relating to them. At lunchtime I went with them to raid the White House Nurseries in Belsize Park. But there was no-one there. We came away with some documents, but I don't think anyone had time to look through them before I left at around 6.30 yesterday evening."

"I imagine Imrie is likely to enquire what was in the foreign documents, lad."

"I was coming to that. They showed a link between a Soviet diamond mining organisation in Siberia to a jewellery wholesalers or shippers in East Germany and a link between them to a company in West Germany and links

117

between them and Jan de Wet's company in Holland. Jan de Wet is Weissman's partner, of course."

"With all that, I suppose Weissman could hardly deny it."

"Not at all. He claimed he knew nothing about the documents and that they'd been left by a customer for safe-keeping. The documents mentioned a name – Louis Davidson – who seems able to travel around the Soviet countries freely and also had paid into the Moscow Narodny Bank in the City around £35 million. The security people are trying to find out who he is and catch him, though there's a chance he's fled the country. Weissman is evidently a lot more scared of people on his own side than of us, so he's saying nothing."

"But he must be pretty well bang to rights on lots of Customs offences."

"Yes. But a few years' gaol are presumably less worrying than being killed."

"Anything else?"

"No. Won't that be enough to satisfy Imrie?"

"It's difficult to tell with that one. We'll just have to see... Make sure you remind him that Iain Cogbill asked you to work with the IB on this, and that you provided not just knowledge of Customs procedures which they lacked, but also your knowledge of German and Russian. I imagine this is as much about his need to maintain his status with his oppo in the IB than anything more substantial."

So we duly arrived in Imrie's office and I told him what I had told Jim, in pretty well the same words, not forgetting to remind him that I had been doing all this at the behest of the IB.

"So you believe that these diamonds were smuggled through here in shipments described as scrap jewellery, is that right?" demanded Imrie, staring at me as if I had somehow been transformed into the criminal, Weissman.

"Yes, sir. If the diamonds were loose, they'd scarcely be noticed among the rest of the consignment. I can't imagine that if the consignment was examined it would be easy to spot that there were several dozen uncut diamonds among all the jewellery, scrap precious metal and other precious stones," I replied staring straight back at him. It was over ten years since I had allowed my father to bully me. I wasn't going to return to such a relationship ever again, whatever the rank of the other person. His rank merited courtesy, not subservience.

"You may be right. But it's also possible there was some form of collusion – either within your lot, Mr Round, or within the Waterguard, or both. This man Davenport, for instance. Why did he take entries relevant to this matter away wi' him when he left for another posting, if he was straight, eh?"

"Well, it's possible," replied Jim. "But it's also possible he had spotted something fishy and was trying to investigate it. If we make that assumption, we might risk missing the real culprit."

"I wasn't making any assumption. I was just airing a theory. What do you think, Storey?"

"I believe some sort of collusion may have occurred. But if someone was colluding, they must either have done it for money or because they were being threatened. At least the first of those is capable of being checked," I replied.

"As we now know which consignments were involved, it would be possible to identify who would've been involved on both the clearance and examination," added Jim. "That would narrow down the number of people who'd need to be checked out."

"Weel then, get that done as fast as you can and report back to me with the names. But discretion is of the essence, Round."

"I'm entirely with you on that, Sir."

"Then get on with it!"

"Is there anyone at AC level and above who's heard of the normal rules of courtesy?" I asked Jim after we had escaped back to his office.

"Oh, yes. The SAC (Senior Assistant Collector) and Higher Collector here are decent enough chaps and won't treat you like a naughty schoolboy. I imagine Imrie is so desperate for promotion that he believes bullying provides the quickest route. After all, it's done pretty well for him so far."

"But he's right about the possibility that someone may have been colluding. I'm sorry, I'd forgotten to mention to you I'd had a similar thought,"

"But it's equally possible that the diamonds could have been spread about in a consignment of scrap jewellery and just not noticed, as you said… Anyway, Imrie has demanded, so Round will do. If you could get me a clean copy of the list of entries and when they came through, I'll work my Yorkshire charm on the Estabs Section to get a peep at the rosters. I can see how the IB or someone could check up on people's bank accounts, but how you'd ever know whether someone or their family were being threatened is beyond me."

I didn't reply. I was feeling a little guilty about not mentioning to him the need to check whether anyone among the Customs staff had been involved in the smuggling operation. But I had been thinking about it primarily in the context of that single import of the 'Fabergé' jewellery on 3 July, which I had said I wouldn't mention. Imrie's intervention had, therefore, been fortuitous and would enable investigation of that particular consignment to be disguised among the many others, in the same way that I suspected the uncut diamonds had been among the scrap jewellery.

Yet again I had to use an unoccupied office to draw up the list of entries. I wasn't at my normal desk for long, but time enough to learn that the raid on Weissman was already widely known throughout the Department. Customs and Excise was really a large village, with the office telephone replacing the garden fence or the front gate as the route for transmitting gossip. My involvement was not only well-known, but was, apparently, already creating annoyance in both London Central and London Port Collections that a junior OCX from Harwich Customs should have been invited by the IB on a raid in their "patch" rather than one of their officers.

"I suppose you also know that Terry Kersey's done a bunk," said Bill Strevens. "And after you went to see him. What on earth did you say to him?"

"I was just trying to trace his copies of those entries the VB asked me about. He had one and not the other. His filing system was a complete mess. What's happening to his entries?"

"Blatherwicks have happily taken them on. Only problem was they couldn't find any records. Someone said Kersey had bagged 'em all up and taken them away with him in his car."

"The power of the VB – isn't it amazing!"

Though, like Imrie and, I suspected, Jim Round, I reckoned that Davenport must have been involved in some way in making sure the 'Fabergé' consignment and possibly those with the uncut diamonds passed through Harwich without being examined, I had picked up enough of Iain Cogbill's thoroughness to remind myself that there was a potentially wider pool of suspects and not to let slip anything to any of them that might alert them to what was afoot.

Not long after the last of the morning's entries had been cleared, I brought the list to Jim's office. No doubt he was still working his charm on the Estabs Section, peopled by glum nonentities who knew every word and punctuation mark of the Estabs Instructions by heart and were probably the only people who read the OWOs from cover to cover. The only thing I had noticed recently – or, more accurately, it had been brought to my attention by Alf Veale – was the formal announcement of the death of Mr N.J.F. Davenport, the sole entry under the "Deaths of Serving Officers" part.

"And they couldn't even get his initials in the right order!" Alf had noted.

I was just working out where to put the list where it wouldn't be seen, when the telephone rang. Out of habit, I answered it.

"Mr Round's phone. Storey here."
"Oh it's you, Storey. You appear to be omnipresent at the moment. Get hold of Round instantly and get over to my office immediately – both of you!" barked Imrie.

I went round to the Estabs Office and found Jim making notes from papers in a file.

"Imrie wants us pronto," I told him.
"I don't believe we could do this any faster – with discretion," Jim said.

We arrived in Imrie's office a few minutes later.

"Weel, now the cat is well and truly among the pigeons!" exclaimed Imrie. "I've just heard by way of the Essex Constabulary that the dead body of a Mr Terence Kersey was found earlier today in a waste tip near Dagenham. He appeared to have been very badly beaten before he was finally shot in the head. Now who do you think might have done that? And why?"

It was plainly a rhetorical question, so neither Jim nor I spoke.

"I believe we can take it that Kersey's accomplices had decided that he knew too much and might blab. Do either of you disagree?"

We both muttered our concurrence.

"And does this not shed an even more suspicious light on the death of Davenport? And presumably his missus?"

"If they were murdered, someone went to considerable trouble to make it not appear to be murder. From what you say about Kersey, someone seems to have gone to the opposite extreme," I said.

"So, what are you trying to say?"

"There isn't a clear pattern, sir. But if it's as you say, the most likely explanation, it seems to me, is that the raid on Weissman's yesterday has let the cat out of the bag and loose ends are being tidied up as rapidly as possible, with the way Kersey was killed providing a warning to anyone else who might be a weak link."

"I can see that working with the IB has rubbed off on you. So where does that line of thought take you?"

"The people involved won't talk. If we want to catch anyone, we're going to need conclusive evidence as there won't be any confessions. Also, there are still people around who are actively trying to stop us getting to the truth... probably working from the Russian or East German embassies."

"Ah, someone from the 'funnies' was with you yesterday, eh? We got the picture and description of a man by fax from Special Branch about an hour ago, to detain and inform. Might be travelling under the name of Louis Davidson, Wilhelm Schmidt or Henk Verhaeren... Mind you, I think he'd be pretty cheeky if he tried to exit through Harwich, don't you?"

"It also suggests that anyone who might've been involved here is going to be even more on the alert for anyone trying to get on their track," said Jim.

"I expect that once they knew we'd raided Weissman, they were on full alert. You know it's common knowledge all round the Department," I commented.

"I'm only too weel aware of that!" exclaimed Imrie. "The SAC has already been on to yours truly twice with unofficial mutterings from his oppos in London Port and London Central. I told him to tell those pricks that it was a Harwich case and, anyway, if they've got any complaints to address them to the IB. SAC is a gent of course. If it'd been me, I'd've told 'em to stuff their complaints up their arses!"

Of course, I thought to myself, this is the sort of stuff that gets you noticed – provided Harwich Customs aren't seen to have ballsed it up. Then Jim and I could expect to be well to the fore to catch the smelly brown stuff!

"Do you wish to indicate to the Essex Police that we have knowledge that may be relevant to Kersey's death?" asked Jim.

"All in good time," replied Imrie. "I reckon Special Branch and your anonymous and secretive friends may decide to involve themselves pretty sharpish, if they haven't done so already. I wouldn't be at all surprised if Mr Storey doesn't get another summons from his new friends in the IB. But until he does, let's get that list of names on my desk soonest!"

Even though days in London were hectic, exhausting and unpredictable, at least they took me the best part of fifty miles away from that deeply unpleasant man.

As the Estabs records could, in practice, only be examined by Surveyors and above, I was spared the tedious task of looking through them on the days when Weissman's and Silberstein's entries came through Harwich and working out who – both in Custom House and in the Waterguard – were rostered on those days.

Meanwhile I returned to my desk and attempted to concentrate on the entries which my DCOs had suggested for physical examination. One was a consignment of diamonds from Amsterdam for Silberstein. I authorised them for physical examination and decided to go over to the examination shed to see what happened.

In all the fuss about Weissman, it seemed to me that we had rather lost sight of Silbersteins. They, too, had used Kersey as their agent and Davenport had taken at least as many of their entries away with him in his suitcase as he had entries from Weissman. Of course, any link to Silberstein was tenuous – and Davenport might even have been using them as a smokescreen. But I couldn't help feeling we were missing something. Also, what had been learnt from the papers taken from the White House Nurseries?

It would have helped to get a better idea of what Davenport might have been up to from his former colleagues in the office, but that was now impossible.

Over in the freight examination shed I was met by Wally French, as usual.

"Diamonds and jewellery are all the rage today, aren't they!" he commented. "With all that's going on it'd be a particularly dim-witted importer who tried to get something fishy through here at the moment."

"Other than valuation. After all, can anyone other than an expert tell the real value of one uncut diamond from another? Or where they've come from, for that matter?"

"If in doubt, we'd send a sample off to the VB. But I take your point. Mostly these diamonds are valued at such a high level we wouldn't challenge the valuation, so it could be twice as much and we certainly couldn't tell."

"I know I'm Jewish and everybody thinks Jews know all there is to know about diamonds," said Morry Gold. "But actually I do know a bit. I couldn't tell where they're from – unless they've got a bit of colour in them, but I reckon I can tell really good stuff from mediocre."

"OK then," said Wally. "You can have the pleasure of examining the stuff for Silbersteins."

"I was at school with a cousin of theirs. I think he's now in New York."

He found the package and opened it. It contained a small metal box, locked, but with the key attached by string. Inside the box was a chamois leather pouch containing two dozen uncut diamonds of various sizes. The entry had valued them at £11, 722 12s 9d.

"Three of them – those three – are too small to be cut into anything of much value. They're worth no more than a few hundred. There's a couple here are what you'd say are 'dirty'. There's a faint colouring that would also prevent them being cut into large, bright stones, so they're not worth much either. This one is a star – worth thousands. The rest are decent enough. Unless they're Russian, I'd say the valuation was pretty well spot on. I could weigh them and give you a more accurate assessment."

"I think that's fine," I said. "But how could you tell they were Russian or not?"

"I couldn't. There are probably a few experts who could. As these are from Edelmann of Amsterdam, you'd never be able to check through the paperwork. Once diamonds get into a large jewellers like Edelman or Silberstein, you wouldn't be able to track where they came from if the trader didn't want you to find out."

"Would they keep their own records?"

"Undoubtedly. But even if you were incredibly lucky and found them, you probably wouldn't be able to decipher them – and I couldn't see them ever helping you."

"You seem to know a lot about the diamond trade."

"I was brought up in a Jewish community. Who didn't know a bit about the jewellery and diamond trades? When I was a kid, I was interested in everything."

"Well, there's no reason not to send Silberstein's diamonds on their way."

"Why don't you join us in the pub?" suggested Wally. "There's a lot of rumour flying around and you seem well placed to firm it up a bit."

"OK. But no more than two pints. I had a very long day yesterday."

"So people have been saying."

I waited until they finished off the final examination of some cut flowers and then headed off with them to the Jolly Jack Tar. Once the first pint had been ordered, we took over a table in one corner of the bar. Wally introduced me to two of the POs, Jack Shepherd and Les McGrory and two APOs, Stan Westcott and Geoff Wilson. The other two I already knew – Hywel Jenkins, my fellow lodger, and Morry Gold.

"Well, you've certainly had an interesting first few weeks here," began Wally, who was sitting next to me. "Bet you didn't expect that when you were told you'd been posted to Harwich."

"No. Is it always like this?" I replied.

"Customs Officers get run over and agents get bumped off every other month here, didn't you know!" said Wally.

"So what happens in the Waterguard?"

"As always – we do all the dirty work," remarked Morry. "The Excise never get themselves dirty climbing around inside ships or underneath lorries."

"Well, they are grammar school boys," added Les McGrory, with a strong Northern Ireland accent. "They probably only just abite know the difference between the front and the back of a ship."

"I rummaged several ships when I was at Holyhead," I said. "Of course, I put on overalls to protect my nice clean suit."

"And did you make any seizures?"

"Ten pounds or so of hand-rolling tobacco. But it wasn't exactly well-concealed. I don't think they were expecting to be rummaged."

"So you're one of those who thinks we shouldn't rummage every ship?" demanded Jack Shepherd.

"I don't think I'm very well qualified to say. It seems to me that if we rummage every ship, it'll stop casual smugglers, but the more determined ones will just use better concealments. Whereas if we only rummage on a random basis, they won't be so careful. Isn't that human nature?"

"The cleverer they are, the cleverer we've got to be."

"But rummaging takes time. If we really wanted to search every possible hiding place on a ship, it'd take days. We couldn't hold up every ship that way. Trade would grind to a standstill," commented Wally.

"You just need a mathematical formula to determine from your random searches what percentage of ships you should rummage thoroughly," added Morry. "Though, if you had two levels of rummaging – say, thorough and a quick once-over – it'd be a bit more complicated. If the IGW had any sense, they'd be doing something like that."

"Morry's passion is mathematics," explained Wally. "He teaches it to remedial sixth formers in his spare time. One day he's going to fly off to the new university and become a professor there."

"And maybe I will. But even when I solve a difficult equation, there's not quite the same satisfaction of making a really good seizure."

"More pecuniary satisfaction too," observed Les McGrory.

"That's not it at all. It's the satisfaction of catching a crook and bringing him to justice afterwards."

"Of course, you don't mean actual justice – but getting them to compound for as much as you can screw out of them."

"Isn't that justice?"

I listened to their conversation. In spite of the reputation of the Waterguard – the so-called "hairy-arsed preventers" – their conversation was intelligent and thoughtful. It seemed to me that they were genuinely keen to do the job as best they could – and had a passion for catching smugglers. Of course, it was a conversation laced with crude jokes and bad language, but beneath that, it was a good deal more serious than what I was used to hearing over lunch with my colleagues from the Custom House, whose interests seemed to be limited to football, cricket, golf and racing – horses or dogs.

On the other hand, the conversation gave me absolutely no inkling as to whether one of these men might be the one who had assisted the smuggling of £35 million worth of diamonds and precious jewellery.

I got back to Customs House feeling slightly less harassed, doubtless the effects of two pints of beer and no food. I had barely sat down at my desk when Jim called me in.

"If we take all the entries Davenport had, there is actually no-one who was on duty on every occasion. So while you were enjoying a leisurely lunch with your Waterguard chums, I tried looking at who had been present when only the jewellery and diamonds came through. That pulled out Davenport, Strevens and Gill here and McGrory and Gold in the Waterguard. Everyone else was on a different roster or on leave for at least one of those imports.

I glanced over the list, mainly to see whether I could make out who was on duty on 3 July, the date of the 'Fabergé' consignment.

"Did you do just the consignments for Weissman?" I asked. "Entries for Silberstein were in Davenport's suitcase, but there's never really been anything to tie them into the Weissman operation."

"No. Haven't had the time. You can do it if you like. My head's starting to spin."

So I took his lists away and looked specifically at 3 July. That added Vernon Turnell from the Custom House and Geoff Wilson from the Waterguard. But Turnell had been on leave for two of the other Weissman imports. So I mentally added Wilson to my list, but deleted Turnell. Then, on reflection, I decided to keep on my list all of those on duty on 3 July. After all, wasn't it possible that this was really the one and only time when a physical examination was absolutely to be avoided? This added Mair and Byrne in the Custom House and Westcott and Jenkins of the Waterguard. Those were the names I would give to Iain Cogbill for the IB to check out. However, when I looked at them, the only name that stood out was that of Davenport. But wouldn't that be too easy? And how could he guarantee that some bolshie PO or APO wouldn't decide to have a look at the consignment just because their "revenue nose" suggested it was fishy, even though Custom House had cleared it without physical examination?

I brought my additional lists back to Jim.

"I'd better get them up to Imrie myself. A messenger definitely won't do for this stuff."

"Could I possibly have a word when you get back?"

"Sure. But not for too long. The shift's pretty well ended and I've got some rugby practice to get away for."

I had learnt that Jim trained several local youth rugby teams. Indeed, some Sunday mornings he could be seen on the touchline, cheering on both teams.

"Well, that was a relief. He wasn't there. Off to see the SAC. What was it you wanted to have a word about?"

"I was thinking about these names. If you assume Davenport was definitely mixed up in this for a moment, is there any way he could have ensured that any individual consignment wasn't opened by the Waterguard, even though he'd given it clearance?"

"What, do you think your Waterguard chums are whiter than driven snow?"

"No. They told me of an APO at Holyhead who got sacked and prosecuted for helping a smuggling ring. It's just this seems to have been well organised and within quite a small circle of people. As far as we can tell, if Davenport was an accomplice, he's the only one we've come across so far. So I was just thinking, why would you want to involve two Customs people if you could do it with only one? It'd be cheaper and there'd be one less person who had some knowledge of what was going on."

"With the amount of money they seem to have been making, I doubt whether one more bribe would've worried them much... But I take your point. I suppose if you cleared and stamped the entry and gave the documents straight to the van driver, provided you could keep the consignment out of the freight shed in the first place, it'd probably go straight through. The easiest way of doing that would be to get the agent to stay with the goods and stop the Waterguard trying to take it over to the freight shed if they appeared to be minded to. If, say, Davenport worked quickly – did the entry first – the stuff would be away before anyone really noticed."

"And Kersey would certainly have co-operated."

"Yes... But I'm still reluctant to believe Davenport was crooked."

"Perhaps he was being threatened or blackmailed. But if it was someone else, you'd think that Kersey's death might've got them a little worried. I can't say I noticed any of the blokes I had lunch with looking at all bothered."

"Unfortunately, neither of us has been in the Long Room enough of the time to tell about the chaps here. Though, again, none of them strikes me as suitable. They're either too junior, too thick or they're people I've known for several years and I'd stake my reputation that they were honest."

"So it seems to come back to Davenport, working on his own."

"Well, I imagine Imrie will be getting someone to check out all the names we've given him."

"Of course, if someone's been threatened. I don't know how anyone would find that out. But, I was just thinking... I said that Davenport stuck out, because he wasn't part of a rather close-knit chain. But he must've done National Service. How old was he?"

"Early forties."

"That means he'd've been called up and might well have fought in Germany and Holland. Is it too implausible to wonder whether he knew one or more of the foreign contacts when he was there?"

"Who knows? I can get a look at his Estabs file. But some of that sort of stuff will only be held by the War Office or this new Ministry of Defence. I think you'd need to get anything like that by way of the IB."

I hung around for a bit, chatting to the 'late' roster, but a ship from the Hook was due, so I went back to my lodgings. I must confess I had been expecting, even hoping for, a call from the IB encouraging me to go to London. But no-one rang. I felt rather at a loose end, but as it continued to rain, I decided to get out one of my old textbooks on Russian and brush up my command of the language, which I realised had got rather rusty over the last two and half years. In reality, I was just passing time until I could phone Rosemary after 6.30.

6.30 came. I dialled the number.

"Hello. WPC Sawney here."
"Hello. I was hoping to speak to WPC Johnson. My name is Storey."
"I'll go and get her."

Within a minute, Rosemary picked up the receiver.

"Hello Nick. How are you?"
"I'm fine. How are you?"
"OK. Did you know that chap who was found dead in Essex today? They said on the tape in the office he was from Harwich."
"Yes. He was a shipping agent here. I'm terribly sorry about last night. I spent all day in London and didn't get back until after nine."
"Busy?"
"My feet didn't touch the floor from before 6 a.m. until I got a car to Harwich more than twelve hours later. I was really annoyed I didn't get a chance to speak to you, if only for a few minutes."
"I missed you too."
"What about this weekend? What do you want to do?"
"I know it's a bind, but could you possibly come to Leicester? I realise I've promised to play for the Leicester WPC's hockey team on Saturday afternoon and there's so few of us, I don't really feel I could duck out. If we met about fiveish and you could stay overnight, we'd have all day Sunday."

"OK. Would you be able to book me somewhere to stay that wouldn't cost the earth?"

"Certainly. I'm really looking forward to seeing you again. It feels rather odd, these short conversations on the phone."

"I'm glad I'm busy at work, otherwise I'd spend most of the time feeling depressed. I really miss you, Rosemary."

"We should really be enjoying ourselves."

"Yes, I know. Let's concentrate on thinking about the weekend."

I felt desperately lonely once she had rung off. The two days until the weekend seemed an eternity. I had never been in love with someone like this before and, though I had hoped I would fall in love, I hadn't expected it to be so painful.

I walked the relatively short distance to the Custom House the following morning feeling depressed. Apart from missing Rosemary, I feared that the IB had now taken over the Weissman case and I would be left on the outside while they did all the interesting and exciting stuff. I felt that I deserved to be properly involved, not least because if it hadn't been for me, the case might well not have started, or would have started so late that the trail would have gone completely cold. However, I felt there were still things I could find out here and I decided to take a suitable opportunity to seek Wally French's or Morry Gold's opinion on whether it would be possible for someone in Custom House to guarantee that no-one in the Waterguard could examine a particular consignment.

But first, there were dozens of entries to be checked, pulled out for examination or cleared. Today's consignments consisted almost entirely of cut flowers, Christmas wreaths and Christmas trees, all destined for reputable importers in Covent Garden. A high proportion were subject to 100% checks as a result of Min of Ag requirements, so I knew the Waterguard would have a busy, albeit unrewarding, morning. The only entry of any interest was described as motor spares for a specialist car-maker in the Midlands. I pulled them for examination, just to give the POs and APOs some variety.

I had just finished and was contemplating wandering over to the freight shed to see whether there was anything dodgy about the 'motor spares', when Jim put his head round the door of the Long Room and beckoned me into his office.

The office felt crowded. There was Jim, Iain Cogbill and two men I hadn't met before.

"This is Storey," Jim began.

"These are Mike Elliott of Special Branch and Don Carvell from Box 500," explained Iain. "We're here to see the 'crime scene', as you might put it – and also to see Kersey's office and where he lived."

"You'll be taking Davenport's envelope of diamonds with you, too, I hope," added Jim.

"Yes," remarked Elliott, a tall, lean man with thick black hair and a matching moustache. "That's something I'd advise you not to do again. Walking off with potential evidence constitutes a criminal offence in itself, even if it was aimed at finding out the truth. Fortunately for you, it's led to the uncovering of a major Soviet operation, otherwise I'd be handing you both over to the tender mercies of the Leicestershire Constabulary."

"So you've taken over looking at the deaths of the Davenports?" I asked.

"No. If we can't locate this man Davidson, there may be very little we can do about the operation, apart from getting Weissman locked up. No-one wants to advertise the fact that the Soviets pulled this stunt. So we'll let the woodentops in Leicester go on believing it was a hit and run and a suicide, even though the former seems highly unlikely."

"We'd like Storey to show us round the set-up here in Harwich," added Carvell, a small, slim man, whose almost bald head made him look much older and less active than I felt he was. "And also Kersey's office."

If Jim thought this should have been his prerogative, he nobly didn't say so. I couldn't imagine Imrie letting someone of junior rank show such exalted visitors around.

"Does the AC know about your visit? He's interested himself in this case recently."

"The Chief was on to him earlier," explained Iain. "He told him that this was a low key visit and we didn't want the staff here to notice anything particularly untoward. They will notice, of course – but I don't want him putting his nose in where it's neither wanted nor needed."

"You realise he's getting someone to check the backgrounds of the staff on duty when the jewellery and diamond consignments came through here?" said Jim.

"Yes. He phoned my DCIO to ask if the IB would do it. We said 'yes', of course."

"Will that include Davenport?" I asked.

"Of course. Him especially."

"What about their records when they were in the Army during the War or doing National Service? I wondered whether Davenport might've had contacts with any of the German or Dutch people involved in this."

"We thought of that in the course of yesterday. It's been set in hand."

"Shall we go?" demanded Elliott.

I took them briefly into the Long Room to show them how entries were handled – from the counter where the agents and occasionally drivers came in to the entry processing area – and explained what we did with the entries. Apparently word was going around, no doubt instigated by Jim, that these were a couple of high-ups from the Secretaries Office in London, familiarising themselves with the entry clearance operation. Since most Customs staff are sceptical, if not downright cynical, and not addicted to believing in co-incidence, I imagined most people reckoned they were something to do with the deaths of Davenport and Kersey and probably the raid on and arrest of Weissman.

I walked them round the arrivals area and then took them over to the freight examination shed. Wally French evidently knew Iain Cogbill and something was clearly on the tip of his tongue, but he evidently decided he would go along with the pretence.

While McGrory showed the others round the examination bays, the bonded areas and the QW, I stayed with Wally.

"I wanted to ask Morry Gold something," I began, "but I can't see him anywhere. I thought from the roster he was on this morning."

"The roster is one thing. Who is here is another," he replied. "Unless the Super is wandering around or there's an IGW inspection, we're pretty flexible. The POs and APOs often swap rosters for all sorts of reasons. Provided we're properly complemented for each shift, no-one really bothers who's there. The only point of the rosters is evidence for the allowances anyway. What did you want to ask Wally?"

"I wanted an APO's view of whether it'd be possible for a consignment to be guaranteed a free run through the port without the slightest chance that you lot could get your hands on it."

"This is presumably to do with this Weissman stuff?"

"Yes. Why Morry?"

"Because if you couldn't guarantee that the Waterguard wouldn't get their hands on a consignment, it'd mean there was a possibility that someone here colluded in these importations. I took the view that it couldn't be Morry."

"Why?"

"It always comes down to your gut feeling doesn't it? But he doesn't seem to fit the type. His passions are inconsistent with being bribed. But he's also too obvious. If you were running a smuggling operation involving one or more Jewish traders in London, would you really use the most obviously Jewish APO?"

"There are quite a few flaws in that, you know."

"Probably. But do you honestly believe Morry could be bribed or coerced?"

"No. But, if I may ask, why didn't you just come directly to me?"

"You're the CPO. I reckoned that the APOs know dodges that their managers might not."

"So you didn't suspect me of being involved?"

"No. Unless the roster lied about you, as well, you weren't around when several of the consignments went through."

"Fortunately for me, I suppose, the roster is accurate for the CPOs. But you now realise…?"

"That any of the POs or APOs could have arranged to get themselves here for any particular consignment. Yes."

"Would it help if I did a bit of checking back through our records to see whether anyone swapped rosters on a particular date? There'll be the original rosters, but also seizure forms and records of exams."

"That would be very helpful. But are you able to do it without anyone else knowing?"

"Yes. What date or dates do you want to check?"

"Potentially there are nearly twenty, but I suggest 21 June and 3 July."

"No problem. I can probably let you know later today. And for the record, if it was handled quickly, it would certainly be possible for a consignment to get here without us getting even a sniff of it."

"Thanks."

Occasionally you have to trust someone and your trust is based on instinct rather than anything firmer. But if there had been any Waterguard involvement in this smuggling operation, once it was clear that the rosters were unreliable, I couldn't see how we could discover who was actually on duty on the critical date of 3 July without the help of someone like Wally.

And come to think of it, if I had to trust any two people in the Department, Jim and Wally would be at the top of my list.

The party of visiting dignitaries rejoined us. As Iain had a large Ford Zephyr with him, we drove to Kersey's office.

"I'm assuming one of you has a key," I remarked.

"Naturally," replied Elliott. I wondered what rank he was. Did he outrank Iain, for instance?

There were several letters on the floor as we went in. Iain picked them up and opened them.

"Nothing of interest to us," he reported.

The front office and Kersey's own office looked unchanged from my last visit, though closer inspection revealed that there was only stationery in the drawers of the desks. However, the back office where Kersey had looked for the files I had demanded was now denuded of all files.

"Do you think he left any papers of any value?" asked Carvell.

"No," I replied, "and I reckon he removed a lot that were of little interest to anyone. I reckon his filing system was so chaotic he just took everything to be on the safe side."

"Was there anything in the rest of this space?" asked Elliott.

"No. I can only guess why he rented so much space when he didn't need it. Whether or not he was set up by Weissman or Silberstein, I think he needed to give the impression that he was a large-scale operator. And he'd have to get more business than just Weissman's and Silberstein's or it'd start to look a bit fishy."

"Why do you think Silbersteins were in on this?"

"From the entries which Davenport took away in his suitcase. I realise it's possible he was just making a smokescreen – as he seems to have done with the notes he left around the place to cover many of the missing entries – but Silbersteins had more entries in Davenport's suitcase than Weissman. They are also diamond importers after all. Wouldn't the best way to hide smuggled Russian diamonds be within consignments of legitimate diamonds travelling between reputable diamond merchants?"

"You have a devious mind, even for a Customs Officer," remarked Carvell. "But we've been aware for some time that elements in the Kremlin nomenklatura wanted to rid themselves of Khrushchev, who they regarded not just as a clown, but soft as well. They've never forgiven him for backing down over Cuba. So the idea that they would try to obtain large amounts of hard currency to buy support in key places wasn't new to us. Furthermore, we had exactly the same thought that you've just had. So we made a series of visits to the Silbersteins of this world and gave them a very severe warning. If we ever found any Russian diamonds in their possession or could prove had been through their hands, without them telling us, we'd put them out of business. They're perfectly aware we have ways of doing that. None of them has particularly clean hands when it comes to the provenance of their diamonds, which are often used as a way of wiping clean dirty money. We've also been monitoring their banking transactions and who does business with them. Mr Davidson nor, as far as we can tell, anyone else of his ilk has been in contact with them. They may not be entirely clean, but we can rule them out of any involvement in this particular operation."

"Would you have expected the Soviets to have tried to use them or one of the other main diamond merchants?"

"Yes – that's why we did what we did."

"So why didn't they? Why did they choose to use someone as down-market and risky as Weissman?"

"Because he imported the right sort of stuff, was already engaged in smuggling stolen jewellery and could be bought."

"I don't think that's Storey's point, with respect, Carvell," said Iain. "What I believe he's suggesting is that, if the Russians would go to someone like Silberstein in the normal course of events but didn't, presumably someone tipped them off. After all, if they had tried to use Silbersteins, say, you might've been able to stop the whole operation and pick up Davidson. The fact that they appear never even to have contacted Silbersteins has turned out pretty conveniently for them."

"In other words, someone from Silbersteins was approached and tipped them off? Is that what you're saying?"

"Yes."

"But it might not have been Silberstein's directly, of course," I added. "They would presumably have alerted their partners in Amsterdam, for instance. It might've been someone there."

"On the other hand, it could equally have been someone among your lot," observed Elliott sourly. "Your lot haven't exactly got a good record when it comes to keeping stuff away from the Russians."

"Let's not go raking all that up again," retorted Carvell. "We now have security procedures on top of security systems on top of security checks. I can scarcely blow my nose without someone trying to check that the snot doesn't contain a microphone or a transmitter made in Leningrad or Leipzig."

"But you take the point about Silbersteins – and the others?" said Iain.

"Of course. But it may be damned difficult to check."

"Let's go on to Kersey's abode," said Elliott.

We got back into the car and drove to Low Road where Kersey apparently rented a semi-detached. The house had a small front lawn, with flower beds consisting of roses. I wondered whether the plants might have come from the White House Nurseries, but quickly dismissed the thought as ludicrous. Elliott produced another key to open the front door. The decoration showed that nothing had been altered since the mid 50s. The furniture was sparse, except for a well-upholstered three piece suite covered in a floral pattern. There was a cheap TV in the lounge and another one in the dining room – a small Russian one, like the one Weissman had kept in his office. The kitchen showed nothing out of place, nor untoward. There was another stainless steel percolator so that Kersey could maintain his heavy caffeine intake at home. Upstairs, one bed showed evidence of having been slept in. The other two rooms looked as though they hadn't been used for some time.

The back garden was small and laid to lawn, apart from narrow flower beds in front of the fences on either side. On a patio made from a dozen paving stones, just outside the back door, was a metal dustbin that had been used to burn papers. There was a large amount of black ash in the bottom and the smell of paraffin remained. Iain raked around in the ashes with the handle end of a broom.

"Nothing decipherable there, I fear," he announced.

"Pity. We can't tell whether he burnt all his papers or whether he took some with him," said Elliott.

"Do you think he might've hidden anything on the premises?" suggested Carvell.

"If he had, I guess the people who killed him got here first. It's difficult to tell, but the loose edges of the carpets suggest a search and there's a couple of places where dents in the carpet or lino suggest that the furniture has been disturbed. We can send a team round to go through the place, but if he had any sense, he'd've hidden any important stuff somewhere a lot less obvious than here. Besides, he was in such a state when he was found, I can't really believe he didn't tell them everything they needed to know."

"So why did they need to search here?"

"My guess is that they've been having to work at great speed. One team went after Kersey and beat out of him what they needed to know before killing him. Another team came here – and probably had a look round his office too. In a way, the dimwittedness of the woodentops in Leicester was helpful. Because they treated the deaths of Mr and Mrs Davenport at face value, it'd seem that the other side began to believe that they'd got away with it. It was probably only when Kersey rang Weissman about the 3 July consignment that they started to realise that they hadn't put the lid on it and then your raid on Weissman meant that they'd have to act extremely fast. After all, they couldn't be certain that Weissman wouldn't squeal."

"Since they've achieved what they wanted, why did they need to kill Kersey?" I asked. "After all, we can't get our hands on the money that went into the Moscow Narodny Bank. Khrushchev has been replaced. They must've assumed that we'd work out what had happened and how sooner or later. I wouldn't have thought Kersey could've identified Davidson, could he?"

"My guess is that Kersey was killed to remind everyone else in the chain to keep their mouths shut," said Elliott. "And whether or not Kersey could identify Davidson, others in the chain certainly could – notably Weissman, Mrs Weissman and the people who bought the diamonds from Davidson. I suspect Davidson has a good reason for remaining here and he's either still here or needs to return at some point fairly soon. He's a big fish and connected in areas that the Soviets value greatly, so if we got our hands on him, it'd be a serious loss for them."

"And he's definitely not Embassy. We've checked all of them out against his photos," Carvell confirmed.

"I assume the bulletin arrived with his details?" asked Iain.

"Yes. We felt he'd be a bit cheeky to try and leave through Harwich," I replied.

"Unless he's still got accomplices here," said Elliott.

"I still find it difficult to understand what Davenport was up to," I observed. "Why did he take those particular entries? Some led us to Weissman and this whole operation. But Silbersteins appear to be only indirectly involved. And where does the White House Nurseries fit in? And how did he lay his hands on the diamonds? And why?"

"Subject to the appropriate people here being checked out," replied Elliott, "it seems likely that he was the accomplice here. I reckon he took those documents either as insurance or because he thought he could blackmail the people concerned. I suspect he intercepted the diamonds, either as payment or to demand a larger pay-off."

"When we get them to London, we'll check whether the rest of them are of Russian origin," added Iain.

"And London is where we should be heading," said Carvell, as if a few hours away from the metropolis would somehow leave him impaired for life.

"We'll drop you off at the Custom House," said Iain. "I'll phone Jim or you in the morning."

"Don't forget to get the diamonds from Jim," I reminded him.

"I think it's best if we take the whole suitcase," he replied with a meaningful look.

"Yes," added Elliott. "The sooner it's in some sort of official custody the better for you, my lad."

TEN – LONDON: AMONG THE TOP BRASS

Not long after I had enjoyed another bitter-sweet few minutes talking to Rosemary on the phone, the phone rang again. It was Iain Cogbill.

"There's a meeting with Mr Salt, one of the Commissioners, at noon tomorrow. The Chief, the Chief Inspector, the IGW and your Collector will all be present. You and I are also bidden – along with your AC, unfortunately. As far as I can tell, it's just to put them in the picture – but I think you can assume neither you nor I will have to say anything. All of the talking will be done by the Chief and your AC, I imagine. We've just been invited along in case any inconvenient details need to be clarified. I expect your chaps will travel by car. If you've got any sense, you'll go early – by rail."

"Where's the meeting taking place?"

"The Board Room in King's Beam House. In Mark Lane in the City."

Much as I would have liked to have known a bit more about my Collector (Higher Collector, actually, but only used when it was necessary to pull rank over Collections with ordinary Collectors, apparently), the thought of spending several hours in a car with Jock Imrie made me determined to follow Iain's advice.

So I went to bed early and called into the office before 6 a.m. to ensure Jim was aware of my summons. There was no message for me from Wally French about the Waterguard rosters he was checking. A little disappointed, I took a train to Liverpool Street that got me there shortly after 11 a.m. Since the Tube journey seemed to be circuitous, as you might expect, via the Circle Line, I walked up Bishopsgate and through Leadenhall Market, a hive of activity, along Fenchurch Street and into Mark Lane. King's Beam House turned out to be a gloomy post-War building of dark red bricks – a terribly undistinguished building for the heart of HM Customs and Excise, I thought. As I was still twenty-five minutes early, I crossed the road and wandered past a handsome church that hadn't been rebuilt since the War, into Lower Thames Street where almost immediately I encountered the

London Custom House, right by the river. Though not particularly distinguished architecturally from that side, it seemed to me a lot more suitable as a main HQ building. Why on earth would the Board choose to be in that nondescript building rather than one that was within close sight and sound of the river – and of the docks? Even though many were now closed or closing, surely that was closer to what the Department did than a mediocre building in an ordinary street in the City?

Realising the time, I returned to King's Beam House. A Revenue Constable, resplendent in a red coat, stopped me and demanded my name and purpose of my visit. After consultation with a colleague and a list of names, I was allowed through the entrance lobby and escorted to a waiting room on the fourth floor. I was ten minutes early, but not surprised to be the only one there.

Within a couple of minutes, Iain Cogbill arrived in the wake of a tall, imposing man who looked as though he was fashioned from oak. He was one of those people you suspected could knock a door down with one blow from his fist or even thump a brick wall and see it crumble away. Reputedly the man who had leapt across the windscreen of a car attempting to flee from an IB operation in Dover, the "Chief" – Stanley Woodruffe – needed no introduction. Naturally, he said nothing to a being as junior as me, though he eyed me over once the moment he arrived.

Indeed, he said nothing until the next contingent arrived a couple of minutes later. On the basis that Imrie would be accompanying the Higher Collector, Harwich and the Chief Inspector, these were evidently they. I guessed that the tall, thin, middle-aged man who looked as though he would rather be on the links playing golf, was probably my Collector and the short, black-haired man with the jaw and swagger of a bulldog was therefore the Chief Inspector.

"Good morning, Ron," said Woodruffe. "Are you going to claim credit or just try to duck away from the blame?"

"Good morning, Stan," replied the short man, confirming himself to be Ronald Mather, Chief Inspector and, so to speak, my ultimate boss. "It seems to me that without the alertness of my people in Harwich, your lot would still know nothing."

I could tell Imrie was itching to add to that, but the Collector, probably wisely, remained silent. When two great beasts lock antlers, he probably felt that the safest place was at some distance and certainly not attempting to intervene.

However, the next sally was interrupted by the arrival of an ordinary-looking, grey-haired man with black rimmed spectacles. By process of elimination, he had to be William Crowther, the IGW.

"Morning Ron. Morning Stan. Morning Frank. Morning Jock," he began. "You must be Cogbill and you Storey? Morning to you, too. What a gathering of men who'd rather be spending this afternoon on the golf course!"

Responses were curtailed by the announcement by a Revenue Constable that the Commissioner was in the Board Room and we were invited to join him there.

We proceeded along a corridor past the lifts and through some swing doors into a quite different world. Here the corridors were lined with dark wood panels and the floor covered with a beige carpet. A couple of large doors announced the occupants as 'Chairman' and 'Deputy Chairman' with 'Private Office' in between. The Board Room was on the other side of the corridor, its windows looking out on to a space between this wing and the rest of the building. The Board Room was long and quite narrow, mostly filled by a long table of shining wood with two dozen chairs around it. On the walls were various charters in frames, a picture of the Queen and a small stained glass representation of Charles II behind which a small electric light was shining.

The Commissioner, Mr Salt, rose from his chair on the far side of the table, as we entered. Next to him was a young man, presumably some sort of assistant, and a tall, cadaverous, white-haired man.

"Good morning to you all," Mr Salt began. "I think we all know each other, so let's start. I've asked the Solicitor along, in case any legal issues might arise."

In front of him was a black leather folder with a small bundle of paper and a handwritten page on top.
"You may not know Mr Cogbill from my office," said Woodruffe, indicating Iain, sat at his side.

"I'm not sure whether you've been to Harwich," added Mather. "At my side is the Higher Collector, one of the Assistant Collectors and the OCX who's been doing the leg work on this case."

"Very well," said Mr Salt. He was another tall man, wearing what appeared to be regulation black jacket and pinstriped trousers. He was tanned, with greying fair hair and seemed very relaxed. He was puffing away at a cigar. Within a couple of minutes, Mather lit a foul-smelling pipe and several others lit up cigarettes. "I've read the papers. Not in detail – but young Tony here has. The salient aspect essentially is whether we have liabilities in relation to the police or anyone else. There are two aspects to this. First, the involvement of our people in facilitating the transit of illicit diamonds through Customs controls and second, the removal of potential police evidence and the failure to inform them. Tigran, I'd welcome your thoughts."

The cadaverous man spoke. "Although at present there seems to be some lack of clear evidence as to the nature of the involvement of Departmental personnel in the operation of these illicit activities, I can see only limited scope to suggest any supervisory negligence. As I understand it, the Investigation Branch check from time to time on the bank accounts and any other wealth of staff who are in a position to benefit from corruptly selling their active or passive participation in activities in breach of the laws assigned to the Department. Such monitoring can only be occasional: that is reasonable. However, it would be helpful if local management could furnish details on how supervision is exercised in situ."

"I suggest that the Higher Collector –" began Mather.

"I'd prefer the Solicitor to finish, as I know he has to dash off for another meeting shortly," interrupted Mr Salt.

"I shall go on to the second issue. There is plainly no doubt that the suitcase was removed from the premises in Leicester, in full knowledge that it contained diamonds of substantial value. There also seems to be no doubt that an official of HM Customs and Excise failed to mention the said diamonds when interviewed by the Leicestershire Constabulary as part of their investigation into the suicide on the same premises and, as such, nothing was recorded on that matter in his statement to the Leicestershire Constabulary. I am given to understand that this was done on the advice of a senior officer. Though no direct falsehood was perpetrated, the said statement plainly omitted a fact potentially relevant to the suicide under investigation. There is no doubt in my mind that a court would regard this as an offence under Section 24 (2) of the Police Evidence Act 1955, carrying a term of imprisonment of up to two years and a fine of up to

142

£1000. The fact that this was done in order to facilitate the investigation of another possible offence is merely a plea in mitigation. It does not erase the original offence. However, the fact that the use of these diamonds and documents in the investigation of a very large series of offences of very considerable value and the subsequent evaluation by the Special Branch of the Metropolitan Police suggests that there is only an insignificant likelihood that this would ever get before a court. Having said that, it will be for the senior managers of those concerned to consider whether any disciplinary action should be taken against them within the relevant parts of the Establishment Instructions Part 11."

"It may be worth adding," said Woodruffe sharply, "that it's virtually certain that the diamonds concerned were illicitly imported from the Soviet Union and thus technically liable to seizure by the Department."

"That may well be the case," replied the Solicitor, "but it still only serves to mitigate the offence of an incomplete and potentially misleading statement to the Leicestershire Constabulary."

"Be that as it may," drawled Mr Salt, "I've got it on pretty good authority that if the Leicestershire Police try to make anything of it, they'll be sat on from a great height. The worst we can expect is that the officer concerned may get a wigging from them. Indeed, if we seem to have imposed something under our own disciplinary procedures on those involved, it probably shouldn't even come to that."

"We'll institute appropriate disciplinary proceedings," confirmed Mather, to my silent discomfiture.

"What really bothers me," Mr Salt went on, "isn't this side of it, which is pretty well sewn up now, but the possible involvement of one or more of our staff in all this. What is it going to look like in the Press? And how will Ministers react? I don't really want the Chairman to be giving the new Financial Secretary this sort of bad news on only the second time they've met. We don't want to give Ministers any excuse to start poking their noses around in matters that don't concern them."

"As I understand it," began Woodruffe, "we don't have to charge the man Weissman with every illicit import, so the courts may only learn about those where it'd seem the diamonds were spread around in an otherwise legitimate importation of scrap jewellery. The fact that we failed to spot this doesn't look brilliant, but it's not culpable, and we've no need to bring to public mention anything about an accomplice within the Department. I can't imagine Weissman wanting to make a point of it. Indeed, I think when we start discussing what offences he should be charged with, beyond the single one he's currently held on, we could guarantee his silence."

"But what about Special Branch and the Security people? They're both pretty leaky – in the latter case whether they intend to or not. Can we guarantee it won't slip out that way?"

"I believe they want as little publicity about this as possible. Unless they can catch the ringleader, all they have is a highly successful Soviet operation to smuggle £35 million worth of diamonds into London, sell them here and get the cash into the Narodny Bank, but three hundred yards from here. Why would they want to advertise such a kick in the nuts? Besides, both of them suspected an operation like this was likely to be coming and failed to stop it. If all this blew up, none of us would come up smelling of roses, so we've a strong mutual interest in playing this close to our chests."

"Have the Press shown any interest in your raid on Weissman?"

"A couple of our tame crime correspondents. We've told them there's a story in it for them in due course. They'll print what we feed them. It'll be a good enough story, but won't let any cats out of bags."

"Is there any news on whether the ringleader is likely to be caught?"

"Opinion is divided. Special Branch think he's left the country. Box 500 believe he's still here. If he does get caught, you may need to reconvene this meeting because this'll just have been promoted directly from Third Division (South) to First Division."

"Very well. I think that's that. Thank you for your attendance, gentlemen."

Mr Salt remained in conversation with the Solicitor and the young man called Tony, while the rest of us left.

Mather left immediately with Imrie in tow.

"I see the Chief Inspector wants his arse licked," remarked Woodruffe unkindly, but memorably.

"Are you off to lunch, Stan?" asked the IGW. "I'd like to sort out some problem our folk seem to be having over the use of the cutters."

"If it's what I think it is, you'd better come to my club."

I was left with my Collector and Iain Cogbill.

"Don't worry about all that disciplinary stuff, Storey," said the former with a pleasant smile. "Actually you seem to have done rather well. I got Jim Round to brief me yesterday evening. You and Jim will get a letter of formal reprimand from me, with a separate note to the Estabs people telling them to remove the letters from your files in three months. But I would advise you never to do anything like that again – even if a senior officer tells you to. You could've landed in gaol, you know."

"Thank you, sir. I was feeling very uncomfortable at certain points in that meeting."

"Never worry about the Sols' Office. They always paint the worst case and Tigran Tigranian is the worst, so I'm told. Still, it's probably safer in the long run than optimistic lawyers, I reckon. I would offer you a lift back, but as this has finished when it did, I'm going to find an old colleague in the CI's Office and persuade him to join me for a round at Sunningdale."

"Well," said Iain after the Collector had departed, "What did you think of that?"

"If I'm perfectly honest – 'much sound and fury signifying nothing'. All the Commissioner was really interested in was whether the Department might come out of it looking bad."

"Well, I suppose it's his job. I'm sure we do better – not least with people like Special Branch and Box 500 – if we're well regarded than if we're seen to be incompetent or corrupt – or both."

"You're right, I'm sure. That's probably why I'm an OCX and clever blokes like that Tony are advising Commissioners."

"Though I probably shouldn't say it in these hallowed portals, I expect that's because some of them are too idle to do the work for themselves."

We had to wait until we could be escorted out of the building, into a grey and cold Mark Lane.

"I would suggest lunch, but I've got a meeting with Mike Elliott in about half an hour."

"No problem. I'll make my way back to Harwich. Just one thing, did anything come out from the papers we got at the… at Belsize Park?"

"Nothing at all. They all seemed in order. Someone's going through their accounts to see if they can pick anything fishy up, but at the moment, it just looks as though it might've been another of Davenport's little smokescreens."

After I had eaten in a gloomy underground restaurant with medieval pretensions called the 'Baronial Rooms', it was about 1.30. I decided it was foolish to return to Harwich, only to have to travel back to London on my way to Leicester the following day, so I decided I would go and stay with my parents that night and, if I felt brave enough, go and see Barbara the following morning and finally break off our engagement.

ELEVEN – SOUTH LONDON AND LEICESTER – MORE UNOFFICAL SLEUTHING

I phoned my mother in advance of my arrival. If nothing else, she deserved the chance to reinforce her natural stock of forbearance and resilience before the Cold War recommenced. Her pleasure at the thought of seeing me for the first time in more months that I wished to count was inevitably muted by what was likely to be in store. I could tell that much from her voice.

When I arrived home, both my father and mother were there.

"It's lovely to see you, Nick," said my mother.

"After such a long time," added my father.

"I had to settle into my new post in Harwich," I replied by way of explanation.

"There's weekends."

"I got dragged into playing rugby on a Saturday."

"Toff's game. I could never understand why you couldn't stick to a proper working-class game like football."

"How's the allotment – full of carrots, tomatoes, red onions and red cabbages?" I fear that since I had become independent of him, I couldn't resist teasing him.

"Have you been to see Barbara?" asked my mother hastily. "She must've wondered what's happened to you."

"I don't think we're going anywhere, Mum," I said. "I was rather hoping she might've found someone else rather nearer home. How is she, anyway?"

"Doing all right. Still teaching in New Cross."

"Why are you 'ere?" suddenly demanded my father.

"I've been working in London today, so I thought I'd come and see you."

"I thought you was working in 'Arwich?"

"I had to go to a meeting at Customs HQ in the City. I actually met some of the top brass."

"'Ow naice for you. Suppose they was all ex-public schoolboys?"

146

"I doubt it. For what it's worth, my impression is that outside the Secretaries Office, the top brass started at the bottom and worked their way up."

"Like you propose to do?"

"I want to do a good job and I want to have a life I enjoy. I don't know whether that means getting promoted or not."

"Have you seen anything of your sister?" asked my mother. My sister, Ellen Nadezhda (named after Lenin's wife) had married a teacher and now lived in the heart of the bourgeoisie in Sutton.

"Not lately. We speak on the phone from time to time. She, Barry and the kids were well the last time we spoke."

"There was that shipping agent from 'Arwich turned up dead on a tip in Dagenham the other day. Anything to do with you?" demanded my father.

"Well, I didn't bump him off, if that's what you think! But yes, I had come across him. I dealt with lots of his Customs entries and had to visit his office a couple of times because of queries about the accuracy of some of them."

"So 'e was a bit of crook."

"I think he was someone who did a 'bi' of duckin' an' divin'' as your mates would say, Dad."

"There's nothing wrong with a working-class accent. That grammar school made you all toffee-nosed and encouraged you to betray your class."

"Not again! I just did what every working-class lad has done for centuries, when he got the chance to better himself, he did. If that's betraying my class, there's been a lot of us at it and there'll be a lot more."

"All it does is delay the inevitable."

"I'm not going to have a dialectical debate with you Dad. I know I haven't got a snowball in hell's chance of changing your views, but you've had your chance to mould mine and it didn't work. You aren't going to succeed now. So why don't we talk about the success or otherwise of Charlton? Or the exciting prospects for the Russian people of the replacement of Khrushchev by Brezhnev and Kosygin? It's surely better than spending all our time every time we meet for the rest of our lives quarrelling over something we'll never resolve and just making Mum's life a misery."

"So you admit bourgeoisie people like you can't win the argument."

"No. But I know when I'm faced by a blinkered old man whose view of the Soviet Union hasn't changed since the 20s, despite the gulags, the show trials and the craven deal with Hitler in 1939. I'm sorry, Mum. I'm going out!"

As it happened it was a fortuitous moment to leave the house and clear my head. It was just after 6.30 and I was due to ring Rosemary to settle arrangements for the next day. Fortunately the second phone box I came to actually worked and I agreed to meet her at Leicester Station as soon after 5 p.m. as she could manage. That was not a conversation I had intended having in my parents' house. I wasn't prepared to face an inquisition about her at this stage.

Less than a day! I could even face my father with something approaching equanimity.

"I'm sorry, Mum," I said as I returned. "But he just keeps winding me up. I don't know why he does it. He's just driven his children away with it."

"He" was in the back yard smoking a pipe.

"He can't help it. I think deep down he's quite proud of both of you. But when you've put so much of yourself into believing something, it's hard to admit you might have been wrong. It isn't the sort of thing where you could be a little bit wrong. It's all or nothing with him."
"Well, he's lucky he's got you."
"I'm lucky I've got him."

Perhaps both of us had been reflecting on our row and on the effect on Mum, so we both stuck to Charlton Athletic's mediocre performances in the Second Division and a discussion about pop music, where, to my surprise, my father turned out to support groups like the Beatles and the Rolling Stones, on the basis that it was British, working-class music rather than foreign classical stuff imposed by the tastes of the bourgeoisie. I ignored this and told him about the other groups emerging on Merseyside, like Billy J. Kramer and the Dakotas, Gerry and the Pacemakers and The Searchers. My mother probably breathed a deep sigh of relief when I announced that I'd been up since quarter past five and would go to bed.

The following morning, conflict was avoided during breakfast for the simple reason that my father was off to his allotment at 8 o'clock, just as I was cleaning my teeth.

Having breakfasted and said goodbye to my mother, I took a bus to Maze Hill and took Barbara and her parents somewhat by surprise. The reason for this surprised embarrassment became rapidly obvious when

Barbara suggested we went for a walk in Greenwich Park, just half a mile away.

"I was hoping…" I began.
"I felt…" she began.
"After you," I continued. "Ladies first."
"I felt I should speak to you directly rather than writing or phoning. You know we agreed a sort of unofficial engagement when we were at college. We were in Greenwich Park then, if I remember… Well, we've seen so little of each other the last year or so, I began to realise that it wasn't that important to either of us, or we'd've made more of an effort. Anyway, I've met one of the teachers at my school and we're both rather keen on each other… I hope you don't mind."
"Not at all. I was going to say something similar. Not that I've met another teacher, you understand…"
"I think it would've been better if we'd just been friends…"
"Possibly… Anyway, I wish you and your teacher friend lots of good luck."

We walked across the park, talking about family and mutual acquaintances. She was about to go up to the Royal Observatory, where, as I recalled, we'd agreed our unofficial engagement. But I wanted to reserve the pleasure of going there again to a time when I was with Rosemary, so I invented an excuse to shoot off to Greenwich Station. I raced there with a burden lifted from my shoulders. In spite of my confrontations with my father, I didn't care for emotional scenes – especially if I was going to be cast in the role of bad guy – so avoiding one as neatly as I had seemed almost as great an escape as avoiding gaol for my part in concealing evidence from the police.

As I didn't want to spend the whole weekend in the clothes I had worn on Friday, I went round the Greenwich shops and market and bought a pair of black jeans with obligatory turn-ups, a black roll-neck jumper and some socks and underwear, along with a small duffle bag to put them in. I made use of some averagely unwholesome gents toilets to change. Though the sports jacket and shoes I wore for work didn't go brilliantly with my new attire, I began to feel that the weekend was starting properly.

I got a train to Cannon Street and realised I had five hours or so ahead of me before I needed to catch a train to Leicester. I didn't want to mooch around the centre of town, just in case Barbara and her teacher friend, Brian, bumped into me. The chances were astronomically slim, but I didn't want to risk being caught out in a lie – even a whiteish one. So I decided to walk from Cannon Street to St Pancras, by a route that kept me well clear of the Hatton Garden/Fetter Lane area. So I made my way up Cheapside to St Paul's and then down Ludgate Hill, up Fleet Street and into the Strand. I finally turned north at the Aldwych and went up Holborn Kingsway. I realised I had gone rather too far west in my desire to avoid areas that overlapped with my recent activities and, after going a short way up Southampton Row, I started to snake my way along and up, as I put it to myself, through the series of streets than run between Theobald's Road and Coram's Fields. To avoid going too far east, I skirted Coram's Fields to the west and found myself in Brunswick Square.

For much of my walk I had been noting to myself how quiet the centre of London was on a Saturday. Most people had presumably headed to the West End or had done their groceries long before I started my perambulations. But all the busy-bee workers of weekdays had vanished, mainly to the suburbs no doubt. Yet coming towards me was a man in the full regalia of a City worker – bowler hat, black jacket and pinstripe trousers. Idly, I glanced at his face. To my shock, it was Louis Davidson, or his doppelganger. I didn't dare stare and quickly looked away.

Had he noticed the look of recognition on my face? I didn't dare turn round for a moment. People like that tended to carry guns. There would be no point confirming my suspicions if I wasn't alive to pass them on to anyone. So I kept walking. After a minute or so – an eternity it felt – I stopped and pretended to tie up my shoe, looking back as surreptitiously as I could. But he had turned the corner into Guildford Street. I ran back to the junction and saw him heading westwards along Guildford Street. I remained where I was, partly obscured by pedestrians if he decided to look back. But he didn't, disappearing from my sight. I raced up Guildford Street, but he was nowhere to be found. In front of me was the Russell Square Tube station. It seemed more than likely he had gone in there. I couldn't see him in any queue for tickets, but I bought a ticket and went down on to the southbound side. There weren't many people about and he wasn't one of them. I chased over to the northbound platform, but as I did so I heard a train pull out. When I got there, the platform was empty, except for a handful of people going out through the "way out" corridor.

I went back to the booking office and had another look around. Then I went back into the street and near Russell Square, in case he had seen me and deliberately tricked me and was now awaiting a bus. But he wasn't there either. He had well and truly vanished. Indeed, I realised that in my haste I had overlooked the possibility that he had gone into one of the nearby houses or hotels.

But I could scarcely search them on my own. The only thing to do was to let someone know. I rang the IB from a phone box bear Russell Street Tube, but all I could get was a bored-sounding duty officer, who promised he'd try to get a message to Iain Cogbill. I didn't want to leave a message that was too obvious, so I asked him to tell Iain "I spotted our mutual friend Louis D close to Russell Square Tube, but lost him. He may be in that area. I have no telephone contact until Sunday evening. I'll ring this number again later."

As I had no means of contacting either Special Branch or Box 500, that had to be it. I made my way up Woburn Place and along Euston Road to St Pancras. Feeling peckish, I got a bowl of Brown Windsor soup and a slice of bread in the station buffet and tried to decide what to do for the next four hours or so. In the end, I concluded that though the delights of St Pancras Station were limited, they beat those of Leicester Station. Moreover, I had no particular desire to hang around Leicester on my own without any obvious purpose. I preferred not to attract the attention of any eagle-eyed, keen young copper in that city more than any other. So I bought a copy of *The Guardian* and learnt how trendy middle-class lefties spent their money – which seemed to be considerably more than you'd expect a socialist to have available to spend.

Shortly before 3 p.m. I rang the IB again, but the same duty officer said he'd been trying to raise Iain Cogbill, but without success. Did I realise Iain was a keen golfer, like all Scots, and was probably enjoying a round and a couple of drams at his local course?

So I boarded a Leicester-bound train and snoozed. In between dozing and waking, I felt uncomfortably that there should have been more that I could have done. But for the life of me, I couldn't figure out what.

I had caught a stopping train, so I arrived shortly before 5 p.m. I was just making my way slowly to the front of the station when Rosemary shot through the front entrance on a bicycle, wearing red and green hockey kit covered by a short, black duffle coat.

"Hello!" she cried out and stopped abruptly. We kissed. A couple of cars hooted.

"The WPC house is in Stoneygate Road. It's about a mile. Do you mind walking? I must have a shower before doing anything else!"

In spite of all the walking I'd been doing already, my feet felt as ready to go as when I'd stepped out of bed. Rosemary walked alongside me, wheeling her bicycle.

"One of the perks of being in the police," she remarked. "It's amazing how many people don't report their bike's been stolen. After six months we're allowed to buy them cheap."

"How are the Davenport cases getting on?" I asked.

"Of course, you have something of a personal interest," she replied with a cheeky grin. "Well, you can put your mind at rest. They're both signed, sealed, closed and filed away. Dear Eric is now investigating a series of burglaries in the Belgrave Road area."

"My actions have been criticised at the highest levels in Customs and Excise and I've had my knuckles rapped by a member of Special Branch, so I shan't ever be doing anything like that again."

"You've obviously had a hectic week."

"You can say that again."

I told her what had been going on, including what I regarded as the key consignment, that of 3 July, the so-called 'Fabergé' one. If I couldn't trust Rosemary, who could I trust?

"Do you think these checks will finally establish what Davenport was up to?" she asked.

"I doubt it. It's the oddest part of the whole thing. Jim Round, my boss, doesn't believe he was capable of colluding in something like this. But what if he'd been threatened? I realise they didn't have any children, but could they have threatened to harm Mrs Davenport? And why did he take those particular things away with him? No-one has ever suggested he left in a great hurry. He even left some notes in our filing system about the entries which he'd taken with him. Everything was neatly in order in his suitcase. But some of the items have drawn a complete blank. Silberstein seems to be clean – as does the White House Nurseries…"

"If they haven't got something to hide, I'd be very surprised. That whole set-up looked really fishy."

152

"I agree, but the papers we picked up when it was raided appear to have shown up nothing. The only strange thing seems to be that the people involved there haven't been back. Presumably they've spotted that the place was being watched."

"So what is the explanation for what was in Davenport's suitcase?"

"The favourite theory is that he was involved and the diamonds either represented his pay-off, or he intercepted them to use to blackmail the people he was involved with. I suppose it's possible that if they were threatening his wife, he intended to use them to bargain with. As to the other entries, it's thought they were just a smokescreen."

"But you're not convinced...?"

"No... I suppose I can't quite understand what he was trying to achieve by creating a smokescreen."

"Well, if you think he was fundamentally honest, but forced to do what he did because of threats, perhaps what he was trying to do was to leave clues that would be sufficiently unobtrusive so that anyone from the people he was involved in might not spot them, but – especially if he got killed – those investigating it might? Of course, part of that might well require a smokescreen –"

"Rosemary! That's brilliant! There must surely be a career for you in the CID!"

"Well, it's just an idea. But, of course, if some of it is smokescreen and some of it genuine clues, you have to try and sort out which is which."

We had arrived at the WPC house in Stoneygate Road.

"There's a common room where you can wait, Nick," she explained. "We aren't allowed gentleman visitors in our rooms. This is not, as I understand it, a rule applied to male PC houses... I won't be long."

The common room was spartan – four easy chairs, a cheap sofa, a TV on a small table and a dartboard, with some rather dog-eared plastic darts sticking out of it. There appeared to be a kitchen at the back. A chunky woman in her late thirties with short, brown hair emerged, eyeing me with the practiced eye of a spotter of potential malefactors and troublemakers.

"So you're him," she remarked in a strong Leicester accent. "Do sit down, you're getting in the way. I need to see the telly to do my pools."

That activity and the subsequent news broadcast maintained her attention until Rosemary reappeared, wearing a navy roll-neck jumper, a grey miniskirt, and the same grey coat and black boots which she'd worn the previous Saturday. She looked fantastic!

"I meant to ask you whether you won?" I began.

"No we lost. We usually do. Still it was only two-nil. We play teams from the colleges round here and they're usually fitter and get a lot more chance to practice together."

"I didn't realise you were sporty as well as musical."

"I'm not particularly. I played hockey and tennis at school and just kept doing them when I went to college. The facilities in Loughborough were brilliant! I hated netball, though."

"I hated cross-country. It always made me sick. I liked football and rugby. I used to play cricket in the summer, but once I left school I stopped. It just took up too much of the day."

"Where do you want to go?"

"I don't know Leicester at all – apart from Aylestone and the police station. So I'm happy to go wherever you fancy… Is where I'm staying tonight reasonably near? I'd quite like to dump this bag."

"It's just round the corner in Alexandra Road. One of the other WPCs always puts her fiancé up there when he comes up from Bristol. She says it's quite nice."

It was a large Victorian house that had been converted into a B&B. The middle-aged lady at the reception desk pointedly stated that there was a single room booked for me and that I had to be in by eleven o'clock or there was no guarantee anyone would be available to open the front door. From her expression, it was obvious she expected Rosemary to be spending the night with me – and plainly disapproved. We went up to my room, which was in the attic, small and with a bed so narrow only two skeletons could possibly sleep in it side by side.

"You weren't anticipating that I would be spending the night with you, were you, Nick?"

"No. Much as I might want you to. I know you're not the sort of girl to go to bed with a man on her second date."

"To be quite honest with you, I'm the sort of girl who goes to bed for the first time with a man on her wedding night. Does that disappoint you?"

"Truthfully – yes and no. There's part of me that finds you incredibly sexy and would like to get you into bed this instant. But the other part is more me, I think. The reason why I love you isn't just because of how you look, but of who you are. I know we don't know each other very well yet, but sometimes you have to trust your feelings… No, it's not your feelings… it's something deeper than that… to me, love is more important than sex. Indeed, on the rare occasions I've been to bed with a woman – the same woman, I should add – it felt very incomplete for that reason… I hope that hasn't put you off me completely, but I love you too much to pretend about things…"

Rosemary said nothing, just put her arms round me and kissed me.

"I think we were born a bit too soon for the 'Swinging Sixties'," I suggested.

"I never really expected – or wanted – to be just like my mum, but here I am…"

"I was thinking about that when I was lying in bed last night. I'd had my usual row with my dad and I was asking myself how my mum could possibly put up with him. But I realised that it was because they both loved each other. She must've known what he was like when they got married, but she loved him in spite of his faults. Deep down he's honest, faithful and cares deeply – about many things, but not least her. Between them, there's a great truth. I contrasted it so much with my relationship with Barbara, which was based on a sort of half-deceitful compromise from the start and continued that way."

"Your previous girlfriend?"

"I saw her this morning and we agreed to formally conclude our relationship. She's got someone else, anyway."

She fell silent, reflecting.

"I'm not sure…" She began, after a while.

"Not sure about what?"

"I'm not sure where we go from here."

"Why do you want it to stop?" I said, inwardly panic-stricken.

"No. It's just…"

"Distance and time?"

"Yes… It doesn't make it very easy."

"We'll think of something. I'm not stuck in Harwich for life. One of the good things about Customs is that you can move around the country."

"This job isn't so wonderful I have to stay in it. It's not that."

"I do want to marry you, you know – though I was hoping to ask you somewhere a bit more romantic."

"I'd like to do it properly. It's just… I'll be twenty-six next April and I don't want to leave it too long to have a family."

"Are you worried I don't?"

"I don't know…"

"I want what you want, Rosemary darling. I'd always envisaged myself having a family – and I wasn't planning to wait until I was a millionaire."

"We could save for a year or two."

"But let's get married first. I think you should take me to dinner somewhere suitable where I can formally propose to you… Or should I seek your father's permission first?"

"You won't need to bother with that. He'll be only too pleased to see me 'off his hands' as he puts it. My younger sister was married four years ago, at nineteen. She's already got two children. My parents thought once I joined the police that I decided never to get married."

"Just so long as you don't want to get married in uniform!"

We took a bus into the centre of the city and Rosemary took me to an Italian restaurant where, beneath a highly-coloured picture of the Isle of Capri, I asked her to marry me and she accepted. We agreed to keep it a secret until the Davenport case was finally completed and we had a clearer idea of where our future lay together. The food and the wine were good, as far as I can remember.

We just wandered round the streets moving slowly up the hill towards Stoneygate Road. Parting outside the front door of the WPC house was worse than ever, but at least it would be one night apart.

Rosemary had arranged to hire a car the following day, so we could see some of the surrounding countryside, which she assured me was beautiful, though not spectacular. We made our way to the London Road where she picked up a Ford Anglia from the rental company.

"I'm sorry it's not very exciting," she said, "but the cost of anything flashier is astronomical."

"You probably know more about cars than I do," I replied. "I'd been even contemplating getting a Beetle because they're supposed to be reliable. What goes on under the bonnet of a car is a complete mystery to me."

"I was planning to drive over to Bradgate Park. It's got some wonderful views and you'll be able to do some walking. There are also some pretty villages with pubs all round there where we could have lunch."

"That sounds good. If I wanted to see where Davenport was run over, would it be very much out of our way?"

"A bit – but it wouldn't take us too far out of our way... Why do you want to see where he was killed?"

"I just want to be able to form my own view as to whether it was an accident or deliberate."

"That might not be as easy as you think. Even if a road is dead straight and well lit, if a driver has had a bit too much to drink, he's quite likely to swerve even if there isn't a bend."

"Did whoever was investigating the death check out any of the local pubs to see whether there had been anyone who'd been drinking heavily around that time and then driving away?"

"I believe so – but I think they'd got it into their heads pretty early on that they'd only find the driver by a stroke of luck. So I doubt they did a particularly thorough job."

We set off in the direction of Aylestone. I recognised the roads sufficiently by now. Just after the turn-off leading to Marsden Lane and on across a bridge over the river and the Grand Union Canal. A little way past the river, Rosemary pulled to the side.

"It was just about here, as best as I can tell," she said. "As you can see, it's pretty straight and there are a fair amount of streetlights."

"The pavement is quite narrow... but even so... Were there any tyre marks showing where the car skidded?"

"Come to think of it, I don't know. I know it's been a while, but you'd think you could still make out something, wouldn't you?"

We got out and peered around, but there were no tyre marks anywhere.

"At what time of day was Davenport killed?" I asked.

"Early evening. His wife said they fancied a stroll along by the canal, but before they went down there, he said he wanted to cross the bridge and get a view of the river and the canal from the other side. It seems rather odd when you say it like that, but people don't necessarily always act as you'd expect."

"And no-one at work seems to have known much about them – certainly not here. I'm not even sure anyone had ever really seen her."

"They liked to keep to themselves..."

"Yes. That sort of goes against one of my theories that Davenport got mixed up with some of these people when he might've been in Germany or Holland at the end of the War. You'd think if he was going to get involved in something nefarious like this, he wouldn't want to be seen as a loner, someone who kept himself to himself. I think I'd expect him to live in

Harwich like most of the other people of his grade, especially as he was renting."

"So you're back to what? He was threatened. He was suddenly offered the chance of great wealth and succumbed, at least initially. He wasn't involved but was trying to find out who was. Any other possibilities?"

"Not that I can think of – and I must say, the last one seems less and less plausible to me."

We set off round the western suburbs of Leicester and eventually reached the countryside. Not long afterwards we reached the village of Newtown Linford, where Rosemary parked.

"This is the historic end of Bradgate Park," she announced. "I assume you know nothing about it?"

"Should I?"

"Did you do any history at school?"

"I got a creditable B at A level."

"Then you'll know all about Lady Jane Grey."

"All would be putting it a bit strong. But I am aware of her – the so-called 'nine days' queen'."

"She lived in Bradgate Park – in a house which we'll now walk along and visit."

Hand in hand, we walked along by a stream until we came to the ruins of Bradgate House, quite evidently a very fine Tudor mansion in its day. Beyond it, Rosemary showed me walled fields where there were two dozen or so wild deer, explaining that at some times of year they could be found all over the park, but generally keeping well away from people. Then we swung round the side of a copse and I saw this strange building at the top of a hill, like a large stone beer-mug, upside down.

"That's called 'Old John'," she explained. "I used to know why, but I can't remember. Do you fancy walking up there? You get an incredible view from the top – across the Soar valley and much of Charnwood Forest."

"After dragging you up Parliament Hill last Saturday, I could hardly refuse."

It was a bracing walk in the cold, sunny air – a walk I felt I would remember for the rest of my life. The view from the monument was exceptional, but the sight of Rosemary's face, her skin flushed by the cool breeze and the exertion of the climb, her happy, smiling eyes, made my heart soar. Such happiness was something I had never imagined would happen to me.

We made our way back and, finding the pubs in the village full of people who had the same plans as us, but had got there earlier, we went on to a small village with the pretty name of Woodhouse Eaves, where we found a pub that did a Sunday roast with all the trimmings and served a decent pint of beer – and, so Rosemary said, proper orange juice. We agreed that we weren't going to fritter away our money on eating out and unnecessary luxuries, but it wasn't every weekend that we'd decided to get married. So we forgave ourselves this once.

Almost as a way of putting off thoughts of having to part for another week, our minds turned to the death of the Davenports.

"Assuming he was deliberately killed," I said, "by professionals. You'd think they must've been watching the house in Marsden Lane. That stretch of road where he was killed was pretty well the first point where they could've picked up enough speed to be almost certain of killing him."

"So someone in Marsden Lane might've seen a strange car parked within sight of the Davenports' house. But I wonder if they knew him? If they did, they could've parked a bit further away and waited 'till he came out on foot."

"But did they follow him here with the express intention of running him over? Or merely killing him in such a way that would seem accidental?"

"In that case, you'd want to make sure Mrs Davenport was out of the way. Though I suppose they could've killed both of them – a burglary gone wrong, a fire?"

"A burglary which led to murder would cause too much of a stir, I reckon. They wanted the police to do as little as possible and file the death away as either virtually impossible to solve or simple suicide. A fire might do it, but it'd have to be very obviously an accident, otherwise it's a bit like the burglary. The police couldn't just go through the motions."

"So you reckon they would've waited, probably in a car, within sight of the house in Marsden Lane waiting for either of them to go out alone – or together, but somewhere he could be killed but it would seem like an accident?"

"Yes. I imagine a parked car would be less conspicuous than some bloke hanging around."

"But you'd've thought one of the neighbours might've noticed something."

"Yes, it's not as though it's a busy road – or a long one."

"Shall we have a peep on our way back?"

"OK. But we need to work out a plausible reason why we're there. I'll leave that to you, as you seem a dab hand at manoeuvring with the truth." She gave a huge smirk.

We parked outside the Davenports' house in Marsden Lane. We wandered along the road and saw that, at one end, it appeared to lead right down to the canal. I thought that might have provided cover for someone to have observed the Davenports' house from on foot, but it wasn't visible from there. We retraced our steps.

There was an elderly man, sweeping leaves off his drive, almost opposite the Davenports' house.

"I'm sure that's the house," I said quite loudly.

"I don't see why it should be. Why do you think it is?" said Rosemary, playing along.

"He said it was a semi-detached, about eight houses from a road going down to the canal. That must be it?"

"There must be half a dozen places like this. Why should this be it?"

"Excuse me," said the man, "What's the problem?"

"We're trying to find something. About three weeks or so ago, a friend of ours who's a private detective was supposed to be watching a house to catch a wife in the arms of her lover, so the husband could get a divorce. But he spent a whole day parked in his car watching the wrong house. He was told it was the eighth house, left-hand semi, from the canal. He forgot to write the name of the road down and the husband is a pilot, so he couldn't get in touch while he was away. So he tried to work it out from the map. We bet him we could find the right house from the same description. I think that's it!"

"About three weeks ago? Hmm… more like four weeks ago there was a grey Morris Oxford parked here most of the day – about three doors up. I'm not sure whether I can remember whether there was anyone in it. Come to think of it, I reckoned whoever's it was had parked it here and gone down to do some fishing or painting. We get a few like that from time to time – but not usually this time of year. Perhaps it was your man watching the wrong house, though."

"It must've been a bit irritating for the people he parked in front of. He told us he was there from the crack of dawn."

"I don't remembering it arriving – or leaving for that matter. So it's possible it was early. I don't get up as early as I used to. Get the wife tea in bed at about 7.30."

"That sounds like a very nice thing to do," said Rosemary. "It sounds an example we should follow."

"Thank you," I said to the man. "I think you may have helped us win our bet."

"You know that was the house where the woman killed herself after her husband got run over?" he said.

"Oh yes," replied Rosemary. "I think I saw something about it in the local paper."

"Funny thing about it was her. I've lived here since Esmee Wilkins was a toddler, when old Fred and Dorothy were still alive over there, but when she came back I barely recognised her, she'd changed so. It's been a fair few years, I know, but she'd lost weight and seemed so careworn. Esmee was always such a carefree child. She barely seemed to recognise me, either."

"Perhaps it was the sadness. If she killed herself, she must've been terribly upset after her husband was killed."

"Oh, I thought it was before that... but you may be right. That's the trouble with getting old."

"Well, thank you awfully, anyway."

We got back in the car and drove back to the car hire place.

"I wonder if that was the car?" she began. "It's not really a very thorough way of checking."

"Not without arousing suspicions... I wonder if they drove up overnight, or stayed somewhere locally overnight?"

"I could probably check up on where they might've stayed locally. It'd have to be somewhere where they'd be fairly anonymous. I might even have a bit of time to ask the odd question if they're within cycling distance."

"Well, be careful and make sure you've got a plausible story."

"I may need to try one out on you over the phone."

"What did you make of what the old man said about Mrs Davenport?"

"It was a bit odd, but if she really knew what her husband was up to, perhaps she really was feeling worried. He wasn't sure whether he'd seen her before or after he was killed either."

"People change when they get older, anyway. If she'd changed her hairstyle and perhaps lost weight because of indigestion – you remember those tins of indigestion powders? She could seem quite different. I wish I'd looked more carefully at those pictures in the bureau of her as a child now. I know people change a lot from when they were children, but there's usually something…"

"Well, it's possible I might be able to lay my hands on something."

"Please, please, don't take any risks. This isn't worth ruining your career over."

"I'll see what's possible within the bounds of being a WPC. I must say I do rather like feeling I'm playing a part in this thing again. I'll let you know on the phone how I'm getting on."

That reminded us of what we'd been ignoring for the last half an hour. I was going to have to get a train back to London and she would have to return to Stoneygate Road. We walked slowly to the station and said our farewells, clinging to each other, with tears streaming down our faces. I deliberately waited until I could hear the London train approaching before giving her a last kiss and telling her I loved her, I had to run across the bridge, down the steps and along the platform.

The other passengers in my compartment must have considered it rather strange, a grown man with red eyes, snuffling into a handkerchief. But I thought I noticed similar behaviour from a young woman, who looked like a student, in the opposite corner. My heart was aching like it had never ached before. I had never felt so happy or so miserable.

Love seemed such a strange thing. I was naturally cool-blooded, cautious. Yet I had asked Rosemary to marry me on only the third time we had met, on our second date. I had no doubt my parents and my friends would consider me barmy. My elder sister would take the view, as elder sisters tend to do, that younger brothers were congenitally foolish. On the other hand, I reminded myself, I was marrying an elder sister. So perhaps even elder sisters didn't act consistently with the wisdom they doled out to their younger siblings.

But I had absolutely no doubts about what I had done. How people could meet and decide so quickly that they were right for each other was a mystery to me. If I was religious, I might have said it was God's will. But, whatever else I had not learnt from my father's lectures on religion being the opium of the people, I had retained a scepticism that had settled into confirmed agnosticism as I had spent my years doing National Service and at university. So was it just pure chance? Or might it have been possible that there were many young women like Rosemary I might have met and fallen just as deeply in love with? As one of my friends at college regularly pointed out in a variety of circumstances, in such cases it's impossible to say because there's never a counterfactual.

Why Rosemary Johnson? At first I was attracted to her physically – in spite of the police uniform. Her face was extremely pretty – but so were lots of other girls. There must have been something about the nature of her face, her eyes, her slightly ironic smile, framed by her short, jet black hair. And her slim, shapely legs. Attractive – but in a way that attracted me. Like many of her generation, she was slim, small-breasted with long legs. I imagined that many men would actually have found Barbara more sexually attractive. She was, without being plump in any way, curvier – with long fair hair and an equally attractive face. Yet, even when I was in bed with her and sexual passion took over large parts of my brain, I had always had this part of me that was telling me I didn't love Barbara. Inevitably, that had an impact on our sex. I wasn't quite sure how or whether I had been brainwashed into believing that love was more important than sex, but it appeared not to be something I could or wished to get out of my system... It wasn't even as though I was predisposed to girls of Rosemary's type. As a six-footer, I'd tended to go for taller girls, generally with long, light hair. Why I should fall in love with her – and pretty well at first sight – I couldn't explain for the life of me. I just had to accept it – and welcome it.

Thinking of her set my heart burning and made my throat sore. I tried to think of something else, to take my mind off the pain of separation. The unexplained actions and deaths of Mr and Mrs Davenport were foremost among the thoughts that swirled through my brain. Lots of ideas and theories came and went. St Pancras suddenly arrived.

Momentarily I contemplated walking back through the Russell Square area to see if I could spot the man who I felt sure was Louis Davidson again, but common sense told me that if I could see him, he was just as likely to see me and rapidly put two and two together. But the likelihood of us encountering each other in the dark streets of north London was infinitesimal. So I did the sensible thing and took the Tube to Liverpool Street and got the next train that stopped at Manningtree.

When I got to my lodgings, there was no message from Iain Cogbill – or anyone else – for me. So I phoned the IB and was informed by the duty officer that my message had been passed on to Mr Cogbill, but that was all.

So I read a bit of my Russian grammar and went to bed.

TWELVE – HARWICH: CHASING AFTER THEORIES

I had barely sat down the following morning when Jim signified I should see him in his office.

"We've been summoned to Imrie, yet again. Is there anything I need to know about Friday's meeting with the Board?"

"The meeting seemed to be mainly about protecting the public reputation of the Board. The Solicitor took some time to explain that I – and you as well – had broken the law and were potentially liable to imprisonment and fines. Our reasons for doing what we did might be good, but they were only mitigation, he said. But he did say that the case involving the Russian diamonds was so important and sensitive that it was pretty well inconceivable that anyone would allow Leicestershire Police to charge us – well, me, at any rate – if they even ever got to learn about what I did. He then spoke about departmental disciplinary action, but the Collector told me afterwards that you'd spoken to him and that the action was going to mean nothing in practice."

"I expect Imrie has got to hear I briefed the Collector in his absence on Thursday afternoon. He doesn't like that sort of thing. I reckon that's why we've been summoned. It's probably exercise book down the back of the pants time!"

It didn't strike me that Jim appeared particularly bothered.

"Weel, it's another Monday morning and here you two are again!" Imrie began. "May I say for starters, I was particularly concerned when I discovered that one of my Surveyors had been briefing the Higher Collector directly, behind my back. You're not going to deny it, are you?"

"Not at all, sir," Jim replied with equanimity. "I was summoned to see the Higher Collector late on Thursday afternoon. I don't refuse such summons, so I attended. I assumed you would also be there, sir. When I found that you weren't, I enquired why you weren't and suggested you should be present. The Higher Collector explained that your presence had been sought, but that unfortunately, you could not be located. In any case, as the Higher Collector reminded us, the two of you were due to travel to London together on the following morning, so you could brief him during the journey. In such circumstances, I couldn't reasonably refuse to brief the Higher Collector, could I, sir?"

"I take it you informed him about Storey's dubious actions in relation to the Leicestershire Constabulary and your part in it?"

"In some detail, sir. The Higher Collector told me that the Chief Inspector had been forewarned that the Solicitor had been asked to look into it and give his legal opinion at the meeting on Friday. Naturally, the Higher Collector wished to know in detail what had occurred and why."

"Did you discuss the nature of any departmental disciplinary action?"

"No, sir. It would have been inappropriate, since it would be the Higher Collector who had to impose any disciplinary penalty and I would be one of those subject to it. So the matter wasn't raised."

"I take it you know what it is?"

"Yes, sir. The Higher Collector informed Mr Storey after the meeting with the Board on Friday. He passed it on to me a few minutes ago."

"It sounds all very plausible – you can't pull the wool over my eyes that easily! Someone, somewhere gave the Higher Collector the idea to let you off with just a nominal, meaningless penalty. I'd've taken great pleasure at throwing the book at you. I advised him to downgrade you back to OCX, Round, and you required to do another three years as a UO, Storey. But no – you get off with bugger all!"

"With the greatest respect, sir, it may be that the Higher Collector realises that as it turned out, the actions of Mr Storey and I contributed significantly to getting a highly important smuggling operation uncovered. It may well be the case that if Mr Storey had told the Leicestershire Constabulary about the diamonds in Mr Davenport's suitcase, they would've cocked the whole thing up, sir."

"That may be what the CIO and his chums in Special Branch believe, but, as the Solicitor made out, it's just mitigation."

"Perhaps the Higher Collector and you differ on the extent it should contribute to mitigating our offence, sir."

"And why do you consider the Leicestershire Constabulary would've cocked it up, as you so eloquently put it?"

"Perhaps I can answer that, sir, as I've been there," I said. "Even not knowing anything about the diamonds, they've done a sloppy job. When I visited the Davenports' house after she'd killed herself, there were all sorts of inconsistencies with a theory they'd already convinced themselves of."

"For instance?"

"Papers and other things that were out of place, suggesting a search – which I know they didn't undertake themselves. The Davenports had a nearly full bottle of sleeping pills in the medicine chest in their bathroom, yet a different bottle was used to kill her. She had drunk several tumblers of brandy, yet the bottle of brandy which the police took away was too large to fit in a medicine chest, yet there were no brandy glasses – or any other sort of glass for drinking spirits – anywhere in the house."

"That doesn't prove she didn't kill herself, laddie!"

"I'm not saying it does, sir. What I'm saying is that they were so convinced it was suicide that they didn't spot any of these. Besides, there's more – in relation to Davenport being run over. I've seen where it happened. Apparently, Mrs Davenport said they'd gone out for a stroll along a road that goes over the river and the canal. He was run over in the first straight part, where a driver could gather sufficient speed and also be certain about who he was aiming at."

"The police said it was a hit and run."

"Yes – because that was the only idea that was in their minds. If you open your mind to the possibility that it might be something else, it takes you in more fruitful directions. For instance, if Davenport was deliberately run over, it occurred at the first convenient moment after he left his house. So it seems likely that his house was being watched. And it seems likely that there was a car parked in the road within sight of his house on the day he was killed – a grey Morris Oxford."

"How in God's name do you know all this?"

"My girlfriend lives in Leicester. We did some digging around at the weekend."

"I'd've thought you would've wanted to be as far away from the Leicestershire Constabulary as possible, laddie!"

"I understand that investigations into both deaths have been completed and the cases have been closed and filed away, sir."

"And the Leicestershire Constabulary kindly informed you of this?"

"Not officially, sir. My girlfriend works there."

"So – are you planning to inform them of the results of your amateur investigations?"

"No, sir. I don't see it as my job to sweep up behind the dustcart. But there is one thing which puzzled me and I was thinking of seeing whether it meant anything to the IB…"

"Spit it out, laddie!"

"We learnt about the Morris Oxford from an old bloke, who's lived in the street ever since Mrs Davenport was a girl. He commented that he thought she'd changed unrecognisably – and also that she didn't recognise him. I didn't think much about it at the time. But since then I've been thinking – what if Mrs Davenport wasn't the real Mrs Davenport? We've always wondered why Davenport may have colluded with this smuggling operation and thought it would either be for gain or because he was being threatened. Perhaps the real Mrs Davenport was being held against her will somewhere, which was why Davenport was compelled to act as he did?"

"So the Mrs Davenport seen in Leicester was some sort of Russian substitute? So the woman you met calling herself Mrs Davenport was this substitute? And then the real one was substituted and killed in a way that looked like suicide? Is that it, laddie?"

"It's a possibility, sir."

"But then, why didn't the substitute just not go off with the diamonds and the incriminating papers in the suitcase, rather than handing them over to you, eh?"

"I don't know, Sir… That's a very telling point. But it still seems odd, what that man said… But I saw quite a few old photos of Mrs Davenport before the War. If we could compare them with those of her when she was married and then more recently, we might find out something that would explain why Davenport acted as he did. Unfortunately, I didn't really look at them properly when I was there after her death, but I reckon I could tell whether I felt the woman I met was her. At any rate, it seemed worth mentioning to the IB."

"I believe you've been reading too many James Bond books, laddie. All these doubles and substitutes and dark secrets. If I was you I'd wish to draw the attention of the Leicestershire Constabulary to this not one bit."

"If the IB are interested, I expect they'd do it on their own – or with Special Branch, sir."

"The ramblings of a senile old man. I reckon they'll just laugh in your face, laddie."

With that we were sent packing.

"Actually, this sort of thing is much more like *The Spy Who Came In From The Cold* by le Carré than any of the Bond books," I remarked to Jim. I had read it about three months earlier and found it fascinating, much more realistic than the James Bond books.

"Do you think it was wise, letting all that out?" was Jim's only comment.

For the next few hours, my attention was concentrated on doing my job, unexciting and predictable as it was. When I had finished I phoned Iain Cogbill, but he wasn't there, so I left a message asking him to call me back.

I wandered over to the freight examination shed to see if I could find out whether Wally French had got anywhere with his checks in relation to the rosters.

"Sorry I haven't been back to you," he said. "We had a tip-off from the IB that there was going to be a big importation of cannabis from Holland over the weekend, so it's been all hands to the pump."

"Did you find anything?"

"Not a sausage! Trouble is, you can't check every consignment, especially when it's bulk. But I can tell you what you were asking. No-one changed from the roster. In other words, if someone needed to be on that shift, either they were lucky or, as I believe, no-one here was involved."

"If one assumes the late Mr Davenport was involved in some way, I always felt that if there was a way of not having to bring anyone else in, that would be the favoured way."

I went back to my desk and, as there was nothing happening, but too early for lunch, I sat and thought. Mainly about the idea that Davenport might have left some clues among the smokescreen intended to thwart those who were threatening him. I was also still intrigued by what the old man had said about Mrs Davenport. Imrie had blown my theory of her being a Russian 'plant', as I think le Carré would have put it, completely out of the water. And, the more I thought about it, the Mrs Davenport I met would have to have been a highly talented actress... But something continued to niggle in my brain and I was determined to tell Iain Cogbill about it.

The telephone rang. I expected it to be Iain, but to my surprise and joy, it was Rosemary.

"I'm sorry, but I've only got a few seconds. I thought I'd better ring from outside the station. I'm just on my way back from a rather nasty RTA (Road Traffic Accident). You remember the nurseries. You said you didn't find anything when you raided the place. Were there any seeds around?"

"From what I remember, quite a lot. Mostly bagged up. I assume they either plant them or sell them in early spring."

"Well, we had a circular today from the Hertfordshire Police. Apparently, they've just uncovered a large cannabis farm near Welwyn

Garden City. Loads of cannabis plants growing in greenhouses, just like tomatoes. They think the plants were brought in to the country as seeds. You don't think it was cannabis seeds that were being imported by the nurseries, do you?"

"It's certainly worth following up... I hope the accident wasn't too horrible for you."

"I'm getting used to them. I don't really mind the dead bodies, it's the people who are hurt and in pain and usually there's not much you can do about it before the ambulance arrives. You feel so helpless!"

"Well, my day has been a lot less awful. My boss and I had a sort of wigging from his boss – but he can't actually do anything. Otherwise it's been routine. Have you thought about where we might go next weekend?"

"Not really yet. The nice thing is I'm free both Saturday and Sunday – but we should try not to spend too much money. I'll keep thinking, if you will."

"I will."

"I'd better go."

"Thanks. I love you."

"I love you."

She rang off. Something else to mention to Iain. I wished he would call.

I went to lunch with my colleagues and realised for the first time how less comfortable they were with me than they had been when I was newly arrived in their midst. This shouldn't have surprised me, but it did. I also understood that there was virtually nothing I could do about it. This affair had to blow over and time would have to pass... and probably even then, in some parts of the Department, I would be seen as someone who didn't fit tidily in any of the pigeonholes, well known and respected throughout. I would always be the file that didn't fit into the filing system.

It was with some relief that I got back to the Long Room to deal with the final ship covered by my shift. The moment the entries began to arrive, Iain Cogbill phoned.

"Thank you for your message at the weekend. The bird had flown, of course. He'd been staying in the Russell Hotel, would you believe, bold as brass."

"Do you think I alerted him?"

"Impossible to tell. People like that have to be trebly cautious. But at least it suggests he's still in the country, presumably for a reason."

"Perhaps he can't go until he's accounted for all the diamonds – including the ones we've seized."

"It's a thought… The duty officer said you wanted to have a word about something?"

"A couple of things actually. As you know, my girlfriend lives in the East Midlands – Leicester actually. I was there last weekend. We had a look at where Davenport was killed and it started me thinking. Anyway, we went to the road where the Davenports were living and spoke to a man who lived there. He said that he thought a grey Morris Oxford had sat within sight of the Davenports' house all day on the day Davenport was killed. If someone had been planning to kill Davenport in a way that looked like an accident, it struck me they'd have to keep a watch on his movements. I realise this is all pretty old stuff – as the Leicester police have filed the deaths away and both Davenports have been cremated. But I thought the car might still turn up if the killers are around."

"I'll pass that on to my colleagues."

"But that wasn't really it. The man said he remembered Mrs Davenport from when she lived in that house before the War. He said he found her greatly changed and that she hadn't recognised him. It got me thinking about Mrs Davenport. Davenport is being checked out, but perhaps we should extend that to her? Also there were quite a lot of photographs in the bureau in the house of her when she was younger, as well as some more recent ones. I wondered whether they might not shed any light on whether there was some guilty secret that might mean Davenport could be blackmailed?"

"It's worth looking into, I agree."

"Finally, a friend in the police mentioned to me that the Hertfordshire police have put out a bulletin about a big cannabis operation they've uncovered, where cannabis plants were being grown in greenhouses in Welwyn Garden City. Apparently the plants were probably grown from imported cannabis seeds. I just wondered whether that was what had been going on at the White House Nurseries. You remember, there were quite a lot of seeds all bagged up, lying around the place."

"Oh hell! I pulled the surveillance off over the weekend. I'll get up there this afternoon and see whether we haven't let this slip through our fingers. Thank you for that. I'll be in touch."

He seemed a lot more interested in the cannabis seeds than the Davenport stuff. Still, I hoped he would do something about it, ideally before Rosemary tried to get into the house in Marsden Lane and get a look at the photographs. Though she didn't seem wholly dedicated to the police as a career, I didn't want her to put it in jeopardy on my account.

Apart from the painful pleasure of my phone calls with Rosemary, the rest of that day and the following one were entirely routine. We agreed to spend the weekend in London and she expressed a desire to see the sights from a river-boat. I agreed to organise what we needed.

The following morning, I had a moment of inspiration. Shortly after we had finished clearing the morning's entries, Alf Veale and Ken Byrne were having an argument about how much Davenport might have been worth.

"I reckon he'd put a tidy sum away," argued Alf. "You never saw him dip his hand into his pocket when we were in the pub. And he used to duck out of as many of those as he could."

"Always dressed quite smart though. Just because someone's a bit mean doesn't mean they've got loads of cash stashed away somewhere," added Ken.

"And they say he owned several houses in the Midlands too. I'll bet he was worth over six figures," Alf went on.

"Well you can find out soon enough. Once the executor gets probate, the value of the Will is available as a public record. Court of Chancery Probate Division or summat like that. When my wife's great-aunt died, there was a great hoo-ha about who got what and how much – and it only really started when they saw how much she was worth when she popped off," explained Ken.

"But suppose I had a distant relative who might've left me money? How'd I know how much?"

"Well the executor is supposed to get in touch with you. But if no-one has and you reckon your relative might be dead, you'd have to find out whether they was dead first."

"And how'd you do that?"

"Registry of Births, Marriages and Deaths. I think they all go to the Public Records Office in London. Or is it Somerset House? I dunno whether you could just ring 'em up. I reckon you might have to fill out a few forms."

"When don't you?"

I suppose there would be no harm in checking whether Mrs Davenport had died, I thought. If he was, for instance, living with someone who wasn't his wife, but pretending she was – for instance to ensure he retained the ownership of the house in Marsden Lane – he could have been vulnerable to blackmail. On the other hand, would the IB or whoever else was checking up on the Davenports do this anyway? Besides, unless you knew roughly when someone had died, it would be like looking for a needle in a haystack.

But something might show up in Davenport's estabs file. A lengthy absence from work not explained by illness or injury might at least indicate a time worth a further look. I wondered whether his file had already gone to Walsall or whether it had still been retained in Harwich. I decided to go over to the Estabs Section and find out.

A sharp-faced woman in her early forties, with dark brown hair tied into a tight bun intercepted me as I entered the section room.

"Who exactly are you and what do you want?"

"My name is Nick Storey. I'm an OCX on Customs Freight Clearance. I wanted to ask a question about my predecessor, Mr N. F. J. Davenport, due to move to Walsall PT, lately deceased."

"You may ask. Depending on the nature of your question, it may be possible to respond."

"OK. Do you still hold his Estabs File here?"

"I believe that's a question I can respond to. But I'll have to check with the Records Clerk."

She went over to the back of the room, near a series of large metal filing cabinets and spoke with a dishevelled-looking, colourless man in his early thirties. It struck me that she was the only woman I had seen working in the place, other than the secretaries working for the Collectorate. Presumably there were some women search officers available at the passenger clearance station. It was a good job I wasn't seeking a bride from within the Department, I said to myself.

"I'm told that we were about to despatch the file when we learnt of Mr Davenport's demise. So it remains here."

"If I wished to examine it or get it examined, who would have to authorise that, please?"

"I believe anyone could, in theory, examine it, but it would require the written authorisation of an officer of Assistant Collector level on Form E119(D)."

"OK. Can I get one of those here?"

"I fear not. Forms and notices can be obtained from Stores Section in the basement, room B024A."

"I'm most grateful for your assistance."

I wondered whether these people thought the same way they spoke. Or whether they just spoke like that during working hours and reverted to being real people once they left for the day. I would probably never know.

Working underground all day in Stores Section would drive me insane, but I had forgotten that there is a type of individual who positively welcomes a trogloditical existence. The man at the hatch, which opened into the stores office, was, however, not a troll. He was about sixteen, with a haircut resembling Brian Jones of the Rolling Stones, and the mannerisms and clothes to match. I got the distinct feeling that modelling himself on his idol used up most of his brain cells as it took me four attempts before he finally came up with Form E119(D). He kept twiddling his fingers as though he was playing an electric guitar. Could he actually play one? I would probably never know that either.

But that was the easy bit. Although in theory I could have got one of the other ACs to sign and stamp the form, I knew I would have to go through Mr D. J. 'Jock' Imrie. As he was probably going to kick me around anyway, I thought I might just as well complete the details and then take it to him personally for signature and authorisation. I planned to mention it to Jim, but he wasn't in his office or in the Long Room.

I handed the form to Imrie's secretary, a plump young woman who seemed to have a perpetual smirk on her face. She told me Imrie was in his office and she would take it in with his tea, which was just brewing. I said I would wait.

While I waited, I wondered how long it would be before Iain Cogbill got back to me, as he had promised. It seemed to me that the operation was cooling down and that only the capture of the man known as Louis Davidson would heat it up again. Of course, there would be little Customs involvement in the search, other than keeping watch at ports and airports. As far as I was concerned, the only loose end was Davenport. What exactly had he been up to, and why?

"What the hell are you up to?" Imrie burst out of his office. "Are you trying to do the work of the IB for them, laddie? Your job is on Customs entry clearance, not investigation. Is that clear?"

"I thought I might be able to save everyone some time and effort, as the file is actually here, sir," I replied, following Jim's example, in remaining calm whatever. "Besides, there's always a certain amount of slack time between freight movements."

"You have cleared this with your Surveyor?"

"He wasn't there, sir. But I know he wouldn't have objected."

"Yes. You have become as thick as thieves, haven't you!"

"Is there any reason why I shouldn't see the file, sir?"

"There's a matter of precedent, laddie. Do we really want it established that OCXs just out of their nappies can get their snouts into estabs files?"

"Even when the file relates to an officer who's dead, sir?"

"I'm going to keep a very close eye on you, laddie! Make sure the file is kept safe while it's in your possession. There've been too many unexplained disappearances from Customs entry clearance in recent months."

But he signed and stamped the form, so before he changed his mind, I went over to the Estabs Section and collected the file from the sour-faced woman. I settled down to read the file, hoping it might tell me more about what Mr Neville Frank Jefferies Davenport SN 34128 was really like.

It was too late that day to start on this work and I knew I wasn't allowed to take such files out of the office. With an incipient headache, spending an hour in some corner reading through old files, often carbon copies or written in faded ancient ink didn't appeal, especially as there was always the risk that someone from the late shift would see me and start to ask the sort of questions I didn't want to have to answer. So I left it for the day and decided to start immediately the morning rush had ended the following morning. So I locked the file way in my desk drawer and headed back to my lodgings, Apart from a brief call with Rosemary, the rest of the day was spent nursing my headache.

The following morning. I decided to start at the beginning of Davenport's file. He had entered the Department as a DCO immediately after being demobbed in early 1946, at the age of twenty-four. As the letter of appointment had been sent to BAOR Mönchengladbach, it seemed certain that he had spent at least the latter part of the war in West Germany. His first appointment was to Birmingham Excise. Within two years he had applied to become an OCX and spent the next three years as a UO, working in Purchase Tax in Stratford – of the East London variety – Excise controls in Burton-on-Trent, entry clearance at Heathrow Airport and PT again, in Leeds. His first fixed appointment was in Stoke-on-Trent and, after he gained sufficient seniority there, he succeeded in transferring back to Walsall PT. All his assessments said almost exactly the same thing – Davenport was conscientious, unambitious, with reasonable intelligence and judgement, quiet and not particularly sociable. "Middle of the class" wrote one of his managers. A couple of managers noted a determined, persistent streak in him and one an element of self-righteousness.

I was just beginning to look at his leave record when my phone rang.

"This is Staff Nurse Kenworthy from Leicester Royal Infirmary. Are you Mr Nicholas Storey?"
"Yes."
"Is WPC Rosemary Johnson a close friend of yours?"
"Yes. What's the matter with Rosemary?"
"She's been shot. Earlier this morning. She's doing all right. But she's asking to see you, if you can come."
"I'll be on my way this instant."

THIRTEEN – LEICESTER – ROSEMARY IS SHOT

Fortunately Jim was in his office.

"I'm sorry, but I've got to leave work this instant. My girlfriend in Leicester was injured earlier this morning and is in hospital."

"Of course. Is it serious?"

"I don't really know. But she's asked to see me."

"Then go. Hire a car by the passenger terminal. I'll get the Department to cough up later."

"Thanks. Can you possibly take the Davenport estabs file and keep it safe? I've been looking through it for clues."

I ran to the passenger terminal. Fortunately there was the inevitable Ford Anglia available. So I paid my deposit and drove away.

I found the car pretty easy to drive, once I'd got used to it. It was a good thing too, as I intended to get to Leicester as fast as I could, without worrying too much about speed limits. Before I left, I bought a cheap road atlas at the car hire place and tried to work out the quickest route. I decided that if I went through Manningtree and joined the A12 as far as Ipswich, I could join the A14 which would take me through Bury St Edmunds, Cambridge and Huntingdon to Kettering. Within a few miles of Kettering I would get on to the A6 which would take me all the way into Leicester.

It looked easier on the map than it was on the road. Apart from the heavy lorries slowing down traffic between towns, there were traffic lights and congestion as I tried to skirt my way round each of the towns I encountered, using what was euphemistically and misleadingly described as a bypass. I guess the frustration kept my mind from wandering too much on to how badly Rosemary had been hurt, but foolishly I still took my life into my hands with some risky overtaking in places. If I had a kindly bomb to drop on anywhere, I would have chosen Cambridge that day rather than Slough, if only to enable someone trying to drive through it to move faster than the proverbial tortoise.

It was early afternoon before I reached the outskirts of Leicester and joined a slow convoy of cars and vans moving into the centre. Eventually I saw a sign for the hospital and turned past a large park and onto the Welford Road. Quite soon I could see what looked like hospital buildings ahead of me, duly confirmed by road signs. I pulled into the hospital and found what seemed to be a visitors' car park, locked up the car and rushed to the main entrance. A stolid young woman listened to what I had to say and advised me to go to the Accident Unit. So I raced to where I was directed, only to be told that WPC Johnson was in the Belvoir Emergency Ward on the second floor, on the other side of the building. I sped as fast as I could along various corridors past wards and offices which didn't say 'Belvoir' on them, got lost twice and had to seek directions, and finally got to the door of the Belvoir ward.

As I was about to go in, a staff nurse stopped me.

"Who are you? You can't just go barging in there!"
"I'm Rosemary Johnson's friend. Somebody rang me from here and said she'd been shot. She said she was asking for me. How bad is she?"
"I'll have to see. Wait here!"

I stood just outside the staff nurse's cubicle. A further set of doors obscured the main ward, so I couldn't see anything. My heart was pumping as though I'd just tried to beat Bob Hayes over 100 metres. What did "I'll have to see" mean? Was Rosemary really badly injured? Where had she been shot? How?

"It's not really visiting time, but I understand you've come all the way from Harwich. So I'll allow an exception – this once," stated the staff nurse firmly.

I followed her through the doors and past a bed shrouded in blue curtains. Rosemary was lying in bed on the other side of the curtains, with two people sitting next to her, on either side. Rosemary was lying back, supported by several pillows, with her right leg outstretched in front of her, bandaged from just above the knee up her thigh, with a smaller bandage on her calf. She also had a bandage round her hand.
As she saw me, she smiled. "I'm so glad you were able to come," she began. It struck me her voice was a little uncertain. "These are my parents. Mum and Dad, this is Nick Storey, who I've been telling you about."

"Pleased to meet you," said Mr Johnson, who seemed more alert and livelier than my idea of a middle-aged bank clerk.

"I'm sorry we've not met in happier circumstances," added his wife, thin and short-haired. I could see where Rosemary got her looks from.

"Yes," I replied. "I never expected to meet you like this. How are you feeling, Rosemary? Were you shot anywhere else?"

"No," she said, with a forced smile. "I thought my leg was probably enough."

Whereupon she burst into tears. I sat on the bed – away from her injured leg – and put my arm round her and let her head rest on my shoulder.

"I was so terrified!" she whispered. "I was certain they were going to kill me!"

"You're safe now," I said, kissing her on the side of her head.

After a while she stopped crying and regained some of her normal composure.

"Mum and Dad? You've sat with me for hours. You know I'm not in any danger. Do you mind if I talk to Nick alone, please? There are things I can only say to him alone."

"Of course not," said Mrs Johnson, even though she did.

"We'll go and get a cup of tea and a biscuit," added her husband.

"Just hold me for a bit, Nick... I felt so frightened! I've never felt anything as bad as that in my life!"

I kept my arm round her shoulder and stroked her hair. She didn't cry again. She just closed her eyes and rested.

"I think I'm probably still in shock. That's what the doctor said. I could probably go home tonight, provided there was someone to look after me, if it wasn't that I lost a fair amount of blood and the shock."

"I hope they're not planning to send you home?"

"No. The doctor was very kind. Actually they've all been very nice. I suppose it's me being a WPC being shot on duty... The trouble was, I wasn't actually on duty."

"Oh God! You were in the Davenports' house, weren't you?"

"Yes. I was on a later shift today and I managed to get my sarge to give me the key to the Davenports' house on the grounds that I feared I'd dropped the spare set of keys to my car when I was there with you. Of course, he had no trouble believing a story like that and just told me to not to be late for my shift. I got there shortly before 7, let myself in and started to put all the photos in the bureau into an envelope which I could put in my bag. I don't know what did it, but I felt I heard a car driving up. Then I saw a grey Morris Oxford had parked opposite and two men were getting out. I ran to the front door and tried to lock it from the inside, but as I was getting the key from my bag, I heard a shot, as one of them fired at the lock. Then he pushed the door open – a big man, with a broad, bland face. He told me to put my hands up, but I'd got my bag in one hand. He told me to put it down, so I leant forward and pretended to fumble with my bag, then I just threw my hands up clenched together under his chin. I didn't think. I was so sure he was going to kill me, I just did it. Anyway, I think I broke his jaw, as he fell backwards against the door, pushing the other man outside. I think his gun must've gone off as he fell, because I felt a sharp stinging in my leg. I assume the bullet must've ricocheted off the floor. I think he must've been quite badly stunned, because he collapsed on to the floor and the other man had to keep pushing at the door to get in. I didn't know what to do. I didn't know how badly he was hurt. I felt trapped. I just ran into the kitchen and picked up a couple of the sharpest knives I could find. I also unlocked the back door into the garden. But it's a small garden with high hedges, so I couldn't see how I could escape that way. I could hear them at the front door, the second man cursing as he tried to push his way in. I hid behind the kitchen door and hoped they might just take the pictures and go. But once the second man had got in, he came looking for me. I pushed the kitchen door against him and he fell back a bit, but he came in, just as I was getting to the back door. He raised his gun at me and fired, but I threw myself out of the back door and ran as fast as I could down the garden. I just dived into the hedge and it seemed to give way. I heard another shot, but I couldn't feel anything and I fell into some bushes in the next door garden. I thought I'd try and get through to the next garden, but then I realised there was blood pouring down my leg. I think I must've been just about to pass out – but all I could hear were sirens

Then I came round and I was still lying in the garden. I could hear someone in the Davenports' garden calling out 'What's going on? Are you all right?' It sounded like that old man we spoke to on Sunday. So I called out to him whether the men in the grey car had gone and he said, 'Yes, they drove away like maniacs a few minutes ago," I told him I'd been shot in the leg and couldn't move very easily, so could he call an ambulance and perhaps tell the people whose garden I was lying in. It seemed a long time before anyone came and I started to feel very cold and get really shivery. Then an ambulance-man poked his head through the hedge. Apparently there was no-one in where I was. Anyway, they bound up my leg and got a stretcher and got me out to the ambulance. I don't know how, because I fainted again. When I woke up, I was in the ambulance on the way here – and you can guess the rest."

"I'm not surprised you're in shock. That was incredibly silly and incredibly brave!"

"Yes. I have an uncomfortable feeling we're too much alike in that. I'm afraid I don't know whether they got the photos. But I can only assume that was what they were after. How did they know…?"

"I didn't tell anyone that you were going to the Davenports' house. As you didn't mention it last night, even I didn't know you were going to be there this morning."

"I hadn't decided last night. It was only first thing when I had the idea about the car keys."

"I've mentioned to a very few people that we needed to look into Mrs Davenport's past because of what the old man opposite said… and I have mentioned the photos to three people, one of whom could've passed it on to others I suppose. So someone has told those men."

"I hope they only went there to get the photos not on purpose to kill me?"

"No. I can't think so. I fear you just happened to be there at precisely the wrong moment."

"But I could certainly recognise the man I hit again. I don't know about the other one."

"Well, if you did break his jaw, they'll be long gone. But do you want me to ask the police to provide a guard?"

"If they haven't got the photos, do you think they might think I had them here?"

"That settles it. I'll speak to one of your colleagues and make sure you're completely safe here."

"Do you know who told those men about the photos?"

"I don't know who. But the field has been narrowed down a great deal."

"Will you go and see whether the photos are still there?"

"As it's the scene of a crime, I expect there'll still be police and experts all over it. Hasn't anyone interviewed you yet?"

"No. I suppose my sarge told them I'd gone there because of my mislaid keys."

"Well, they're either being kind or they're extremely gullible."

"If you tell them to guard me, won't you get yourself into trouble?"

"What worries me is that it's likely to get you into trouble. If I tell them why I think you're in danger, they're bound to realise that your story about the keys was a blind."

"It's a pity I didn't have time to put the photos into my bag – but I know I hadn't put them in. I just can't remember where they were…"

"Anyhow, it isn't really urgent. Either those men have got them or, if they're still there, your people aren't going to go off with them. So we may be able to get hold of them. It's possible I might be able to enquire about the photos without giving the game away."

"If anyone can, you can," she said with a weak smile.

"Does your leg hurt much?"

"Not really. The doctor told me it was essentially a flesh wound, but it just bled a lot. I probably passed out the first time as much from shock as from the injury… Not much of a policewoman, really."

"Too bloody much of a policewoman, if you ask me! You stood in front of a professional killer with a gun and dared to knock him out! That's the bravest thing I've ever heard anybody do!"

"And possibly the most stupid…"

"That too…! I hope you won't spend your career as a policewoman doing things like that."

"Once is enough… Will you stay with me tonight, Nick? I know if I'm on my own…"

"Of course. Nothing and no-one will stop me."

At that moment, the Staff Nurse interrupted us. I feared she was going to try and throw me out.

"Dr Peacock wants to examine WPC Johnson. Will you wait outside until he's finished."

I went into the area outside the staff nurse's cubicle. Rosemary's parents and Mike Elliott of Special Branch were standing there.

"How is our daughter?" asked Mrs Johnson.

"She's still in shock, but I don't think there's anything to worry about," I replied. "I expect the doctor is just checking that there's no bleeding from her stitches."

"Do you…" began Mr Johnson, but he was quickly interrupted by Mike Elliott.

"Do you mind if I take Mr Storey away for a few words in private?" he said firmly. "I'm a colleague of WPC Johnson's."

We went outside into the corridor and Elliott found – or had already laid claim to – an empty room. He put a large buff envelope on the table.

"Was this why WPC Johnson was in the Davenport house?" he asked, in a tone that suggested he already knew the answer.

"Yes," I replied.

"Why didn't you get us to do it, rather than putting your girlfriend's life in danger?"

"I spoke to Iain Cogbill about it a couple of days ago. I didn't know Rosemary was actually going to go to the house today. We spoke about getting the photos when I was here at the weekend, but she hadn't thought up a plausible reason for going there when I spoke to her on the phone last night. I must say I'd expected your lot to have got there first."

"We've had no request from Iain, as far as I'm aware. Anyway, why did you want these photos so desperately?"

"As I explained to Iain, when Rosemary and I were there on Sunday –"

"On Sunday! Don't you two ever have a day off and let the professionals deal with this sort of thing?"

"I just wanted to see where Davenport was killed. But when you've seen it you'll realise that if you're not convinced it was an accidental hit and run, Davenport had to have been followed. That suggested that the house must've been watched. So we made up a story and found an old man in the street who remembered seeing a grey Morris Oxford at about the right time."

"You may wish to know that said grey Morris Oxford was found in the car park of the Blue Boar services on the M1 early this afternoon. There was some blood on one of the seats and a couple of bloodstained handkerchiefs, presumably the result of your girlfriend's handiwork."

"How did you know that? She told me no-one from the police had spoken to her."

"There was actually a policeman with her in the ambulance. Apparently she was rather in and out of it, but she did give a pretty graphic account of what happened. Of course, her colleagues want to know what she was really up to, so I've told her we'd asked them to do a bit of hush-hush work for Special Branch, on the basis that she already knew the layout of the house from when she went there with you. But you were attempting to explain the real reason why she was there…"

"What the old man told us was at least a plausible explanation of what happened to Davenport. Of course, they wouldn't have done it again with Mrs Davenport. I imagine they parked further away and just made their way into the house after dark."

"But that doesn't explain why you were after these photos."

"Sorry. Just before we left, the old man said he remembered Mrs Davenport from before the War and the woman who'd been there recently seemed to have changed enormously. Also she didn't recognise him. That led us to all sorts of theories – some of them that clearly didn't hold water – about Mrs Davenport. But we thought if we could see the photos from before the War which I'd seen in the bureau, alongside wedding photos and later ones, of which I'd also seen several there, it might give a clue as to whether the woman who was killed really was Mrs Davenport. You see, I've always wondered about why Mr Davenport got involved in this."

"So who did you tell about this?"

"My boss, Jim Round. My AC, Mr Imrie… and Iain Cogbill. Of course, they could've mentioned it to other people."

"So you've worked out why I'm asking."

"Yes. Someone must've tipped off the men who were at the house today. I think Rosemary being there was just bad luck."

"So when they hear your girlfriend's been shot, presumably they'll twig that you at least will probably work it out."

"I didn't tell anyone where she was shot – not least because I didn't know."

"But the KGB hoods will doubtless tell their masters what happened when they get back to the Embassy – where I imagine they are by now."

"You believe they've gone back to London?"

"If your girlfriend really did break his jaw, they'll need to get it seen to. Clearly, they couldn't risk going to a hospital in this country."

"So, what are you going to do – arrest Round, Imrie and Cogbill?"

"No. I'll arrange to have them all watched. If one of them tries to scarper, we can be reasonably sure he's been tipped off by our Soviet friends. I might even be able to get their phones tapped. Just give me a moment to make a couple of phone calls. While you're waiting, you could take a look at these photos and see whether they were worth the risk."

I opened the envelope. There were a couple of small books of pre-War photographs, one per page and one slightly larger album with two photos per page. There were also about a dozen miscellaneous photos, including the two I'd seen in Davenport's suitcase. Now that really did seem a long time ago! Oddly enough, there were no wedding photos – but it might be that they were kept at the Davenports' main home in Shire Oak.

Unfortunately, none of the photos in the albums were titled, so I had no idea which of two daughters was the future Mrs Davenport. Both were angular, with short wavy hair and thin, rather unsmiling faces. I don't know whether they disliked being photographed, but it was a rare photo in which they were smiling. Not that their parents and relatives were the cheeriest bunch, either. The most recent album stopped with a picture of one of the girls dressed in some sort of military uniform. I would have said that it must have been some time after the War had begun. The only post-War photos were the two I'd already seen. It seemed likely, therefore, that Esmee Wilkins had met Neville Davenport during or shortly after the War and had not returned home. The two photos were puzzling. The one taken in about 1954 or 55 seemed to me to bear more of a resemblance to the girls in the pre-War photos than the one of the Davenports as a couple, taken, I'd guess, two or three years ago, judging by their clothes. In the later picture, she appeared taller and thinner and there was something about her face that seemed different. But she had changed her hairstyle a bit, too, while invariably wearing quite heavy make-up. I really couldn't tell whether it was the same woman or not. What I could tell for certain was that the most recent picture was of the same woman I had met in the house in Marsden Lane.

"Well?" said Elliott, coming back into the room and closing the door firmly behind him. "That's in hand. Now – have the pictures proved any of your theories or not?"

"I'm really not sure. The trouble with photos is that they don't necessarily give a very good likeness."

"As most people say. Let me see…"

"Probably the best to look at are the two framed ones."

"Card frames? I bet these were taken out of proper glass frames. This is just black mounting, I think… But I see what you mean. It's not conclusive – but I'd say it wasn't the same woman. I think the woman in the later photo is trying to look as much like the other as possible… Look at that make-up. Doesn't it look to you as though it's being used to alter her face?"

"It could be. I wonder whether they've any photos in their house in Shire Oak that might help?"

"Shire Oak?"

"Apparently it's between Walsall and Brownhills in the Black Country. I think that's their main home – where they were planning to move back to."

"I expect we could get someone to have a look. In any case, it'd be interesting to see whether our friends have been there first."

"So what happens now?"

"Well, I suggest you go back to your girlfriend and look after her. It's more than likely that I'll be heading to Harwich tomorrow, so I could give you a lift back if you like."

"I've got a hire car in the car park here."

"If you like I can get that sorted out."

I gave him the hire car keys and returned to Rosemary's bedside, content that my car was being taken care of and that both the Leicestershire Constabulary and the Russian hoods were off our backs. Of course, I couldn't mention most of this to her, as her parents were ensconced in the same chairs they had been in when I first arrived.

"The nurse wants us to leave," said Mrs Johnson. "Apparently visiting hours are two until three and from six until seven."

"Would you like me to be difficult with them?" I asked. "I'm quite prepared to."

"No, thank you," replied Mr Johnson. "It's kind of you, but we don't really like any scenes."

"Rosemary asked me to stay, so I'll probably have to make a scene in any case."

"We'd probably best be off anyway," said Mrs Johnson. "Now we know our daughter's all right and in good hands. We really ought to let her sister know. We didn't have time before. We just rushed over here as fast as we could." I doubted that when she said 'in good hands', she was referring to me.

"Perhaps while you're here, Mr Storey, you might encourage our headstrong daughter to think about a less dangerous career," added Mr Johnson.

Having said their farewells, they left. I was beginning to tell Rosemary about my conversation with Mike Elliott when the staff nurse returned.

"I thought I explained that all of you had to go. You can come back at six."

"I'm sorry. I'm not leaving. Rosemary has asked me to stay with her and that's what I intend to do."

"Well, you can't. The hospital has its rules –"

"Perhaps they need to be more flexible. Just to make myself clear, when I said Rosemary asked me to stay with her, I meant all night."

"That's completely out of the question!"

"I'm not asking to have a double bed, you know. Just a chair so I can sit next to her."

"It's quite impossible! I shall have to inform Matron! We can't have the ward disrupted in this way!"

"There must surely be smaller rooms where you could put a single bed with a chair at the side?"

"It just can't be done!"

"Can't, or is it that you don't want to?"

"It'd mean moving the patient – or her bed."

"Is that impossible?"

"Matron will absolutely forbid anything of the sort!"

"Then perhaps I'd better speak to her. But when you see her you could perhaps tell her that WPC Johnson came here after being shot in the course of her duty. She is plainly suffering from shock, resulting both from being shot and facing the prospect of death when a gun was pointed at her. She has merely asked that I should remain with her tonight. Not surprisingly while she is still in shock, she still feels those moments of fear. Surely, the best way you can care for your patient is to let me stay with her as she asks."

"A sedative will have the same effect without disrupting the routines of the hospital."

"So if I felt minded to tell all of this to the *Leicester Mercury*, that would be the message the hospital would like to be made public, is it?"

"You wouldn't!"

"Just try me!"

She strode off, presumably to speak to the all-powerful matron.

"I wouldn't like to get on the wrong side of you," remarked Rosemary.

"Let's hope it works. I have absolutely no idea how to get in touch with the *Mercury*."

"I think you did rather well to know it even existed."

"I noticed people reading it on the train."

I told her about my conversation with Mike Elliott, which gave both of us a greater feeling of comfort. We had started discussing who might have been responsible for telling the two Soviet hoods about the photos, when the staff nurse and two porters appeared – to take Rosemary to a room of her own, where, the nurse informed me coldly, there would be a chair for me. But whereas Rosemary would enjoy the delights of a hospital dinner, I would have to fend for myself. There turned out to be three chairs, each one chosen, I would have said, for lack of comfort and apparent hardness.

The room was on a different corridor, overlooking the central well of the building. Looking across you could see lots of different wards, with doctors, nurses and porters making their way round them in what appeared to be an entirely random fashion.

At 6 p.m., Rosemary's parents reappeared, along with a young woman who I instantly guessed was their younger daughter. She was slightly shorter, rounder, with long, dyed blonde hair and was dressed in the latest gear, notably a white, shiny plastic coat. Though her face was like Rosemary's, she used make-up heavily, so it was a little difficult to tell what she really looked like.

"This is Simone," explained Mrs Johnson, "Rosie's little sister."

"Enough of the 'little', Mother. You're Rosie's intended are you? Where do you work?" Simone had a determinedly 'posh' accent.

"We told you, he works for the Customs and Excise," said Mr Johnson.

"I thought they all wore uniforms."

"Only the Waterguard," I explained. "They work at ports and airports. The bit I'm in works all over the country, but not in uniform."

As there were only three chairs, I agreed to leave them for a family chat, while I found my way to the hospital buffet to get myself something by way of an evening meal. Given the choice between a slightly tired cheese and tomato roll with a slice of fruitcake and a mug of coffee and the rather unpleasant-looking stuff they had given Rosemary to eat, I thought I had done rather better. I also managed to get several chocolate bars of various sorts and a couple of apples, to give Rosemary some sustenance, after she had pushed most of her dinner away, and to keep me going during the night, as I did not anticipate getting much sleep on any of the chairs provided for me.

When I got back, the visitors rose, almost as one.

"We've got to go," explained Mr Johnson. "We drove Simone here…"

"And I've got to get back to my babies," added Simone. "There's no way Don can be trusted with them for more than an hour or so."

After they had gone Rosemary explained, "Simone and I spent most of our lives fighting like two cats in a sack. She spent her whole time wanting – and taking – what I'd got and I spent all my time being beastly to her in return. My mother must've had the patience of a saint!"

"I just got bossed around by my elder sister – but she's five years older than me. Do you want me to call you 'Rosie'?"

"No. I detest being called that! It's what you call a little girl. I'm grown up – and I wish they'd stop calling me it."

"I've smuggled some food back in case you were still hungry. We'd better hide it away somewhere in case that nurse comes back. Will she be round again?"

"She'll want to check all visitors have gone at seven and then I expect they come round later for sedatives. I wonder if they bring cocoa? On the telly, hospitals always give you a mug of cocoa last thing."

But when a rather more amiable nurse brought Rosemary her mug of cocoa later on, she had fallen asleep. I took the cocoa and the nurse gave me a saucer to put on it to keep it warm in case Rosemary awoke. But after a day like that, the best thing she needed was a good night's sleep.

FOURTEEN – LEICESTER AND HARWICH – ALARMS AND EXCURSIONS

I sat beside Rosemary in a chair that quickly confirmed my view that it had been chosen by the unhelpful staff nurse as the most uncomfortable in the whole hospital.

I got up and stood by the window, watching the wards opposite. By now, all the main lights had been turned down and there were low, orangey night lights everywhere, except in the corridors behind, of which I could see glimpses when someone left the ward – presumably a nurse or orderly or a patient going out to the toilet. I wondered how many were sleeping. Lights out at nine o'clock would be far too early for me. Unless I had been sedated, I knew I'd spend the next two hours tossing and turning, with my head full of unruly ideas, completely unable to sleep.

Inevitably, just as I had worked out a way of sitting on the chair that seemed to enable me to doze, Rosemary woke up. It was about 11.30. She sipped some of the cold cocoa.

"Did you try any of this?" she whispered.
"No. I'm not really here as far as the hospital is concerned."
"Lucky you! You can barely taste the cocoa for the sugar."
"Perhaps it's supposed to build you up."
"Have you been able to rest?"
"Not really. But then I'm supposed to be guarding you, remember."
"So have you seen anything suspicious?"
"A man in the ward opposite went out to the toilet about twenty minutes ago – and came back."

I was peering across at the ward opposite. Suddenly, it occurred to me that there was something odd about it. A light seemed to be flashing. I looked more carefully. There seemed to be two doctors or possibly orderlies in long white hospital coats making their way up the ward, checking on each patient.

189

"I don't understand that," I said. "Why should you need two doctors to check on the patients at this hour of night? You might need one – but not two... I don't like the look of this at all!"

"What do you mean?"

"I think those two men over there are searching for you."

"So, what can we do?"

"I'll bet the only outside phones are downstairs in the lobby by the buffet and the waiting room. There's no point alerting staff. If these are like the men who shot you, they'll have guns and I can't imagine they'd hesitate to use them. Besides, how many staff will be around at this time of night? We're going to have to hide you and I'll set a trap for them."

"I can help."

"Not with that leg you can't. Wasn't there some sort of linen room we came past earlier? I'll sneak out and have a look."

Almost opposite was a linen cupboard with piles of sheets, blankets, pillows, bedclothes, dressing gowns and towels. There was also somewhere for Rosemary to be concealed. I went back to Rosemary's room.

"I have an idea. But I'll need to get you into the linen room. Can you see where those men have got to?"

"They're just in the ward in the corner over there."

"We should have enough time then."

I got her to sit up and swing round with her feet facing me. Then I picked her up in my arms. She was lighter than I'd expected. She was trembling. I carried her across the corridor and into the linen room. There, she put on a dressing gown for warmth and I helped her lie down on some blankets behind a cupboard. Then I covered her carefully with more blankets. From the doorway it just looked like a couple of piles of blankets.

"Don't move or say anything until I come and tell you!" I whispered. "I love you."

I took several blankets and pillows back into her room and did my best to put them in the bed as if there was a body asleep there. Then, checking that the two men had moved round the corner, I removed the bulb from the night light, so that the room was dark, lit only by the dim lights from the wards on the opposite side of the well and from the corridor, when the door was opened. Then I made sure that Rosemary's chart was in full view in the holder on the outside of the door.

About ten yards down the corridor I found the other thing I needed – a fire extinguisher. Rosemary's room was next to a staircase and I hid myself at the top of the stairs, with my fire extinguisher ready to use.

I was hoping that they would go into the room, shoot at the bed and then either just dash away or check, realise their mistake and come out, irritated, but cautious. I needed to get them just as they were coming out, before they could shoot at me. At least, that's what I hoped.

As I heard the measured steps coming along the corridor, halting and examining the charts on the outside of each door, I asked myself whether it wouldn't have been better just to have hidden or fled. But Rosemary wasn't in any state for sustained flight and it seemed to me that these people had the persistent bravado to keep on searching until we were found. Besides, if we got away this time, they'd just come back. There were probably lots of other things I could have done. But anyway, I was stuck with the decisions I had taken.

The footsteps came closer. I thought I could detect a whispered "*Nyet*" and the footsteps moved closer still. "*Ah! Shto eto!*" said the same voice and I heard the door of Rosemary's room open. Immediately half a dozen sharp clicks announced that one or both had fired into the bed with a silencer. That was my cue.

I stepped quickly round the corner of the stairs and fired the fire extinguisher into the face of the first man and then the second as he followed his fellow killer from the room. Both of them instinctively put their hands to their eyes. As the second one did, I smashed the fire extinguisher into the midriff of the first man who doubled up in pain and dropped his gun on to the floor. Wiping his stinging eyes with one hand, the second man attempted to fire at me, but as he did so, I moved to one side and thrust the bottom of the fire extinguisher into his face. He staggered back into the room. I grabbed the first man's gun from the floor. He was still doubled up, his blindness adding to his bewildered agony. I left him and followed the second man into the room, where he was lying backwards against my chair, having fallen against it and knocked it over. His face was a mass of blood, but he still tried to raise his gun to fire at me. But his shot was aimless and I heard the bullet fizz a couple of feet past my head. I then put a shot from his partner's gun into his thigh and told him in Russian to drop his gun or I'd put the next one through his brains. Slightly to my surprise he did. But then, he, too, was pretty well blinded by the extinguisher foam and in no condition to fight. I took his gun and went back into the corridor. Amazingly, the only person there was the other man, trying to crawl away. I gave way to the temptation to hit him with the fire extinguisher again, remembering how close his compatriots had come to killing Rosemary the previous morning. So I smacked it down on the middle of his back as hard as I could. He screamed with pain and lay still.

As no-one appeared to have noticed anything, I decided I needed to secure them before I sought help. So I dragged the second man out of the bedroom into the corridor and tied their shoelaces together. I removed their belts and tied them round their arms, as best I could. Then I used their ties to secure their wrists. Having done that. I sprayed each of them in the face again, just to make sure they weren't tempted to do anything. By this stage however, they were groaning and I suspected would probably be going no further this night than the emergency ward. I realised I had injured both of them quite severely. It's amazing how fear can brutalise someone.

I went into the linen room, explaining to Rosemary that it was all right and that the men had been disposed of. I helped her to her feet and carried her into the corridor.

"That was them?" she exclaimed. "What on earth have you done to them?"

"I used a fire extinguisher on them," I explained, suddenly feeling quite tired and shaky.

"I'm glad you're on my side."

"I need to go and ring the police. Can you keep an eye on them? I've got both their guns, but I don't think there's much ammo in them. They emptied most of it into your bed."

"Well, it never was a particularly comfortable mattress," she replied with a tearful smile.

We sat opposite them for a few minutes, with my arm round her, until the thought of what might easily have happened passed.

"Give me both guns," she said with a firmer voice. "I want to make sure I don't miss."

I raced downstairs to the lobby. There was some sort of night attendant on duty .

"There's been a shooting and two men are seriously injured on the second floor by the linen room – 224A was the number, I think. I need to ring the police. Have you got an outside line?"

Within seconds, I had rung 999 and was informed that a police car was on its way.

As I ran back up the stairs, I overtook a young doctor heading in the same direction.

"Do you know anything about some incident that's just been reported?" he enquired in a leisurely drawl. He was about my age, with short sandy hair and a deeply unfashionable Anthony Eden moustache.

"Yes. I reported it."

"What sort of injuries do you know?"

"Both men have had fire extinguisher foam in their eyes. They've both been hit several times by a fire extinguisher and one has a bullet wound in his thigh."

"How do you know all this?"

"I did it to them. They're Russian hoods who came here to kill my girlfriend. You can only do what you can for them without allowing them the chance to escape. The police are on their way and then they can decide what to do."

"Who's that?" he demanded, as we turned into the corridor, initially seeing Rosemary sitting on the floor, holding two semi-automatic pistols in front of her.

"This is WPC Rosemary Johnson, the bravest person I'll ever meet."

"They haven't tried to escape," said Rosemary. "I think they're probably quite badly hurt."

"Good!" I replied.

The doctor hadn't long started to examine the men when four uniformed policemen arrived. I explained briefly what had happened and Rosemary told her part of it. A couple of the policemen knew her anyway and at least one had some knowledge of the reason why she was in the hospital in the first place.

"There'll have to be a bit of explaining," remarked the policeman who had been checking the two men. "These are employees of the Soviet Embassy – Mr Konstantin Fyodorov and Mr Yevgeniy Golovzhkin – who have diplomatic immunity apparently."

"I suggest you have a look at the bed in there, where Rosemary was supposed to be sleeping," I said. "I'm not sure whether that sort of thing is covered by diplomatic immunity."

"These men are badly injured," said the doctor. "I need to get some colleagues and get them treated, whatever they've done."

"I'll call in for some back-up," said a policeman. "Doctor, you can take them to be treated, but they'll need to be secure. These men are not, repeat not, going to leave without our say-so."

"I think you can safely say they won't be able to go anywhere for some time."

"Before you start sorting them out," I said, "can you please find somewhere where Rosemary can lie down in comfort."

"Just wait there a moment."

He popped into the linen room and evidently roused someone on an internal telephone. Why the hell hadn't I noticed that? I could probably have avoided any risk to myself if I'd used that to alert the hospital staff. But it was too late for recriminations – and, anyway, quite a lot of me felt considerable satisfaction at what I'd done to those men.

Anyhow, within a couple of minutes, hospital staff began to appear. Some assisted with getting the men on to trolleys, to which a wrist was immediately handcuffed by a policeman. Others, including one with an invalid chair, led Rosemary and me to an empty room further down the corridor, where there was a bed and two comfortable armchairs. Much more professionally than I had got her out of bed, they got her back in. She lay back and gave a deep sigh.

"Do you think that's it?"

"Yes. I think if there'd been anyone else around, they'd've done what they needed to do by now. I think you really can sleep safely now."

"I'm not sure I'll sleep properly for ages… Think what could've happened if we hadn't seen them!"

"We should never have assumed that because one team of hoods went back to London, there wasn't another around. You'd think Special Branch would've thought of that."

"But why did they want to kill me?"

"I suppose those two might say. But I expect they're well trained to keep silent. I guess it was either because you could identify the man you hit in the face or because they thought you still had those damned photos."

"They're not still here are they?"

"No. I gave them to the man from Special Branch, Mike Elliott. Now try to get some sleep."

But it was impossible. Within ten minutes a doctor came in to check Rosemary's leg and blood pressure, etc. Then Detective Sergeant Barnes came in, asking to know what happened and suggesting that we might wish to make statements. I asked him whether all that was necessary at one o'clock in the morning and he said all he really needed was a quick summary for his bosses. So I gave him the two-minute version and he left.

"You realise the cleaners will start coming round in about four hours time," said Rosemary. "Do you think you could come and sit next to me and put your arm round me? I want to feel really and truly safe."

So I sat close to her pillow and did as she asked. Within ten minutes, she was fast asleep. Though it wasn't particularly comfortable, I dozed for a bit. It seemed like no time at all when I could heard the sound of a hoover in the corridor accompanied by someone whistling tunelessly.

"Another day dawns – and here we are," I whispered.
"Only it's not dawn for at least another hour," observed Rosemary sleepily. "But it's nice to be able to wake up to another day… Did last night really happen, or did I dream it?"
"What? I carried you into a linen cupboard and hid you there, then attacked two Russian hoods with a fire extinguisher and then the police came? That's surely just the stuff of dreams…! Actually, it does seem a little unreal. But I know it's true because we're in a different room, with comfortable chairs."
"No bullet holes in this bed either!"
"God, that was stupid! Did you realise there was an internal phone in that linen room? I could've alerted the hospital authorities and not run quite such a risk of us being killed by those men."
"I'm just glad you stayed with me."

At that moment an orderly appeared, offering both of us a mug of tea, which we gratefully accepted. She also pointed out that in these rooms, there was a radio and we could listen to the news or music if we wanted to. We decided it was too early in the day to listen to the news on the BBC Home Service and managed to find Radio Luxembourg playing pop music. This led to a lively debate between us as to whether the Beatles were better than the Rolling Stones and whether *The House of the Rising Sun* was the best single of the year or not. A few hours' sleep had helped Rosemary recover completely from the shock of the previous day. She was back to being her usual self. In fact, I suspected that if it wasn't for the stitches in her leg and a certain amount of weakness from the blood she had lost, she would have got up and gone to work. Needless to say, the doctors would have none of that.

At 6.30 breakfast arrived – for both of us. It was surprisingly good, but then it takes a fair bit of skill to mess up a good fried breakfast. Breakfast was followed by an inspection of Rosemary's stitches by a nurse, who even allowed me to remain in the room, presumably on the basis that, in these days of miniskirts, I might have caught a glimpse of her thigh before.

"You realise that we've just spent the night alone together?" I observed after she'd gone. "In some cultures, we'd have to get married or you'd be a ruined woman."

"Well, if I'm forced to, I suppose I'll have to put up with it. Though I'm not sure it ever felt we were actually alone for long."

We listened to the Four Tops hit *Rag Doll*, *I get around* by the Beach Boys. *Oh Pretty Woman* by Roy Orbison and *I'm Into Something Good* by Herman's Hermits.

"Now that is truly awful!" I exclaimed.

"Whenever I see them on the telly, I want to throw something at them," added Rosemary

"So that's not going to be 'our song', then."

"No. I think *A Hard Day's Night* or the *Pink Panther* might be more appropriate."

"The way I feel this morning, it should be *Dancing in the Street*."

"I don't think I've heard that."

"It's the best Motown song I've heard – by Martha and the Vandellas. I'll get you the single."

"Remember what we said about spending money."

"OK. Well you'll just have to stay here all day listening out for it on the radio."

A nurse came in. "Your parents are outside, WPC Johnson. And there's a policeman outside who wants to speak to you Mr Storey."

"How's our daughter?" asked Mr Johnson, as I followed the nurse out of the room.

"She's absolutely fine. You've managed to avoid visiting hours."

"The police contacted us first thing and arranged everything. They said someone tried to attack Rosie during the night," said Mrs Johnson.

"They failed. In fact, they didn't lay a finger on her. But let her tell you herself."

They went in. I had a suspicion that the policeman might be Mike Elliott of Special Branch and I wasn't disappointed.

"I see you're in fine form," he remarked. "You seem to have a way with fire extinguishers."

"It wasn't entirely my idea. I was in the NAAFI when I was in West Berlin and watched a rather drunken brawl, where eventually a corporal saw off three squaddies attacking him by using a fire extinguisher. I never thought it'd come in handy, though."

"Your girlfriend in there is lucky to have someone like you around."

"No. Every day since I've met Rosemary I've thanked my lucky star and every god there may or not be that we met and fell in love! How are those two men doing?"

"Do you care?"

"I probably hit them a few more times than was needed. I suppose it was a mixture of fear and anger."

"They'll live. One has a broken jaw, cheekbone and collarbone – and a bullet hole in his thigh. The other has broken ribs, a ruptured spleen and cracked vertebrae in his back. And, of course, neither will see very well for quite a while."

"You've got a very accurate picture."

"I've just come from seeing our medic. Fyodorov and Golovzhkin have been removed from here. Far too insecure. They'll be treated somewhere the Russians can't get at them. Then they'll probably be horse-traded. The Russians know that if their men get caught trying to kill people here, there's a price to pay. Doubtless Carvell and his colleagues will be working out what those two are worth."

"Are they likely to make another attempt to kill Rosemary?"

"No. With these two in our charge after what they tried to do, the Russians will either try to get Davidson out or leave him to our tender mercies. You should also be aware that your girlfriend's continued safety will be an essential part of any horse-trading. By now or very shortly, they'll be aware of that."

"That's good of you."

"Don't thank me. I think there's a general view going around that trying to guard your girlfriend and you would take up too many police resources."

"What about the suspects in Customs? Has anything happened with them?"

"Well, as of first thing this morning, all were sticking to their normal routines. I didn't get phone taps on until about midnight last night. Since then, no-one's had any interesting calls. But, of course, they could've been contacted earlier. How is your girlfriend this morning, really?"

"She's got over the shock of yesterday. Apart from her leg, she's as strong and brave as ever."

"Well, do you think she'd let you escape for a few hours? I think it's time to stir the pot a little. What do you say?"

"I'll see what she thinks – but I'm pretty clear what the answer will be. I don't suppose you know somewhere I could get myself tidied up and ideally get some clean underwear, do you?"

"I'm sure that can be arranged – But you'll need to be quick."

"Twenty minutes?"

I went back into the room.

"Nick," began Rosemary. "The police have told Mum and Dad that it'll be completely safe for me to stay with them for a few days when I get out of here. I expect they'll kick me out later today or tomorrow. I realise you'll have to go back to work. Do you mind if we postpone my trip on the river to another weekend and you could come and stay in Thurmaston at the weekend?"

"If Mr and Mrs Johnson don't mind having me."

"After what Rosie – Rosemary's been telling us, we couldn't possibly refuse," said her mother.

"Besides, we ought to get to know you better," added her father.

"Then I'll leave you in good hands. If you can give me your home phone number, I'll be able to get you this evening wherever you are. I've got to go back to Harwich now."

Rosemary and I kissed longer and more passionately than was comfortable for her parents, I guessed. But you don't often experience a twenty-four hours like that.

True to my word, within twenty minutes, a clean and spruced-up version of me got into a Special Branch black Rover and sped off out of

Leicester towards Kettering and then on to Huntingdon and Cambridge. When we hit any slow-moving vehicles or traffic jams, the driver turned on the police siren and blue lights and we whizzed past with ease. I wished I had enjoyed the same facilities when I'd been driving in the opposite direction.

At Cambridge we made a small detour into the city to a police station.

"This is where we stir the pot," explained Mike Elliott. "You need to ring them and put a small fire under them. Then we'll see what happens?"

"OK. So I'm the spoon. What do you want the spoon to say?"

"First you need to tell them you're phoning from Leicester, but you'll be driving back shortly. Then you tell them that your girlfriend wasn't hurt badly and you've managed to get hold of the photos. From that you're convinced that the woman calling herself Mrs Davenport wasn't the woman Davenport married and that therefore it seems likely that Davenport was being blackmailed in some way. Tell them that you've just told Special Branch this and that they're now checking death records over the last ten years in every Registry of Births, Marriages and Deaths in the country, as well as Somerset House. Oh, and Special Branch expect to get a result today and that will narrow down the list of those who could've been blackmailing Davenport to two or three people at most."

"Do you think that'll convince someone to make their move? Why don't we tell them about the two Russian hoods you've got stashed away who'll be bargained for the person who was blackmailing Davenport?"

"If they've got any sense at all, they'll know that such a process could take weeks, certainly days. That would enable them to make a more surreptitious exit. I want them to panic and try to get out in a hurry."

"OK. You're used to this sort of thing."

So I phoned Jim and Iain, in both cases feeling like a complete blackguard. Both expressed concern about Rosemary. Iain explained that, as he hadn't yet done anything about the photographs, obviously he wouldn't now Special Branch were involved. He offered apologies for not having done anything about it, but that was because a second raid on the White House Nurseries had turned up sufficient cannabis seeds to fill a hundred acres. Two of the 'hired hands' had been at the nursery and had been arrested. They were now singing like canaries and the IB were on the tracks of the main organiser, a man called Devaney, who had got the seeds from our old friend, Jan de Wet, in Holland. I suggested that they might check the maiden name of Kersey's wife, as that might be the connection which Davenport knew about.

Speaking to Imrie needed a cover story.

"I'm sorry to bother you, Sir," I began, after his secretary put me on to him, "but I wasn't sure whether my Surveyor could authorise my use of a hire car between Harwich and Leicester and back –"

"What the hell are you on about, laddie? What in God's name required you to go to Leicester?"

"I got a phone call yesterday telling me my girlfriend had been shot, trying to get hold of the pictures of Mrs Davenport we were talking about the other day, sir."

"Shot? Is she dead?"

"No, sir. Just a flesh wound. The gunmen fled apparently because they thought the police were arriving. So we managed to recover the pictures and they show that the Mrs Davenport who I saw and who killed herself wasn't the same person as the woman who married Davenport – Esmee Wilkins was her maiden name. Special Branch are checking all round the country to find out when the real Mrs Davenport died and expect to know by tonight. I'm just about to drive back from Leicester and I'd thought I'd better get your authorisation to come back by hire car, sir."

"You don't need me to authorise. Round can do it. But I don't see what good these pictures are to you, laddie? I thought I'd shown you that they were of no value when we spoke the other day. Why in hell's name are you still bothering with then?"

"Because if, as we believe, the woman calling herself Mrs Davenport wasn't the real Mrs Davenport, Davenport was open to blackmail. And Special Branch believe their enquiries today will narrow the field of suspects down to two or three people – all in Customs."

"I've seen more than a few Special Branch castles of sand blow away in the air, but if that's how they want to waste their time…! Report to me, with Round, when you get here, laddie."

As we proceeded on our way, my mind turned to the three suspects. I found it extremely hard. Because I knew Jim and Iain better and liked them, it was difficult to regard them as blackmailers and traitors. But then pointing the finger at Imrie was almost too easy, because he was so deeply unpleasant. Besides, what was in it for him? He was an AC, with presumably prospects for further promotion. In view of his age, I guessed Jim might well have reached his ceiling. But he seemed too open, honest, blunt – so typically 'Yorkshire' – and fanatical in his devotion to the game of rugby to be the one. And Iain – well, I suppose I knew less about Iain – but I reckoned he was young enough to enjoy several promotions before he was due to retire. Moreover, he seemed to me to be made of that Scottish Presbyterian steel that was pretty well immune to rust and corruption.

"Why are you going to Harwich?" I asked Elliott. "Iain Cogbill isn't there, surely. I spoke to him on his IB number in London."

"From the latest information, he set off for Harwich first thing this morning and should've been there half an hour ago. It's entirely unclear why."

"And his phone?"

"Didn't you know? Your investigation people have a system like ours. You ring a particular number. If the person on it has left another number somewhere else, the operator transfers the call automatically. Didn't you notice a few extra clicks and whirrs when you rang him?"

"I thought it was probably your phone taps."

We sped on towards Harwich. After we passed through Manningtree, Elliott said, "When we get there, you and I will both go directly to see your Higher Collector, as I believe he's known. I've got men around the place to spot any unusual activity on the part of our suspects."

"Since none of them are now suspect, I'd strongly advise you to let me tell the Waterguard people – the uniformed lot. They're a lot closer on the ground and will spot something unusual a lot faster than your people are likely to be able to do."

"Can you do it without being seen yourself?"

"If the driver goes where I indicate, yes."

As we arrived, I told the driver to swing round behind the freight examination shed. Immediately Morry Gold rushed out.

"You can't park that bloody car there! Oh, it's you, Storey. What the hell are you up to?"

"Is Wally French around? I need to speak to him urgently."

"He's having a quick cup of tea. I'll get him."

Wally appeared. True to form, Morry stood at his shoulder.

"I assume you've noticed that there's a police operation on today?" I asked.

"Of course," replied Wally. "They're not bad. It's just when you're around the docks all day as we are, you can spot 'em a mile off. I suppose you know why they're here?"

"Yes. I expect you've worked out that a lot of diamonds and expensive jewellery got smuggled through here earlier in the year."

"That's been rumoured, but not confirmed, of course."

"It probably never will be. But it was facilitated by my predecessor, Davenport. But he was being blackmailed by the real traitor, who is expected to try and flee sometime today. It'll be a senior member of the Department, but I can't say who. But if you see anyone, either from Harwich Customs or elsewhere in the Department at Surveyor level or above, please signal to the police or, if in doubt, detain them."

"I take it there'll be some sort of subsequent authorisation if we get it wrong?"

"Yes. You have my word on it."

"That'll have to do I suppose."

"What's that chap from the IB, Cogbill, doing here today?" asked Morry. "Is he part of your operation or not?"

"Not. I've no idea why he's here. But I'm still keeping an open mind."

"Yes. I've not got a lot of time for the posers in the IB, but Cogbill has always seemed pretty straight."

I got back into the car and we drove up outside the Custom House as though we had just arrived. Showing his warrant card, Mike Elliott breezed past the Revenue Constable and allowed me to lead him up to the Higher Collector's office. We were admitted rapidly – possibly because the Collector had already been notified – and Elliott explained what was going on. From time to time he got crackly messages on his walkie-talkie, but they seemed to be in some sort of code.

Lunchtime swiftly arrived and plates of tea and sandwiches arrived and were consumed. Iain Cogbill had told me that the work of the IB while you were on surveillance was 98% boredom and 2% terrified excitement when you took action. I wondered whether he knew he was the subject of today's surveillances?

"You expect whoever it is to flee by ship?" asked the Collector.

"We believe they reckon it's the least obtrusive route. Any of them could legitimately approach a ship and then be on board without anyone really noticing," explained Elliott.

"Well, Jim Round will have to be pretty sharp, if it's him," I said, "He'll go off shift at three and there's only one ship departing between now and then."

"When he leaves, we've got men to tail him."

At ten past three, a virtually unintelligible message on his walkie-talkie informed Elliott that Jim had got on his bicycle and was heading in the direction of his house in Upper Dovercourt. Deep inside me, I felt a warm glow of relief.

At 3.45 p.m., a ferry from the Hook arrived. After about twenty minutes, the walkie-talkie started going mad.

"We'd better get down there," exclaimed Elliott. I set off with him.

We walked as fast as we could over to the passenger terminal. In a corridor was a group of men, arguing furiously. As I got closer I could see Iain Cogbill in the middle of it, white with rage. Surrounding him were several men in Waterguard uniforms and others in plain clothes, who I guessed were Elliott's men.

"He was planning to go on board," explained one of the Special Branch officers. "We thought we'd better detain him."

"Ditto," said Hywel Jenkins.

"Of course I wasn't trying to get on fucking board!" cried Iain, "I was attempting to detain a major suspect."

"Who, exactly?" demanded Elliott.

"You! I should've known this was some Special Branch cock-up!"

"We'll see about that. I repeat who was it you say you were planning to detain?"

"Bloody Jan de Wet! When we raided the nurseries in Belsize Park, we picked up a couple of the legmen. Thanks to your information, Storey. I'm sorry to see you're mixed up in all this. And in the course of singing, one let slip there was a code their boss had used to communicate with his Dutch partner. In return for a promise of a quiet life in the Antipodes hereafter, he gave us the code. I used it to summon Jan de Wet here so I could detain him as a key player in several dirty operations.

"Now you idiots have let him walk. He's probably back on the boat and paying out to make sure we couldn't find him."

"No he isn't," said Morry Gold. "I saw this character on 3 July when, as we guessed later, some very fishy consignment went through. He travelled with the consignment, took it all the way to Custom House and then went back on the boat. Exactly the sort of behaviour that would encourage us to examine – but before we could even get a sniff, the van had driven off and he was back on the boat. Anyway, to cut a long story short, he's sitting in an interview room just along the corridor, staying schtumm apart from demanding a lawyer, with Wally and Geoff Wilson keeping an eye on him. I think you'd do well to trust the Waterguard a bit more, Mr Cogbill…"

"To be quite honest, after what's been going on here, I wasn't sure I could trust anyone in Harwich, expect for Jim Round and Nick Storey – and I see that he didn't trust me!"

"It wasn't a matter of trust," I replied. "It was a matter of evidence. But while we've been getting into this argy-bargy, has anyone been keeping tabs on the other suspects?"

Mike Elliott immediately checked on his walkie-talkie, but it was clear that not everyone had been in the right place to observe who had been boarding the ship. The team in the passenger departure line confirmed that no-one had gone through that way – nor were they in the queue.

"If I thought I was being watched, I'd just take a van and drive on," said Morry. "If I was known to the staff and had a plausible excuse, I'd be on board before you knew it."

"Bugger!" exclaimed Elliott. "We'd better check."

Several vans had gone on board, but none driven by either Jim Round or Jock Imrie.

Time moved on and all we could do was wait, the Special Branch operation hopelessly blown by the fracas with Iain Cogbill, now restored to liberty and trying to extract information out of Jan de Wet. The ferry began to prepare to sail.

"We've blown this bloody thing!" muttered Elliott. "If only those buggers in your investigation side were prepared to trust anyone else, we could've avoided this mess. Now whoever it is will be doubly cautious now."

The ferry started to move away from the dockside. I looked up. On the top deck was Jock Imrie. He gave me a cheery little wave. I signalled a telephone at my ear.

Just a moment of irrepressible arrogance. Customs contacted the ferry by radio and it returned back to its berth. Just as it did so, Imrie appeared again, in virtually the same place. He repeated his little wave and then launched himself out of the boat on to the dock. His body hit the concrete with a remarkably quiet thud, but it was immediately apparent that he was dead.

"Well that's pretty well that," remarked Elliott.

FIFTEEN – HARWICH – A CAPTURE BY THE CUTTERS

Of course, Imrie's suicide meant that it was unlikely we would ever know about how he had manipulated Davenport into helping all those illicit consignments to get through Harwich. Indeed, it was still conceivably possible that Davenport had not actually been involved, though that now seemed highly unlikely. A search of the Davenport's home in Shire Oak revealed no photographs but evidence of a search. Special Branch assumed that the two men I had attacked had probably been there and were sent on to Leicester after the unsuccessful attempt to get hold of the photos there by their colleagues. As nothing was found in their car, it was reasonable to assume that they had destroyed them.

The following day evidence emerged that Mrs Esmee Davenport had indeed been killed in a car accident in Devon in 1957. Her body, identified by her husband, had been cremated locally. Her will, if she ever had one, had never been proved. Who the substitute Mrs Davenport was would be hard to discover and Special Branch appeared to believe it was not a trail worth following up. When Davenport's and Mrs Davenport's will and financial accounts were gathered together, it seemed that the house in Leicester and several thousands of pounds in shares would have reverted to Mrs Davenport's sister, if she died without children. That seemed to provide sufficient motive for Davenport to have wished to maintain the fiction that Mrs Davenport was still alive. How Imrie had found out about it was a complete mystery and was likely to remain so. I suspected that Imrie had somehow come across the real Mrs Davenport and, encountering 'Mrs Davenport' by chance after Davenport started working in Harwich, had realised it was a different woman. It was as good a theory as any other.

When I got a chance I borrowed Davenport's estabs file back from Jim and confirmed leave dates that fitted around the time of Mrs Davenport's death in Devon. Doubtless, if I got the Estabs Section to check, I could have found out whether Imrie had travelled down this route too. But there didn't seem much point now.

What gave rise to more speculation was why Imrie had been involved. Jim Round's view, with which I generally agreed, was that Imrie had reached an age where he believed he wasn't going to be promoted further. Frustration and the possibility of substantial wealth were sufficient to corrupt a man who felt he'd given the Department much, but not received sufficient back in return. Where he had stashed his wealth was not, however, readily apparent. Unlike Iain Cogbill, of course, Jim appeared never to have the slightest suspicion that he had been one of those suspected of being the traitor.

As for the contents of Davenport's suitcase and the various notes he had left for someone following his tracks to find, it was still difficult to be sure whether he had attempted to leave clues as to what had happened. It seemed likely that he had been blackmailed by Imrie and that the diamonds were not just a pay-off, but a way of ensuring he didn't talk subsequently. That might explain why he hadn't attempted to hide them away or sell them – because at heart he was an honourable man, trapped in a desperate situation, trying to get out of it in the only way he could. Hence the reference in the registries to Imrie, the selection of files that pointed to Weissman and his attempts to get information out of Kersey. But I still found it difficult to believe that the Silberstein and White House Nursery entries had been taken purely as a smokescreen. The fact that they probably identified a large operation to smuggle cannabis seeds seemed to be too much of a coincidence. Perhaps it was just that Davenport knew of the link to Jan de Wet? But then, what about the Silbersteins? I could puzzle about it, there seemed to be little I could do about it now.

Iain Cogbill had returned grumpily to London with Jan de Wet. It emerged – by way of Wally French's 'grapevine' – that de Wet was refusing to co-operate in any way, claiming that any documents naming him were forgeries and that if he had shipped any illicit goods, that was unknown to him. He had merely acted in good faith for his clients in the Netherlands and customers in Britain. He also was demanding to see the representatives from the Dutch Embassy. The documents in the possession of the IB were, as I was well aware, unlikely to guarantee a conviction. I suspected that de Wet's fate probably depended on the negotiations that were doubtless taking place between the Russians and Carvell's people, who might well have other fish to fry. To my mind, Iain had made a gallant attempt to catch this fish, but time was against him and Jan de Wet was slippery enough to escape the net. Wally also told me that Iain was in a bit of hot water with his bosses for running a solo operation to catch de Wet with neither authorisation nor back-up. Iain was claiming the need for speed and absolute security, but it wasn't going down very well.

Naturally, I returned to my normal job and enjoyed a quiet, routine day which, for once, was entirely welcome. There were inevitably loads of rumours going round about the reason for Imrie's death, and the official story – that he had some suspicions about something on the ferry, tried to pursue them, but unfortunately fell to his death – was widely disbelieved. A few people tried to pump me for the 'truth', but I just feigned ignorance. Another cause for the increasing gap between my colleagues in the Long Room and me.

On the other hand, the Waterguard were more welcoming – not least because they had a clearer idea of what had occurred and probably why, but also the discretion to know when not to ask questions or go telling the rest of the world what they knew. Wally French was a canny man and I suspect managed to bargain for a good price.

I barely had time to speak to Jim, currently acting as temporary AC as well as doing his 'day job'. As I left the Custom House on the Friday evening, I felt rather alone. But doubtless time would pass and these matters fade into a distorted reflection in the long and varied history of the Department.

I travelled to Leicester via London, as usual. I had told Rosemary which train I was getting, but was still surprised to find Mr Johnson waiting for me, with his car parked a couple of streets away. We passed the journey in routine conversation.

The village of Thurmaston was only a little way beyond the city boundary. We quickly arrived at a pleasant street, with 30s semis with bow windows and neat front gardens. Mr Johnson let me into the house while he parked the car in the garage. Rosemary met me in the hall with an enthusiastic hug and kiss.

"It's wonderful to see you!" she cried. "Did you have a good journey?"
"Yes. How are you? How's your leg?"
"Funnily enough I can barely notice it, but my knuckles are still quite sore."
They were indeed very badly bruised and discoloured.

"You didn't break any bones there? The doctor did check?"

"No. Just bruises. I hope that man's jaw was jolly well broken, though."

"Well, I hope the Russian doctors do a thoroughly rotten job on him. Elliott – the Special Branch bloke – reckoned that they'd send both of those men back to Russia."

"And the other two? – the ones in the hospital?"

"Special Branch have them under guard in some sort of secure hospital unit. I've no idea where, of course. Apparently they'll be used in some sort of deal with the Russians. Apparently one bit of it is for them to keep well away from you, though Elliott thought that after all that had gone on, you were unlikely to be of interest to them now, anyway…"

"Not even for revenge?"

"No. Apparently that would be unprofessional. It seems possible that they might use those two men to get their hands on Davidson."

"Now then you two, stop filling up the hall and come in and sit down. I'm sure Mr Storey could do with a cup of tea and something to eat," said Mrs Johnson.

"Please call me Nick," I began.

"I think we'll stick with Mr Storey," said Rosemary and, somewhat rudely but irrepressibly, we burst into fits of laughter, "Sorry, Mum. That's what I said to Nick when we first met…! I wasn't particularly friendly."

"Well you seem to have made up for it subsequently. I assume it is all right to call you Nick?"

"Of course," I replied.

They turned out to be what I had expected – a very pleasant couple. It seemed inconceivable to me that Rosemary could have been the child of unpleasant or strange or domineering parents. Marjorie Johnson was a keen gardener and cook. Harold Johnson was one of those people who could fix anything and make anything. He had made all the kitchen cupboards, assembled the radios and the TV and did all the maintenance on his car. At present he was making a record player for Simone and her family and was eager to make something for Rosemary and me.

I imagine it was the shock of leaning that their daughter had been shot in the course of duty that persuaded them that she had actually grown up sufficiently to be called 'Rosemary'. But I never heard her referred to as 'Rosie' while I stayed there. Rosemary had been told to rest her leg as much as possible, so Mr Johnson allowed us to borrow his car on the Saturday and I drove through the beautiful small villages of north-east Leicestershire to Belvoir Castle, whose elevated site gave it a medieval grandeur which belied its Victorian reality. Obviously, we didn't walk round the castle, but we stopped in various places and enjoyed looking at the scenery. We also found a pub in the village of Thorpe Satchville, which provided a decent Sunday roast accompanied by... apple juice. Rosemary wasn't a policewoman for nothing.

It wasn't a weekend to talk about our future. That could come soon enough. Rosemary just needed to rest and recuperate. We didn't talk about the events in Marsden Lane or those in the hospital. I told her what had happened in Harwich and at the White House Nurseries. But otherwise it was time to enjoy being in each other's company and to breathe deep sighs of silent relief that things had turned out as they had.

Saturday night was remarkable. At about ten o'clock, Mr Johnson announced that he and Mrs Johnson were going to bed.

"We realise you two are grown-up people, so you mustn't feel we are imposing any rules on you."

After he had gone, Rosemary whispered to me, "I think he means that they won't object if you spend the night in my bed."

"Oh!"

"I would very much like you too – but not in the way my parents may be expecting. I said I wanted to be a bride who wore white honestly and that's still what I want. So if sleeping with me, but not having sex, would be too difficult, I'd completely understand it if you preferred to stay in your own bed."

"Don't be silly. I can't say I have the same feeling for the bride wearing white, but I love you and I'll do whatever you want. You really think I'd rather spend tonight in a bed on my own than being next to you?"

Not that it was easy. Her nightdress was quite short and her naked legs troubling for a man determined to be in control of himself. As she lay against me, it seemed I could feel her naked body through the cotton of the nightdress and feel her bare legs against mine. As she moved, I could see her small breasts pressing against the cotton. I stiffened. But I knew that when we did make love – at the right time, in the right place – it would be so great that it was worth waiting for. We slept, innocently, in each other's arms. And waking up, with Rosemary by my side, felt so good, I could scarcely believe it.

As he drove me back to Leicester station the following evening, Mr Johnson asked me about my intentions towards his daughter. I replied that she and I intended to get married and quite soon. My job was flexible enough for me to move so that we could be together. We planned to buy somewhere to live as soon as possible and I knew Rosemary wanted to start a family in a year or two.

"I'm pleased about that. We've been getting a bit worried lately. Rosemary has broken up with a couple of boyfriends and then became a policewoman. We'd begun to think she might've decided not to get married. Her sister was so desperate to beat her at something, she married at nineteen, virtually to the first man who'd have her. I don't feel they're as happy as she pretends."

"Life is very strange, it seems to me. A month ago, I didn't even know Rosemary existed. Now I can't imagine living without her. It's as though I'd been going around with a large part of me missing and suddenly I've discovered what it was."

"I believe we've worked out from what Rosemary's told us what she means to you, and we're very grateful. I just hope that the two of you realise you mightn't be so lucky another time."

"I sincerely hope there won't be another time."

"If you and my daughter settle down into a life of contented domestic bliss, I'll be astounded."

"Who knows what the future holds? If someone had told me what would happen over the last month, I'd've told them they were insane."

The following week consisted almost entirely of routine. I learnt that the IB had been compelled to release Jan de Wet, who had returned to Amsterdam. Information had been sent to Dutch Customs, but whether they would act on it was anyone's guess. From time to time I wondered whether somehow a piece of this puzzle had been missed in the absence of anything significant in regard to Silbersteins, but I wasn't in a position to do anything about it. Besides, I'd probably been pushing my luck with the Department enough as it was.

I returned to Thurmaston the following weekend and agreed with Rosemary when we would get married – in April – and that it would be a registry office affair. Though I suspected Mrs Johnson would have preferred a church wedding, Mr Johnson – somewhat to my surprise – supported his daughter who felt it would be hypocritical for her to get married in church. I was happy to do whatever she wanted – but I knew for certain that my father would not have set foot inside a church. I realised that I would have to inform them in the course of the next few days. Rosemary felt her leg was sufficiently recovered to come to London the following weekend and we would take the opportunity to introduce her to my parents. She was also adamant that she would start back at work the following Monday.

By Monday evening, I felt I was slipping back into my normal routine. The only real difference was that I took a sudden interest in OWOs, in particular the part that advertised vacancies. Though I was probably ineligible under existing rules to apply for another post, I thought that there might be the odd favour I could call in. But Harwich was too far from Leicester and though Rosemary had suggested that she would happily resign and look for a job nearer me, I felt I should do my best to get a post that was located more conveniently – or, failing that, we might both move somewhere where we could both continue our existing careers, even if that probably meant London or Birmingham. Certainly, as I looked through the vacancies, those were the places where there were plenty of suitable openings. Though I didn't greatly welcome the idea of leaving a port and doing Purchase Tax or excise, especially as excise in big cities tended to have too much betting and gaming work, it was a sacrifice worth making for the two of us to be together all the time. I don't know whether I would ever have settled happily in Harwich, but being at least three hours' journey away from Rosemary meant that I had developed no great love for the place.

On Tuesday, just before the first lot of entries began to arrived, I was summoned to the AC's office, temporarily occupied by Jim Round. Iain Cogbill was with him and Mr Jones from Box 500.

"What's going on?" I asked, somewhat impolitely.

"All in good time," replied Jim. "You need to be briefed. I think that's the word, isn't it, Iain?"

"First I should just say I'm sorry for my behaviour when we last met," said Iain. "It's not nice thinking you were suspected of something like that, but, as you said, evidence is evidence and I'd've done the same thing if the boot was on the other foot. You could hardly say I wasn't acting suspiciously either. I fear I'd got it into my head I could catch de Wet all on my own – because I feared he had a contact in Harwich who'd tip him off if I arrived mob-handed. It's a sorry lesson in realising you need to know who to trust and when."

"I didn't ever really believe it was you..."

"Past history. Let's get to the present. Perhaps Jones might explain where things stand at his end."

"After you conveniently got Fyodorov and Golovzhkin into our custody with a very nice murder attempt, we've been bargaining with the Russians for their release, without charge. Of course, once your man Imrie was unmasked and killed himself, there was no need to protect your girlfriend, Mr Storey, so we've been concentrating on getting our hands on this man who, until recently, was calling himself Louis Davidson. I assume they know his real name, but they aren't telling. He isn't part of the Embassy, nor has he ever been there, as far as we can tell. Clearly, he's not a lone wolf, so he must be being run by the KGB or one of their other security outfits through a contact in this country. Davidson probably wouldn't talk, but he's sufficiently well-connected that he could do the West damage again – after all, next time the money got from selling their diamonds could be used to suborn politicians or fund disruptive groups in the West. So we'd like him off our streets. Of course, the Russians have been doing their best to outfox us. We reckon they've been trying to work out where Fyodorov and Golovzhkin are, so they could try to spring them – or kill them – but they haven't succeeded. So last week we put the pressure on and told them that if we weren't given Davidson by midnight last night, Fyodorov and Golovzhkin would be formally charged with attempted murder in absentia, getting a date set for trial. So just before midnight, they told us his whereabouts and his current alias – Joseph Friedlander. But when we went to the place, he wasn't there. Of course, we were immediately on to the Russians, but they claimed they hadn't told him. We've now informed them that if either they don't come up with him or we haven't got our hands on him by midnight tonight, the deal will be off. We suspect they tipped off his contact and he's now trying to flee the country. We can only guess that there's been some sort of power struggle back in Moscow about whether Friedlander/Davidson could be sacrificed or not and the upshot is he's been given a chance to get out. He can't use any official means. The Russians know we're monitoring all flights to the Soviet Bloc, all traffic from the embassy, the Diplomatic Bag, all Soviet Bloc ships in UK ports and territorial waters. So he's essentially on his own – to a certain point. A small Soviet submarine moved into the North Sea from the Baltic during the last week. Its last reported position was about twelve miles opposite the mouth of the River Blackwater. We believe that it is there to pick him up."

"So couldn't you just stick a naval ship or two alongside?" I asked.

"At the moment, it's just outside the twelve mile limit. But more important, our new political masters have told us that they do not want a major international incident with the Russians at this juncture. Aircraft may fly over, to keep tabs on the sub. Air-sea rescue helicopters may buzz around discretely. Even lifeboats may be on standby. But not any naval craft."

"So essentially it's up to the Department," added Iain. "It's assumed that he'll try to get out there by motorboat, perhaps even a yacht if he's smart. We've got three cutters in the area, one just east of Foulness, one lying off Clacton and the other one's just about to arrive here. We've no idea where he'll set off from. It's unlikely to be too obvious I'd guess from what we know of the man. It's been suggested that you should join us on the cutter, not least because you're the only person who's actually see him."

"Of course, it's always possible that the sub is a decoy and he'll be flown out by private light aircraft from some obscure airstrip in the south-west," observed the saturnine Jones. "But trying to prevent that really would be looking for a needle in a haystack, so we'll give this our best shot."

"Can't you do something with radar and the normal controls on planes?" I asked.

"Well, to tell the truth, an exercise has been put in hand. If you hear on the news later today about a light aircraft that mysteriously and unfortunately crashed, you might believe it had been shot down, but, of course, you'd never know. But it's still a thousand to one chance."

Wally French appeared to inform us that the cutter had arrived. He led us to the boat, HMRC *Vigilant*, joining us on board. The skipper and crew were unknown to me, apart from Morry Gold, who apparently had previous service in the cutters and was known to be a useful man if someone had to be restrained.

We cast off and were quickly past the old town of Harwich and Landguard Point and into the open sea. The cutter bounced about a bit, but the expectancy of the chase prevented any of us from feeling seasick.

"We're going to sit about four miles off the Naze," explained the skipper, a bearded stocky man named Arthur Nash. "Then we'll see what comes up on the radar. We've got the location of the sub, so anything on a direct course and we'll go and have a sniff around."

"Will the Russian submarine know that we're there?" I asked.

"He'll know there's a vessel – but he won't be able to tell it's us. On his radar we won't look any different to a large fishing boat or even a trawler. Why did you ask?"

"Well, I suppose I was wondering whether Davidson would be able to contact the submarine in some way."

"By radio, you mean? They'd have to surface and I assume they don't intend to do that until he's pretty close – especially if they have to go within the twelve mile limit. So basically, they'll be doing the same as us, tracking ships on their radar and they'll surface when they're confident it's the right ship. That's about the size of it."

After a while I got the hang of how to make sense of the radar screen. Of course, it was less the nature or position of the various dots, but plotting their course. True to the traditions of the Department, no dot was regarded as innocent until it dropped off the screen. Even those heading in a steady line along the coast weren't dismissed, as there was always the chance that they might suddenly veer out to sea.

Fortunately, as it was December, there was not much traffic about. Equally fortunately, there was a bleak sun and white clouds in a pale blue sky, with only a light wind. We were given thick woollen sweaters to put on under our jackets to ward off the cold. It could very easily have been a much nastier day. The day before had seen a Force 8 gale with leaden clouds chasing across the sky and teeming rain.

"What would you do, if you were this chap?" began Wally French, a tin mug of steaming sweet instant coffee in his hand. "A dash out to sea in a fast motorboat to try and outrun us? Or a motor yacht, pretending to head in a different direction and then make a last-minute feint?"

"From what we know of him, I'd have to say the latter," replied Jones.

"Do you think he's had a boat waiting for him all the time?" I asked. "Or do we think he's going to head for somewhere like Burnham and steal a boat? Or if they've had to set this escape up quickly in the last week or so, did someone get a boat ready for him somewhere?"

"I see what you're getting at," said Iain. "It's possible that the CPMs (Coast Preventive Men) round here might've noticed a new ship appearing in the last week or so. We can radio back to get them to check."

"But, of course, half of them won't be on duty or they'll be off on their bikes round the cliffs somewhere," remarked Wally. "But it's worth a shot. I don't expect all that many ships get new moorings this time of year."

"No – the problem will be tracking down the CPMs. Don't forget to try their favourite pubs as well," added Morry.

A message was duly sent. Whether it would prove to be any help, who knew?

Shortly after 11 a.m., a boat seemed to be heading on the right track – and within our area. We let it get to within about a mile and then moved to intercept it. It turned out to be a trawler, well known to the crew of the *Vigilant* and to Harwich Waterguard. After it left us, we could see it on the radar heading out into the North Sea.

As the next couple of hours drifted slowly by, we heard from both *Venturous* and *Valiant* further south that they had made similar fruitless interceptions. At last a few sightings of ships newly moored in the area started to come through. In all cases the message back was to check – extremely unobtrusively – whether the ships were still there and, if so, to maintain watch on them.

"Let's hope this isn't a wild goose chase," remarked Wally, "or there'll be a lot of annoyed CPMs who've spent the day freezing their arses for nothing."
"Let 'em earn their money for a change," said Morry.

At around 3p.m., Skipper Nash reminded Iain that the cutters couldn't remain at sea indefinitely.

"How long do you anticipate keeping this up?" he asked. "We won't be able to deploy three cutters indefinitely."
"What do you think, Jones?" asked Iain.
"Ideally, I'd like to keep up a watch until that sub departs. But I accept you can only do what you can."
"Well, may I suggest," said Nash, "that you allow one of the cutters to go off station in at 4 p.m., say, and the other two cover until 10 p.m., then the first one will return and one of the others will go off-watch for six hours. If we move about six miles south and *Valiant* moves four or five miles north from off Foulness, we could cover the area while *Venturous* went off.
"You're supplied sufficiently for an all-night watch?" asked Jones.
"Yes – but you'll have to make do with sausages, baked beans and tinned potatoes for your supper."

"If this chap is going to try and reach the sub, he's got some difficult choices," observed Nash. "If he goes out while it's still light, he can see where he's going better and he can see the sub better. On the other hand, there's more ships about and if he thinks there are ships trying to intercept him, he's more easily spotted. But, assuming he knows about radar, he should know that there's much less traffic once it gets dark, so we can track him much more easily."

"So, if you were him you'd try to make it in daylight?" asked Iain.

"Just before twilight. There'll be lots of ships coming back into harbour, which might be his best hope."

About half an hour later, we got a message on the radio to say that a motor yacht that had been moored in the small harbour at Tollesbury since Saturday had taken advantage of the high tide to set off out towards the sea.

"Odd spot to try and conceal a vessel," remarked Wally. "Tollesbury is so quiet an inflatable rubber duck would stick out like a sore thumb!"

"It seems to me that Davidson would like somewhere quiet. He can look around and see if he's being watched. In somewhere like Burnham or Clacton, the place would be too busy and he could never be sure," suggested Iain. "But, of course, there's no special reason it should be him."

But as we gathered round the radar screen, a vessel emerging into the Virley Channel was heading in broadly the right direction.

"I don't believe they've had time or the people to set up a whole load of diversions," observed Jones. "If we suspect this is our man, let's make sure he doesn't give us the slip."

We moved gently southwards. The dot on the radar screen continued on a heading that would take it three or four miles south of the submarine.

"Check the position of the sub," called out Nash. "If it moves, let me know instantly."

About two miles west of us, the dot changed direction, on to a new course that would take it directly to the submarine.

"Right!" said Nash. "We'll go for him."

"Would it be worth getting *Venturous* in as well in case he tries to outmanoeuvre us?" suggested Iain.

"Fat chance!" retorted Nash. "But better safe than sorry."

HMRC *Venturous* was encouraged to join us. They claimed they had already spotted the ship and were on their way.

The light was beginning to fade, but within twenty minutes we could see the ship heading out towards us. To the south, I could also make out the dim outline of *Venturous*. The two cutters acted in concert. *Vigilant* moved across the front of the ship, while *Venturous* approached from the side.

It was a small motorised yacht, with a mast but no sail. It was being steered from within an enclosed cabin. Davidson, assuming it was him, attempted to swing away round us, but he was evidently not an experienced sailor, and ended up with his bow against our starboard side. *Venturous* stood off about sixty feet away.

Suddenly a man appeared. I recognised Davidson. He had a sub-machinegun in his hand and fired several rounds at the *Vigilant*. I could hear the bullets rattling against the side of the ship. From experience, I knew weapons like that were effective at close quarters, but their range was pathetic.

Nash pulled out a loudhailer from a locker,

"Do that again and we'll ram you!" he called out. "Are you going to come quietly or do you want to make it unpleasant for yourself?"
"Why don't you just give him a couple of shots across his bows or shoot the bastard!" declared Jones.
"Customs and Excise staff never carry guns – not even the cutters," explained Iain.

Some more shots spat against the side of the ship.

"But we do have ways of making ourselves understood," said Nash.

Several members of the crew wheeled out a fire hose. A couple of minutes pumping got it into condition to start firing a steady stream of icy water directly at Davidson. Soaked to the skin, he threw his gun into the air and dived into the sea.

"That bastard is not going to kill himself on my watch!" cried out Nash. "Throw a couple of lifebuoys in and get after him!"

A couple of the crew leapt over the side and, held up by buoyancy jackets, splashed over to where Davidson was struggling in the water. Evidently he was trying to kill himself as he tried to fight them off, but one of them knocked him cold. Between the two of them, he was secured in a lifebuoy and all three were slowly and painstakingly dragged on board. There they were covered in blankets and Davidson was put in handcuffs.

"Skipper, you should know that the sub has just surfaced," called out the radar operator.

"Send 'em a message on the radio that their passenger is unavoidably detained and won't be able to make it," said Iain.

"You don't think they might try and intercept us?" I asked.

"The moment they surfaced, there'd've been an RAF plane launched to fly over. If they attempted anything hostile in UK territorial waters, we'd be in our rights to blow the bastards out of the water, so I think their next course of action will be to head home with their tails between their legs," said Jones.

Sure enough – within five minutes of our message being sent, the radar operator announced that the submarine had submerged again and appeared to be heading away. Shortly afterwards, the roar of a jet engine could be heard in the sky a couple of miles to the east of us.

The journey back was something of an anticlimax. While we all celebrated with mugs of sweet instant coffee flavoured with a tot of rum, Davidson sat under his blanket, shivering a bit, saying absolutely nothing. Nobody spoke to him. I peered at him once, just to confirm he was the man I'd seen by Russell Square Tube station, but he gave not a flicker of recognition of having seen me. I wondered what was going on in his mind. Did he think the Russians had sold him out? Did he expect that if he said nothing, he'd be exchanged at some future date? Did he think his contacts in the UK might help him escape? Or was he just coming to terms with the realisation that he'd been caught and that there might be no escape?

We arrived back in Harwich in darkness. Police cars and others were at the quayside to meet us and Davidson was whisked away, along with Iain Cogbill and a quietly elated Mr Jones.

Wally French, Morry Gold and I repaired to the Jolly Jack Tar and enjoyed a celebratory couple of pints. Then I rang Rosemary and told her the good news – though I probably shouldn't have done on an open line – and made my way to bed, exhausted.

SIXTEEN – HARWICH AND LONDON – YET MORE UNOFFICAL SLEUTHING

I arrived at work the following day feeling tremendously refreshed. In addition, on my way walking to work, something clicked belatedly in my brain that had been twitching away below the surface.

After the bulk of the entries had been cleared by ten o'clock, I went over to the AC's office, to seek a few words with Jim.

"I trust you enjoyed your sea trip yesterday," he began. "I understand it was successful and that we're now winding up our part of the Davenport stuff."

"Has Iain Cogbill been in touch?"

"Yes. They're concentrating on trying to catch this Devaney chap and leaving the funnies to deal with Davidson. But knowing you, you still think it's not over yet."

"Perhaps I just don't like loose ends."

"You mean you're preternaturally nosey. Don't forget curiosity killed the cat."

"I reckon I've got a few lives left yet."

"Well, spill the beans."

"It's about Imrie. It seems to me that everyone has forgotten that someone had to contact him, to tell him what needed to be done, presumably mainly to tell Davenport to get a Russian consignment through without difficulties. Perhaps it was even this person who told Imrie about Davenport's guilty little secret, so he could blackmail him. Who was this person? I can't imagine the Russian Embassy just rang him up. So who did it and how?"

"What, do you want to get the Essex Constabulary to check his phone records?"

"Well, first perhaps we could check what happened here. It seems possible that it might've been necessary to contact him here. We might see what his secretary can tell us."

The secretary, smirking as ever, was summoned.

"Did Mr Imrie ever have telephone calls that you considered unusual?" asked Jim.

"Not that I can recall," she replied in a defensive tone.

"It's all right. No-one's trying to get at you. It's just that it's likely Mr Imrie received phone calls that neither he nor they wanted anyone to know about – certainly not the subject of their conversations. That might suggest that shortly after getting a particular phone call, Mr Imrie went out for a while. Far enough, I guess, to use a public phone. Now can you think really hard about that please, Pam?"

"Recently there might have been one a week ago last Wednesday and possibly the following day," I added.

"Well, he often nipped out, so it wouldn't be obvious…"

"Please think hard," said Jim. "This is important."

"Well, the only ones I can think of were to do with his golf. He was keen on his golf, Mr Imrie. But mostly it was other Scottish men who rang to arrange games. Just occasionally he'd get a message from Mr Wilson, who once told me he was an old friend from back home – but he definitely wasn't a Scottish man… and he had a rather high voice. I remember that. It was rather an odd voice. He would just say, the game is on for one o'clock, two o'clock or three o'clock. Sometimes Mr Imrie would go out a while after one of these calls but not always. If I remember, Mr Wilson did call a week last Wednesday and I think he said the game was on for three o'clock – but I'm pretty sure Mr Imrie didn't go out for quite a long time afterwards."

"Didn't it strike you as a bit odd, a golf game starting at three o'clock?" exclaimed Jim.

"I don't know nothing about golf."

"You'd be lucky to get a round in under three hours. At this time of year you'd've been playing in the dark for the best part of two."

"Evidently a code as to whether Imrie needed to telephone back and I guess how urgently. Perhaps three o'clock meant that he needed to get in touch but it wasn't urgent," I suggested.

"That sounds about right. But that only gets us a step down the path."

"Miss Leadbitter," I began, "Can you possibly remember what time Mr Imrie next left the office for any length of time after he received that phone call?"

"The call was about 2 p.m. I logged it in the office diary… The only time he went out that afternoon was at 3.30, when he said he had a meeting with the SAC. It wasn't in the diary, but he said they'd bumped into each other in the corridor at lunchtime. He came back about 4.15."

"Could you check with the SAC's secretary whether any such meeting took place, please, Pam?" said Jim.

She returned five minutes later.

"She can't remember any meeting."

"Then I suggest I wander around and see whether I can spot any potential payphones in the vicinity. It'll have to be somewhere he couldn't be spotted. Otherwise it would be bound to strike anyone here as rather odd," I said.

In the event I found it remarkably quickly. Just beyond the main entrance lobby was a sort of large cubbyhole where agents could use a payphone. Because they had apparently argued that their calls were sometimes private and Customs staff should not be allowed to spy on them, this little room had a wooden door. So anyone inside could be neither seen nor heard.

The time between 3.30 and 4.15 on that Wednesday fitted between times when the room was likely to have been used by agents. Imrie presumably knew this. He would hardly want to be seen queuing for a payphone when he had a perfectly good telephone of his own.

I rang the local telephone exchange and asked whether they kept records of calls from payphones. They confirmed that they did, but that they were only available to the police. Stretching the truth somewhat, I explained that I was trying to sort out the position after a man had killed himself and was believed to have made his last phone call for this number between 3.35 and 4.10 on that particular day. It was believed that this was to a relative. But from the records we had there was no way of getting in touch with any relative.

My voice was evidently more honest than I was, as the girl agreed to check the records and when I rang back a quarter of an hour later, she told me that there had only been one call during that time from this number, to 01 242 7668. Apart from knowing this was a London number, it meant nothing to me.

On an impulse, I rang the number. A rather high voice with a strong central European accent answered. "Hallo. Who is it there?"

"Is that Pfeiffers?" I asked, plucking a name pretty well out of the air.

"No. This is not Pfeiffer. It is a private number. Good day to you."

He put the phone down.

Of course, I could easily be wrong, but the voice sounded identical to that of the young man who had met Iain Cogbill and me when we did our check on Silberstein's ledgers.

As it was a Friday, I knew that the Waterguard wouldn't go to lunch until they went off shift and would then head to the pub for several hours. I wanted to pick Morry Gold's brains, but first I had to tell Jim part of the truth, but not all of it. My reason for doing so was that I feared he would pass what I'd learnt on to the police and that they would just drop it – or take so long over it any trail would have gone completely cold. So I told him that I had found what I thought was likely to have been the phone, but that only the police could have access to the records. He expressed doubts as to whether the local police would be interested and suggested that if I wanted to take it further, I'd best talk to Iain Cogbill or my 'friends' among the 'funnies'. We had different perspectives on this and I reckoned he was more concerned to ensure that the reputation of Harwich as an uncorrupt and effective organisation was re-established than tracking down Imrie's shady contact.

So I made my way over to the freight examination shed and met Morry apparently heading in the opposite direction.

"I was just coming to see you," he began.
"Ditto," I replied.
"Wally tells me that they're planning to fold this operation up now," he said almost indignantly.
"That's the message I've been getting."
"Well, don't you think they've completely missed something?"
"There are certainly a number of loose ends."
"Loose ends! This is a bloody great bit of the rope that held the whole thing together!"
"Go on."
"From what we've been able to work out about this lot, a load of Russian diamonds get smuggled through here, assisted by Imrie and Davenport. Weissman takes custody and then the Russians get loads of hard currency carried into the Moscow Narodny Bank by that bloke we fished out of the sea yesterday. So what's missing?"

"How the diamonds get turned into hard currency."

"Exactly. Weissman isn't a mensch. There's no way anyone serious is going to buy millions of pounds' worth of hot Russian diamonds from him. Davidson may be the contact who ferries them around, puts the right people in touch with the right people, that sort of thing. But someone has to be cooling those diamonds down, mixing them up with *echte*, sorry, legit ones, guaranteeing no fuss and no comebacks. The moment I heard a bit of this, I've been keeping my ear to the ground and word is that around thirty million's worth of diamonds and next to ten million's worth of top class jewellery has been washed clean and sent on its way. That requires people with a name, with contacts, with the size to mix the stock around and the greed to see the profit. That forty million that Davidson got back to the Russians will also have lined someone's pockets to the tune of twenty million or so."

"It's nice to know that communism can do its bit to benefit capitalists."

"They may have a legitimate part of their business, but to me, they're just crooks."

"So, have you any idea who?"

"There are half a dozen candidates in Hatton Garden, big enough, respectable enough on the outside, and greedy enough."

"I take it one of those would be Silberstein?"

"Yes – at the top or close to the top of the list. Why have you come up with them?"

"Two reasons. One – they were among the clues I believe Davenport intended to leave or possibly intended to buy his way out of being blackmailed. Two – the person I believe was Imrie's contact about the illegal consignments works for Silbersteins. Or I'm pretty certain that's him."

"So?"

"I'm trying to think what best to do. I ought to tell Jim Round and Iain Cogbill or try to get in touch with someone from Special Branch who helped me…"

"But…" Morry peered at me quite fiercely.

"No-one seems very keen to have a go at Silbersteins and I'm afraid that if I tell them, nothing will happen. Though I shouldn't, a little voice is telling me to take this further myself without telling anyone."

"And you have some sort of plan?"

"No. Not yet. I need to think about it for a bit… My girlfriend is coming down to meet my parents in London tomorrow. In fact I'm meeting her this evening at St Pancras. I'll let it puzzle around in my brain over the weekend."

"Is this the 'meet the parents before the wedding' sort of meeting?"

"Yes... Now an idea is starting to come. I haven't bought Rosemary a ring. What if we went to Silbersteins to buy a diamond ring? Will they be open on Saturday?"

"Yes. The Sabbath is today."

"Suppose we claimed to be a bit in the know and after we'd seen a few quite pricey diamonds, we asked to see some cheaper diamonds of the same quality but more questionable provenance, say Russian ones? Would they just boot us out or would they take the bait?"

"Saturday would be a good day as they'll have some weekend staff on – you know, sons who are at college or training as lawyers or accountants are likely to have to take a turn at the weekend. You'd need to name a plausible contact, though."

"Do you know of anyone?"

"Hmm... I'll need to think about that. But if you get offered some Russian diamonds, so what?"

"I ask how they can guarantee that someone from the authorities won't come along later and confiscate my girlfriend's ring because it has an illegally-imported stone in it. If we can tape-record the conversation, we'd surely have enough to bring to Iain Cogbill or Special Branch. That'd get them in to act on the rest."

"If they actually were Davidson's contact, it could be extremely dangerous. If they suspected anything, you and your girlfriend might easily just disappear for good."

"Before I did anything I'd have to be absolutely certain Rosemary was prepared to go along with it. She's already faced death twice as a result of me not thinking through what I'd been doing and saying. I probably shouldn't even be asking her."

"But you will."

"She'll want to know what's happening – and I don't want to lie to her. Unfortunately, I fear she'll want to do it, even though I try my hardest to persuade her not to. We're too much alike in some things."

"Well, if you do decide to do something like that, you should plan it carefully and then talk it through with someone wise and experienced, like Wally French. And then make sure you've got a plan to get you out or, failing that, back-up."

"Do you think Wally would mind us talking this through with him now?"

"I believe it would be an excellent idea."

I returned to the Long Room for the final rush of entries to be cleared from the Esbjerg ferry, with a rather more carefully conceived plan, which I told myself I would do my level best to dissuade Rosemary from taking part in.

I met her at St Pancras Station and we made our way to a cheap hotel I had found in Pimlico. Our room turned out to have an enormous double bed, but was so cold that we clung together so tightly we could just as well have done with a single. There was a gas fire that appeared to give off a minimal amount of light but no heat and the bedclothes were as thin as one could get without them being translucent. We ended up putting on jeans and sweaters and two pairs of socks, and still barely warmed up enough to get to sleep.

"I think we can tick this place off our list for the first night of our honeymoon," she remarked as we devoured some hot porridge the following morning.

However, the previous evening over dinner in a hamburger place near Victoria Station, I had explained what I'd been up to during the previous week, including Davidson's capture, and where my thinking had led me about Silbersteins. As I both feared and expected, she was eager to go ahead with the plan to visit them and get their nefarious dealings out into the open.

"If I've managed to survive being attacked by Russian assassins, surely I can avoid getting killed by some jewellers," she remarked.

Besides, with Wally's help, I had devised a plan that should allow us to use injured innocence or customer frustration to get ourselves out of any tricky situation. It would really be only if someone tried to examine Rosemary's handbag, where the tape recorder and microphone would be concealed, that we might find ourselves in serious trouble. And we had set in hand a plan for such an eventuality.

We caught a bus up to the Strand and wandered round the Civil Service Stores until we found a suitable tape recorder and microphone – and a couple of tapes. Unfortunately, once we started to play it, its insuperable defect was only too readily apparent. As the tape reels turned round, the machine made a continuous whirring noise which would be impossible to disguise or fail to be noticed. The shop assistant mentioned a shop further along the Strand that might sell more sophisticated equipment. Indeed, it had – but the cheapest one that was silent enough for us to use was well beyond what we could afford. So we decided that as a good deal of what we were about to do was dependent on bluff, we would return to the Civil Service Stores and buy a machine that resembled the other one, run the tape so that it looked as though it had been recording, but actually not run it at all, apart from possibly when we entered the premises, so that when we came to claim the conversations had been taped, we had a grain of verisimilitude to offer.

We ought perhaps to have reflected that this was not the most propitious start to our 'bit of amateur sleuthing', as Rosemary liked to call it. In any event, we caught another bus up to Holborn Circus and walked to Hatton Garden.

The first bit would be easy. We didn't need to pretend to be a young couple deeply in love – apart from the diamond engagement ring bit, as Rosemary had made very clear that if I wasted money on something unnecessary like that she'd be deeply hurt and upset. On entering the shop, I was relieved to see that the young fair-haired man with the high voice and central European accent was not behind the counter, but a willowy Jewish lad of about seventeen. He was exactly what I'd hoped for.

"Good morning. My fiancée and I have just got engaged and I want to buy her a nice diamond engagement ring." (We had, of course, changed out of our sweaters and jeans and now, especially Rosemary, looked as though we might actually be able to afford an expensive diamond ring).
"You've come to the right place, sir. What sort of price range were you thinking of?"
"Fifty or sixty pounds, I guess."
"You should get a very nice stone for that amount. Your fiancée is a very lucky lady."
"I know," said Rosemary, giving me a passionate kiss. "It's so nice the boutique in Carnaby Street is doing so well."
"You know I'd do anything for you, darling."
"Let me get some rings out for you."

We looked through a dozen or so rings in various settings, Rosemary playing a full part in an indecisive adoration of the diamonds.
"But you don't get as much as you think you'll get – even for £60," she remarked.

"I see what you mean… A friend of ours knows people in the diamond business and she said you could get better value if the diamonds were Russian. Do you have any Russian diamonds?" I asked.

"I think your friend must be mistaken," replied the youth, looking a little troubled.

"Genevieve? She's not usually mistaken about that sort of thing! Her father – Mr van Hoogstraaten – is in the diamond business, so she told us. She said she her engagement ring from Philip has a Russian diamond – and the stone is a lot bigger than any of these."

"I'll have to ask my colleague."

He disappeared to the back of the shop. This was the critical moment. If Martin Klugman or the fair-haired man with the east European accent appeared with him, they were likely to recognise me and we would have blown it. In any event, they might decide not to take the bait. Rosemary took the opportunity to switch off the tape recorder.

To my relief a tall, skinny young man of about my age, with a traditional Jewish beard and haircut appeared.

"My name is Bernard Silberstein. My cousin says you seem to know a bit about the diamond business and want to get yourselves a bargain by getting a Russian stone?"

"That's right. We haven't been making so much money in the boutique without going for the best bargains we can," I replied.

"Well, I believe we may be able to accommodate you, sir and madam. Would you like to come through? For obvious reasons such stock isn't kept on public display."

"Not that a passer-by could tell, I imagine."

"Who knows when a customer isn't a rival, who might wish to damage you?"

"A good point. We face the same problem in Carnaby Street."

We went along a corridor, past the room where Iain Cogbill and I had interviewed Mr Klugman and into a similar office, cupboards with small drawers all round the room and a table with four chairs round it squeezed into the middle.

"Well, these are the sort of stones that would be in your price range. We would put them in a setting of your choice, of course."

"They're lovely!" cried Rosemary enthusiastically. "So much bigger!"

"If we bought one of these, would there be any risk that the police or someone like that would confiscate the ring because it was Russian?"

"If you didn't tell then I don't know how they'd ever find out. In any case, we could give you a guarantee on the basis of 'as far as we are aware' – something like that."

"Stop bothering the nice man, darling," said Rosemary. "Let me just have a closer look at these diamonds."

At that moment, Martin Klugman chose to put his head round the door.

"Bernie, where's that invoice for Kempinskis?" he began and then spotted me. "What the hell are you doing here! Bernie – do you know who this fellow is? He's from Customs and Excise! He was here a few weeks ago going through the books!"

"What's your game?" demanded Silberstein.

He shot outside and came back within a few seconds with a semi-automatic pistol in his hand.

"Bernie! What do you think you're playing at!" demanded Klugman.

"Come on! Spit it out!" shouted Silberstein. "What are you two up to?"

"That's an interesting gun you've got there," I replied. "Russian is it?"

While he had gone out, I'd surreptitiously moved my leg away from the chair, so I was free to swing it round – much as I had done in my early years as a rather dirty football player – and catch him behind and just below his knee. As he started to fall backwards, I grabbed hold of his wrist and held the gun on the table. I then hit his wrist as hard as I could with my other hand. He released the gun on to the table and I picked it up.

"Before you start pointing guns at anyone, you really ought to release the safety catch, like so," I explained. Silberstein was getting himself to his feet.

"Like this," added Rosemary, pulling back the innocuous safety catch on a small replica revolver which we had bought in a shop about six doors east from the Civil Service Stores. Pointing it at Silberstein's young cousin who appeared also to be contemplating violence, she added, "Stay where you are!"

"You're not going to shoot us!" cried Silberstein.

"No," I replied. "Not to kill, anyway. Now I think we'll go into a larger office. You too, Mr Klugman. You will all keep your hands above your heads please."

We found a much larger room and sat the three of them down where we could see them.

"Is there anyone else here?" asked Rosemary.

"No," replied Klugman.

"If you do anything, we'll report you to the police as robbers," said Silberstein.

"Go ahead and call them," I retorted. "I don't mind being arrested as a robber. At the trial however, a vast amount would come out about how Silberstein & Co were the route through which illegally smuggled Russian diamonds and Faberge jewellery were turned into hard cash which was then sent back to Russia, for a total sum of over £60 million, out of which you made £20 million profit –"

"What!" exclaimed Klugman, his face as white as a sheet.

"Moreover, you employed and continue to employ a man who's the main contact for the Soviet Embassy and Louis Davidson, who you probably know was caught trying to escape to Russia a couple of days ago and is now in police custody."

"What is all this about? Are you mad?" demanded Klugman.

"Ask your colleague, Mr Silberstein there," I replied. "He can confirm what I've just said, can't you?"

"It's all lies."

"Well, perhaps I should ring the police and tell them there's a robbery in progress here?" suggested Rosemary.

Bernard Silberstein gave her a venomous look, but waved his hands in defeat.

"The question which you need to consider is whether Silberstein & Co can be saved as a business – and, if so, how much of it," I continued.

"What do you mean?" said Klugman.

"Well, we've been tape-recording ever since we came in here."

Rosemary opened her bag and showed them the tape recorder, playing a bit of our initial conversation with the youth. Meanwhile, I kept an eye on them. But with Silberstein's gun in my hand, no-one seemed at all interested in trying anything. Rosemary had been right. These were jewellers, not Russian hoods.

"I knew nothing of any of this, I swear." began Klugman.

"I'm prepared to believe you. But the innocence of some people in the company won't save it. We already know enough to ensure that there'll be a full-scale search of these premises, in such a way that the press are bound to find out. It'll go to court and the press and TV will have a field day. The only way you can save something of the company is to co-operate. By the way, in a couple of minutes two men will come into the shop. You –" I pointed to the youth. "– will go and get them and bring them through here. They are colleagues of ours."

"What do you mean by co-operate?" asked Klugman.

"First, I want the real books where you recorded these illegal transactions managed by Davidson."

"We recorded nothing – for obvious reasons," said Silberstein.

"Don't take us for idiots! I don't believe you. Besides, compliance isn't optional. Either you do what we ask or any deal is off and Silberstein & Co will be destroyed, either in court, the press or both."

"Get the books, Bernie," said Klugman. "You evidently know where they are."

"Just wait a moment. One of my colleagues will accompany you. Second, I want a written and signed statement by you, Mr Silberstein, setting out exactly what went on in relation to the sale of these illegal Russian diamonds and the Faberge jewellery. Third, I want to know the name and whereabouts of the fair-haired young man who I met when I came here before, who's your link to Davidson and the Russian Embassy."

"That's easy," said Klugman, eager to keep on the right side of us, "That's Karel Jesensky. Edelmann's cousin's cousin. Or so I was told."

At that moment, Wally French and Morry Gold came into the shop. Within a minute, they joined us.

"Guns?" said Wally. "I thought we never carried guns."

"This was his," I replied, pointing it in Silberstein's direction.

Morry went off with Silberstein and returned within a few minutes with the real set of books, which I examined, while Silberstein wrote out his statement.

When he had written it and signed it, witnessed by Klugman and Wally French, I marked the various books and papers in which the diamond and jewellery transactions were recorded with 'C&ES' and a separate number for each one. Then I wrote out two copies of a receipt using carbon paper helpfully supplied by Klugman, which Wally French, Klugman and Silberstein and I all signed.

"These will be taken immediately to a highly secure place," I told them. "I'm also going to hang on to the gun for now. I'll get it back to you later. Now the final thing, I need you to tell us the address of this Karel Jesensky. If he's not there or appears to be have been tipped off, our agreement with you is dead. Do you understand me?"

"Yes," replied Silberstein wearily. "He's got a flat in 24 Millman Street. It's off Guildford Street, west of Grays Inn Road."

"Can you get him on the phone there?" asked Rosemary.

"Yes. Do you want the number?"

"Yes."

He wrote it down.

"If he went missing for any reason, were there any particular numbers you would have needed to ring? You know what I mean."

He wrote down a couple more numbers.

We had done all we could there and had achieved what we had set out to do. We set off at once for the nearby IB offices in Fetter Lane.

"Even if they do ring someone up to try and stop us," said Wally, "we'll be in Fetter Lane before they can do anything."

It being a Saturday, there were only a couple of duty officers around. Wally dealt with them. Seniority and age have their advantages. The duty officer solemnly agreed to put all the papers we had given him and sealed in an envelope with 'TOP SECRET – To be opened only by Mr Iain Cogbill' written on it, into the most secure safe in the most secure part of the building and to inform Mr Cogbill as soon as possible that there was an important package of evidence for him 'with the compliments of Harwich Customs'.

"I hope you don't mind not being mentioned," Wally said to Rosemary. "But I'd assumed you regarded this as strictly unofficial."

"Quite so."

Though she protested, I insisted that we got a cab up to Guildford Street, to give her leg a rest. Morry went to 24 Millman Street and found that Mr Jesensky wasn't in. The woman who lived in the basement, who appeared to act as a sort of concierge, told him that Jesensky always took his lunch on a Saturday in a little Polish café in Exmouth Market, staying on to play chess with friends.

Rosemary insisted on walking and it certainly wasn't a long walk. We spotted the café quickly enough – café Wroclaw. Wally and Morry went in and ordered a couple of coffees and cakes at the counter. They were mainly there to prevent Jesensky from trying to escape round the back when he saw me. As it happened, when Rosemary and I entered, he was so engrossed in his game of chess, he didn't notice us. But I saw him almost immediately, at a table of four – Jesensky playing against another man, with two onlookers. Two of the others were men, a little older than Jesensky. The other was a woman with long, dark hair.

Rosemary and I made our way over to the table and stood behind Jesensky.

"Checkmate!" we both said at the same time, and couldn't resist laughing.

"Oh God!" she cried. "We're even getting to think like each other!"

Jesensky turned round. Seeing me, he rose immediately, but I waved Silberstein's gun at him and he sat down.

"What's going on?" demanded one of the men, in a strong Polish accent.

"You may regard this man as a friend," I said. "But he's actually a stool pigeon for the Russians. We're from Customs and Excise to talk to him about illegal activities that have greatly helped the Russians."

"It's nonsense!" retorted Jesensky. But the damage had been done. Even the slightest whiff of Soviet connections would frighten off Polish émigrés.

"But we know it isn't, don't we?" I said sitting opposite him. Rosemary took up a seat next to me and, grabbing an extra chair, Wally and Morry joined us. "You see we've just come from Silberstein & Co and they've given us a very full statement concerning your activities."

"They're lying!"

"They weren't really in a position to do that. Besides, when I discovered the number Imrie at Harwich rang in emergencies – and who phoned him from time to time – you answered."

"I just happened to be there. Anyone at Silberstein could've answered it."

"That's not what they told us. Anyway, I'm sure you're quite happy to stonewall us."

"Stonewall?"

"Admit to nothing. But you see, Mr Gold is just about to take our picture on his camera."

"There's plenty of background to show where we are," said Morry as he pressed the button.

"Though your friends at the Russian Embassy probably don't know who we are, we'll make sure they learn that we're Customs & Excise officials investigating the illegal import of diamonds and Fabergé jewellery worth around £40 million. Of course, that won't come as a great surprise to them. But when we charge various people from Silberstein & Co and Louis Davidson, we might just decide that rather than compel you to talk, we could just let you go. This photo will just find its way to the Embassy or one of the stool pigeons known to our colleagues in the Security Services."

"You know what would happen then?"

"I believe I can guess. But you have a choice. You can talk to us and the Security Services may be prepared to look after you. It's up to you Mr Jesensky."

"You are a fucking bastard!"

"I'm pleased you've learnt British slang so well, Mr Jesensky. Does that indicate you're willing to co-operate?"

"Yes," he said in a tone of resignation.

"Right. Will you please write down on these sheets of paper exactly what your role was in the illegal import of the diamonds and the Faberge jewellery, who your contacts were and how you made contact with them."

"While he's doing that, do you think we could get something to eat?" said Rosemary. "All this sleuthing has made me absolutely starving."

So while Jesensky wrote, we enjoyed slices of Polish kabanos sausage on light rye bread with pickled cucumber, Russian salad and sour cream. As we decided we'd earned it, we washed it down with a glass of Polish Zywiec beer each.

"So now I've done this, what are you going to do to protect me?" he demanded.

"Let me read it first," I replied. "Assuming it's satisfactory, it will be put in a place of highest security. Though it's unlikely that the Russian Embassy will know anything about it until Monday, I'd advise you to go to Scotland Yard – or a closer police station, if you wish – and say that you have important information for Special Branch about matters of national security and if they let you go your life will be in danger and the information which you have will be lost. Or you can hide and hope."

I read through the statement, which largely tallied with that of Bernard Silberstein, though it also mentioned Silberstein's father as being involved. Jesensky had been Davidson's contact and, in effect, worked as a sort of postbox, keeping Weissman and Imrie informed as required.

"I'm sorry," I said firmly. "You haven't set out here how you contacted the Russian Embassy and who your contact was there."

"If I do that, I'm a dead man. Nothing will protect me."

"They can scarcely kill you twice. What you've written down here is more than enough to get you killed once, don't you agree?"

"You're not going to be able to touch them. Surely you know that!"

"Yes. But I've a tidy mind."

"Perhaps if you just told us the name and telephone number?" suggested Rosemary. "After all, it's possible we might've got them from someone else. Is it this number written down here?"

"The second one. But I never actually knew the name. You must believe me. That number isn't a direct line. It's a phone with some sort of tape-recorder linked to it. I'd leave a message and a voice would get back to me with instructions or information. Honestly, I never knew who it was!"

"Honesty and you don't strike me as sitting close together. I simply don't believe you. You must've had a plan for meeting your contact. After all, there might well be times when you couldn't say things on the phone."

"I never knew his name. There was a place where we met – but only once. By the canal, in Camden Town. I'd go to Camden Town Tube and walk north until I reached the canal. Then I'd go down on to the path by the side of the canal. He'd come from the other end. But I swear on my mother's life, I never knew his name."

"So how did you get into this in the first place? You can't have been recruited over the phone," I said.

"I was recruited in Kosice, my home town. I got to live in the West and keep all I earn, plus extra payments for anything I can give them on Czech, Slovak and Polish émigré groups. Also my family get to do well. Not so well if I mess up."

"All that's a matter for the security people. Will you sign and date this, please, and we'll witness your signature. Then you're free to go, after one more little task."

"Which is?"

"I want you to phone the contact number and leave a message that you need to meet urgently – within an hour. Would you say why in your message?"

"I'd say something like there'd been unwelcome visitors."

"Then you can tell the truth and say the jewellers have had unwelcome visitors. Let's keep you out of it."

So, having signed his statement and telephoned his contact number – with me listening in carefully – Jesensky was off, looking not unlike a rabbit caught in a car's headlights.

As we paid for our lunch, the proprietor, a Pole with an immense moustache, asked whether he really was a stool pigeon for the Russians. Wally confirmed that he was. The proprietor refused to accept our money. It was evident there would be a scene if we tried to argue, so we just left a five-pound tip for the service, which they wouldn't find until after we had gone.

We made our way back to Fetter Lane and deposited another document for Iain Cogbill.

"Remind me if I ever commit a crime, not to ask you two to interrogate me," remarked Wally. "You've a talent for it which is wasted in the Long Room and I'll bet as a WPC you don't get near any suspects."

"I thought we made a good team," I replied. "I always reckoned that if they got too uncooperative I could ask Morry to give them a hug."

"You heard about that?" he asked.

"I saw you do it. My first day in Harwich."

"So what are you planning next? Are you actually going to confront this Russian?"

"Yes. If you'll come with us. He's the last loose end to be tidied up."

"But he won't sign anything, like this lot. He's got diplomatic immunity. He'll say nothing, knowing you can't touch him."

"I'd just like him to come out of the shadows and be recognised for what he is – a man who sends out killers to murder anyone who gets in his way."

"I imagine he might bring a couple of hoods with him."

"Yes, but they don't know we're going to be there. So if we do it properly, we have the element of surprise."

"But Jesensky might ring again and warn him."

"Jesensky has a simple choice. Either he gets himself within the safety of a police station or he runs as fast and as far as he can. Telling his contact what he's been up to isn't going to save him. Even if he's guessed what we're thinking of doing, if he rang his contact, all that would do is mean that the contact knew about his confession sooner. Why would he want that?"

"Let's hope you're right."

We caught a bus up to Camden Town and found the place Jesensky had mentioned. Evidently, the contact would come along College Road and make his way down some steps to the towpath of the Grand Union Canal. Technically, it was part of the same canal close to where Davenport had been run down in Leicester. It was a strange co-incidence that the beginning and what seemed likely to be the end of this tale would take place by the same canal.

Morry declined the replica gun that I had bought at the shop in the Strand. It seemed unlikely that the Russians would send anyone to the Camden Road steps down to the canal, and he expressed a strong aversion to guns. So we agreed a system of whistles to alert each other to any signs of danger. Wally remained a little way along College Street, near a convenient telephone box, in case we needed to make an emergency 999 call. Rosemary and I loitered not far from the steps, needing no excuse to pose as a courting couple.

It was a chilly, grey afternoon and this particular stretch of towpath seemed deserted.

Just over an hour after Jesensky's phone call, a black Rover drew up. A man with steel-grey hair and a military manner got out and went quickly down the steps to the towpath.

Meanwhile, Rosemary and I approached the car, with a guide book open in our hands. I tapped on the driver's window, waving the guide book at him. He waved his hands at me to go away. I tapped again. He wound down the window.

"Fuck off!" he cried.

"Language, language!" I replied, sticking Silberstein's revolver against the side of his head. "Now, tell your colleague to wind down his window and both of you keep your hands where I can see them.

As the other man wound down his window, Rosemary pressed her replica gun against his head.

"Now, very slowly. With your left hands, please take your guns out and throw them out of the window."

They did as they were told. The driver muttered to his colleague in Russian.

"Under the dashboard, you say," I said. "Thank you. Take it out slowly, with your left hand and throw it out of the car.

"Now," I continued, "both of you take off your ties and lay them on the window."

While Rosemary covered the other man – with a real loaded gun – I tied the driver's hands tightly to the steering wheel column, so his face was pretty well pressed into the wheel. Then I went round to the other side of the car and tied the other man's hands behind his seat.

We found a couple more guns in the front of the car.

"You people do like your guns don't you!" I remarked, pulling the keys from the ignition.

Rosemary and I wound up the windows and I locked all the car doors, leaving just a small vent open at the back so that they wouldn't suffocate. Then I unlocked the boot, where there were a couple of small machine-guns, tossed all the other guns in, except for mine (actually Bernie Silberstein's) and the one Rosemary was holding, and locked it again.

Then we made our way down the steps where the contact was pacing up and down, looking at his watch and appearing thoroughly fed up. We were about ten yards away, when he suddenly appeared to make up his mind and turned on his heel to set off back to his car. He obviously saw us as a courting couple and came towards us.

We blocked his way.

"Excuse me," he said irritably. "Will you get out of my way!"

"Mr Jesensky's compliments," I said, "but he's been unavoidably detained. We've come instead of him to have a few words."

We both drew our guns.

"What are you going to do? You can't do anything to me. I'm a Soviet diplomat."

He turned as if he was thinking about making a run for it. I whistled and Morry appeared coming down the steps from the Camden Road end.

"That is one of our colleagues. Like us, he is armed. So if you were thinking of shooting your way out –"

"I'm not armed! But –"

"But your colleagues in your car are? Were – to be accurate. I fear they aren't in any position to come to your aid."

"What are you going to do to me?"

"Just a little chat. But I like to know who I'm talking to. What is your name? I can easily search you and find out, if you'd prefer it."

"I am Khrestinsky. I am a Counsellor at the Soviet Embassy."

"And you are the mastermind of a large operation to smuggle Russian diamonds into this country to sell for hard currency to put Brezhnev and Kosygin in power back home. You're also the man who sends out his hoods to kill people, just because they might be getting in your way."

"You have me mistaken for someone else."

"Are you incapable of speaking the truth? How do you think you were summoned here? If you weren't that person, why did you come? And why did you come with two armed hoods?"

"I have to protect myself from fascist fanatics like you! I thought I was meeting a trade contact. I'm the Counsellor for commercial matters at the Embassy."

"So this is where you hold your business meetings? And, for the record, we're not fascist fanatics. We work for the Government. That's why we wanted to see you and why my colleague is going to take your photograph for our records. You see, I'm sure you don't realise it, but the men you send out to do your dirty work have tried to kill my girlfriend here twice. They didn't do a very good job. We've got two of them in safekeeping and the others got shipped home, one with a broken jaw…"

"I wonder what you'd feel like if someone was about to kill you!" said Rosemary quietly but fiercely.

She clicked the safety catch back on her pistol and put it directly under Khrestinsky's chin. Then she pulled the trigger back ever so slightly, but the sound seemed to echo across the canal to the walls opposite.

There was a sound of water being released.

"He's wet himself," observed Morry.

"In that case, you need a good wash," said Rosemary and pushed him into the canal. "Now he knows what it's like!" she remarked.

We whistled to Wally who had been watching from the College Street steps. He rang 999 to inform them that there was a car with crooks and guns in it by the canal entrance in College Street and a man seemed to have gone into the canal nearby. Then we all made our way to Camden Town Tube station.

"I do believe spending Saturday with you two puts a bit too much strain on my heart," said Wally. "But I take it even you think this is all over."

"As far as we're concerned," I confirmed.

SEVENTEEN – LONDON: A NEW START

And so it pretty well was. Rosemary and I went back to our hotel to pick up our bags and made our way to my parents' house. Whether my mother had insisted he behaved, my father was as good as gold and didn't try to preach to Rosemary or criticise her for her choice of profession. As I expected, however, my parents were rather more traditional in their view of bedroom arrangements.

The following morning was a beautiful December day, bright and cold. I took Rosemary to Greenwich Park and we stood by the Royal Observatory and looked down to the buildings that used to represent such an important centre for the Navy and beyond to the river and the decaying docks.

"What a beautiful view!" exclaimed Rosemary, putting her arm round my waist and leaning against my shoulder. "It just feels so wonderful to be alive! I feel so incredibly lucky!"

I said nothing – just kissed her. Even for me, there were times when words weren't needed.

We walked and found a nice historic pub by the river where we had an indifferent lunch. Then we talked about our future. We decided that we would have to come to London. Both Customs & Excise and the Metropolitan Police were seeking more people and we didn't want to be apart. Though London would be more expensive we knew, from looking at an old copy of the *Standard* we found on a bus, that we could afford to rent reasonably close to the centre, with a fair prospect of affording a flat somewhere like Romford or Wimbledon or Beckenham once we could get a deposit together. It would be nose to the grindstone and saving hard for a couple of years, so that we could buy somewhere and start a family. But we would be together and that was what counted.

Though I hated parting and those long five days before I saw her again, the time when we would be together seemed a much more real prospect now. I arrived at work the following morning, eager to examine again recent OWO vacancies and if I found any suitable ones in London, seek to speak to Jim Round to see whether he would be prepared to support my application.

However, I had barely sat down when I received an urgent summons from Jim.

"Iain Cogbill's been on the phone. You're to go to London at once. Not Fetter Lane but 140 Gower Street. I assume you and your girlfriend were up to something at the weekend again. I won't ask."

I got the next train and was in London by eight o'clock. I took the Central Line to Tottenham Court Road, as I had no idea at which at end of Gower Street number 140 was located. The building gave nothing away about its occupants, but I went up to the front door and rang the bell anyway. There was a buzzing sound and the door opened. I went in.

Inside was a very small lobby, with four doors going off it and a reception manned by an elderly man who looked ex-military.

"Who are you?" he asked.

"Nick Storey. I got a message from my boss in Customs & Excise to come here."

"Are you with Mr Woodruffe? He's from Customs."

"Mr Woodruffe? Is there a Mr Cogbill with him?"

"Yes."

" I'm with them. I'm called Storey."

"Oh yes. There you are. Well, you've got a bit of a wait. The meeting isn't due to start until 9.30."

"Is there anywhere I can wait?"

"I'll get a messenger to take you through to the room. But you'll need to complete these forms first."

After I had completed the formalities and had been given a "visitor" tag to pin on to the top pocket of my jacket, I was taken through the central door, along a gloomy corridor, and ushered into a meeting room, whereupon the door was locked behind me. The room gave little away about the organisation. There was a picture of the Queen on the wall, which indicated it might well be part of Government. Otherwise, there was a large, well-scrubbed blackboard and two copies of engravings of the Crystal Palace and the Banqueting House. But I would have been completely unsurprised if Mr Carvell or Mr Jones walked into the room next.

However, the next person who entered the room was a complete and wonderful surprise. Rosemary was led in and ceremoniously locked in with me. We embraced and kissed.

"I wonder if we're being filmed or bugged?" she said. "This is the Security Service, I assume?"

"I reckon it is. I wasn't told. My boss just told me to get down here as soon as possible."

"Same here. I hoped I might see you."

"I'm glad you're early as well. I didn't fancy the prospect of waiting nearly an hour here on my own. Now I hope no-one else comes."

Indeed, we had a very pleasant half hour to ourselves. If we were being watched or bugged, our observers would have heard little conversation and a lot of smooching.

It took no brains to work out why we were there and we had no plans to conceal or deny what we'd been up to. So we made best use of an unexpected opportunity.

At about quarter past nine, we heard feet in the corridor and Stanley Woodruffe entered the room, followed by Iain Cogbill. Iain introduced me and I introduced Rosemary.

"So it's you two I have to thank for a completely ruined Sunday's golf, is it?" said Woodruffe magisterially. He was the kind of man of whom it was impossible to tell whether he was using a very dry humour or having a go at you. I suspected that it could be either, depending on your response.

I decided that silence was the safest response. He could make the first move.

"I don't know what the hell you thought you were doing. This thing is a lot bigger than you think."

"Let's see what Special Branch and Box have to say about it, Chief," counselled Iain.

Special Branch, in the form of Mike Elliott and Assistant Commissioner McTeague, appeared within a couple of minutes. Elliot gave Rosemary and me a cheery smile, McTeague glared at us and promptly ignored us, preferring to chat about golf to Woodruffe.

At just after 9.30, Jones arrived with an ordinary-looking man, with thinning hair, a sailor's complexion and a ready smile.

"Good morning all," began the unknown man as he sat down at the top of the table. "I think everyone knows each other and those that don't, don't need to, eh?"

Everyone sat down. Special Branch sat next to the IB, while Rosemary and I remained where we had been – on the opposite side of the table. It felt a little bit as though we were the defendants.

"Mr Storey, WPC Johnson," he continued, looking at us, "you've had an active weekend. Is there anything you wish to say at this juncture?"

"I'm assuming that the documents we left in Fetter Lane for Mr Cogbill are the reason for this meeting. They resulted from some of us in Harwich Customs following up some loose ends after the capture of Mr Davidson. I hope Mr Khrestinsky and his colleagues are safely back in their embassy after their little mishap?"

"We'll come to that incident later. You were presumably aware that the Silberstein premises were under observation?"

"No. How long had that been going on?"

"Ever since Customs arrested Weissman, I believe. If I may ask, why did you feel you in Harwich Customs should, as you put it, follow up loose ends in London?"

"It was a Customs Officer from Harwich who was killed first. It was clear that the illegal consignments came through Harwich helped by him and Imrie. I've long felt that Davenport did what he did unwillingly and what he left us was a series of clues to help us find out what had been going on. After Davidson was caught, I was told that that was the end of it. So as there seemed to us there were some loose ends, we decided if we didn't follow them up nobody would."

"Why didn't you inform the IB?" demanded Woodruffe.

"Because we only expected to get a little bit of information and then I would've passed it on to Mr Cogbill to take further. When Rosemary – WPC Johnson – and I went into the shop, we really only expected to discover that Silbersteins would offer us Russian diamonds. It seemed to me that would be enough for the IB to raid the place."

"But why did you go to Silbersteins in the first place?" asked the unknown man from the Security Service.

"Two reasons. First, there were too many documents involving them left by Davenport. But more important, I was trying to follow up who

Imrie's contact was. I managed to track down a phone number and I was certain I recognised the voice at the other end. The man Mr Cogbill and I met when we visited Silbersteins a few weeks ago. He had a very distinctive voice."

"Jesensky," observed Jones.

"Yes."

"So why did you go and get them to hand over their accounts and write out a statement?"

"Klugman, who I met when I was there before, recognised me and Bernard Silberstein pulled a gun on us. I got it off him and the situation it created seemed too good to miss – especially as Klugman seemed not to have been aware what had been going on."

"And I suppose you had to follow up Jesensky in case they informed him and he made his escape?"

"Exactly."

"Did you not think to contact Special Branch or your investigation people?"

"How would we contact Special Branch? Do you think an ordinary police station would've taken us seriously? There were only duty officers around in the IB. Or that's what they told us. If we'd wasted time doing all that, Bernie Silberstein might've alerted Jesensky and the bird would've flown."

"Did you threaten Jesensky?"

"I encouraged him to believe that if he didn't spill the beans, we'd let the Russian Embassy know informally that it was him who'd dropped Silbersteins in it. So he had a choice of going off on his own without talking or telling us what he knew and getting some form of protection."

"I see you follow traditional Customs interrogation methods."

"I've no idea what they are. Actually, I got the idea from when Mr Jones interviewed Weissman."

"Perhaps you could explain under what powers you did all this?"

"Under the Customs and Excise Act 1952. I was pursuing people involved in the illegal importation of goods contrary to that Act. I agree, you might say Jesensky was some way removed – but actually he was the person who tipped Imrie off about when the importations were coming through. I didn't ask him about Jan de Wet, who's probably tied up in all of this, but we'd got enough at that stage – and, to be honest, I completely forgot about him. But if Jesensky has turned himself in as seemed likely on Saturday, you can probably get that out of him."

"Regrettably, he chose not to do what you suggested. He has disappeared."

"Well, I thought we must've given him a bit of a head start after we met Khrestinsky."

"Yes. I was going to come on to that. What the hell were you playing at? Apart from the fact that these people are pros, threatening a Russian diplomat and chucking him in the Grand Union Canal could've provoked an international incident."

"As I've said, I like to tidy up loose ends. Khrestinsky was the last one. As for his bodyguards, I feel we can score that Russia nil, England six."

"This isn't a matter to be flippant!" growled McTeague.

"I wanted to drag the man out from the shadows where he lurks so happily, sending his men off to kill people, even innocent people like WPC Johnson who happen to get in their way. And then they were ordered back to try and kill her just because she'd seen the face of one of them. I wanted to see the sort of person who could order such things."

"And I wanted him to feel what it's like when someone's pointing a gun at you intending to kill you," added Rosemary.

"Besides, would Khrestinsky really want to make an international incident over it? With his men tied up in a car full of weapons?" I added.

"But you'd no idea whether you weren't watched. This sort of incident can easily get into the press and where would we be then?"

"Exactly. That's what really bothers you, isn't it Jacob?" remarked McTeague. "You want all of this to remain hidden for at least thirty years."

"That's really why we wanted to get you two here this morning," continued the man called Jacob, looking at Rosemary and me again. "What you did turned out to be extremely helpful. You probably turned up stuff we'd not felt necessary to take forward. You've also allowed us to understand how an operation like this works, so that we've a better chance of stopping one like it again. And the bath didn't really do Khrestinsky any harm. He certainly deserved it."

"But you could very easily have buggered it up," added McTeague. "You bumbled into a situation you knew nothing about. You'd no idea Silbersteins was under surveillance. If there'd been a serious incident with them or with Khrestinsky and his men – with you getting shot or one of them – it might well have been impossible to keep this stuff out of the press."

"I don't wish to be difficult," said Iain Cogbill sharply, "but this meeting is solely because you're concerned that this massive operation by the Russians should be kept out of the press?"

I noticed Woodruffe looking daggers at him.

"In a word, yes," replied 'Jacob'. "Our new political masters want to turn a new page in our relationship with the Soviets. Mr Wilson would like to be the first Western leader to meet Brezhnev and Kosygin. If something like this blew up, it'd scupper all that."

"Besides," added Elliott, "it'd add yet another fiasco with the Russians to our growing list of failures. We don't want the press or Parliament knowing that, do we?"

I saw McTeague in his turn give his subordinate a withering stare.

"I understand what you're saying," I said. "I did what I believed was the right thing to do. Others didn't seem to be doing anything and it seemed to me that I had the honour of Harwich Customs to restore. If anything like this ever came up in future I'd certainly be more careful and would try and do more to inform the right people. I accept that there is a wider picture that I didn't grasp."

"I don't believe either you or WPC Johnson have anything to apologise for," said Elliott firmly. "If it wasn't for the two of you, we'd still understand less than half of this. Besides, of all those in this room, you are the only two who've actually risked your lives to get this information. No-one else here has had guns pointed at them with a real intention to kill them. The wider picture be blowed! There'd be a whole bunch of Russians and their stooges rubbing their hands together and waiting for the next time to run this little show if it hadn't been for these two."

"Well said," added Iain Cogbill loudly.

We got no endorsements from anyone else, however. I suppose that those close to where the work was done had one perspective. The senior people were more influenced by the bigger picture.

Anyway, that appeared to be that. Without formally closing the meeting, 'Jacob' drifted away, followed by Jones. A messenger led the rest of us out and we went our separate ways, not without firm handshakes from Iain Cogbill and Mike Elliott.

Rosemary and I decided it was too good an opportunity not to spend at least until lunchtime together. So we walked towards Shaftesbury Avenue and found a cinema that was showing *From Russia With Love* and sat and watched that, at least part of the time.

Over lunch in a sandwich bar, Rosemary suddenly remarked. "You know, one thing I've never quite understood is why the Russians didn't just take Davenport's suitcase and photos after they'd run him down, especially while Mrs Davenport was still in hospital? If they had, all this would never have started."

"It's one loose end which won't ever be tied up. And I'm not even going to try. If you want a guess, I reckon they were hoping to tidy this thing up quietly as quietly as possible. That's why they took such care in killing the Davenports, so it didn't look like murder. They might've been worried that someone would spot their car again and start asking questions. Perhaps they didn't even know about the suitcase at that stage? After all, would you assume that someone trying to negotiate himself out of being blackmailed would keep all the relevant evidence in a suitcase he carried around with him? I wouldn't. I'd assume he'd got it safely stashed away in a safety deposit box in a bank. Would you expect anyone to be running around with what I gather was around £50,000 in diamonds in a suitcase?"

"So they only knew about it when they came across your receipt when they killed Mrs Davenport?"

"I guess so. Somebody did try to break into the Queen's Warehouse in Harwich some time after I'd brought the suitcase back. But they didn't get in – and the suitcase wasn't there either. I wonder who's got it now?"

"Oh well, we can stop worrying about all that now and think about us and our future."

We got married at the end of April 1965 at the Registry Office in Leicester and, after a reception in a local hotel in Thurmaston, set off for our honeymoon in the Lake District. We spent the first night in a small hotel in Matlock, a joyous time I shall never forget, and definitely one worth waiting for. We returned after a week, to a small flat in Stoke Newington and new jobs. To my astonishment, within a fortnight of my asking Jim Round if he would support my application for a transfer to London because of my forthcoming marriage, I received a phone call from Estabs in the Secretaries Office offering me the post of Higher Executive Officer in a branch that was being newly set up to look at ways of reducing imports and encouraging exports through Customs levies and rebates. The salary was significantly better than what I was currently getting. Rosemary had been offered a post in Scotland Yard, which involved helping to set up better records of crimes and criminals. Neither of us fancied jobs that were so office-bound and heavy on paperwork much, but the hours were regular and we could live as a happily married couple.

Jesensky never turned up and nor did I hear what happened to Davidson or the two Russian hoods I maimed with a fire extinguisher. I never heard anything about Silberstein & Co in the press, though Morry Gold told me when we met for dinner one Saturday several months later that the business was in the process of being taken over by a formerly detested competitor. Weissman pleaded guilty to several Customs offences and received a heavy fine and two years in gaol. Iain Cogbill managed to catch up with Devaney, the mastermind behind the smuggling of the cannabis seeds and got him sent down for five years. Jan de Wet was never brought before British justice – or Netherlands justice for that matter. Iain continues to reserve judgment on his Dutch counterparts to this day. Jim Round failed to get the well-merited promotion to AC at Harwich, but the grapevine was already saying that both he and Iain were marked for promotion soon. Whether the Leicestershire Constabulary ever caught on to my misleading and incomplete statement or not, it remains buried in a closed case file somewhere in their records.

That is enough loose ends tied up.

As we lay in bed together, after the end of our first week in our new jobs and our new home, no longer requiring the restraint of night attire, Rosemary said, "Well, Mr Storey, what next?"

"WPC Storey. I think we should just enjoy ourselves for as long as we can. Starting now!"

Hierarchy in Customs & Excise 1964

The Board

Chief Inspector	Inspector-General of the	Secretaries Office
	Waterguard	(London HQ)

(Higher) Collector--Chief Investigation Officer

Deputy Collector/   Deputy Chief Investigation Officer

Senior Assistant Collector   (DCIO)

Assistant Collector (AC)	Waterguard Superintendant	Assistant Chief Investig-ation Officer (ACIO)
Surveyor	Chief Preventive Officer (CPO)	Senior Investigation Officer (SIO)
Officer of Customs & Excise (OCX)	Preventive Officer (PO)	Higher Investigation Officer (HIO)
Unattached Officer (UO)	Assistant Preventive Officer (APO)	Investigation Officer (IO)
Departmental Clerical Officer (DCO)	Coast Preventive Man (CPM)	
Departmental Clerical Assistant (DCA)/ Revenue Assistant (RA)		
Revenue Constable		